B H Turner studied Modern History rather a long time ago then worked for more than thirty years in residential social care.

The Sultan's Kul series is the eventual result of a lifetime's somewhat eclectic interests and enjoyment of the written word.

ISBN 978-0-244-05017-7

The Paper-cuts of the Horseman and the hand-drawn Maps all by Alison Eradus

YLDERIM

An historical novel

by B H Turner

Book Two of *The Sultan's Kul* series

ALSO BY B H TURNER

ALL THE SEA
Book One in The Sultan's Kul series

Prologue

Summer 1487. Moulins, Duchy of Bourbonnais.
'Your position in Europe has become too dangerous. What happened here in Moulins has proved that!'

The mute Jew smiled a little grimly. Things have become very difficult even in Nice, he acknowledged, the shorthand marks concise on his battered tablet.

Jews had been banished from the kingdom of France a century before but Savoyard Nice, with its Genoese heritage, had remained largely tolerant of a people who were very useful to its commercial way of life. True, for the past fifty years the Jews of Nice had been nominally restricted to the Rue Guidaria, enclosed with chains and iron fences "for their own protection", but everyone knew and accepted that there were hundreds of ways in and out of the area via the maze of caves, cellars and sewers. Now it seemed that even the Niçois, following the lead of Ferdinand the Catholic and his equally devout wife Isabella, in their newly united kingdoms of Aragon and Castile, were intent on removing any remaining heathen blot on the Christian landscape.

Isaac's stylus moved again. That's what I came north to discuss with you.

Hosé scowled at him; even disguised as a *converso* and travelling under the protection of the redoubtable Donna Annette Grimaldo that had been a very risky undertaking. 'You could have written to me in code, as usual,' he said.

The Jew smiled again. A lucky thing for you that I didn't!

Hosé was forced to acknowledge the truth of that statement: but for the skills of the Jewish physician the Moulins cooper would have died and Hosé, wrongly accused of attacking him, would have hanged for murder. 'The Grimaldi can't continue to shelter you?' he said eventually.

Isaac shook his head. I think not, he wrote. Yes, he acknowledged Hosé's frown, they are well rewarded by the Sultan for the valuable assistance they render me and the House of Osman, but standing out against popular opinion would draw attention to what needs to be unnoticed.

Hosé frowned.

He had been accompanying the renegade Ottoman Prince Cem and his "protectors", the Knights of St John, into increasingly remote parts of central France for the past five years, but always, somehow, it had been possible to maintain a link with Isaac in the Grimaldo office in Nice, with Isaac and his remarkable knowledge, constantly updated through correspondence from Islambul and many other places.

The thought of continuing without that was daunting. Hosé considered it for a few moments. 'And there is nobody who could take your place in Nice?'

It was a forlorn question. Isaac held a unique place in the employ of the Sultan Bayezit for good reason.

The Jew stroked his clean shaven and bony jaw. The main concern, of course, remains the Prince.

Hosé shook his head in frustration 'The Knights have managed to keep him in their "safekeeping" but there have been constant plots and intrigues. This most recent one by the Duke of Bourbon will surely not be the last. De Blanchefort and the other Knights have done their best to keep the Prince secure, including the building of the Tour at Bourganeuf, but perhaps in the end all their efforts will not be enough: Bourbon's plot was not thwarted because of any precautions the Knights had taken.' He paused and added sourly, 'Nor, indeed, because of anything I was able to do.'

Isaac nodded his head; that was true. He looked at Hosé. It could also be that your position with the Knights will now be compromised. What will de Blanchefort make of what has happened here in Moulins?

The same thing had been worrying Hosé. He rubbed his arm absently. 'If he hears the tale, would he identify me as the cooper's labourer?'

A labourer who fought like a professional soldier but whom de Blanchefort believed to be a lame clerk.

The Jew sucked the end of his stylus thoughtfully. It is too risky.

'So, what about keeping surveillance on the Prince?'

Isaac shrugged. Perhaps that will no longer be possible, from within the castle. However, it should be possible to keep a watch on the comings and goings; for as long as it is necessary.

Hosé looked at him sharply. 'What does that mean? You expect Prince Cem to leave Bourganeuf?'

There has been news from Rome.

'Rome? The Knights can't let the Prince go to Rome. The Sultan's been paying them a fortune specifically to prevent it! That would be all Pope Innocent VIII needs to head up a new crusade.'

Isaac smiled, without humour. The Sultan has indeed been paying the Knights well, but the Vatican can offer Pierre d'Aubusson, Grand Master of the Knights of St John, something more than money.

Hosé slammed his hand on the table. D'Aubusson had been receiving huge sums from the Sultan over the past five years for keeping the Prince in safe custody. And had used much of it to increase fortifications on the Knights' island of Rhodes, Hosé reflected bitterly. Meanwhile d'Aubusson had also been receiving money from Cem's wife and mother, in exile in Egypt; their hope being to *free* the Prince from custody. Pierre d'Aubusson was the Grand Master of intrigue, as well as being Grand Master of the warrior monks of St John.

The younger man swallowed his anger with difficulty. 'And what would that be?'

What every Christian monk would aspire to.

Hosé's eyes narrowed. 'A cardinalate.'

Isaac nodded.

'And that will happen soon?'

The Jew shrugged. The news from Rome cannot be that specific. You will appreciate that such negotiations are not cried on every corner!

It was, after all, not surprising that Pierre d'Aubusson was as ambitious for himself as he was for his Order.

'And after Cardinal?' Hosé's thoughts continued. 'One day Pontiff?' He shook his head at the idea.

Isaac grimaced. We have to cross one bridge at a time. I believe there are already a good number of cardinals who have the Papacy in mind; d'Aubusson would have plenty of competition!

He wiped his tablet and went back to more immediate matters. For the moment, we need to inform d'Aubusson's nephew, de Blanchefort, that you will not be returning to Bourganeuf; that Nicolas Grimaldo needs you back in Nice. If for any reason de Blanchefort does come to suspect you, at least you will be out of the way.

Hosé pulled a rueful face. 'If he came to suspect me, he would also suspect the part the Grimaldi have played.'

Isaac inclined his head. Possibly; but they could claim to have been deceived. They could point to the genuine help they have given to the Knights over the years. He smiled. And Nicolas Grimaldo could remind de Blanchefort that he advised strongly against employing you in the first place!

Hosé grimaced at the memory. The guise of sullen and rebellious youth had only been partly simulated. The young janissary, Hasan, had resented being recruited by Isaac and being removed from his orta for such a devious mission. 'So?' he queried. 'Should I write a letter to de Blanchefort?'

Isaac nodded. And Annette shall deliver it.

Hosé was startled.

Together with the one that her father has written.

Hosé gave a small laugh. 'You came prepared.' Of course. 'Will it be safe for Annette?' And would she be able to collect his few possessions?

I think so. If she goes immediately, she should get to Bourganeuf before any news from Moulins. The Jew paused. Then I believe we shall still be able to visit Évaux les Bains on the way back south; I am curious to see the place.

Hosé nodded. Évaux les Bains was the ostensible reason for this journey of Annette Grimaldo and her personal physician. It was a spa, its waters well known for their healing properties; a woman who had suffered illness like Annette might well visit the town. The waters could do nothing for her pocked face but they could perhaps help the body that had to live with such terrible scars.

'How will she feel about going to Bourganeuf?' Hosé was curious.

Isaac's sunken eyes gleamed. I know she agreed to this trip for reasons of her own, as much as to help me!

Hosé shifted uncomfortably. When they had first met in the Grimaldo palace, on the Cimiez heights above Nice, he had despised her flagrant affaire with Prince Cem and resisted all her attempts to seduce himself. After he had left Nice Annette had fallen victim to the *variole* and only escaped death because of Isaac's care. The illness had changed more than her striking looks. She had given new purpose to her blighted life by learning many of the Jew's clerical skills and putting them to good use in her father's business. Among those skills was a facility with the ciphers used to exchange news and information throughout the far-flung Grimaldo commercial domain. She and Hosé had begun a coded correspondence and achieved a sympathy at a distance which he, at least, had certainly not enjoyed in proximity.

Hosé was not sure, however, that meeting her now was any easier than before: his mission, that she might well suspect but was not a part of, lay between them. There were imperatives in his life that did not coincide with her ambitions.

And the relationship that had existed between her and the Prince? Since they had last met she had lost her looks and he had lost his hopes. Would anything remain?

Hosé grimaced. It had nothing to do with him; did it?

The Prince, Isaac smiled slyly, was one of the reasons.

Chapter 1

Early 1488. Nice, Duchy of Savoy.

Hosé scowled at the Jew. 'What can one tell from such a message?' He thrust the letter back at Isaac. 'If I had still been there we could have known for sure!'

But you are not, Isaac reminded him calmly. For good reason. He eased his hand. But if we put such a scrap together with what we have heard from other quarters then we can make a good guess at what is happening.

Hosé took a deep breath; he knew Isaac was right, but even after all these months he was still not reconciled to this way of gleaning information. Furthermore, Isaac would leave soon, when the new sailing season opened; and Hosé would have to work on his own: for which he felt less than adequate, in spite of the knowledge and skills the Jew had been cramming into him since the return to Nice.

Isaac had not gone back to the Rue Guidaria. He would no longer have been able to reach the Grimaldo office near the port; nor would Hosé have been able to visit him as he had once done with relative ease. Instead Isaac had moved into the Grimaldo palace; there Annette and her father could shelter him from the general hostility of the Niçois and insist at least that those they employed accord him civility. Nevertheless, the Jew's position was restricted and uncomfortable; although perhaps Hosé chafed more under the conditions on his behalf than Isaac did himself.

Isaac of Córdoba had seen it all before.

'But in Islambul it is not like this! The Sultan insists that all are free to live there, even those who do not share the Faith.'

Isaac nodded gravely. It will be good to live like that again, he agreed. But, he pointed a bony finger at Hosé, first there is still much to do here.

The Jew pulled forward several other messages that had been received over the past weeks. He picked out one in particular: a note from Antonio Rericho, or Antoine Rorijo as he was often called in France.

Hosé had already read it. Rericho acted as an agent for the Sultan; once Hosé had been suspected by de Blanchefort of being just such a person. That suspicion had been laid by the English merchant Clough for his own ends and Hosé had dispelled it with considerable difficulty.

That had not been the only time Clough had caused him problems. He had been very much part of the trouble in Moulins. His schemes there to eliminate Hosé, as well as to kidnap the Prince, had barely been thwarted.

Hosé paused for a moment to think of another message, received from the Lowlands. Somehow the merchant had wriggled out of Medici custody, although his standing had been severely damaged. He had retired to England to lick his wounds. But that recent message from Antwerp suggested he had begun to rebuild his commercial enterprise. Hosé had good professional reasons to keep a very close eye on William Clough's affairs. He also had personal reasons for mistrusting the Englishman's interest in the van Damme family in Antwerp, although the woollen cloth trade was an obvious link.

Hosé returned to the news Rericho had sent. The Sultan's agent had made several visits to the French court, particularly since Charles VIII had become monarch. The youthful French king was both a zealous Christian and a romantic, which made him particularly interested in the striking Ottoman Prince being held by the Knights of St John. The king's uncle, the Duke of Savoy, had described to Charles his meetings at Rumilly with the well-educated, French-speaking Prince Cem; Savoy had been captivated by the personality and charm of the Prince and wished to help him reclaim the throne in Constantinople from his elder brother Bayezit. Rericho feared King Charles would also see this as both a noble deed, and one that could strengthen the cause of Christendom.

Rericho had done what he could to persuade the young King Charles rather to help send Cem back in peace to the brother who offered him a safe and respected place, in the land of his birth. The agent's latest note said his efforts had recently been aided by the protestations of the Knights of St John at the French court: Prince Cem was not the noble figure the Duke of Savoy claimed, but a violent and humourless man who condemned the King of France and his religion.

Well might the Prince be humourless, reflected Hosé, after six years in custody, the last two confined in the specially built Tour in Bourganeuf designed to resist any army.

He compared the news with the first note Isaac had read. That had come from the town of Bourganeuf where the best information about the Prince now came via a laundrywoman who worked in the castle. She liked to drink at the same wine shop as a travelling peddler, who regularly visited a certain Lyon warehouse with commercial links to the Grimaldi. Hosé pulled a face. It was a tortuous connection but it was better than nothing. And, as Isaac said, put together with the note from Rericho it gave some sort of credible picture.

Hosé sighed. 'It would not be the first time that the Prince has despaired and fallen into depression,' he confirmed.

De Blanchefort had had a difficult balancing act to perform: on the one hand to keep the Prince under secure guard and on the other to keep up his spirits (since the mortal decline of this most prestigious of hostages would have been a catastrophic loss to the Knights). Over the years there had been all sorts of attempts to keep the Prince entertained: hunting expeditions, chess games, special foods from the East, books and tapestries, prostitutes and Turkish baths; and there had been Philippine-Hélène de Sassenage. She had been the daughter of one of his many custodians; another of those who fell for the exotic prince. Perhaps it had truly been a love match; certainly, there had been a love child (although little Constantin bore a Frankish sire-name). Prince Cem had gone into a dark mood after that affaire came to an end; he had threatened to go on hunger strike. Was that what was happening now? Hosé imagined the Tour in Bourganeuf as it must be in the dark days of a bitter winter. Here in Nice it was easy to forget the intense cold and barrenness of the season up in the central mountains.

'If the Prince were to pine away, it would solve the Sultan's problems,' Hosé put to Isaac a little defiantly. That had been his own balancing act: to reconcile his oath to Lord Bayezit to keep Prince Cem safe, with his personal inclination to save the Sultan all the misery and expense his brother's continued existence caused.

Isaac looked calmly at Hosé. He had wondered about the young janissary; once upon a time.

Hosé looked at the figures: the Grimaldo trade from the Levant had been particularly successful this last year.

Nicolas Grimaldo himself was in the office at the warehouse. Granted only daughters, he had always assumed a son in law would become head of the family concern, but none had come up to his standards. As age brought him physical frailty, he had worried increasingly that the prizes secured by generations of the Genoese family would be lost to ineptitude or lack of ambition. Of late, however, he had come to realise that they would be safest in Annette's elegant white hands. Once he had imagined that it would be her fair face that would secure the future, but the *variole* had put an end to her betrothal; and perhaps the English merchant would not have been the right answer: too many other interests, Isaac had informed him tersely. Now Nicolas Grimaldo accepted that his daughter had a mind as acute and devious as any merchant or banker he had ever met and recognised that the training she had received from the Jew had made her a formidable player in the deadly serious game of commerce.

He greeted his daughter as she entered the room. She pushed the vizard aside to receive his kiss on her scarred cheek then took his arm as they moved together around the desks, looking at accounts, reading letters, discussing supplies and prices, putting detail on the plans for the new season.

They stopped near where Hosé was sitting on a stool, looking through the window at the boats in the harbour. There were not many yet and those mostly local craft; but there was one vessel newly arrived and he was staring at it. It had been many years since he had seen its like and even longer since he had seen one in the Middle Sea. He could hardly believe they still existed, even less that this one had managed the voyage down the Atlantic seaboard and through the Strait.

'Pardon?' He turned to face the Grimaldi.

Annette looked to see what had caught his attention. 'What on earth is that?'

Her father peered out of the window. 'A northern cog.' An international merchant had good reason to know about boats. 'I haven't seen one of those for years.' His words echoed Hosé's astonishment. 'We used to see them sometimes when I was a boy; there were a number which used to come each year for the salt and the wine. But more usually it was the bigger hulks, with two or three masts.' He smiled. 'Now most merchants use carracks or sometimes the Portuguese caravels: more storage space and better able to withstand the ocean conditions.'

Hosé looked at the small boat with its distinctive straight stem and stern. Its single square sail was neatly furled, the platform at the rear deserted. 'Carvel built,' he remarked.

Nicolas Grimaldo laughed. 'And ancient!'

'I wonder where she is from?' Hosé mused, mostly to himself.

'Antwerp,' said a voice with an odd note of excitement in it.

Hosé turned sharply. He had not noticed the boy before. He was standing near Annette, holding the tools of the clerk's trade. Hosé almost smiled at the familiar picture: it was how *he* had served Guy de Blanchefort, following the Knight with tablet, quill and ink, listening in on the conversations of the Turkish Prince and his followers.

'Your clerk?' Hosé raised an eyebrow at Annette.

She nodded. 'Rab has worked for me for more than a year.'

Hosé looked more closely at the dark skin and cropped glossy black hair. What were his origins? he wondered. And, he added to himself, why had he not seen the boy before?

'He usually works in my private office,' Annette answered the unspoken question, meeting Hosé's gaze unblinkingly.

He was not deceived.

He addressed the boy directly. 'Have you spoken to the crew?'

The boy flushed. 'Yes,' he answered cautiously.

'Jij spreekt erg goed Diets?'

'*Vrij goed!*' came the immediate response. 'But they speak good Catalan,' he admitted.

Hosé nodded; another collector of languages. He glanced at Annette. She was remarkably competent in ciphers and figures, but she did not have the languages that an international merchant needed; the languages that both Isaac and Hosé had.

He looked at the lad again. The colouring and the slight accent in the Niçois Genoese would have led a betting man to place a safe wager on the boy's Arabic origins. Annette could have a good commercial asset there. 'They are regular traders to these parts then?'

The boy shrugged. 'They have not been to Nice before.'

And yet the lad knew about them. 'And what brings them here now?' Hosé made the question as casual as possible.

Another shrug of the narrow shoulders. 'Trade perhaps.' The boy looked uncomfortable.

Well, that covered a multitude of possibilities, reflected Hosé. 'Does the boat have a name?'

'Of course.'

Hosé acknowledged the stupidity of his question with a slight smile. 'Do you know the name of the boat?' he amended.

'The *Liesabeta*.'

Hosé considered that; the name had no particular significance although the St Elizabeth's Day flood came into his mind.

'And the crew?'

The boy hesitated.

He wished he had not started this conversation, realised Hosé.

'The one I know best is Job,' the boy admitted.

'Job? Just Job?'

'His family name is van Damme.'

Chapter 2

Hosé entered the wine shop. He had visited it several times since his return to Nice, but the man he had hoped to find had not been there. This time he spotted the Arab immediately, in his accustomed place, his head bent in conversation with a man whose clothes proclaimed him a seaman. The style of the man's jacket also suggested he was local or from down the coast. His shoes would probably have revealed more, but these were out of Hosé's sight under the table.

Sayf had frequented Nice for a long time. Nobody remembered when or why he had first arrived there; he was just part of the port and all its dealings. He came and went as frequently as any Genoese round-ship. He traded in every kind of good that passed this way: olives, oil, wine from inland; fish and salt from the coast; dates, leather and metal ware from across the Middle Sea; occasionally fabrics and spices from further afield, although mostly he was a local dealer. Nobody knew more about what was happening in this corner of the world and nobody had more contacts. He shared much of the news he gathered with anyone who cared to ask: it was good for business. But some things he was paid very well to keep to himself.

Hosé settled on the bench and with the rest of the wine shop's customers listened in on the conversation. He took a few mouthfuls of the wine he had bought. At least wine tasted better than beer; his face almost contracted with the memory and he pulled himself up sharply. He knew why that particular memory had surfaced. The mention of the name van Damme had recalled a journey to the Lowlands some fourteen years before; not that it had been Antwerp where the van Damme brothers had introduced a Genoese boy to some of the "best" Hamburg beer: it had been in the toll port of Amsterdam.

After the Ottomans took Caffa, that Genoese boy had become the kul Hasan, now serving Sultan Bayezit under the name of Hosé. And Hosé should keep his reminiscing for later, he reminded himself sharply, concentrating on what Sayf was saying.

Hosé had been right about the seaman: he came from Marseille. He had recently been upriver to Lyon and Hosé listened with increased interest, picturing the great market town where the Saône joined the Rhône. He waited for the boatman to disclose what goods he had loaded there, but it was not books or silk; it had been salt meat.

Hosé listened as Sayf spoke to another man, a Niçois fisherman, who was lamenting the lateness of the season this year.

Then the Arab left the wine shop.

Hosé spoke to a couple of local people he knew. He exchanged banter with one of the serving girls then emptied his mug and made his way outside. The alley leading to Sayf's house was as foetid as ever beneath his uneven step.

He spent more than an hour with Sayf, listening to the news that had not been shared in the wine shop and mentally comparing the information with what he and Isaac had gathered from their own reports.

Sayf started with Spain. The Moors, he said, were on the verge of defeat. The Christians were firmly in control of all areas except Granada. They had also strengthened the hold on their forts over on the coast of Africa. Sayf said with a shrug that Arab power in the western end of the Middle Sea was weakening: too much quarrelling amongst themselves.

The young French King Charles was very busy sending messages back and forth with the Duke of Milan, the Arab continued.

The Milanese Duke, Ludovico Sforza, would be a good match for anyone's intrigues, thought Hosé dryly.

There were all sorts of other tales too coming out of Milan: about fantastical machines contrived for the Sforza entertainments by the Florentine engineer, Leonardo; about many other civil and military works too.

Engineer? Hosé had heard from Isaac about this Leonardo, but not as an engineer; apparently a man of many talents.

In Florence, the Magnificent Lorenzo da Medici in his declining years was ruling a declining state. Banks had been closed, the Tolfa alum concession had been lost and the Papacy had gone to bank elsewhere. Money might have been lavished on art and architecture but the people of Florence had seen little of it and were listening with great interest to the seditious preaching of the monk, Savonarola.

Very much what Isaac had predicted, reflected Hosé.

Sayf spat with great accuracy towards a brass pot.

The Venetians continued to poke their long noses into the east and their *stato da mar* seemed well secured with the fortifications on Cyprus. At the same time, they had taken the Ottoman warning to heart and had successfully staked out their *stato da terra firma* nearer home, as insurance.

Hosé frowned at these extensions to Venetian power. He was no longer Genoese but the Ottomans also had good reason to hold a deep-seated suspicion of the Lagoon dwellers.

Over in Urbino the stripling Duke, Guidobaldo da Montefeltro, was trying hard to fill his father Federico's shoes but he needed to watch the Vatican carefully: the Ottoman Prince was only one small part of what Pope not-so Innocent VIII was interested in.

The Italian city states were always at war with each other; that was nothing new. The more resources they spent on that, the less they would have for any concerted campaign against anyone else; such as a crusade.

Hosé nodded and changed the subject slightly. 'What about Portugal?'

The Arab sniffed. 'They say Portuguese boats have gone down through the Green Sea of Darkness and sailed home again.'

Hosé frowned: *the Green Sea Of Darkness where a ship would stick fast in gelatinous slime, while loathsome monsters hovered in the depths and men turned black beneath a scorching sun.* Was it possible to go there and return alive?

His head was buzzing by the time he left the Arab's house. He picked his way back to the wine shop.

He sat on a bench against the wall, sunk in thought. It was a while before he became aware of the voices from the far corner of the room. Standing out from the local tongue was a very different language, sounding, he had once thought, as if the speaker had a fish bone lodged in the throat. He listened hard. Until that morning it had been a long time since he had used Diets himself; there had been no reason. Now he found himself struggling to follow the conversation although odd words struck his memory.

He was also trying to identify any familiar tones in the voices, but the adult bass bore no similarity to any remembered adolescent treble. He noticed, with wry amusement, that the conversation was decidedly one-sided. One man was doing all the talking, with only the the odd word or noise of response from the other. That would certainly fit with his memories of the van Damme brothers.

He listened harder. There was one word at least that he recognised; he would have recognised it in any language. It was as he had feared: the appearance of the van Dammes was definitely related to the merchant Clough. Had the Englishman made the final connection after all? In Moulins it had been obvious Clough knew Hosé served the Sultan. But Hosé had hoped the man had not recognised the former Guido Lomellino, the Genoese boy who had visited Antwerp and the van Dammes with his father; and who had saved the Englishman from drowning in a quayside accident. Strangely the incident had only fuelled the rivalry that already existed between the boy's father and the merchant, over trade and also over negotiations for the hand of Caterina Sforza, ward to Battista da

Montefeltro. That bitter rivalry had pursued the Lomellini to Caffa, and even as far as the Topkapi palace.

Hosé frowned. Did Clough know that Hosé was back in Nice? How good were the merchant's communications since his disgrace in Moulins? Was *he* really the deciding factor in what the merchant Clough might now be scheming?

But why otherwise were the van Damme brothers here in Nice?

Perhaps Hosé was adding two and two and making five. The frown was replaced by a grimace. Perhaps, but it was always wise to assume the worst if Clough was involved.

Another voice joined the conversation in the corner. Hosé glanced that way and saw a boy had joined the two men. He was about ten years old with sun-bleached hair, fair even in the dim light of the oil lamps. He did not look much like the man he was talking to, but he did remind Hosé strongly of another Lowlander he had met: she had been not much more than ten herself at that time and, dressed in the boy's clothes she had stolen, had looked remarkably similar.

So, the betrothal had not been called off after that disastrous episode in Amsterdam! Cornelius van Damme had married Katrin Molle after all: this had to be their son. Was this the Job that Rab had mentioned?

Hosé tried to look more closely at the two men but he did not want to stare. Both the talkative one and the bigger more silent one, surely Pieter, had shaved since coming into harbour, but new growth now shaded their faces and Hosé was not certain he would have recognised them, if he had not been looking for a resemblance.

Another lad moved between the tables and joined them.

Another son? A twin perhaps? The second boy looked much of an age with Job. However, there was no family likeness and this boy held himself differently. Hosé had learned much from Isaac about the language of the body: this boy was not addressing a father.

The boys squeezed onto a bench.

A man nearby spoke to them in Catalan. 'First time in Nice?'

'Yes,' Job replied in the same language.

'That's a rare boat you have.' The irony was barely disguised.

'She may seem old fashioned, but she is solid and very well balanced.' It was the other boy who responded to this. His Catalan was careful; Hosé could not place the accent.

A nudge brought Hosé's attention to the person intent on sharing his bench. He moved impatiently and focused his attention once more on the group in the corner.

'You were friendly enough earlier,' complained a voice in his ear.

Contrition got the better of annoyance and his fingers touched the rough hand on his sleeve. 'It's busy, Marianne, for so early in the season.' He nodded at the visiting seamen.

'Who cares for them?' she inquired, looking sideways at him.

'Don't you enjoy hearing about what is happening in the great world outside Nice?' he teased her.

'*Hein.* What does that have to do with me?' She moved closer. 'They will leave again soon enough. It is those who live here that interest me.'

'Oh dear,' he pretended disappointment. 'That rules me out then.'

She paused for a moment. 'But you live here!'

He shrugged. 'For the moment; but who knows for how long? Grimaldo business can take me away at any time.'

'But you will come back,' she said confidently.

What was this? 'And what makes you so sure of that?'

She continued to look at him, her eyes narrowed. 'You will have to, won't you?'

He looked his puzzlement.

'Old Grimaldo won't live for ever.'

'Nobody lives for ever,' he agreed.

'Then someone will need to run his business.'

He laughed. 'I'm just one of his clerks!'

She smiled knowingly. 'A bit closer to the family than that,' she said meaningfully.

He frowned and forced a certain bitterness into his tone. 'I would have thought people would have tired of that old gossip.' That had been the story put out when he first came to Nice; it was quite possible that cousin Gaspard Grimaldo at the Mallorca office had a previously unknown bastard son; it was equally believable that "uncle" Nicolas Grimaldo would have employed the boy, Hosé.

'It's true though?' she persisted.

He shrugged. 'Why should I deny it? And it can't be that interesting.'

She smiled again and he was suddenly wary. 'The interesting thing is whether you are Gaspard's son.' He tensed. 'Or actually a by-blow of old Nicolas himself?'

He relaxed; that suggestion too had circulated before; it had not seemed to matter much. 'Either way,' he said, refusing to answer her question, 'The Grimaldo business and fortune is not going to go to someone born the wrong side of the blanket!'

She chuckled as if he had said the most amusing thing she had heard all day and he struggled to contain his increasing irritation. 'But old Nicolas only has daughters.'

That was not news.

'And they say that none of the husbands he has chosen for them has the talent for the family business.'

That was not news either. What on earth was she leading up to? What had the gossip-mongers invented this time?

He swallowed and reminded himself that he came here to hear the latest gossip, didn't he? And if it seemed to be about himself, that was all the more reason to listen to it and to listen carefully. 'So?' he prompted.

She giggled this time and shook a finger at him, as one might at a tiresome child. 'He still has one daughter unmarried.'

Hosé thought of what might have happened if Annette's marriage to William Clough had taken place and repressed a shudder. 'The *variole* was cruel indeed,' he said neutrally.

It was Marianne who shrugged this time. 'It was God's will,' she dismissed this. 'However, she may have lost her looks but she still has her fortune.' There was no hint of resentment: God also ordered such things. 'Many a man would overlook a few pock marks for that.'

"Few" did not quite cover the reality but Hosé could see now where Marianne was leading. He could also see why the question of his own supposed paternity should suddenly have become a matter of general interest, in Nice anyway. He let out a careful breath.

In fact, he was dumbfounded. He spent much of his life picking up snippets of hearsay and information and weaving them together. He had missed this one completely. He was silent for several minutes thinking about it. It was not such a surprising fabrication really, when one looked at it from Marianne's point of view, from what she thought she knew.

How to handle this one?

'You may be a bastard,' she continued, 'But at least you are part of the Grimaldo family.' Her fingers lingered on his ink-stained cuff. 'And,' she continued, 'They say that the Holy Father can change that, being a bastard.'

Hosé did not doubt it.

'But even if you had to stay a bastard,' she went on happily, 'You could still marry the Donna Annette and .....'

He put a hasty finger against her lips; he had got the point.

She pouted a little; she had been enjoying the tale. She had also been savouring the possibilities of being a special friend to someone who might soon be a person of such consequence. She said nothing for a few moments then added a little crossly, 'But obviously, you could not if you were her brother.'

Obviously, he could not even though he was not Annette's brother!

Had the Donna herself heard of this interesting suggestion?

A suspicion came into his mind.

He carefully disentangled himself from the girl; going out would give him some time to think. He stumbled out of the back door. He leaned against the wall hardly noticing the stench as he tried to get his thoughts in order.

At the far end of the alley there was the noise of a scuffle and a sudden scream. As Hosé looked that way, a figure pushed past him.

'*Nee*!' shouted Job van Damme, the muck kicked up by his flying feet spattering the front of Hosé's gown.

'Ayyub!'

Hosé moved quickly down the alley; he could just make out three bodies locked together.

There was a vicious curse in Spanish from the largest figure. A raised arm was silhouetted against the evening sky, the solid limb chopped downwards like a woodman's axe and one of the smaller figures dropped away.

Hosé pulled up sharply to avoid treading on the fallen form. As he hesitated, the boy groaned and moved. There was the sound of more people emerging from the wine shop. They would care for the lad.

Hosé set off after the others.

At the end of the alley he paused. In front of him was the harbour. On the quay were fishing nets and baskets, barrels and stacks of timber, heaps of rough quarried stone and the myriad other items that littered a busy port readying itself for a new season. But everyone had finished for the day; the area was deserted.

He held his breath, straining to hear. There was only the slap of the waves against the wooden piles, the faint grinding of a nearby vessel at its mooring. The only human sound was the voices in the alley behind him.

Then his ear caught a faint noise; to his left. He moved carefully towards one of the sturdier storerooms. His steps were silent; he had long since learned to compensate for the false sole in his boot.

The noise came again: strangled sounds and the distinctive thump of flesh on flesh.

Then the heavy breathing of an aroused man; desperate scrabbling.

Hosé tucked his gown firmly into his belt. He reached for the door with his left hand and flung it wide. He barely had time to make out piles of jars, before there was a loud Spanish oath and a large figure launched itself at him from the back of the room. Hosé dodged the attack; but in the confined space caught one of the piles with his elbow. Pots crashed to the ground.

His adversary leaped across the shard strewn floor. Hosé dodged again.

This time his hand dislodged more pots on purpose. The man struggled to keep his footing as heavy pottery struck his shins.

There was a brief moment for Hosé to assess his opponent. The man had recovered well from the sudden interruption to his other activities, it seemed: an instinctive, or well-practised, fighter then.

Hosé reached for another pot.

The man anticipated it this time, and jumped out of the way. His long arms reached out. His eager hands clutched at air.

With a roar, he leaped forward.

This time Hosé moved to meet him. He grasped a burly forearm and used the man's own momentum to swing him, and slam him onto his back.

The breath whooshed out of the man's chest as he landed and gasped like a stranded fish. He managed a ragged gulp and struggled to his knees.

Hosé's foot caught him under the jaw and threw him backwards again.

The man rolled over and made another attempt to get up.

Hosé's boot connected unerringly and the man screamed. It would be a little while before he sought any further sexual pleasures, Hosé thought with some satisfaction and repeated the action.

The man retched violently.

Hosé grasped the man's neck; his fingers found the point they were seeking and squeezed. The man thrashed desperately. Definitely a man who trained; hard. Hosé applied more pressure to the thick muscles. He gauged his moment as the struggles grew less and the big body went slack.

Hosé released his hold; he did not want to face another accusation of murder.

He smiled grimly to himself as he seized the unfastened lacing of the man's points and jerked them free; using them to tie the large hands.

He rose to his feet; the slight figure who had been watching him moved back.

'It's all right,' he said, his own breath a little short.

There was silence.

'It will be some time before he comes around.' Hosé tried to sound reassuring.

There was a loud sniff and the figure moved.

Hosé stepped forward, then retreated hastily as the fingers aimed at his eyes raked down his cheek. He caught the hand tightly and struggled to prevent the other one from pulling out a large tuft of his hair. He was too busy defending himself to make more than one or two gasped protests. In any case, he doubted if he could have made himself heard over the stream of invective. It was a mixture of harbour language from several parts of the Middle Sea; in other circumstances, he might have found it entertaining.

He was suddenly exasperated; being considerate was achieving nothing. He took the offensive, capturing the marauding hands and twisting them fiercely behind the slight form. There was a gasp of pain.

'Sorry,' he said insincerely, increasing the pressure.

'Let go of me!'

'With pleasure,' he said, 'If you stop attacking me.'

Spittle sprayed his face.

His grip tightened. 'This is ridiculous,' he said. 'I just rescued you from that man.'

'So, I should show my gratitude!'

'What?

'It's always the same thing.'

'It is not.' Hosé was angry. 'Not all men prey on boys.'

'Boys?' The figure suddenly stilled.

There was a long silence and Hosé cautiously relaxed his hold a little. 'Can I let you go?' he asked. 'Or will you try to gouge my eyes out?'

There was no answer.

He stood back, poised for a renewed attack. 'I'm sorry,' he said, with some truth now. 'You have obviously been badly treated.' He put out his hand. 'I can see you home,' he offered. 'Or,' he added hastily, pulling his hand back again, 'Not.'

There was no response.

'What were you doing in this part of town anyway, on your own at this hour?' He had time now to be curious.

'I think I can answer that question.' A voice spoke from behind them.

Hosé half turned.

A figure pushed past him. 'Rab, are you all right?' Job van Damme demanded.

A gulp and an impatient sniff. 'What about you?' came the rejoinder. 'That Spanish oaf hit you!'

'I'm fine.'

'I'm not so sure about that, Jakob.' said his father. 'That is a nasty cut on your head. Maybe it should be stitched.' He hesitated.

Hosé thoughts instantly went to the Jew, but he wanted to extricate himself from this situation as soon as possible; he did not know why these Lowlanders were here, but their connection with Clough was danger enough.

Before he could say anything, however, Rab spoke. 'Isaac lives in the Grimaldo villa.'

There was something about the wording that bothered Hosé.

'But will he see us at this time of night? Perhaps it could wait until the morning.' Cornelius sounded doubtful.

Job suddenly swayed on his feet. It was Pieter who caught him.

'He'll see us,' said Rab confidently.

Why would Rab be that confident? Another question added itself to the considerable list building in Hosé's mind.

Rab led the way out onto the quay as Pieter carried a now senseless Job along the wharf and up through the town.

Isaac responded almost instantly to Rab's knock.

A candle on the table behind him illuminated the book he had been reading.

Hosé did not need to see the title page to know what it was: *Continens, Being a Comprehensive Book of Medicine translated from the Notebooks of al-Razi, including Extracts from earlier Writers and a Criticism of Galen - Breschia 1486.* The book may have been printed in Breschia but Hosé had bought it in Lyons. He was glad that Isaac had refrained from asking either its cost or where Hosé could possibly have got that sort of money. The Jew had accepted the gift gravely, turning it over several times before finally cutting open the first pages with surgical precision and perusing the neat print.

The margins, Hosé noted, were now crowded with tiny hand written notes.

The physician's deep-sunk eyes took in the group at the door, resting on Rab's dishevelled appearance for a moment, before moving onto Job. The Jew made a gesture of invitation, his gaze scanning the two seamen as they entered with their bloodied burden.

He moved quietly and efficiently to gather what he needed and nodded at Rab to light more candles. Rab knew exactly where to find everything.

A bony finger attracted Hosé's wandering attention. Hosé recounted, briefly, what had happened.

The physician nodded as he gently removed the soaked cloth from around Job's head. The gash, somewhere near the left temple, had bled a lot but Hosé could see that it was only oozing now. The Jew continued his examination carefully, moving the boy's head gently and lifting the closed eyelids.

He rinsed his hands in a bowl that smelled vaguely of the herbs that grew on the local hillside. Maybe he fainted only from loss of blood, he wrote. Maybe there is bruising inside the head. He will rest and we shall see. First, I shall stitch the wound.

He had not used his usual shorthand but written this in full to show to Cornelius.

The Lowlander nodded.

Rab stretched to see what Isaac had written. 'But he will be all right, won't he?'

The Jew moved his hand. Probably.

Hosé had watched Isaac at work before; he had even been required to help on occasion but he did not relish the task. Now he watched with a mixture of relief and a strange resentment as Rab assisted the physician, seemingly unbothered by the sticky mess and the deep cut. The Jew used wine to cleanse the area and expose the jagged edges of the laceration. He then uncorked a jar and extracted a fine curved steel needle from the pungent oil inside; he used this with a length of silk thread to insert several swift and neat stitches. Finally, he applied a salve from his store.

'What is it?' asked Rab.

Isaac pointed to the label on the jar.

Rab's lipped moved hesitantly.

Isaac finished his work and cleaned his hands carefully before writing something; from right to left. This time Rab nodded.

Isaac cleared the battered tablet.

Cornelius moved as if to gather up the boy, but the Jew stopped him. He must stay here, at least until he wakes properly.

The seaman paused doubtfully. 'How long will that be?'

The Hebrew shrugged. Perhaps a few hours, perhaps a few days.

Cornelius frowned. 'We must go back to the *Liesabeta*. Thomas is on his own there.'

'We can go,' said his usually silent brother. 'Jakob will be fine here.'

Isaac looked hard at the big Lowlander and slowly nodded his head.

'Of course he'll be all right here,' put in Rab. 'We'll look after him.'

Cornelius hesitated a moment longer, staring at his pale and unconscious son.

Hosé watched the expression on the seaman's face then turned away a little impatiently. He found Pieter looking at him, the light grey eyes direct and placid. 'Jakob will be fine here,' repeated the big man.

Cornelius reached out a hand, lifting a lock of stained hair away from the boy's brow with a weather-beaten forefinger. 'I'm sure you are right, Pieter,' he replied over his shoulder. 'You usually are.'

About many things, recalled Hosé; like when the fog would lift at sea and a good wind would get up; things that could not usually be predicted by men. There had always been an other-worldliness to Pieter.

'I'll see you out,' Hosé said to Cornelius. 'I'll send a couple of the Grimaldo men with you in case you meet the watch on your way back to the port.' He smiled a little without humour; sometimes watchmen jumped to wrong conclusions. 'And give instructions to let you visit whenever you wish.' He added to Isaac, 'I won't be long.' He had many questions to put, although he feared the Jew might have a few of his own; better to get it over.

Tomorrow will be soon enough, read the note on the Jew's tablet.

Hosé glanced at Rab and back at the physician. So, they had more immediate things to discuss, did they?

He turned and led the Lowlanders out.

Chapter 3

Hosé swallowed the cold salt mutton and bread and rose from the board.

He liked to break his fast early: it meant he could generally avoid having to eat with any members of the Grimaldo family. This particular morning, he also wanted to see Isaac before work started in the office.

A servant appeared at his side. The Donna Annette presented her compliments and would like to see him.

Hosé hesitated. 'Where?'

He was not too surprised by the answer.

He greeted her formally.

She looked with interest at his face. 'Fighting again?' she inquired. 'Another ambush?'

'A misunderstanding,' he said shortly. It was more than likely she already knew about it, but he did not think that was what she wanted to talk about; he certainly didn't; not until he had talked to Isaac at any rate.

He waited politely for her to seat herself by the little fountain in the centre of the garden. The air was still chill but a brightness in the eastern sky promised sunshine.

'A bit early in the season for a rendezvous in a flowery bower,' he remarked.

She shrugged. 'As you once pointed out, this is a good place to meet and not be overheard.'

He looked around at the open space with its low growing plants and shrubs; the nearest place of concealment was some tamarisk a little way away, and even their feathery branches offered little cover.

He had also chosen the garden as a meeting place on a previous occasion because while one could not be overheard one could certainly be seen; that offered its own protection.

Annette pushed aside the vizard and her smile mocked him. 'It was the only place I was sure you would agree to meet me alone. Was I right?'

'Perhaps,' he acknowledged. 'You also know why that is so,' he added deliberately.

'You still do not trust me,' she said quietly, her pale eyes watched him. 'Or you still do not trust yourself with me.'

'A bit of both,' he answered evenly.

'You are attracted to me?'

He drew a breath. 'We have had this conversation before.'

'The *variole* has made me repulsive.'

'Don't use that trick,' he said sharply. 'I will not be manoeuvred into paying you empty compliments.'

'No,' she said. 'You are not to be manoeuvred, are you?' She tucked her long white hands into a fold of her gown.

'You're cold?'

She shook her head. 'I have always found that a challenge: a man who could not be brought to heel.'

'But those that come at your beck and call are no longer interesting. An insoluble dilemma,' he smiled a little.

'I realise that now.'

He lifted an eyebrow.

'Don't you believe I have changed at all?' she demanded.

'Your interests may lie elsewhere these days, my lady, but you still have the same need to find and overcome challenges.'

'Don't call me "my lady",' she said.

'Why not?'

'Because I know very well you are not any bastard clerk.'

'But everyone else believes it.' He watched her closely.

She continued. 'I do not know who you really are.....'

He interrupted her. 'Do you not think that might be part of the challenge?'

She shook her head. 'I have thought about that. I have thought a lot, these last years, believe it or not.'

'And what is your latest thinking?' he inquired evenly.

She looked at him closely. 'Damn you,' she said, but mildly. 'You know!'

'As does half of Nice it seems.'

'Oh?'

'It is talked of in the wine shops,' he said.

'What do they say about it then?'

'They can already smell the ox that will be roasted for them in celebration of the nuptials.'

She smiled a little at his tone. 'But would it be such a bad idea?'

'For whom?'

'For you, for the Grimaldo business.'

'And for you?' he inquired. 'It would be a way of getting what you said a long time ago that you were determined to have.'

She flushed angrily. 'That was a very long time ago. I didn't mean it.' She amended, 'At least I don't mean it now.'

'No?'

'No!' She lifted her hands then pushed them back under her gown with determination. 'I am not going to beg,' she said.

'It would get you nowhere,' he agreed. 'And it would not become you.' He shifted a little on the cold bench. 'I thought we had left all this behind. I hoped we could work together without all the old games, Annette.' He said her name softly, without the title. 'I have come to respect how you run the business. You have a good head. You have learned well. If I have somehow given you the impression that my admiration was more personal, then I am sorry.'

She shook her head and wisps of her pale blond hair escaped the headdress; the *variole* had not diminished its silky brilliance. She tucked it back impatiently. 'No,' she said. 'You have been quite honest about that.' She looked at him steadily. 'I do not really know who you are,' she repeated her words, then added, 'Or what you are doing here.' She paused, but he did not help her. 'Even my father cannot tell me that.'

'You have discussed it with him?' he asked politely.

She nodded. 'Of course. He accepts that I need to know everything about the business and the payments from Sultan Bayezit are part of that. The agreement is that the Grimaldi make it possible for you and Isaac to be here and I realised a long time ago that that had to be connected with Prince Cem.' She looked at him curiously. 'I would have thought the Sultan would want his brother out of the way. Such a rival must be a constant danger.' She watched him, 'I would have expected the Sultan to hire an assassin to rid him of the problem.'

Hosé said nothing.

'You must have had plenty of opportunity for that over the past five years,' she continued, 'But you didn't.' She waited for some response. 'I can understand why the Sultan is paying us, but I don't understand what he is paying you for.'

She was right about a lot of it; she was wrong about the last part. But Hosé did not think Annette would understand, even if he were free to tell her.

'Anyway,' she said briskly, returning to the original point of the conversation, 'What better way for you to stay here in Nice, doing whatever it is you are doing, than to be a real part of the Grimaldo family?'

'Your concern for me is touching,' he commented. 'And have you discussed this with your father?'

She hesitated. 'No,' she said finally.

'And you think he will not hear what is said in the wine-shops?'

She was silent.

'Which raises the interesting question of how the idea spread in the first place.' He looked hard at her. 'I think,' he persisted, 'That you deliberately started the gossip yourself. You must have known I would hear it, although you may pretend otherwise; but the real target was not me anyway, was it? It was your father.' The pale eyes met his, unremorseful. 'You thought he would not like the idea but if it were already public it would restrict his opposition. He could hardly suddenly deny my supposed blood relationship to the family.'

'Pah!' she was suddenly impatient. 'What does it matter? It is a good idea; for everyone, including Papa. He will see that afterwards.'

Hosé took a deep breath, savouring the clean chill air. He shook his head slowly. 'To be successful in business one undoubtedly has to be cunning, at least as clever as the others; perhaps that applies to other things in life too, but is scheming the way to deal with relationships between people?'

She looked surprised. 'But this *is* about successful business.' She stared at him. 'What else would it be?'

He laughed.

'Why are you laughing at me?'

'I'm not,' he said, shaking his head. 'I'm laughing at myself.' He smiled at her. 'Try to tell me about it; without any ciphers, without any coded messages, without any hidden meanings, without any manipulating or manoeuvring. Just tell me in clear language what you have in mind. Is that possible?'

'You mean you might agree?'

'I can hardly say that until I have heard about it,' he pointed out.

She accepted that. 'All right then. I'll try.'

Hosé resisted another laugh at the effort it cost her.

'You're right, of course, that I enjoy the challenges of commerce and trade. It's not just that someone *has* to run things now Papa is getting old, but I actually like it. And I'm good at it.'

He nodded. 'Very good,' he agreed.

'Better than most men.'

He nodded again.

'Certainly, better than those types that Papa married my sisters to.' She paused to consider her next words. 'When Isaac first suggested it, Papa only agreed because Isaac said it was essential for my health that I find an interest in life. Now Papa accepts that I can do it and I pretty much run the business, but he still worries about what will happen when he dies. A woman has little power or position in her own right: she depends on her father, then her husband for that. We have talked about this quite a lot and reluctantly I accept he is right. When he is gone, I will have to fight prejudice as well as our rivals. And,' she continued, 'Even if I manage to keep it all going successfully what will happen to it after me? Who will keep it going for the family?'

'And the answer?'

'A husband, of course; to provide the status. And,' she glanced mischievously at the fountain, 'To provide an heir who can be taught the business.'

Hosé ignored the outrageous innuendo and repressed a shudder; he had been just such an heir, once upon a time.

Annette continued. 'Within that simple answer there are several problems; the first one is obviously who to choose for a husband.'

'At least you have some say in that, this time,' he pointed out.

She nodded. 'Although Clough rejected me after the *variole* I know most men will pretend not to mind if they think the Grimaldo fortune is involved.' She pulled a wry face as she put this truth into words. 'But that is part of the difficulty, you see, because I shall keep control over that. Any marriage settlement would make my husband a generous allowance but no direct access to the returns of the business. In the event of my death without an heir, the business would be broken up among various cousins.'

'That does not seem to be asking that much,' Hosé commented. 'There must surely be men without dynastic ambitions; men who would be happy to marry a "generous allowance".'

'Mm, quite possibly,' she agreed. 'But would such a man then make a good ambitious son?'

Hosé shrugged. 'You may arrange who you marry but you cannot arrange such things.' *God rules over the heavens and the earth. He creates what He wills. He gives daughters to whom He wills and sons to whom He pleases. To some he gives both sons and daughters and He makes sterile whom he wills. Omniscient is God, and mighty.* 'Maybe there will be no children; maybe there will be only daughters!' He smiled at her as he emphasised the "only" slightly. 'Maybe any sons will be feeble, or,' he added with feeling, 'Not be interested in trade and banking.'

She looked puzzled at his tone. 'You can't be talking about yourself; you do excellent work in the office.'

'I have other reasons for being there,' he said shortly.

'Was your father a trader?'

'I believe Gaspard made a good living.' Hosé took refuge in a facetious response.

'I thought this was supposed to be a frank discussion.'

Hosé pulled a face. 'I don't believe my father is relevant.'

'He might be,' she said seriously. 'Perhaps your talents come from him. Such things can go down families as much as hair colour or the shape of a nose.'

Isaac had once made a similar remark in relation to Hosé's facility with languages. Hosé did not want to think about his father; blood relationship had no part in his life. 'But often they don't,' he replied. 'Just look at you and all your sisters; you are the only one with a good head on your shoulders.'

'But that could be because our mother was such a goose.' She continued her idea. 'I have been talking to Jean-Paul l'Écurie.'

Hosé started. 'About the stables?'

'About the horses; how they are bred. He says it is important to choose both a good mare and a good stallion to get a good colt.'

Hosé winced.

'But don't you see,' she persisted, 'The family connections are always regarded as so important in arranging a marriage, to make alliances, to increase power and wealth, but unless the couple breed well it will all come to nothing.'

'All right.' Hosé was not really sure he wanted to hear the rest of what she had to say.

'You don't have important connections,' she said, 'At least as far as I know.' She waited hopefully. 'But,' she continued after a moment, 'Even if we start with the fiction that you are Gaspard's son that has a lot to recommend it. That would make you a Grimaldo by blood.'

'A bastard.'

'That might be changed.' She knew about Papal edicts too.

'Would it be a good idea to invite closer inspection of the circumstances?' Why was he even talking about it?

She nodded. 'I thought about that too; perhaps it would be better to leave that as it is. In the end, I don't think it would matter if the man I married was a bastard; the fact that he was apparently a Grimaldo would be more important. People might secretly point a finger and snigger but who cares? People already do that about my face.'

No point in denying that.

'So, you see,' she concluded, 'It is a perfect solution.' She lifted her hands and told off the points on her elegant fingers. 'You get a secure position in Nice; I get the status of being a married woman; and there is a good chance of creating an heir who will carry on the family company.' She waited for his reaction. 'Well? Don't you see?'

He was thinking hard. 'I may not stay in Nice,' he said eventually. 'I might have to leave.' He emphasised the next point, 'And not come back.' Who knew what would happen? And Hosé's future was not in his own hands.

She nodded calmly. 'I realise that, but I believe you will stay here as long as the Prince is around.'

Hosé stiffened. Had she heard about the rumours of Rome?

'He is young and strong and the Knights look after him well; he will live a long time yet.'

Hosé relaxed a little.

'And I would not try to stop you going,' she said. She added with mock gravity, 'If you never came back I would be sad.' She smiled. 'But I would not die of a broken heart. And a wealthy widow may do much as she pleases.'

He smiled with her.

'See,' she said. 'We understand each other very well. Would it be so terrible?'

He could see her point of view. For himself, of course, quite apart from anything else, he was not free to marry. But he could not talk to her about that; or any of the other considerations.

He picked up another point. 'You feel it necessary to force your father's hand,' he said. 'Does he have some other candidate in mind?'

She nodded. 'Since we started talking about it, he has been very busy.'

'And what fortunate man has he identified?'

She frowned at his choice of words then laughed a little. 'At first he came up with all sorts of proposals: the son of a wine merchant he deals with in Lisbon; the heir to a title and a large estate near Barcelona; a trader in leather from Marseille….'

'François de Beaumont?' The man had escorted Annette on her journey north the previous year.

She nodded.

'I thought you said he was an old man.'

'He is; not quite as old as my father, but definitely the wrong side of forty.'

Not what Annette had in mind.

'Some distant cousin to the Duke of Savoy,' she continued. 'Even a Greek whose family owns goodness knows what in the Levant.' She shivered a little, although the sun had now appeared and was spreading a faint warmth across the garden. 'Then he thought about how powerful the neighbouring kingdom of France is growing and how our family is isolated here in Nice; and that perhaps the best idea would be to strengthen links with one of the Genoese *Alberghi*.'

Hosé was not convinced about the reasoning but he was curious to know where Nicolas Grimaldo's choice had fallen. 'Which Albergo is he considering?' he asked casually.

'The Spinola.'

'One of the most important,' he commented.

'Yes,' she said, 'And the Spinola Albergo has widespread trade links.'

Very useful to the Grimaldi no doubt.

'Although it did suffer at Caffa.'

He looked politely interested.

'The Spinola family itself only lost one member, but there were other families from the Albergo that were hit much harder. The Lomellini for instance.'

'Oh?'

'The head of the family and his sons all died.'

Not quite.

'And?' He watched her.

'The head of the Lomellini now is a weak-minded young man called Gianmaria.' Her voice was scornful.

Not very clever perhaps, but not weak-minded. 'And your father thinks he would make the ideal husband for you?'

'Exactly!' she spat out the word. 'He is not even a real Genoese nobleman. The family was only adopted into the Albergo because his uncle managed to plant a few olive trees.'

She had not got that quite right either: he had pioneered a new and highly successful way of managing the olive groves; but Hosé did not explain. 'Has your father opened negotiations?'

Annette looked furious. 'He sent a messenger; without consulting me!'

Ah. Not the way to gain her cooperation.

'So now you are negotiating for yourself,' Hosé smiled.

'Of course,' she said fiercely. 'I don't want an idiot to father my children.'

'Perhaps he is not really such an idiot,' Hosé said cautiously. 'Maybe he only seems weak in comparison with the Spinolas. And,' he reminded her, 'You need someone who will not meddle in Grimaldo affairs.' Why on earth was he arguing for the match? He could not see Gianmaria being happy in such a position and with such a firebrand for a wife.

'You will not meddle; you as good as said so.'

Hosé moved to stand up.

'You can't go; you haven't given me an answer yet.'

'I can't say yes, Annette. The most I can say is that I will think about your situation.'

She looked as if she would keep him there, then thought better of it. She offered him her hand and rose from her seat. 'It is a good idea,' she made one more plea. 'If you think it over you will see for yourself. At least promise me you will consider it and we can talk about it again.'

'I will think about your situation,' he repeated. 'And,' he added, 'Please do not stir up any more gossip. It will not help your cause.'

'Maybe it has already served some purpose,' she said looking sideways at him.

He laughed reluctantly.

He headed for Isaac's rooms, but was intercepted by yet another servant. This time it was a note from the office; there was a despatch from Egypt that needed urgent attention.

Wasn't there anyone else?

It was well after noon when Hosé finally got back to the villa.

Rab answered his knock at the door and reluctantly allowed him to enter.

'Where is Isaac?'

A shrug of the narrow shoulders.

'When will he be back?'

Another shrug.

'How is Jakob?' Hosé knew Isaac would not have left the boy if he was still in any danger.

'I'm fine,' said a voice.

Hosé turned. The boy was sitting up, his face almost as white as the bandage around his head, but his eyes alert. He gave a watery smile. Hosé was reminded again of the boy's mother. 'Good,' he said a little shortly.

He paused. Where was Isaac?

'Has your father been here today?' Hosé needed to resolve the question of why Cornelius was in Nice.

The boy began to shake his head then thought better of it. 'No,' he said. 'But that's all right,' he assured Hosé. 'I'll be going back to the *Liesabeta* soon.'

'Not today,' put in Rab quickly. 'Isaac said you must stay here at least until tomorrow.'

'No need really,' protested Jakob. 'I feel fine.'

'You said your head aches,' Rab argued.

Jakob grimaced. 'Not much.'

'Isaac said it might be a sign of something more serious. You must stay here and I must keep a watch on you.'

Hosé moved towards the door.

'I bet that was a good fight.' Jakob's voice was a little wistful.

Hosé half turned.

'Rab says he is a soldier, that Spanish oaf.'

'Oh?' Hosé looked at Rab. He really did want to ask Isaac some questions.

Rab would not meet his gaze.

'It didn't take you long to deal with him,' persisted Jakob.

Hosé shrugged.

'And you a clerk.' A faint flush lit the pale cheeks and he made haste to add, 'At least that is what Rab says.' He stopped, embarrassed.

'And what else does Rab have to say?'

Jakob looked uncertainly from one to the other. 'We were just talking,' he said awkwardly.

'Job was teaching me some Diets,' put in Rab sullenly.

Hosé nodded. '*Goed zo!*' He watched the boy.

'*U spreekt Diets?*'

'*Nog maar een klein beetje.* Perhaps I should join the lessons.'

Jakob's open face lit up. Hosé wanted to believe the boy was as innocent as he looked.

Rab's face on the other hand was tight with animosity.

Hosé nodded to them both. 'Later, perhaps,' he said.

He turned once more towards the door.

He looked around the wine shop. It was not so busy at this time of day, although a handful of seamen was conversing loudly with the local boatmen and even more loudly with the local women.

Marianne spotted him and detached herself immediately from the group. She put a possessive hand on his arm and pulled him towards a bench at the back of the room.

Hosé followed reluctantly. He had been hoping to find Sayf; the Arab had not been at his house.

'You missed the fun,' she said, placing a hand on his knee.

He lifted it. 'What fun?'

'This morning,' she said, her eyes bright with the memory. 'Philippe found his store had been wrecked, smashed pots everywhere. He was furious. Then he found Garcia tied up.'

'Garcia?'

'Garcia de Tineo. He is a Spanish mercenary from the castle. He used to come here often for a drink. And,' she pulled a face, 'For other things.'

'Oh?'

She shifted. 'He is very fond of the girls, that one.'

'A soldier; what else do you expect?'

She was silent.

'The girls here serve favours as well as drinks,' he pointed out.

Marianne looked angry. 'Of course,' she was not disputing that. 'But he is violent with it. His tastes,' she paused, 'Are beyond decency.'

Her choice of words could have been amusing if she had not been so obviously upset. 'Oh?' he said again.

'A girl may favour a man if she wishes, but if she does not wish it she is entitled to keep herself to herself.' Her eyes flashed. 'None of the girls here would go with him once they knew what he demanded.'

'Did he hurt you?' Hosé enquired quietly.

She shook her head. 'No, not me, but a couple of the other girls. Then when he realised he could not get what he wanted here he stopped coming. There were stories of him finding his sport elsewhere.'

So.

'Now,' her face brightened. 'It seems he has got his deserts. Someone beat him and left him tied up by the waterside.' She gave a tight laugh. 'He had been bound with the laces from his own points.' She smiled more broadly, 'And Philippe blamed him for all the smashed pots and threatened to throw him into the harbour.' She pulled a face. 'Pity he didn't.'

'What happened?'

'Antoine de la Forêt arrived, with the guard.

'The Governor?'

'The Governor,' she confirmed. 'He stood there,' she gestured towards the doorway, 'And gave a long speech about how the town had had enough of the soldiers and no citizen was safe anymore in the streets and how he would take up the matter personally with the captain at the castle.' She grinned at the memory. 'He demanded to know if Garcia could explain how Philippe's pots had got broken. The Spaniard opened his mouth a couple of times like a stranded fish then let fly in his own tongue. The guards hauled him away,' she finished her tale abruptly and looked at him. 'The Governor never asked how Garcia came to be tied up.' She lifted a finger to the marks on his face. 'How did you get those scratches?'

'Not from a Spanish soldier,' said Hosé firmly.

'You went out the back last night and never returned.'

He shrugged. 'I had other things to attend to.'

'Those Lowlanders went out about the same time and never came back either.' She pursed her lips.

'But Garcia did not accuse anyone?'

She shook her head. 'I'll bet he had been up to his usual evil tricks. He wouldn't want to talk about that!'

Hosé hoped it stayed that way.

'They have not been in tonight, the Lowlanders?' he asked.

'No,' she said.

'Nor Sayf?'

She pouted. 'You ask about everyone but me,' she protested.

He ran a finger across the rough skin of the hand still resting in his. 'Let me see,' he said lightly. 'Peeling onions I think and scaling fish; perhaps crushing some garlic and undoubtedly pitting olives; certainly, pouring out Jean Paul's red wine.'

She tried to hide her work-stained hand.

He kept hold of it and laid his own alongside, blackened as it was with ink. 'Is there shame in serving others?'

Hosé left as soon as he decently could. He limped into the town. He paused as he passed the Rue Guidaria and looked for a moment at the chains and iron fence. There might still be some ways in and out but they would be dangerous. He stood considering, then turned and retraced his steps towards the harbour.

He looked for the cog. At first, he could not see it because a couple of bigger boats had arrived and the little craft had been moved to the end of the quay. He walked slowly, studying the little vessel. She certainly looked out of place here in the Middle Sea: her flat bottom and single sail suited her perfectly to her home waters, the myriad shallow inlets of the Lowland coast, but she was hardly designed for the wider and wilder seas of the ocean. What had prompted the van Dammes to make such a voyage? He looked more carefully as he drew closer. The carvel planking showed evidence of many repairs, the boards scarred and battered, around the projecting deck beams.

Hosé nearly bumped into the boy who was standing staring at one of the bigger craft.

'Where do you think she's from?' asked Hosé casually, in Catalan.

The boy did not turn his head but answered in the same language. 'She's a northern caravel. She is built on the same lines as that Portuguese caravel.' He nodded at the other new arrival. 'But she is longer in width and her rudder is heavier; see, it's hung from the stern post with pivot pins.'

Hosé looked.

'She can carry a lot of sail too.'

'Fine as long as the wind blows,' Hosé returned, thinking of oar-driven galleys that skimmed across the water whatever the weather.

'Coming up or down the Atlantic there's nearly always wind of some sort, and even if it's contrary she can beat into it pretty close with her sails rigged like that.'

Hosé took that in.

'Diaz would never have made it in any other vessel.'

'Diaz?' Hosé queried.

'The Portuguese who found the tip of Africa and rounded the Cape of Torments,' the boy answered absently, still staring at the caravel.

Cape of Torments? 'He actually rounded the tip and managed to return?'

'We had to stop at Lisbon on the way here to make some repairs,' said the boy. 'Diaz was all the talk along the Tagus.'

Hosé pondered the news for a moment, trying to adjust his thoughts. He looked at the boy and found his companion was now staring out over the water, his eyes focused on the darkening horizon. 'It'll be caravels that make the next trip and sail as far as the Indies; one way or the other.'

'One way or the other?'

'Down Africa again and then east from the Cape; or perhaps all the way to the west as far as Cipangu and Cathay.'

Hosé wracked his mind.

'The Genoese Colombo was in Lisbon too. The Spanish weren't willing to finance the voyage he wants to make to the west so he was trying the Portuguese. He spent years in Portugal and what with Diaz's success I suppose he hoped the Portuguese might help.'

'But?' said Hosé, struggling to keep up.

'The Portuguese will surely follow up the passage Diaz found; at least they know for certain that it exists.'

'So, what will he do now, this Colombo?'

The boy's face lit up. 'They say he might try the King of England. Imagine if he did. Then they would sail out of Bristol most likely. Other boats have sailed from there and found great fishing grounds and land beyond Greenland.'

'Cathay?'

'It must be, I suppose.' The boy looked uncertain. 'Father says it would take a lot of money and there is no guarantee that there would be a decent return on the investment. He says King Henry is not rich enough, for the wars between the Lancastrians and the Yorkists have cost England dear.'

Father? Hosé filed that question for later. 'So, it will be Diaz who sails next, not Colombo?'

The boy shrugged. 'The Portuguese are bound to send another expedition sooner or later, aren't they? But Diaz said the caravels he took last time were too small. They need to be heavier and stronger and he thinks square rigged sails would be better. They'll take some time to build.' He sighed. 'It would be interesting to see if he is right.'

Hosé tried to share his vision, but he still had trouble seeing beyond the

Green Sea of Darkness. Would the Portuguese seamen really sail safely round into the Indian seas?

He came back to England; he had more than a passing interest in England.

'You talked of the King of England and a port called Bristol. Where is that?'

'In the west of England,' came the reply. 'It is much better placed for voyages to the west.'

'Better than?'

'Ipswich or Norwich.'

Hosé swallowed. 'Have you been to these places?'

'I only went to Bristol once,' the boy said regretfully, 'But I know Ipswich well.'

'And Norwich?'

'Of course,' the boy's voice was low. 'I live there.' He paused. 'Or at least I used to.' He turned his gaze back to the northern caravel. 'They build some fine boats there.'

'For the wool trade?' hazarded Hosé.

The boy nodded.

'There are big wool merchants?'

The boy nodded again.

Hosé could still only see his face from the side but he could see the tightening of the jaw muscles. 'You know a lot about boats,' he said, steering a slightly different course, looking for the right wind.

'I'm…,' another slight pause. 'I was apprenticed to a boat builder.'

'Now you are here in Nice.' Hosé invited an explanation.

But the boy was silent and turned abruptly. 'I should go back to the *Liesabeta*.'

'*Liesabeta?*' Hosé queried.

The boy indicated the cog.

'That is a very interesting boat.' Hosé still hoped for more.

'Interesting?' The boy suddenly laughed. 'That is not the word most people use about it, especially in these parts.'

'A little old-fashioned perhaps,' admitted Hosé with a smile, *but solid and well-balanced.*

'She handles well-enough with the bottom boards flooded,' the boy said. He stopped and turned, looking once more at the two caravels. 'But boatbuilding has changed completely with skeleton-build designs.'

Hosé did not get the chance to pursue the subject. At that moment, there were voices aboard the cog.

'Hey, Thomas!' Cornelius called. He added something in Diets.

Hosé caught the word "*finished*".

Cornelius turned to the figure behind him and offered him a hand. Isaac took it and stepped onto the gangplank. As he reached the quay the Jew looked around. For a moment his eyes swept past Hosé, then they returned and regarded him with a querying look.

Hosé swallowed his surprise and also looked around; he knew what Isaac was looking for. Given the mood of the times, the Hebrew needed an escort whenever he ventured away from the Grimaldo villa. Even then he avoided busy times and crowded streets. It was likely he had left the palace early in the morning and had waited until late in the day to return; apparently using the time in between to visit the van Dammes.

Hosé scowled. What had they been talking about?

'Where are they then?' he asked instead.

Isaac looked around again and indicated with a finger where the guards should have been. Then made a gesture, clearly suggesting they had probably legged it to the nearest wine shop.

'Well they weren't at Jean Paul's.'

Isaac's expression showed he knew there were many other wine shops. He also knew the guard needed no excuse to distance themselves from their charge.

Cornelius put in, 'You are welcome to wait here,' he said. 'Or we can go with you up to the villa. I would like to see Jakob. And,' he gestured at Hosé, 'With him along it should be safe enough.' He peered through the gathering gloom. 'Hosé isn't it?'

Hosé was acutely aware of Pieter's eyes on him. And of Isaac's on Pieter.

'It was you who floored the Spanish soldier?' Thomas put in.

Hosé nodded again.

'Why did he attack Rab anyway?'

Hosé glared at Isaac; he had been waiting all day to ask the same question.

The Jew returned the look blandly and took out his tablet. I think we could return to the villa. It is almost dark now.

'And the....' Hosé nearly used a most unflattering word. 'The guard?'

The Jew's eyes gleamed. They will find me gone and then they will have some explaining to do, won't they?

Hosé gave a small smile: the Swiss mercenary captain would not be very sympathetic.

Thomas had been watching the exchange, with a deepening frown.

Isaac looked at him and raised a grizzled brow.

'I've been wondering,' began Thomas then stopped, flushing. He took a breath and finished with a rush. 'Why you can't talk.'

Cornelius frowned in rebuke but Isaac shook his head.

The Jew regarded Thomas solemnly for a moment before lowering his eyes and writing. Men do ungodly things in the name of God.

Thomas read the words, looked up at Isaac, then read the words a second time. 'God?' he said the word softly, almost to himself. 'I hadn't thought of that before,' he said. 'At least not really.' His young face twisted as he tried to explain himself. 'But Jews and Christians acknowledge the same God, don't they? God the Father that is.' He stopped.

Cornelius looked uncomfortable.

Isaac, however, smiled at the boy. He wrote again, at some length, pausing uncharacteristically as he searched to translate a word. Finally, he showed it to Thomas.

The boy again read it through twice before finally looking up. 'Of course,' he exclaimed, 'I know that. "*O Lord, how excellent is your name in all the earth! who has set your glory above the heavens.*" It is one of the Psalms!'

So, Thomas was well educated. Thomas who? Hosé was interrupted in his speculation.

' "*When I consider your heavens, the work of your fingers, the moon and the stars.*" ' Thomas's eyes gleamed. 'It also talks of the beasts of the fields, the birds of the air, and all creatures that travel the paths of the sea.'

Isaac looked at him appreciatively and wrote again. *Do you not see that those in the heavens and the earth, the sun and the moon and the stars, the mountains and the trees, the beasts and the countless men – all do homage to God?*

Thomas read out the words carefully. 'Also from the Bible?'

From the Recitation, wrote Isaac.

Thomas frowned. 'The Recitation?'

The Book of those the Franks call Infidels.

Cornelius shifted uneasily.

Isaac underlined: *All do homage to God*.

'I see.' Thomas's frown belied his words.

Isaac smiled wryly. Jews, Christians and Muslims all worship the same God. If every one really listened to what God ordains, instead of misusing His words to cloak their own base inhumanity, such things could not happen.

He opened his empty mouth and pointed with a bony finger.

Thomas's frown deepened.

'There's the guard!' Cornelius's relief was undisguised.

Chapter 4

'Oh, no!' Hosé placed himself firmly across the doorway.

Isaac glared at him.

'I have some questions that need answering,' said Hosé grimly.

The bony shoulders shrugged and the tablet appeared in the Jew's hand. Perhaps I have one of my own. He thrust the tablet at Hosé.

Hosé hesitated.

You know the van Dammes. Isaac's words were not a question.

'It was all a long time ago,' Hosé said. 'In another life. It has no significance now.'

No? Then why not tell me? You told me about a lot of other things, after Clough just failed to get you hanged in Moulins! The tablet clacked onto the table.

Hosé sighed. 'All right. But I still want answers to *my* questions,' he warned.

Isaac's face promised nothing.

Hosé perched himself on a stool and took a breath, and told Isaac about the voyage of a young Genoese boy to the Lowlands all those years ago.

The Jew did not interrupt then sat thinking for some time. Is it coincidence that these Lowlanders should appear in Nice now? he wrote finally.

Hosé grimaced. Trust Isaac to grasp the essential. 'I don't know. The other night in the wine shop they mentioned Clough. But,' he scowled, 'I couldn't understand what else they said.'

Isaac's gaunt features relaxed a little. Couldn't remember the language? He shook his head in mock rebuke.

Hosé gave a reluctant smile. 'But don't *you* know why they are here? You seem on pretty friendly terms with them.' Just one of Hosé's questions.

No, I do not know why they are here. But, yes, I do think they may be friends.

Hosé lifted an eyebrow as Isaac paused.

Somewhere in the distance he heard voices as servants finished the last tasks of the day; nearer at hand mice started about their business of the night.

He looked down as Isaac started to write.

I did not meet them at that time, but last year they rendered a kind service.

Hosé recognised circumlocution but ignored it for the moment. 'This is the first time they have been in Nice; Rab said so.' His tone was even as he continued, 'Where does Rab fit into this?' Another, perhaps more complex, question.

Rab went along the coast for me last year to collect various plants that I needed. Somehow young Jakob became involved and they spent some weeks on the task together. Isaac paused. I believe they enjoyed the time.

There was something about that pause. Hosé waited.

There has been little for Rab to enjoy in life. The Jew sighed softly.

'Why?' Hosé finally prompted. 'And how did you come to be involved?' He added, 'And Annette?'

Isaac hesitated.

Hosé said impatiently, 'I realise that Rab is not a boy, which,' he pulled a face, 'Makes the situation even more curious, you must admit!'

The Jew chewed the end of his stylus although he nodded, accepting Hosé's point.

Hosé had a sudden suspicion. 'She's been your patient, hasn't she?' he demanded.

The physician slowly nodded again.

Hosé made an exasperated sound. He knew Isaac set himself strict limits on discussing such matters. Mostly Hosé respected him for it. At that moment the young man felt only frustration. He got off the stool and paced around the room before coming to a stop and staring unseeingly at a shelf of jars and boxes.

'If it had just been a broken arm,' he flung at the Jew, 'You wouldn't be so reticent. So, I have to assume it was something more sensitive than that.' He glared at Isaac. 'How old is she? Or is that confidential information too?'

Isaac still hesitated then lifted his tablet. She is coming up for twelve. I treated her last year, but her problems started before that.

Hosé did not understand the last part, but his mind seized on the bit about last year. 'Garcia de Tineo,' he said slowly.

Isaac made no sign, but Hosé knew he was right. He remembered what Marianne had said about the Spaniard. He understood now what had happened recently down by the harbour: that was not the first time Garcia had met Rab, and the soldier had good reason to know she was a girl.

'Rab?' he asked suddenly. 'Is that her real name?'

Rabia, wrote Isaac.

The name did not mean anything to Hosé at first, then he remembered who had first spoken of a woman called Rabia. He smiled.

It was Isaac's turn to be curious. He prodded Hosé's arm.

'Prince Bayezit,' Hosé said softly, 'Once mentioned the name to me.'

Isaac's deep eyes gleamed. Ah yes, before he was Sultan; when he took an errant palace kul into his household.

Hosé put that memory back in its private place. 'She was a famous Sufi ascetic, was she not?'

Yes. She died some two hundred years after the Prophet. She believed people saw only a God of strict justice in the Recitation. For her He is also a God of love. He added, To be found through intense and earnest meditation.

Hosé's face sobered. There were some members of the Divan who wished the Sultan spent less time on such practices. Just as some of his "feet", notably the Vizier Muhammad, did not accept the Sultan's attitude to his renegade brother Cem.

'Have you heard direct from Lord Bayezit?' he asked Isaac abruptly.

The Jew nodded.

Hosé felt a pang of envy. 'After you leave Nice, I might receive such correspondence.'

Perhaps.

Hosé savoured the possibility for a few moments before returning to his quest for news of the Topkapi.

Isaac's face was grave. When I return there, it will be easier to discuss with the Sultan such matters as the Vizier Muhammad. It is difficult to do so from this distance.

Hosé was equally solemn. It was Vizier Muhammad who had sought to bring about the death of Prince Cem through the English merchant Clough.

Clough. So many things came back to Clough.

'Do you think the *Liesabeta* is here because of Clough?' Hosé asked quietly.

Isaac pondered. I really do not know. The van Dammes were already in these waters last year. As far as I can gather they were trading around the western end of the Middle Sea.

'Then returned to the Lowlands?'

Isaac shook his head. They spent the winter in Mallorca. Cornelius was telling me the news from there.

Hosé nodded; the Balearics were a busy crossroads.

Isaac hesitated before adding, They seem honest people and last summer they helped Rab and Jakob reach certain cliffs to gather herbs for me.

'They believe Rab is a boy?'

I think so.

'Even Jakob?'

Isaac nodded.

'She must be good at the deception.' Hosé's tone was not approving.

The Jew nodded slightly.

'Whose idea was it?'

Isaac shrugged.

Light suddenly dawned. 'Annette's?'

Isaac did not deny it.

'Why should she be involved?' Again, Hosé provided his own answer. 'She owes you a favour of course, and it would be just the sort of trick she would like to play!' That reminded him of her latest trick. Did Isaac know about that one too?

He hastily put another of his questions. 'Who is the other boy, Thomas?'

Now that is interesting.

'It is all interesting,' said Hosé a little sarcastically. 'What is his family name?'

Langton I believe. Isaac paused for effect.

Hosé scowled at him.

His mother was Ann Langton.

Hosé scowled again.

Thomas said, Isaac was drawing it out with considerable aplomb, that the first boat he ever built would be called the *Ann* for her.

'Get on with it.' Hosé did not know whether to be cross or amused.

His mother was a widow and remarried when Thomas was two. She died a year later in childbirth.

'And how does Thomas come to be sailing with the van Dammes? He mentioned something about being apprenticed to a boat builder.'

Ah! Been doing some investigation of your own? Isaac nodded in exaggerated admiration.

Hosé raised his eyes to the ceiling.

It seems his mother's second husband was never very interested in Thomas, although Cornelius told me the man had considered her ability to produce a son an additional advantage to the marriage contract.

'Additional?'

Isaac nodded approval as Hosé picked up the point. The main attraction of the marriage was that Ann Langton was a wealthy woman. She had inherited her first husband's business.

'What was this business?'

He had been a very successful silk merchant.

'Where?'

England.

'And the name of the second husband? Or can I guess?'

I should expect you to.

Clough; yet again. 'So how does the boy come to be here?'

I don't know. The stylus paused. But there is no sign that the boy is involved in Clough's devious activities. The Jew looked at Hosé. What did you make of him?

Hosé said almost reluctantly, 'He did not seem to know who I was or be interested in me.' He reflected for a moment. 'Unless he is exceptionally cunning....' He stopped again. 'No, I really don't think so.' He smiled. 'He has something of Pieter about him: an interest in something just out of sight of most people.'

Pieter is a remarkable man.

'But Thomas's "vision" is not really otherworldly,' Hosé continued his thought. 'Thomas has "visions" about this world.' He repeated some of what the boy had said about sailing to Cipangu and Cathay. 'And he wasn't talking about making a fortune trading; his interest seemed to be in the boats and the problems of navigating them.'

Isaac wrote. Perhaps the Franks will finally manage at last a little of what other seamen have been doing for centuries.

'You mean Muslim traders?'

Muslim traders, Isaac agreed, And others.

'Others?' Hosé was puzzled.

There are stories about seamen from beyond Islam.

Hosé frowned. Beyond Islam: the fabulous lands described by the Venetian Polos. He had heard those stories often enough when he was a boy. 'Stories?' he said out loud. 'Isn't that all they are?'

Maybe. Maybe not. Who first learned to use lodestone to direct a boat on a featureless sea?

'Muslim seamen,' Hosé answered promptly, 'Who also learned from the astronomers how to observe the stars and navigate by them.'

Isaac nodded. Astronomers such as the Persian Nassiruddin Tusi who worked in the famous observatory in Maraghah. They undoubtedly added much to the knowledge of man. But there were seamen using the lodestone hundreds of years before that; it was from them the Arab traders learned.

Hosé looked a little sceptical.

The old Hebrew continued. When I was a young man in Fez, Ibn Battuta was often talked about.

'Was Ibn Battuta a seaman?' Hosé added with a little laugh, 'Fez is nowhere near the sea!'

Isaac shook his head. He was at one time chief Qadi in Delhi but was also sent from there to Cathay. He learned much from his travels and in his old age in Fez he wrote of them and shared this knowledge with all who cared to listen. Isaac looked pointedly at Hosé.

'I should listen a bit more?' Hosé bridled. He felt he had certainly learned that lesson since coming to Nice.

Yes! Isaac's shorthand marks were uncompromising. And do not dismiss what at first may seem unlikely or strange. Keep all things in your mind. You would be surprised how many things link together later. But perhaps you have not lived long enough to see that yet.

Hosé swallowed hard; his age was hardly something he could do anything about. 'So,' he inquired pointedly, 'The use of the compass was discovered in Cathay?'

Almost certainly and almost certainly boats from Cathay have sailed oceans undreamed of by your Diaz or Colombo.

'Ibn Battuta spoke of such voyages?'

No. He died about a hundred years ago.

Hosé looked his scepticism.

There are, however, reliable reports of huge expeditions leaving Cathay and sailing to the four points of the compass.

'When?'

Isaac shrugged. Thirty or forty years ago.

Hosé felt a prick of excitement. 'But why have I not heard of them?' He thought of his original background. 'If anyone should know of such matters it is the Genoese. I never heard tales of such a thing.'

Yes, Isaac's face was ironic. The Genoese do tend to consider all the seas their own private lake.

'They are no longer the "Superb" power they were,' Hosé said absently. He returned to the much more interesting subject. 'So, there were large expeditions; perhaps they failed?'

Isaac shook his head. No, they met great hazards and lost men and boats but some returned safely after long voyages.

'How do you know about them?'

The Jew was lost for a moment in unusual reminiscence before his stylus moved again. When I still lived in Córdoba I had correspondence with another Jewish physician in Castile where he had been called to treat a member of a Christian family. It was not the medical facts of the case that struck him but conversations he overheard between the head of the family, Pedro Tafur, and a visiting Venetian.

It was on the tip of Hosé's tongue to say he might have guessed it would be a Venetian, but he refrained. 'Who was he?' he asked instead.

Niccolò da Conti

Hosé shook his head.

He had traded in Iskandariya before travelling south.

'But the Mamelukes do not permit Christians to go further than Cairo.'

Very true, Isaac agreed, But da Conti had married a Muslim woman and converted to Islam.

Hosé's attention was now total.

He travelled down through India, ending up at Calicut.

Hosé nodded as he placed in his mind the port far down the western coast of India.

Da Conti told Pedro Tafur of the fleet that had visited Calicut while he was there. Isaac paused as he recalled the words. *Boats like great houses and not fashioned at all like those of Europe. They have ten or twelve sails and great cisterns of water within. The lower part is constructed of triple planks. Some boats are built in compartments, so that should one part be shattered, the other part remaining entire, they may accomplish the voyage.*

'Ten or twelve sails?' queried Hosé.

Isaac delved into his memory again. Large sails, reinforced with strips of some very light but strong wood. He added, Four-sided and hanging at an angle.

Hosé tried to picture it but could not. 'Ten or twelve,' he repeated to himself. 'The boats must have been enormous.'

Da Conti compared one of the boats with a caravel he had recently sailed on out of Barcelona. Isaac sucked his stylus. My memory for facts and figures is not what it used to be.

Hosé snorted.

The Jew wrote again. I believe da Conti worked out the Cathay boat was more than six times as long and more than ten times as wide, able to carry forty times as much cargo.

To think of a boat that size was staggering. Apart from size Hosé realised that such a vessel had very different proportions from the boats he was used to. He did some rapid calculations in his head. 'That's width more than a third of the length. Even round-ships are sleeker than that.' He did some other figuring. 'And a galley usually has its length something like six times its width.' He looked at Isaac. 'A boat that broad must flounder like a butter tub.'

Isaac shook his head. Tafur made a similar comment but da Conti said there was a clever construction at the prow to channel the water and there was a way of lowering the keel of what was basically a flat-bottomed boat.

Hosé could not imagine the design at all. 'There isn't a drawing of this marvel?' he asked, half hopeful and half incredulous.

Isaac shook his head. But da Conti gave a very detailed description, as if he had actually been aboard, not just seen it from land.

'Why didn't da Conti tell all this to Frankish boat builders?'

Perhaps he did, but only met sceptics like you!

Hosé pulled a face. 'But,' he said doggedly, 'You need very clear plans to build a good boat. The boat builders I have seen have all learned every detail from their Masters and they know that to change even a small thing may make a bad boat.' He had a sudden thought and smiled a little. 'I'm sure you would find Thomas less sceptical, and certainly more knowledgeable, than me!'

The Jew nodded. His hand paused. Never mind all that for the moment. The most important thing is to find out what the connection is between the van Dammes and Clough and whether their presence here is a problem. He looked hard at Hosé. "*It was in another life. It has no significance now*," Isaac quoted Hosé's earlier words. But perhaps they know who you are?

Hosé grimaced. 'I believe Pieter recognised me.'

Hardly surprising. And Cornelius?

'I do not think so and it seems Pieter has not told him.'

Isaac nodded. Pieter ponders much within himself. I wonder.... He paused with the thought.

Hosé waited.

I wonder if Rab could find out anything from Jakob.

Hosé was not at all keen to involve Rab. He rose from his seat and stretched his legs, 'I can discover what Jakob knows.'

Hosé left a little later, deep in thought. He needed to clear his head before trying to sleep and made his way towards the door that led out onto the gardens. There were no lamps burning in this part of the villa but a faint light filtered through the cracks of the shutters and Hosé knew the way well enough. He moved confidently but quietly.

As he rounded a corner of the passage he bumped into someone hurrying the other way. He made an instinctive move to steady himself against the wall with one hand; his other hand reached out to the other person.

His nostrils caught the unmistakeable odour of the garde-robe; someone had been caught short, he thought. What had that meat been at supper time? By this time of year, it was sometimes hard to tell.

'Pardon me,' he said, straightening up.

There was a gasp; the figure lurched away and fled back the way it had come.

Hosé was mildly concerned. If the call back to the garde-robe was so urgent perhaps there was something to worry about.

He continued on his way, his silent steps a little slower. He reached the point where an opening gave on to the noisome closet protruding beyond the walls of the villa.

It seemed unoccupied. He paused. When he had first come to the villa he had often climbed through one such closet to gain access to a space behind a wall of Prince Cem's chamber. He had spent many uncomfortable hours there listening in on the conversations and, he reminded himself sourly, on other equally loud non-verbal activities. When he had returned to the palace the previous year with Isaac he had made very sure the rooms allotted to the Jew could not be similarly spied on.

He had checked out all the possibilities. Nothing short of a small and very agile mountain goat could have got anywhere near.

Moreover, he reflected, he and Isaac used a mixture of non-local languages when they conversed: it seemed safer and kept them both in practice.

Hosé shook his head.

The walk in the garden did not have the desired effect: Hosé turned restlessly on his pallet and thought through what he and Isaac had discussed.

Greek, Arabic, Persian and Turkish phrases chased each other through his head, finally turning into small goats that leaped in an unruly troupe up rugged Anatolian mountains.

'Where's Jakob?' The day had been filled with an unrelenting succession of dispatches and accounts and myriad queries from those who helped administer the Grimaldo enterprise. Hosé had finally reached Isaac's rooms well after noon.

His father came to collect him this morning. The Jew added, He seemed quite well enough to leave.

'Even Rab was satisfied on that point?'

Isaac nodded. Actually, it was her suggestion. She felt he had been shut up in here long enough. The stylus paused. She could sympathise with that.

'She was not shut up here the other night when she ran into Garcia!'

The Jew frowned. She is not a prisoner. But normally she knows it is safer for her not to go into the town.

'But the call of young Jakob was too strong?' suggested Hosé.

Isaac inclined his head. Yes, she had undoubtedly been hoping the *Liesabeta* would come this way.

Hosé recalled what Marianne had said. 'It may well be that Garcia de

Tineo will not be in Nice long; not if the Governor has his way. Wouldn't Rab be safe then?'

Isaac pointed his stylus at Hosé in mild rebuke.

Hosé flushed in annoyance that his "fishing" had been so obvious. 'Am I allowed to ask if Rab went with Jakob?'

You can ask. I can't answer, because I don't know.

'Don't you care?' Hosé was provoked into the rather aggressive question by frustration and a recurrence of a more unworthy feeling.

Isaac looked at Hosé in surprise for a moment but did not reply. We have many other things to discuss, he wrote instead. Time is short.

The *Santa Giovanna* was Genoese. Hosé carried Isaac's bags aboard and reflected that that was only to be expected: after all, Nice (like the Grimaldo family) was still, in many ways, an outpost of Genoa.

He narrowed his eyes: the two men-at-arms playing dice were supposed to see Isaac safely through the first leg of his journey.

The galley was bound for Tunis. From there Isaac would find a boat heading west for Algiers where there was a sizeable community of both Moors and Jews. He could hope to find there some distant relatives but more importantly treatment from the famed Arab physicians for the crab-disease that was finally ending his long employment with the Grimaldi. So the story ran. In reality, from Tunis Isaac would head east to Chios, where he could get a passage for Islambul.

Isaac scowled as Hosé handed him the last heavy packet. The old Jew clutched *Continens* protectively with one hand as he grasped Hosé's arm with the other. For a moment, the Hebrew looked from the book to the young man and back again.

'It's better if you don't know,' Hosé's voice was not quite even. 'Better for me, that is,' he added with an attempt at lightening the moment.

The sunken eyes regarded him fiercely.

Hosé stared back for several moments before turning abruptly on his heel.

His apprenticeship was served. The young journeyman would now have to apply the craft he had learned on his own. Would he have the skill to become the master Isaac was?

Chapter 5

Hosé had been on his own during the years he had accompanied Prince Cem with de Blanchefort and he had certainly missed Isaac then, but now somehow it seemed worse. Perhaps it was because the villa held so many reminders of the old Jew. Everywhere Hosé went, he expected to see the physician annotating his notebooks, mixing unguents, labelling his medical stores, transcribing despatches.

Hosé frowned. Isaac had left many instructions before he left but it was his final request that bothered Hosé most; as if there was not enough to do. And why should it matter?

Rab had resumed her usual duties with Annette and Hosé rarely saw her. His question as to where the *Liesabeta* might have gone was met with icy silence and he made no further efforts to speak to her. She seemed equally keen to avoid him.

He shook his head and grasped the latest despatch impatiently. Although it looked no different from the dozens of others he had read and decoded since Isaac left, he knew immediately where it came from.

He willed himself to go through his usual routine, turning the package carefully, looking for marks or signs, scrutinising the seal. Finally, he allowed himself to open it and unfold its single sheet.

He scanned the contents quickly. It was immediately obvious that it had not been written by the Jew: Hosé would have recognised his hand in any language or script.

He read it more slowly, identifying the code and interpreting the words.

It came from Islambul all right, but it made no reference to Isaac.

Hosé frowned then his face cleared a little. Even the Sultan's most senior servants did not know who the Ottoman agent in Nice had been for the past five years.

But why had Isaac not written himself?

Hosé fingered the despatch absently. Even if Clough had identified Hosé as Bayezit's man and associated Isaac with him, would the Englishman have informed the Vizier Muhammad? He would probably only have bothered if it brought either payment or some other benefit, Hosé reflected sourly.

Did the Vizier know about Isaac?

And if he did, did he know that Isaac knew about *him*; and *his* dealings with Clough?

Unanswerable questions.

But, Isaac had argued calmly, what the Vizier does not know is that I am returning to the Topkapi.

Hosé hoped the Hebrew had been right.

A hand slid through his arm. 'You have been working too hard,' the voice was full of sympathy, yet carried its usual slight undertone of mockery.

'There has been a lot to do.' Hosé detached himself and folded the despatch.

'True,' Annette agreed, 'And work can help fill other gaps in life.'

Hosé turned. Was she speaking of her own experience after her illness?

'But perhaps you could spare me a little of your precious time.'

Hosé was instantly on his guard.

Amusement lit up her light eyes. 'I need your help.'

'With what?' he asked suspiciously.

'I want to get into the Jewish quarter.' Annette spoke softly and her face was serious now.

Hosé looked at her curiously.

She looked around the room. The door into the large accounting office stood open and she moved to close it. 'After all you are part of the family.' The mocking note was back for a moment. 'Social rules will not be offended.'

'Why would you want to visit the Rue Guidaria?' he inquired, 'And why should you think I can help?' He was still faced from time to time with the infuriating fact that he did not know how much or how little Isaac had shared with Annette. He often suspected that the old Jew had trusted her a good deal more than Hosé did.

That was true of Rab too, he thought with irritation.

He turned his attention to Annette as she answered. 'When I was so ill with the *variole*, Sarah helped to nurse me.' Her mouth tightened. 'The faithful family servants fled.' Her slim white hands straightened an ink pot on the desk beside her. 'So much for Christian charity.'

'Charity is not the monopoly of Christians,' Hosé said a little stiffly.

She looked at him curiously. 'So I realise!'

She tidied a bunch of uncut quills. 'For a while it was easy to send things that Sarah and her family might need, but now you know what the situation is: they are shut in like mangy bears.'

Hosé knew that very well.

'Isaac would have liked to say farewell to Sarah before he left but there did not seem any way to gain entrance.' The light eyes looked to see Hosé's reaction. 'He left something for Sarah in the hope I could deliver it but I have not been able to get in myself and I do not trust the guards who inspect every basket and parcel that goes through the gate.'

'So how did you think to do it?' he inquired evenly.

'I told you,' she said impatiently, 'With your help.'

'Your faith in me is touching,' he returned, 'But what makes you think I could help.'

'Sarah let it slip that you had been there.'

He did not deny it. 'But the situation as you say is different now.'

Her face fell. 'You haven't been recently then?'

He shook his head. 'Not since I returned to Nice last year.' He thought about it for a few moments then shook his head again.

'But?' she prompted him.

'Maybe there are still ways,' he said reluctantly.

He should have kept quiet.

Annette fixed those pale eyes on him.

'There is a maze of tunnels and drains that pass under that quarter. They carry the water and waste of the town down into the river.'

'You have tried them?' she demanded.

He had got as far as investigating them; that had been enough. He shook his head.

The eyes narrowed. 'Why can't you use the way you used before?'

'It does not exist anymore.'

'Why?' She was never diverted easily from anything she had set her mind on, as Hosé already knew only too well.

'There was a baker in a neighbouring street; his cellar joined others .....'

Annette waited.

'The Governor had it closed off.'

'Oh.' Still she looked at him.

'He also had the shop flattened and the baker summoned to answer to the authorities.' Hosé's voice betrayed something of his anger.

Annette's face coloured a little. She took a breath and thought again. 'Which other cellars did the baker's link up to?'

Hosé hesitated, then impatiently made a sketch for her; he had investigated those too. 'The Governor's men have visited them all.' He added, 'With a gang of masons.'

Annette shifted the quills to the other side of the desk as she considered. 'All of them?'

'Yes.' Hosé confirmed.

'All of them?' she repeated; she had picked up the slightest hesitation in his answer.

'Except….' His thin smile was humourless.

'Except?'

'The Governor's brother.' Hosé added another property to the map. 'I found myself in his cellar once, by accident.'

'Bertrand de la Forêt has access to the Jewish quarter?' Annette was incredulous.

'I am sure he would be horrified to know it.'

She smiled. 'I'm sure he would.' She tilted her head on one side. 'Now how could we use that interesting bit of information I wonder? Perhaps Bertrand could help us.'

Hosé looked at her askance.

'Without being aware of it, of course.'

Hosé was not reassured.

'Bertrand.' She said the name again. 'Before,' she said softly, 'It would have been easy. He was a regular visitor to the villa.' She continued, 'He was one of the throng of admirers.'

Hosé did not have to ask what she meant by "*before*".

'Still,' she mused to herself, 'He is no great beauty himself these days; too many rich dinners with his brother. And,' she said, 'Perhaps I still have a few attractions worth something.' She looked directly at Hosé and could not resist adding, 'At least to some people.'

He ignored her. 'Are you seriously suggesting,' he asked, 'Seducing Bertrand de la Forêt?'

'Don't you think I could?' she challenged.

'I have full confidence in you in such matters,' he retorted.

'Oh dear,' she murmured, 'I seem to have upset your sensibilities.'

'I thought you had put such things behind you.'

'And become a decent chaste woman.' She pulled a face. 'But it would be worth something to see if I could still do it.'

He opened his mouth to speak then stopped.

She lifted an elegant finger to his cheek. 'It would also be worth something to think that your concern was jealousy, but I fear it is nothing more than the old prudery.'

He pulled back from her touch and looked at her for a long moment. 'I do wish,' he said, 'That every conversation with you did not end up on the same subject.' He moved towards the door.

She caught his arm. 'I'm sorry,' she said quickly. 'We'll just talk about Bertrand.'

'Is there anything more to say about him?'

'Of course.'

Hosé hesitated.

'Never mind sulking,' she said, 'The important thing is how to get

Isaac's parcel to Sarah.'

Hosé sighed.

'And,' she persisted, 'I really do think I could do it.'

'It?'

'Distract Bertrand,' she said impatiently, 'While you go down through his cellar.'

'Distract?'

'Yes, distract. I'll do whatever it needs to distract him and,' she was suddenly angry, 'I don't need your approval.'

'Just my help?'

She glared at him then smiled and finally laughed.

Reluctantly he smiled back. She was totally impossible.

Annette had lost no time working out the details. She was delighted to find that Bertrand had pretensions of grandeur: he was planning a fountain. She would love to share with an old friend her enthusiasm and expertise on the subject.

'Your what? You don't have the slightest idea. You do not even know how the fountain here works.' Hosé reminded her that he had asked her once about the water supply to the villa.

'Ah, but I have learned many things since then,' she said smugly. She laughed at his disbelief. 'It's true. After my illness, Isaac insisted I should take walks in the fresh air.' She pulled a face. 'As if I was not already as ugly as a peasant.' She shook her head. 'Obviously, it was not a good idea to go into the town so Isaac and I got into the habit of walking around the old Roman remains.'

Hosé had been there himself. So had the Englishman Clough.

'There is a cistern fed from the old Roman system. It still supplies much of the town. Can you imagine that? After all these years.'

Hosé could indeed imagine it. 'So,' he conceded. 'You know something of fountains. Am I expected to be equally knowledgeable?'

She considered him for a moment. 'I thought that might be a bit hard to believe.'

He feigned offence.

'You are my cousin, my protector.' She ignored his look. 'You insist on accompanying me; you are attentive in all things.'

'And that would be easier to believe?'

'But of course!' She continued seriously, 'You follow us closely, as I ask Bertrand to show us everything: the fountain, his water supply, his cellar...... You never leave us alone for a moment.'

'And how will that help?'

'At last there is a message from the villa; you are urgently needed to attend to something. You do not want to go; you must stay with me. But finally you are persuaded; after all, my maid will be with me.'

Hosé knew how much that was worth. 'But I do not want to leave the house,' he pointed out.

She shook her head. 'Bertrand will have other things on his mind by then; he will not care where you go.'

Hosé had a thought. 'Does Bertrand not have a wife? What will she think of your visit?'

Annette laughed. 'I understand she is staying with her ailing sister. She has been away for some time.' Her head tilted. 'Poor Bertrand must be very lonely.'

Hosé should have been prepared for how well Annette would do her part but he was almost caught napping. He hastily put himself between her and Bertrand de la Forêt and started a rapid discourse on the rising cost of Spanish olives. He quoted a string of figures. 'And only last week they went up again!' He managed to sound outraged. 'Now if you compare that with the prices from Nyons,' and he rattled off more numbers.

Bertrand de la Forêt tried to edge around him. 'Perhaps Donna you would be interested.....'

'Why only last season,' Hosé attempted to reposition himself.

Annette beat him to it and Hosé saw colour flood the fat jowls as her small hand, aimed for Bertrand de la Forêt's arm, inexplicably missed its target. She carefully placed it in its proper place and smiled at Bertrand.

Hosé tried again. As they proceeded along a passage towards the back of the house Annette was forced to let go of de la Forêt's arm and Hosé placed himself quickly at the man's shoulder.

'Perhaps you have plenty of space to store olives?' he inquired. He did not wait for a reply. 'If so then you should certainly buy now. I am sure the prices will only rise further if you wait.' He started to quote more figures about the possible savings that could be made but his boot caught on an uneven flagstone and he stumbled.

'Take care,' said Bertrand de la Forêt curtly.

'My leg, you see,' Hosé began the usual tale.

'That is unfortunate.' Bertrand de la Forêt clearly wished Hosé had been completely crippled.

'What a lovely spot!' Annette had emerged into a cramped courtyard and was surveying it with solemn admiration. 'What vision you have Bertrand.' She moved around the confined area looking earnestly at the channels in the foundations of a tiny circular pool. She seemed lost in wonder as she flitted to and fro, before somehow finding herself beside a stack of white stone blocks where she perched in wide-eyed contemplation.

Hosé and Bertrand both spotted their opportunity. Again, Hosé's lameness betrayed him and it was the bulky Bertrand who won the race.

Annette seemed to wake from her reverie as his bulky thighs fitted themselves into the space she had allotted. She moved a little as if to make more room.

Bertrand de la Forêt almost gasped. He swallowed and clenched his sizeable fists on his considerable lap.

Hosé watched the man's florid face. He suddenly hoped that Annette's attentions did not provoke an apoplexy. Or perhaps he did not exactly hope that. He ceded the minor victory to Bertrand with ill-grace and started to talk to Annette about details of some accounts they had worked on together that morning.

'Cousin,' she chided him reproachfully. 'Bertrand does not want to hear us talk of such dry matters.'

Hosé could not imagine why not. He pouted and turned pointedly. He watched a lizard run up the nearby wall of the house; like most sensible creatures it had stayed in the shade until the greatest heat of the afternoon had passed. Hosé moved to study the spot where it had disappeared and looked at the bare stonework long enough for Annette to start explaining to a rapt Bertrand the intricacies of the old Roman waterworks.

Hosé moved behind them and interrupted with a long and tedious description of his own.

Bertrand turned and glared.

Annette tightened her hold on his arm in a show of sympathy and his colour rose another notch. 'Perhaps, Bertrand,' she said soothingly, 'You could show us how the water reaches your house?'

Bertrand was not sure how that would help him achieve what, by that time, he very much wanted, but it gave him the opportunity to grasp Annette's hand and help her to her feet. He kept firm hold of it as he guided her across the rough ground.

He reclaimed it with equal force after he had placed the lamp on its ledge in the cellar wall. He led her to where water splashed into a stone trough.

Hosé kept close behind them but his eyes searched a different corner. 'Those jars,' he said.

'What?' Bertrand turned irritably.

Hosé pointed.

'What about them?'

'They would store plenty of olives,' Hosé said.

'Olives!' Bertrand de la Forêt had heard enough about olives.

Hosé began to tell him once more how much better it would be to buy olives now before the price rose again.

He was saved from hearing de la Forêt's opinion on olives, and probably on Hosé too, by the arrival of Annette's maid.

She stopped at the bottom of the steps and delivered the message she had just received from the villa.

Hosé was certain he could not go.

Bertrand was certain he should.

Annette was sure she would be quite all right, with her maid.

Bertrand was equally sure.

Hosé very reluctantly agreed; but he did want to look more closely at the jars. He would make a quick assessment about their capacity and give Bertrand an estimate of how much he could save; with the price of Nyons olives at....

Bertrand de la Forêt could not bear to hear it all again. 'Look at what you want,' he said desperately, 'Then get one of my servants to let you out. I am sure Donna Annette would appreciate some refreshment in the cool of my private parlour.' He hastened to guide Annette back up the steps with a last contemptuous look at Hosé and a honeyed smile at the maid.

Hosé spent a short time examining the jars, moving them a little as though to count them better. The lamplight reached as far as a protrusion of natural rock, left when the cellar had first been dug out. It was as he remembered.

He climbed the stairs and listened to the faint murmur of voices above, then there was the thump of a door closing and the sound of a servant's wooden soles clattering along the passage towards the kitchen.

He shut the cellar door and went back down the steps. In the corner, he pulled his gown over his head and stuffed it into his satchel. He took the lamp and slid around the rock. A crack there narrowed into darkness. He did what he could to drag jars into the opening behind him then dropped to his knees and, pushing the lamp ahead of him, squeezed into the small space. He suddenly feared that it was a blind-end; he was stuffing himself headfirst into a trap.

He stopped for a moment and breathed carefully. He looked at the lamp, at the flame burning evenly. There was air here, good air; there was space somewhere in front of him. It confirmed what his mind remembered and calmed his panic. All he had to do was keep crawling forward.

Surely, it had not taken this long last time when he had come from the other direction? His knees protested as sharp stones pressed through his hose. He moved the lamp again and his elbow hit the side of the passage, tearing the sleeve of his shirt and grazing his arm.

He caught the oath before it was uttered and moved with greater care.

He came to a stop, his heart thudding painfully. That pile of rocks had not been here last time he came this way, but he should have expected something of the sort. He cursed himself for a fool. He would have to go back.

He tried unsuccessfully to turn around. The space was far too narrow.

He tried to inch his way backwards. However, it was a bit like a barb on an arrow head, he realised: it went in smoothly but was impossible to pull out again, with the satchel which he had dragged behind him acting now like a bung in a barrel.

Sweat ran down into his eyes. He could also feel it trickling under his torso from his armpits.

He forced himself to stillness and took a few deep breaths. Think! he told himself.

He managed to get a hand to his face and wiped his stinging eyes; he closed them and gradually gained some composure. He opened them again and looked at the flame of the lamp. Think! he told himself again.

In the yellow glow, he surveyed the rocks that surrounded him, enclosed him; entombed him. He shook his head. Think of something else!

The lamp. He looked at its bright flame; it was reassuring, but how long would it last?

To be stuck was bad enough; to be stuck in complete darkness was unthinkable.

Find something else to think about.

His thoughts raced madly in his head. His eyes kept returning to the lamp; had it dimmed? Was it beginning to run out of oil? Out of air?

The flame wavered.

Hosé reached forward and shook the lamp; there was a faint swish of oil in its round belly.

The flame flickered again.

Hosé's thoughts stopped spinning: in spite of the rocks in front of him, there was a draught.

He wriggled forward and used his fingers to explore. Up near the roof of the passage he found a gap. He pushed at the top stone. It would barely move but he thought he heard a sound beyond it. He hunched his shoulders up as far as he could and pushed again. The stone gave way and tumbled back with a loud noise; there was space behind.

Hosé tackled the next rock with increasing hope.

Finally, there was a gap large enough for him to crawl over.

Suddenly, the walls and roof of the passage opened out and he got slowly to his feet, easing his cramped body and taking grateful gulps. He held the lamp higher and recognised the broad tunnel. To his left, its walls were marked with the scratches of the hundreds of people who had used it before him. Immediately to his right, new stones blocked the way, mortared tightly in place; a few strides further in and they would have stopped the passage Hosé had just used. He allowed himself a small prayer of thanks then resolutely crawled back into the passage and replaced the rocks he had dislodged.

Finally, he shook out his gown as best he could and tugged it rather desperately over his grimy shirt and hose.

Sarah was much as he remembered her. The intervening years may have added a sprinkling of grey to her black hair but her face was smooth and her dark eyes smiled almost shyly.

Hosé's guts gave a small lurch: as an awkward youth, his mind had once been filled with thoughts of Sarah. He looked at her now and with a flash of understanding wondered if perhaps she had shared some of his dreams.

He smiled back. 'Do your customs permit?' he asked as he lifted her hand in his.

She replied softly. 'I am sure my husband would not object, in the circumstances.'

'I'm glad.' Hosé accepted the information with a laugh. 'He has no need to.'

She returned the pressure of his fingers for a moment before removing her hand and inviting him to sit.

He looked down at his dishevelled clothes and hesitated. 'I would do better in the servants' quarters,' he said wryly.

Sarah shook her head. 'No,' she said firmly. 'You are not a servant. You now stand in Isaac's shoes.'

'But do not fill them,' he said ruefully. 'You know then that he has left Nice?'

'Yes. We manage to get some news in spite of everything.' Her words carried only a trace of bitterness.

Hosé reached for his satchel. 'He left something for you.'

Sarah slowly undid the small package and was still, holding the contents in her hands with wonder. She carefully laid the small branched candlestick on the table and unfolded the paper that had been with it.

Hosé could see the note was written in Hebrew script but he had never learned more than a smattering; in any case this was a private matter between Isaac and Sarah. Hosé looked away.

'I knew he would not have abandoned his faith,' she said soberly. 'Life is difficult for all of us in these times.' She paused. 'I hope it will be better for him wherever he has gone.'

Hosé sincerely hoped so too.

She picked up the candlestick again with its nine branches. 'Do you know what this is?' she asked.

'I think so,' Hosé returned. 'It was Chanukah when I visited once.'

She nodded. 'The menorah is a long-honoured symbol of our people.' She fingered it lightly. 'A converso would not have kept it.' She placed it on the table. 'He must have carried it with him through many years and many dangers.' She was lost in her thoughts for a moment. 'He says it was made by a smith in Córdoba more than two hundred years ago, when,' she frowned, ' "*People of different faiths managed to live in the same town without persecuting or butchering each other.*" '

Isaac had described that to Hosé once, too. By contrast he had also described how, in the same land, in more recent times, he had been set upon and mutilated in the name of Christianity and how the shock had killed his wife. Following that, Isaac had travelled through north Africa, the Ottoman lands and the Levant before returning five years ago to Europe.

And all that time he had kept safe this small symbol of his faith and his people.

They both looked at it for a while longer, remembering the physician.

Hosé eventually reached into his satchel again and brought out the other package from Annette.

Sarah looked in gratitude at each packet of dried herbs and powders. She weighed a leather pouch in her hand for a moment before opening it and lifting a few of the gold coins.

She peered more closely and gave a little laugh. 'How like her!' she exclaimed.

Hosé raised a brow.

Sarah handed him one of the coins. It was old, its face worn smooth by many fingers but its soft edges proclaimed its purity and value. 'New coins would have aroused suspicion.'

Hosé saw her point.

'She is a good woman.'

Hosé was startled for a moment. He knew something of Annette's qualities himself but it had never occurred to him to think of her as "good". He laughed. 'I shall tell her.'

'Please give her my heartfelt thanks.'

Hosé rose to his feet. 'I have to go.' He hesitated. 'I planned to get out down the sewers.' It had seemed a reasonable thought at the time.

Sarah frowned as she stood up. 'I believe it is possible but it is dangerous.'

So was the way he had come. He was caught between Scylla and Charybdis.

'The sewers are apparently impossible from the other direction,' Sarah added, 'But from here all you have to do is follow them downhill to the river.' Her voice did not carry the conviction Hosé would have liked.

He picked up the word "*all*" and wondered if he was completely mad.

'So Mosh says.'

Hosé felt a flicker of hope.

Mosh turned out to be a skinny lad of about fourteen. His pale skin seemed to bear testimony to the time he spent underground. He eyed Hosé with considerable suspicion. The mention of Isaac did not entirely remove the wariness from his face, although he lifted a hand instinctively to one shoulder, which Hosé could see sat higher than the other. Even Isaac could not work miracles.

Sarah interrupted his thoughts. 'Will you be able to come again?'

Hosé was honest. 'I doubt it.'

Sarah shook her head sadly. 'You have done a lot by coming today,' she said. Her face looked old for the first time. 'My husband thinks it will not be long before we all have to leave Nice. Unless,' her lips tightened, 'We convert.'

'What will you do?' Hosé did not deny her fears.

'What our people have done so many times before,' she replied quietly. 'With God's help, we will survive.'

Mosh made some kind of noise as his black eyes flashed the defiance of youth.

Hosé took his leave of Sarah and followed the stiff, narrow back.

They turned down a passage. The stench hit his nose and made him gag.

Mosh turned a withering look on him. 'This is nothing.'

Hosé swallowed hard and tried breathing through his mouth. It was better; slightly.

He reminded himself that he had been in filthy places before and survived. For a while he used the thought to distract him from the reality of the slime and muck under his feet. He suspected his boots would never be the same again. He had toyed with the idea of going barefoot like Mosh but had realised that his feet needed the protection: it was years since he had gone without shoes. He had, however, removed his gown again.

He slopped along, bent almost double, following the flickering light of

Mosh's lamp.

They reached a junction where another drain poured down from a higher level. Mosh ducked around the noisome fall and Hosé did his best to copy him. He avoided the worst but he could not protect his satchel from a drenching.

So much for keeping his gown clean.

A very large rat dropped past his face and scurried over his feet. It fled back the way they had come.

Mosh laughed. 'Goliath,' he said. 'He's usually somewhere round here.'

Hosé grimaced. His back was hurting. 'Do the tunnels get bigger?' he asked hopefully. That would be logical; wouldn't it?

Mosh laughed again. 'Oh yes,' he threw over his crooked shoulder, 'Much bigger.'

Hosé did not like that laugh.

They trudged along in silence for a while, moving from one passage into another, left, right, right again. Without Mosh, Hosé would have been in great difficulty.

They dropped down a considerable distance.

'How do you get back?' Hosé asked as he struggled to keep his footing on the pile of ordure that had provided a soft but treacherous landing.

Mosh turned impatiently and held up the lamp.

Hosé could see the smallest of footholds in the stonework where water (and worse) trickled down. 'Rather slippery.'

Mosh's teeth gleamed white. 'Yes,' he said. 'Rather.' He cocked his head, raising his shoulder even higher. 'Don't reckon you could do it, eh?' There was a challenge in his black eyes.

'I'm not sure I could,' Hosé admitted; climbing was not one of his favourite pastimes. 'And I'd much rather not have to try.'

Mosh laughed and Hosé did not begrudge him his moment of triumph.

Mosh savoured it to the full, then turned abruptly and headed into another passage. Hosé blundered after him, catching his elbow again; his shirt sleeve hung in tatters and his arm would fast go the same way if he was not careful. He concentrated hard, as he had to bend once more through a low section.

The floor was as foul as ever and now sloped more steeply. Hosé succeeded in guarding his abused elbow but he ripped his hose and banged his knee as he slithered sideways and fetched up with a gasp in a sodden heap.

Mosh waited impatiently for him to pick himself up. The lad seemed to have no trouble keeping his footing. 'Watch out,' he said ironically.

Hosé stood up carefully. He pulled a face; his leg hurt but it worked. He struggled on.

Finally, they came to a passage that was wide and high; the lamplight hardly reached the roof. The floor was steeper than ever and a considerable torrent threatened to knock Hosé off his feet. He knew now what the bigger sewers involved. He managed a wry smile at Mosh.

Mosh suddenly grinned back. 'This is as far as I go,' he announced. He pointed along the tunnel. 'It drops down into the river.'

Hosé could hear the sound.

Mosh produced a ball of twine. 'I'll lower the lamp down so you can see what you are doing.' He was still smiling.

Hosé was not.

'You'll need to be careful.'

Hosé certainly intended to be. 'Any suggestions?' This was no time for false pride.

The descent was not pleasant. It might not quite match climbing to the top of the mainmast or being suspended over the battlements of a castle but it was close.

Hosé took a deep stinking breath and moved down a few more feet.

His nails tore as he scrabbled to catch a hold.

'Hey!' Mosh's voice reached him from somewhere above the cataract. 'Are you all right?' The lamp bobbed up and down.

Hosé slid to a halt. 'Still in one piece,' he said when could trust himself to speak.

He climbed down the next part, feeling for every foothold and testing it before he transferred his weight, his fingers clinging desperately to the sodden stonework. His hands were shaking and he cursed to himself; he had had little opportunity to use them for anything other than pushing a quill since he returned to Nice. His legs too were protesting against the unusual exercise.

He paused to allow the trembling to ease.

'Hey!' Mosh's voice came again, fainter this time.

'Nearly there,' Hosé called, in desperate hope. He had not dared look downwards.

The lamp swung wildly as Mosh tried to be helpful and illuminate a wider space.

'Watch out!' The lamp narrowly missed the falling stream.

'Sorry.'

Hosé barely picked up the word. He forced his legs back into motion and climbed downwards.

His left foot found a hold and his right foot found the ledge was broad enough to share. He tested it and carefully lowered his weight. Very cautiously he looked around. The spinning lamp revealed what his ears had been trying to tell him: he had reached the bottom.

He turned his body away from the wall and waited for the pounding in his chest to lessen.

He stared in disbelief. He shouted some very uncomplimentary words upwards and there was a distant laugh.

'It's only a short swim.' The words floated down faintly.

That was not the point.

Hosé had little doubt the boy had enjoyed keeping this little surprise secret. 'Thanks for your help!' The irony would probably be lost in the noise of the falling water. Perhaps that was another faint laugh.

He stretched out and drew the lamp towards him. He gave the twine a couple of sharp tugs and the lamp began to move upwards; darkness closed in.

Hosé shut his eyes. When he opened them, there was total blackness.

He kept his back firmly against the wall being careful not to turn; he could not afford to lose his bearings. He closed his eyes again and waited.

This time when he opened them there was the faintest light to his left. He was thankful he had not stayed longer with Sarah: if he had tarried until evening, he would have been in trouble.

The sewer debouched into the river all right. In his exploring Hosé had found one or two that discharged above water level, but he should have guessed that there would be others like this one that came out underwater. Now he peered anxiously and tried to gauge how far he would have to swim in the water-filled tunnel. Logic told him the daylight would not penetrate far through the densely laden water.

The thought of submerging himself in the liquid was not attractive.

He bent down carefully and removed his boots; they would only be a hindrance at this point. He stuffed them into the satchel, fastening it again, his fingers clumsy in the darkness.

He lowered himself into the stinking wetness and took a deep breath.

The soft evening sun was dazzling as he surfaced and he trod water for a few moments breathing in air which he knew was clean although his abused nose refused to believe it. He moved towards the wooden pilings that lined the bank and reached up. The wood was blessedly dry and warm.

He tested it, found it firm and climbed upwards.

Chapter 6

He had ducked into the Grimaldo warehouse and waited until after dark before making his way back to the villa. He could have asked the servants to bring him warm water; he had that much standing in the household now he thought wryly; but it was late and his state would have aroused unnecessary curiosity.

Instead he had used the horse trough near the stables, then picked his dripping way to Isaac's old room. He wanted something for his elbow; not that it was badly grazed but Hosé gave heed to Isaac's quaint notions. He also wanted arnica ointment for his knee which was causing him a genuine and painful limp. He smiled ironically to himself as his uneven footfall echoed off the walls; he could usually move as quietly as anyone when he wished.

Hosé stepped inside and closed the door behind him. He stood for a moment blinking in the dark then found his way across the room and opened the shutters. A half-moon had risen and he stood looking out over the grounds of the villa. He pulled off his wet clothes, flinging them away with distaste. The smell of the sewer still filled his nostrils in spite of his efforts and overpowered the aroma of the herbs hanging above his head. It also hid the pungent scent of a recently snuffed candle.

The air was warm and he stood allowing it to dry his body. It was a good feeling and he stretched his tired limbs, thinking through the recent events. He breathed in the night air and leaning on the sill turned his thoughts to the next day. Reluctantly he reached for the shutters again; he would find the things he needed and then get some sleep.

The lamp outside in the passage marked a faint yellow line around the door. Hosé limped towards it and groped for the light that usually stood just inside the room. His fingers found the tinder box. He searched further and his hand touched the candle, its beeswax surface smooth beneath his fingers. He tensed and gently felt the top; the wax had set but in the warm weather it had been slow to harden. He might still have no sense of smell but all his other senses were suddenly alert.

He paused: he could light the candle and reveal whoever was in the room, but the light would also reveal him: no clothes and no weapon.

He cursed out loud, fumbling with the things on the shelf, as his mind explored the possibilities. Who was it? And where were they? He strained his ears but could hear nothing except his own breathing.

He thought about the layout of the room: there were no cupboards, no other doorways.

He stretched out a hand and groped across the back of the door. To his relief his fingers found the tabard Isaac kept there. That could help with one of his problems.

It refused to move; it had become caught on its peg. Hosé nearly swore again as he tried to free it in the dark.

He stopped, certain someone had moved to his left. He listened intently.

He could hear nothing in the room, but he was suddenly aware of footsteps in the passage. They stopped outside the door.

As the latch lifted, Hosé gave a last desperate tug. He had just pulled the old garment over his head when lamplight flooded the room.

'Hosé?' Annette's voice was surprised. 'And Rab!'

He could see the girl now, crouched back against the wall.

'In the dark?' The tone was arch. 'And *déshabillé.*'

Hosé looked from her to Rab and back again. 'Don't be ridiculous,' he said shortly.

'Is it me who looks ridiculous?' she asked, staring at him.

'I didn't even know Rab was here.'

'Of course not,' Annette was enjoying herself.

Hosé scowled.

'And yet she has achieved more than I ever managed.' Annette was looking appreciatively at him.

The tabard concealed a good deal less than Hosé would have wished; his limbs usually well hidden under his clerk's gown were clearly visible. He shifted uncomfortably under her gaze. At least the wretched thing covered the essentials.

'Hm,' she mused, making the most of the moment, 'Even better than I had imagined.'

'And you with such a fertile imagination!'

'Pity it all has to be in the imagination, isn't it? When it doesn't need to be,' she pouted at him.

In other circumstances Hosé might have responded to this familiar verbal jousting.

He turned his head and looked at Rab. She was staring at his leg, her gaze like that of a rabbit spellbound by a snake. With a cold feeling in the pit of his stomach Hosé knew what she was looking at and that she understood its significance.

Isaac had threatened to obliterate the tattoo, which Hosé had himself so proudly executed after Yenişehir, when life as a janissary seemed finally assured. Hosé had resisted passionately, asserting that the mark was not likely to be recognised in the west. And, he had pointed out, there was no way to disguise the sign of Abraham and once that was revealed little else would matter anyway.

It appeared, however, that someone did recognise it.

How did Rab come to know about such things? Hosé realised yet again how little he knew about her. But Isaac had trusted her, and she had trusted Isaac.

He needed to talk to her, to get some crucial things straight, but he could hardly do that in front of Annette.

All this flashed through his mind, as he saw Rab's eyes manage to tear themselves away from the black mark and reach his face. Her white lips parted.

'Please don't say it,' he said quickly in Arabic, 'For Isaac's sake if not for mine. We can talk about it later, when we are alone.'

'Alone?' she gasped. 'You think I would be alone with you?'

At least she had replied in the same tongue.

'What is it Rab?' Annette inquired.

'This deceiving bastard,' Rab spat out, now in plain Genoese, 'Is.......'

Hosé had run out of options. He lunged at her and clamped a hand firmly over her mouth, watching out for her fingernails this time, pinning her arms tightly.

Annette looked at him in amazement. 'That empty jibe doesn't bother you that much surely?'

'Stupid, ungrateful child,' he said, facing Annette, but aiming the words at Rab.

Annette was still holding the lamp. She turned now and put it on the shelf. 'Let her go, Hosé,' she said quietly. 'She may be a child but she has had enough of men manhandling her.'

Men? He noted the plural in passing. 'I have absolutely no wish to "*manhandle*" her,' he said. 'Provided,' he added significantly, 'She curbs her tongue.'

Annette looked at Rab. 'Stop it at once!' she ordered Hosé. 'This has gone far enough.' She moved forward and put a hand on his arm. 'I know what she was going to say.'

Rab's dark eyes reproached Annette.

'I'm sorry Rab,' Annette apologised. 'It was irresistible seeing Hosé flailing like a hooked fish.'

Hosé stared at her. This was no game. Was she bluffing?

She shook her head. 'I wondered about it for a long time of course.' She tilted her head. 'It was a tantalising puzzle. In the end, I almost didn't want to know the true answer, because then the game would be over.'

But? The inevitable word in his head.

'But then it was suddenly more important to know.'

He waited.

'After all,' she smiled, 'It would not do for the bedding ceremony to reveal my "cousin" as a Saracen.' The smile was a little sad, 'However perfect he would have been as a husband in every other way.'

A snort escaped from Rab.

'Yes,' Annette continued, 'I asked Isaac.' She saw his look. 'And yes, I did tell him why I wanted to know.'

Hosé was almost surprised the old Jew had not given the match his blessing!

He looked down at Rab. 'But he obviously did not tell you, did he?' She had been shocked by the discovery this evening. Hosé matched her scowl.

Annette shook his arm. 'Let go of her,' she said.

Hosé did not really have any alternative. He loosened his hold warily.

Rab pulled away and immediately moved behind Annette.

Hosé moved just as quickly: to put his back to the door; nobody was leaving yet. He winced.

'Are you hurt?' Annette had noticed.

'Nothing much,' he answered shortly. 'I twisted my knee. It was not easy getting out through the sewers.'

She wrinkled her nose. 'Rather smelly too.'

'You would have thought someone would have cleaned them, wouldn't you?' He returned. 'Most inconsiderate!'

She laughed. 'Mind you I could almost say the same thing about Bertrand.' She pulled a face.

'I'm not sure I want to know.'

She considered him for a moment. 'I don't think your wretched sensibilities would have been too offended,' she said in the end.

Rab stared at her.

Annette caught the look and smiled. 'Rab,' she said gently, 'Not many people are saints, but,' she added, 'Not many are complete monsters either.'

Rab looked unconvinced.

'Long ago I realised I could manipulate men,' Annette told her baldly. 'Now I try only to do so for some good reason.' She flushed. 'Goodness I sound almost prudish.' She avoided Hosé's eye.

He ignored the reference. 'Sarah was grateful,' he said quietly, 'Very grateful.' He hesitated. 'She said you are a good woman.' He was not smiling.

Annette glanced at him then looked away quickly. 'Hardly!' She sniffed,

'And I couldn't have achieved it without you.' She grinned at him, 'And your olives!'

Hosé smiled reluctantly.

'Oh Rab,' Annette saw her bewildered look, 'I know you don't trust Hosé because of things that happened to you before.' She missed Rab's sharp intake of breath, 'But if you could have seen him today you would think differently.' She took the girl's arm and half turned her towards Hosé. 'He would be a star turn with any strolling players.'

'Good at deception, you mean?'

'Ouch!' Hosé grimaced. 'I think you said the wrong thing Annette.'

She ignored him. 'But in a good cause,' she insisted to Rab. 'Otherwise we would never have been able to get the things to Sarah.'

Obviously Rab knew about those, he noted; interesting.

'And what he did was dangerous.'

It was not something he wanted to repeat.

He watched the girl's face. He would have preferred to leave Annette to plead his cause. 'There's something else isn't there Rab?' he joined in reluctantly. 'It's not only what you found out tonight; not only what happened to you before.' He used Annette's words because he still did not know what that was. 'It was something else you heard,' he was feeling his way, 'Or thought you heard.'

She looked daggers at him.

Annette was puzzled.

Hosé lifted a hand and pointed to the corner of the room. 'It's over there, isn't it?' he asked quietly.

Annette looked in that direction. 'What on earth are you talking about?'

He half smiled, 'Even you don't know about that one then?'

'That one what?'

'Being born and raised here in the villa I would have thought you would have known about all of them,' he said.

'All of what?' But then she understood. 'There are no secret spy holes out in this wing,' she said firmly.

'Not one most people could use,' he conceded, 'But a small, agile goat might manage it.' He looked at the girl with grudging admiration. 'One that did not mind climbing up a very steep and narrow opening from the garde-robe.' He had a thought, 'A pity you can't meet Mosh.'

'Mosh?' Annette queried.

'I'll tell you about him later.'

Annette looked across the room again. 'I don't see anything, not from here anyway.'

'Not from close to either, 'Hosé said ruefully. 'I checked carefully when

Isaac moved in here but missed it. Perhaps just a small crack in the plaster, but big enough if you have your ear pressed to the other side I would say.' He looked enquiringly at Rab but she glowered at him in silence. 'So why did you do it? And what did you hear?' His voice was a little more insistent.

She still would not reply although Annette also looked at her for an answer.

'All right,' he continued, 'I'll try and guess again shall I?'

'Do what you like,' she said sharply, muttering something in Arabic under her breath that Hosé only just caught. He raised his eyebrows; he would love to know sometime where she had learned that one.

'I would guess,' he said deliberately, 'That it all hinges on young Jakob.' He did not bother to make it a question and her face showed him he was right. He half expected another colourful imprecation about his fate in the hereafter, but she was silent. 'For some reason, you suspect me of wishing harm to the boy?' That was the question he had been unable to fathom.

She maintained her silence.

He sighed. 'For whatever unknown and totally wrongheaded reason,' he went on a little more impatiently, 'You thought Jakob was in some sort of danger.' He waited in vain for some explanation. 'Though you can hardly have suspected Isaac?'

'Of course not,' Rab was finally goaded into replying.

'Just me then?'

The answer to that one was plain enough.

'But I am Isaac's colleague,' he added in exasperation, although that was hardly an adequate description.

'You deceived him, like you deceive everyone!' she spat.

Annette was about to speak but Hosé stopped her. 'What?'

'You pretended you did not know Jakob's family.'

Ah.

'But Pieter recognised you!'

Hosé ignored Annette's query. He would much rather have had this out with Rab on her own but he could see now that that would be impossible. 'Pieter spoke to you about me?' he asked.

'I saw the way he looked at you. I asked him.'

'And what did he say?' Hosé was curious.

Rab hesitated. 'He would not say much. But,' she insisted, 'He knew you.'

'And why do you think he would not say much?'

She was silent.

'You think he was afraid to?'

She scoffed, 'Pieter would not be afraid of you.'

'Exactly,' said Hosé. 'And did he say anything about me to Cornelius? Or warn Jakob to beware of me?'

She reluctantly shook her head.

'Do you really imagine Pieter would not protect them if he felt them to be in any danger?'

She barely moved her head.

'Pieter understands more than most people, Rab.'

She was motionless.

'Admit it to yourself if you won't say it to me,' he insisted. 'Pieter accepted that I preferred to keep quiet.'

She was obviously debating the point with herself. 'But Isaac was angry with you over it.'

Hosé looked at her. She was right, but how had she reached that conclusion?

'He banged his tablet down on the table.' Her face challenged him.

Hosé thought about that.

Finally, he nodded. 'Yes,' he admitted, 'Isaac thought I should have told him before.'

'Because of some man called Clough.'

Annette drew a sharp breath. 'Where does that evil toad fit into this?'

Rab looked at her in surprise. 'You know him too?'

'Oh yes,' confirmed Annette bitterly. She looked at Hosé. 'And what is his connection with the *Liesabeta*?'

He shrugged and looked in turn at Rab. 'That was my main concern.'

'And you said you could beat it out of Jakob!'

Hosé gaped at the girl. 'Where did you get that idea from?'

'You said so to Isaac.'

He certainly had not What on earth had he said? 'I can't remember exactly what I said,' he admitted, 'But I did not say anything like that. And,' he added, 'You can't think Isaac would have agreed?'

'You didn't say it to him.'

He frowned at her; that was even more nonsensical.

'You said it quietly, to yourself,' she said. 'But I heard you!'

'What are you talking about?' he was exasperated. 'Tell me exactly what you thought I said.'

' "*I can discover what Jakob knows.*" ' She spat the words at him in Turkish, then translated them for Annette's benefit.

Hosé leaned back against the door. His knee was protesting painfully but he had far more important things on his mind. He remembered now; it had been at the end of the conversation: he had got up; he had moved to ease the stiffness in his legs: away from where Rab had been listening; his voice would have sounded fainter. She would realise that if she thought about it, but her reason had been drowned by her fear. The apparent threat to Jakob would have been enough, but it had also been said in Turkish; she understood the language and had imbued the words with the abhorrence she so obviously felt towards all things Turkish.

He let out a long breath and shook his head. 'So, you urged young Jakob to leave the villa next day.'

'Of course.'

'And persuaded the *Liesabeta* to set sail.'

She hesitated. 'I was thankful she did, 'she said, 'But that had nothing to do with me.'

Hosé thought he believed her. He chewed his lip. 'And you didn't talk to Isaac about this, obviously.'

She shook her head.

'Why not?' he inquired.

'Jakob had gone; he was safe.'

'And?' Hosé had noticed the slight pause.

'Isaac was getting ready to leave,' she said. 'And in any case,' she stopped.

'And in any case?'

She glared at him with renewed animosity.

'Please continue,' he said.

'And in any case, he thinks the sun shines out of you!'

Hosé was speechless.

'It was all different before you came back with him.'

Hosé flushed. Something pricked at his conscience and he bit off his retort.

'He helped me,' the words tumbled out, 'And Annette was kind. And there were the three of us. And it was ….. .' Hosé opened his mouth but she continued, 'Then afterwards you were always talking to one of them, talking about things I had no part in.'

Annette put an arm around Rab's shaking body. 'I'm sorry,' she said softly, 'I didn't realise.'

Hosé was sorry too, but he had more than thoughtlessness to be sorry about. ' "*I seek refuge in the Lord of Daybreak from the mischief of His creation; from the mischief of the night when she spreads her darkness; from the mischief of conjuring witches; from the mischief of the envier, when he envies.*" ' He recited the verses quietly and saw her recognise them. For a moment, she flushed angrily. 'We should heed the words,' he said quietly. 'Both of us, I think.'

'Please?' Annette had only understood the last part.

Hosé nodded at Rab. She wiped her eyes impatiently with the back of one hand, started the translation, stopped, then picked it up again, searching for the right words.

She had been taught well, he thought; once upon a time.

Annette looked at Hosé over the top of the dark head. 'That is beautiful,' she said.

He wished the girl would stop crying.

Annette smiled. 'It is a good thing,' she said. 'I have never seen Rab cry before.'

Hosé could not appreciate her logic.

'See if Isaac left any of his mint tea.' Annette nodded towards the shelves.

Hosé was glad of the practical activity. He moved stiffly and found all the things in their old place. He lifted the little brass kettle and heard the swish of water in it.

'Is it fresh?' he asked the back of Rab's head, which bobbed in response.

He struck a light and put the kettle to heat.

By the time he had arranged things and let the tea infuse, Rab had recovered her composure.

He lifted the beaker and allowed the sweet fresh aroma to penetrate the lingering legacy of the sewers. 'What were you doing in here earlier?' His curiosity got the better of his prudence.

'Reading one of the books Isaac left.'

He sipped the tea. 'But you blew out the light when you heard me coming?'

She flushed slightly. 'It was stupid really,' she admitted at last. 'Why shouldn't I be here? Isaac said I could.' She met his eyes defiantly.

He nodded. He was not sure about a girl learning about medical matters but he was not going to contradict whatever Isaac had said. 'Do you happen to know where the arnica ointment is?' He drained his cup.

'Of course.' Rab went to the shelf and reached for a pot.

Annette looked sideways at Hosé as she stretched out her elegant white hand for the jar. Suddenly she changed her mind. 'You should apply it,' she said to Rab. 'I'm sure Isaac showed you how.'

Rab froze and Hosé looked at Annette appalled.

'That would be the best thing to do,' Annette urged the girl softly.

Rab looked at her then at Hosé.

'Really it would,' Annette insisted. 'Sooner or later one has to face one's fears you know, to get the better of them.'

Rab still looked unconvinced.

Hosé forced a tight smile. 'After all, Annette is here.'

He stretched out his leg.

Rab pulled out the cork stopper and stuck her fingers into the jar. She sank to her knees and Hosé saw her close her eyes. The salve was cool but the tension in her fingers was obvious.

Nevertheless, she worked the ointment in and around his knee, sensing the hollows. Gradually her fingers established a rhythm.

'Look what you are doing.' Annette insisted, quietly but firmly.

Hosé saw the girl's eyes slowly open and focus. Her fingers stopped.

'You can do it,' Annette encouraged her. 'It's just a knee like any other knee and it needs treatment.'

The girl's slight body shuddered. She shut her eyes again for a moment and took a deep breath. Finally, she opened them, and took some more ointment.

'You should keep it warm,' she said as she finished and got to her feet. Her voice was not quite steady and she could not look at him, but she had managed the worst part. She busied herself wiping her fingers and corking the jar, finding a length of material.

'It's silk,' she said. 'Isaac says wool is good but silk is better, if you have it of course.' She was talking a bit too fast.

Annette took it from her.

The woman was wicked, Hosé decided, as Annette's fingers fastened off the cloth and sent shivers exactly where she intended. She had no scruples about taking advantage of the situation.

'What is it?' Annette asked curiously, pointing at the tattoo. Its lines were not as sharp as they had once been, but still showed clearly enough a slender-waisted flower with long pointed petals.

Why couldn't she drop the subject? She had done well by the girl; but surely that was enough.

It was Rab who answered. 'A *lale*, a lily; the sort that grows in the hills of Anatolia.'

'Anatolia?' Annette was puzzled for a moment. 'Ah yes, Prince Cem talked of it.'

Hosé did not like to remember when Annette and the Prince had been on intimate terms; nor was he comfortable discussing Anatolia: he had spent the past five years being very careful not to talk about it, or anything else to do with his Ottoman background.

'There was very good hunting in the hills around there, the Prince said: boar, fox, brown bear, even panther; but sometimes they would go out into the desert instead.'

Hosé had not spent his time there in sport.

'He was very young, of course, when he became Governor of Konya.

His brother Moustaffa had been Governor before, but he had died, hadn't he?' Annette interrupted Hosé's thoughts.

Hosé nodded.

Cem had been fifteen in fact; and twenty-two when he claimed to be the legitimate heir to the Ottoman throne and lands. Although he had suggested sharing the empire: his elder brother Bayezit should have Anatolia while he himself would take Rumelia, including Islambul. The battle at Yenişehir had put an end to such pretensions but the Prince had escaped and taken refuge with, of all people, the Knights of St John on Rhodes.

The irony of it twisted Hosé's lips into a sour smile.

The most Christian Knights had hardly been able to believe that such a valuable hostage had fallen straight into their hands; not that they had treated him like a hostage to begin with. For months, they had allowed him to continue in his belief that they would assist him. Even when they brought him to France it was with the promise that they would help him raise an army to invade his homeland. But gradually the truth had dawned, as the Prince had been moved firstly from the welcoming Grimaldo palace in Nice, then from one castle stronghold to another; as his followers had been gradually separated from him; as finally he had ended up in the Tour specially built at Bourganeuf to "protect" him.

But perhaps not for much longer, if what Isaac had said was true.

'You know Anatolia?'

Hosé brought his thoughts back and nodded cautiously at Annette's question.

'Is that why you have that flower?'

Damn her persistence! 'The hills look beautiful in the spring when the *lale* flowers,' he said, 'But that is not the reason,' he admitted, looking at Rab.

'It's the mark of a soldier,' the girl said.

If only, Hosé thought bitterly.

Annette ran her eyes over him. 'Now that's a surprise!'

'The different regiments have different marks,' continued Rab. 'The *lale* orta claims to be one of the best!'

'Who told you that?' Hosé asked quietly; the subject was obviously not going to be dropped.

'The soldier who was the best of the best,' her voice shook a little. 'So good he was too good for the rest of them! So he said.'

'Where did you meet him?'

'Oran.'

A regular cesspit of renegades and pirates. 'Do you come from there?'

She shook her head. 'No, from Fez.'

Hosé smiled a little and Annette looked at him puzzled. 'Isaac lived in Fez for some years. I imagine he and Rab found a lot to reminisce about.' He addressed the girl, 'Am I right?'

She nodded.

'Who was he, this soldier? What was his name?' Hosé looked at Annette. He would like to know who this man was and what had happened, but would talking about it make things better or worse?

Annette lifted her shoulders slightly.

Rab shivered but answered, 'Hasan.'

'That is a common enough name.' Hosé hoped he sounded casual.

'They call him Kara Hasan.'

'Black Hasan.' Hosé did not recognise it.

'Black in his looks and black in his soul.' Her voice was bitter. 'If he has one.'

'How long has he lived in Oran?'

She shrugged. 'Too long.'

'You don't know when he left the orta?'

She shrugged again.

Hosé gave up. Perhaps someone in Islambul knew about the man, although it would be an odd question to include in his regular despatch.

'Do you want to know what happened today?' He looked at Annette. 'After you and de la Forêt left.'

'Yes, tell me all about Sarah,' she said eagerly.

'And Mosh!' He said, looking at Rab.

Chapter 7

1488

The summer wore on. Hosé was not comfortable with the fact that Annette and Rab knew so much about him but he had to live with it. He saw Annette regularly in the course of his work for the Grimaldi. Rab still kept largely out of the way. There was an embarrassing meeting with Annette and her father. Nicolas Grimaldo had heard the rumours and made it very clear that however much he might want to secure the future of the family and the business, he would certainly not accept Hosé as a husband for his daughter. People might believe Hosé was related to the family but Nicolas knew differently. Heaven alone knew the clerk's true origins!

Hosé reflected wryly on the negotiations between Nicolas Grimaldo and the Lomellini, concerning Gianmaria, but he managed a straight face as he happily conceded the point.

Annette maintained her most innocent expression as she claimed that she had no idea where the rumours had come from and that she had absolutely no intention of marrying Hosé.

Nicolas Grimaldo looked at his daughter with suspicion. Negotiations would continue, he said firmly, with suitable persons and families.

As autumn approached, Hosé was seriously worried: there had still been no word from Isaac.

Inquiries made by Sayf had elicited the information that the *Santa Giovanna* had been seen in both Tunis and Ciutat de Mallorca during the season but nobody mentioned an old Jewish passenger, nor the men-at-arms who were supposed to be with him.

Hosé was also concerned about other matters. Intelligence from Rome confirmed that earlier in the year the Pope had appointed Pierre d'Aubusson, Grand Master of the Knights of St John, to be Cardinal Saint-Adrien but there appeared to be some delay in his taking up the position. Agents in Rome did not know why this was but Hosé was convinced it involved the Prince. D'Aubusson's strengthening of Rhodes against the Ottomans and his recent elimination of the Jews from the island would certainly have paid part of the price for the cardinalate, but Hosé had no doubt as to the nature of the outstanding fee: the Pope wanted *the* prize, for his lifelong ambition of mounting a new crusade, an ambition apparently shared by the devout young French King Charles VIII.

Would the Knights withstand pressure from both the Pope and the French king? Or would they hand over the Prince? Would Cem be moved from Bourganeuf to Rome? When might that be and which route would they take?

If only Hosé had still been with Guy de Blanchefort instead of blundering around in the dark in Nice!

The laundry woman in Bourganeuf could report nothing more than that the Prince's humour had lifted. He had been in black despair during the bitter months of the last winter but summer had apparently warmed his spirits. Perhaps it was just the season, reasoned Hosé; or perhaps the Prince glimpsed the possibility of escape. He must have long since recognised that the Knights would never allow him to raise a campaign against his brother, Sultan Bayezit; but perhaps the Pope and the French King would be willing allies. The thought made Hosé sick at heart.

As if all that was not enough to fret about, Hosé also had scraps of information from Flanders where Nicolas Grimaldo traded with the Genoese community in Bruges. The rival Brabant city of Antwerp was growing, particularly in relation to English wool and cloth. The name of Clough came up several times, linked almost inseparably to that of the van Dammes.

Where was the *Liesabeta* and what had she been doing all summer?

Autumn came to an early and abrupt end, with lashing rain and gales sweeping away any boats that had not been safely beached. Then cruel frosts stretched their icy fingers to the very edge of the Middle Sea, decking the tamarisk and mimosa in glittering finery, freezing the fountains and keeping the inhabitants of Nice huddled around their cooking fires or squeezed together in the fug of the wine shops.

Correspondence dwindled as first the seas then the roads became impassable. Hosé paced around the office in frustration.

'If only the bad weather had come a bit earlier.' Annette had her own worries. François de Beaumont had managed to travel from Marseille to Nice a few weeks before and had spent the time since in earnest pursuit of Annette's fair white hand.

'That would only have delayed the matter,' Hosé pointed out shortly. 'And in any case the choice is still yours: either you accept de Beaumont or you look for another suitor.'

She frowned, the pitted skin of her forehead wrinkling. She no longer wore a vizard: she had abandoned it on de Beaumont's first visit. Hosé had refrained from commenting.

She chewed her lip pensively and he looked at her sharply. 'Now what?'

'De Beaumont is a kind man,' she said. 'He is a successful merchant in his own right and would not interfere in Grimaldo matters.'

'But?'

'He is old.'

'Not too old!' Hosé had seen the look in the man's eyes: definitely not paternal.

'But would he beget a good healthy heir?'

Hosé shrugged. How could anyone answer that?

'His first wife never bore him children,' she continued. 'Perhaps he is lacking.' Even as Hosé prepared to question that conclusion, Annette went on, 'But I might marry him, then couple with a more likely man to father my sons.'

He stared at her. He thought he had grown used to the flagrant way she discussed such matters, but he was shocked by what he was sure she was suggesting this time. 'Oh no,' he said firmly. 'Definitely not.'

She smiled at his discomfiture. 'Or,' she added, with her head slightly on one side, 'Perhaps I should couple with de Beaumont before we wed to make sure of his potency.'

He swallowed. 'Have you broached the subject with him?' he inquired a little faintly.

'*Hein*, he would agree to anything.' Of course, she could read any man's eyes. 'But do I wish to?'

'Annette I cannot tell you what to decide.'

'No,' she shook her head a little sadly. 'But,' her face brightened and she put her hand on his arm, 'It is good to be able to talk to you about it, you know.'

'I'm not sure about that,' he said.

'You are the only person around here who really knows how to keep his own counsel. Who else should I talk to?' She looked at him quizzically. 'Perhaps I should not take you to bed after all; that would probably spoil everything.' She smiled. 'But I do think I should like it.'

Hosé refused absolutely to pursue his own thoughts on the matter.

'François and I had a very interesting talk last evening.'

'Do I want to know about it?' Hosé glanced up at her and returned to the accounts he was checking.

She considered him. 'Perhaps not all of it,' she conceded. 'But I shall tell you that I think he is not so stuffy and we may deal quite well after all.'

Hosé accepted the implied criticism with a shrug.

'He has seen many places and many different customs.' She looked at him. 'Travel can broaden the mind so.' She pulled her mouth down. 'At least in some people.'

'Possibly,' he answered shortly, striking a line through a row of figures: the winter weather seemed to have frozen the wits of the clerks.

'He has connections in so many places.'

'That could be a useful asset.' Hosé turned a page.

She nodded. 'For instance, he has just received news from Lyon.'

Hosé gave her the attention she wanted. 'Are the roads open again?'

'The mud has frozen solid and the snow is not too deep; a rider arrived yesterday.'

Hosé frowned. He had missed that.

'There was news of a consignment of leather François was worried about.' She looked at him. 'Lots of things happen in Lyon, even in the winter.'

'Such as?'

'Guillaume Archinault came there on a visit.'

Hosé's mouth tightened. The Governor of Provence had been one of d'Aubusson's carefully chosen escort when the Knights first brought the Prince to Europe. More recently he had been reported to be close to the young French king Charles VIII.

'And is it known why the Governor of Provence should be in those parts?'

'Nobody would say, but about two weeks before All Saints Day a group of heavily armed men arrived: a large group, on the road from the west.'

Hosé drew a breath.

'After a few days, they were seen departing again and the Governor went with them.'

'Heading which way?'

'They embarked in a number of small boats and went down river.'

Hosé dropped the forgotten accounts onto his desk and stared at her.

'Raymond de Glandèves was in the group.'

Hosé remembered him: the Seigneur de Faulcon, also a loyal supporter of the Knights of St John.

'And they were led by Antoine de Blanchefort.'

'Not Guy?'

She shook her head. 'He was not seen in the group.'

But Pierre d'Aubusson could count on any member of his sister's family.

'And is it known what they were guarding so well?'

'Nobody was allowed close enough to see, but there were guesses.'

Hosé could make his own guess.

Annette looked at him. 'They are moving the Prince again,' she said softly, 'From the Tour. Why and where to this time?'

Hosé did not reply, lost in his own speculation.

Annette prodded his arm. 'I think you could tell me what you know.' Her eyes studied him closely.

Hosé stared. She had volunteered this new information; would it hurt to repay her? The news of d'Aubusson's cardinalate would likely reach her soon in any case. 'I know a few things,' he said finally.

She nodded as he repeated what he had heard from Rome. 'Not to be wondered at,' she commented. She pondered the situation. 'Will a guest of the Pope be allowed any more freedom than a guest of the Knights though?'

Her tone held its customary light irony but she had, of course, put her slim white finger exactly on the point.

'Would you wish it for him?' asked Hosé curiously.

She shrugged. 'Once I would have said yes. You know how things were and how much I hoped for.' She gave a little laugh. 'It all seemed so possible then.' She paused. 'He was an exciting man, an energetic lover. I can't say I did not enjoy his attentions but now I know bed-sport was no more to him than a good day's hunting.' She paused. 'When I saw him again last year at Bourganeuf, he had changed. He has become dark and sullen of feature; his body tends towards corpulence; he speaks with bitterness. He no longer has,' she searched for the word, 'Nobility.' She continued pensively, 'Of course, he has suffered from his confinement. I can find it in myself to feel sorry for him.'

The Prince had chosen his own path. 'Down river?' Hosé reverted to more immediate matters. 'As far as Avignon?'

'That would be the usual practice,' Annette confirmed. 'The Bouches du Rhône are too difficult to navigate.'

'Then overland to Marseille?'

'That would seem the obvious direction, if they are to take boat for Rome.'

Hosé thought hard. 'The winter is a bad time to sail.'

'They might travel further east before embarking,' Annette suggested. She gave a short laugh. 'Perhaps they intend to sail from Nice!'

Hosé started.

'After all, we proved very hospitable last time.' She looked at him demurely.

'But not appropriate in the current circumstances I think,' Hosé replied evenly. 'Given Nice's connection with the Duke of Savoy.' The youthful Duke Charles of Savoy had been another romantic captivated by the

Prince's charm and eager to free him from the Knights' "protection". Hosé had only just managed to prevent him doing so.

'To say nothing of a certain Grimaldo clerk who got himself involved in curious matters in Moulins.'

Hosé grimaced. Had de Blanchefort learned of that?

'No,' Annette pretended regret, 'I think we will not see the Prince here.'

Where then? Hosé followed his own train of thought.

'Perhaps François will get more news.'

1489

The next news actually came through Sayf. Hosé chewed the end of his quill. A group of travellers had embarked in Marseille, the day after the Christian Feast of the Purification, and had headed east. Where were they now? Sayf had no information on that; nor did François de Beaumont.

Outside the wind tore at the shutters of the villa sending icy draughts through every crack.

For the best part of two weeks the stormy weather continued, matching Hosé's feelings. He felt like a boat on a rough sea, unable to see over the crests of the waves and with no idea where land lay.

Marianne laid a sympathetic hand on his arm. 'It is too bad,' she said, 'Marrying her off to that old leather merchant rather than to you.' She squeezed up closer. 'Even if she has become as ugly as sin.'

Hosé managed a grunt.

A gust of cold air swept into the room as the door opened, and smoke billowed out from the smouldering logs in the fireplace.

Marianne coughed and wiped her eyes on the corner of the coarse cloth tied around her shoulders.

'Here,' Hosé offered her his cup.

She drank some of the wine, coughed again and took another gulp.

The voices of the newcomers reached Hosé's ears and he looked up sharply.

'Her father must be desperate.' Marianne continued with her thoughts on the proposed nuptials. 'Do you think he is?' She prodded Hosé.

'What?'

The guttural accent was unmistakeable.

'Well it seems a pity, doesn't it?'

'Hey Marianne!' the shop keeper called across to her. 'Customers to be served.'

The woman half turned her head and gave a nod. 'You being half his age, and so much more handsome.' Her finger traced a path up his sleeve.

What had brought them back here, now? And where had they been?

'Definitely more handsome.' Her voice had dropped and the finger had reached his shoulder.

'Marianne, you lazy trollop!'

She gave another nod but made no effort to move. She took advantage of Hosé's inattention and slid her other hand across his knee.

'....*tegen de wind in....*'

"*Wind*', Hosé picked out the word.

'And so strong.' The hand measured his thigh and Hosé jerked his gaze back. What might well have been an unfortunate reaction was prevented by the arrival of the bar keeper, who laid hold of Marianne and heaved her up from the bench.

'Customers!' The man roared. 'There are others beside this tight-fisted pen-pushing Grimaldo b......' He did not finish the word but he glared at Hosé. He made small profit out of Hosé's visits and Marianne was always impossible when the clerk was around.

The woman shrugged off his hand. For a moment, she seemed inclined to sit down again but finally she gave Hosé a wink and turned towards the counter.

'You want to do "business" with her, you do it somewhere else and some other time.' The man glared at Hosé.

Hosé averted his eyes and buried his face in the now empty cup.

'Good evening.' The greeting was in Catalan.

Hosé looked up to see Pieter's large form by his table. The calm eyes met his. 'May I talk with you?'

Hosé glanced past him.

'I will speak for myself,' Pieter smiled, 'For once. But perhaps not in here.'

Hosé returned the smile but a little warily. He looked at the other customers. Most of them were crowding eagerly around Cornelius, hungry for news and seamen's gossip, but a few were still within hearing. He nodded.

'The *Liesabeta* does not offer much shelter.' Pieter was apologetic.

Hosé rose. 'Come.'

There was no brazier in the warehouse but at least it was deserted and when Hosé barred the door it kept out most of the wind. The flame of the candle flickered but did not die.

'The weather is not good for sailing.' Hosé suddenly pictured the ancient cog boat in high seas and strong winds. The *Liesabeta* was built for shallow inshore waters.

'*Nee*. The wind has been against us most of the way.' Pieter's quiet voice was matter of fact.

Hosé thought of the square sail and frowned.

'Cornelius has altered the rig.' Pieter answered the unspoken question. 'It was Thomas's idea and it has answered well into the wind.'

Hosé would like to see it.

'We have been in Genoa.'

The back of Hosé's neck prickled. 'Oh.'

'We traded well over the summer. The winds were kind to us then.'

Quite likely Pieter had known where to find them.

'We intended to winter in Mallorca but at Genoa the *Liesabeta* sprang a leak, again!' He smiled his slow smile. 'She is getting old, although Cornelius does not like to admit it. Anyway, we stayed for repairs. They took longer than we expected, winter came early and we remained there.'

Hosé watched the big man's face.

'It is an interesting place, Genoa.'

No doubt.

'We met seamen who have been to many places.'

Such as?

'We talked with a ship's master called Molfino. He was at Caffa when the Turks took the city.' Pieter looked at Hosé. 'What he had to say explained many things for me.'

As well it might. 'And for Cornelius?'

Pieter shook his head. 'He has not recognised you.'

'And you have not told him?'

'*Nee*. You have some reason for what you do and I see that it offers us no harm. You may tell him yourself, or,' that smile again, 'He will see it for himself sometime.'

Hosé nodded his thanks.

'But all this is not what I have to talk about; or perhaps it is connected; you will know.'

Hosé was puzzled.

'A few weeks ago, we heard of the physician.'

'Isaac? In Genoa?'

Pieter nodded.

Hosé gaped. 'Have you seen him?'

Pieter shook his head. 'We only heard about him.'

'But you are sure it is him?'

'How many old Jewish physicians named Isaac can there be who have been robbed of their tongues?'

Hosé frowned. 'How on earth did he get there?'

'On the *Santa Giovanna.*'

'She was bound for Tunis!'

Pieter nodded, 'But she is owned by the Spinola.'

Hosé cursed himself for a fool. That was hardly surprising. Why hadn't he thought to check?

'One of the family turned up just as she was about to leave Nice and ordered the master to Genoa.'

'And Isaac could not get a passage on from there?'

'It is said that the Jew left the boat; in the company of Oberto Spinola.'

Hosé scowled. After his education in Urbino, Oberto Spinola had joined the Papal guard in Rome. That he made visits to Genoa was hardly surprising, but what had he been doing in Nice? And what damnable timing!

Hosé felt the knot tighten in the pit of his stomach.

'Cornelius tried everything to find out where they had gone.' Pieter added simply, 'Isaac is a good man.'

Isaac was much more than that.

'I am sorry,' Pieter said. 'We thought we should stop in Nice and tell you.'

Hosé's face was bleak. 'I'm not sure what I can do.' There were other commitments. 'First I have to think about it.'

The following day Hosé learned that the *Liesabeta* was not the only boat to have put into the usually dormant harbour; three galleys had taken refuge from the elements.

He hurried down to see for himself.

The *Liesabeta* had once more been unceremoniously ordered out of the way. Hosé peered at her for a moment: there was certainly something different about her mast but he could not see clearly.

In any case his immediate interest was the galleys which had the quay to themselves. He huddled against a fisherman's hut, clutching his cloak as the wind attempted to whip it away, and appraised the craft; the lateen sails were lashed tightly on the long sloping yards to form a canopy and the oars were drawn inboard. The boats looked a bit like large flies whose wings and legs had been pulled off, he reflected.

Unusually they were moored abreast. Only the nearest one was alongside the quay and anyone wanting to reach the others would have to climb across. Nobody seemed to be leaving or boarding and on the nearest galley there were guards clearly visible along the length of the boat. In addition, there was a semicircle of heavily armed men on the quay, their legs braced against the force of the wind; over scarlet tunics they wore black cloaks; and on the left breast of each was the white eight-pointed star of the Knights of St John.

Hosé peered at each of the figures. At that distance and with their helmets fastened he could not recognise any of them, but he pulled his hood further over his face just in case.

He looked across the boats.

Would the Prince be in the galley furthest from the shore? Or perhaps in the middle one, protected from both sides? He must be there, mustn't he?

What else could the Knights possibly be carrying and guarding so carefully?

But perhaps this was a diversion; perhaps the Prince was really being carried in another vessel, or even being escorted overland.

Hosé stared and frowned. He needed sight of the Prince to be sure.

He surveyed the boats yet again. It would be impossible to get aboard from the quay. From the sea then? He thought he could board all right: the lack of freeboard was the crucial weakness of the galleys and no doubt what had forced them to take shelter from the high seas.

He ran his eyes in a slower more careful inspection of each boat; they were light and slender, built for speed. They were biremes: two men to each of the twenty or so oars that would extend through the leather washers he could count along the sides.

Within the shelter of the apostis then there would be eighty men on each galley, chained to their benches. Hosé caught whiffs of the distinctive and foul odour even in the strong wind.

The galleys were also designed for war. Hosé looked with respect at the wicked beaks that protruded from each bow. He tried to guess how many seamen and soldiers were taking shelter in the cabins on the raised forecastles. But most of all he looked at the carosses, the cabins built high up at the stern, extending over and beyond the great central rudders. The Prince would be accommodated in the carosse; but which carosse, which galley?

The Knights would not allow the Prince ashore; they would almost as certainly keep him confined to his cabin. There would be no chance of seeing him emerge to take exercise or some fresh air.

Hosé drew back behind the hut and eased his chilled limbs, thinking hard. After one more look he set off back to the villa in search of the things he would need.

This was probably not the use Isaac had imagined, Hosé reflected ruefully, as he plastered goose grease over his body. He had no doubt he would have to explain to Rab in the morning why he had taken three whole pots.

With some difficulty, he hauled on his hose; the grease would keep out the water and the cold but the hose would offer some protection from scrapes and bruises. He also donned an old brown tunic, his knife and a short stick tied safely within its folds. He left the rest of his clothing in a corner in the warehouse. Finally, he smeared grease mixed with soot over his face and neck and wiped his hands carefully; he would need as much grip as possible.

He eased himself out of the rear door of the building, bare feet silent if a bit tender on the stony roadway.

The heavy clouds were driven by the unrelenting wind but the half-moon seized her chances, and it was not pitch black. The water, even in the shelter of the harbour, was rough; waves slapped angrily against his head as he slid down the wooden piles. He drew some deep breaths to ease the shock of the cold then swam with steady strokes, beginning to enjoy the battle with the water. He stopped and trod water, waiting for a wave to lift him high enough to see the pricks of light that were the lanterns on the galleys.

He had drifted a little from his course but not too much. He set off again, keeping the splash of his limbs to a minimum, taking his time.

Twice more he stopped to check his position; the third time he could make out the dim outlines of the galleys above him. A figure appeared leaning over the side and Hosé ducked under the water just in time to avoid the stream of urine. He surfaced again further aft and made his way to the stern of the outermost boat cautiously; any sounds would transmit through the wooden hull and even a galley slave could suffer from curiosity.

He stopped by the stern post and grasped the central rudder with one hand. Some distance above his head was the overhang of the carosse. He listened intently: above the thump of the waves he could pick out the creak of the boards and the irritable flap of a loose rope somewhere. He managed to get his ear against the hull long enough to hear faint snores, then a wave lifted him and he pushed away.

He swam along the side. Plaited and coiled rope fenders hung between the galleys, preventing the hulls from clashing. Hosé stretched up tentatively at the nearest one but it was just beyond his reach. He swam in further and tried the next one which was a little lower. He trod water for a moment then thrust as hard as he could with his legs and pushed himself upwards; his fingers grasped the wet rope and slipped. He dropped back into the water with a splash.

He waited anxiously but there were no signs of alarm so he tried again.

This time he caught hold of the fender with his left hand. He swung there, his arm protesting at the sudden insult as he desperately tried to get a purchase with his other hand. His flailing feet struck the hull with a thud. He searched with his right hand, his cold wet fingers trying to bury themselves in the even colder and wetter rope.

The muscles of his left shoulder were shrieking; his feet hit the boards of the galley again; his left hand was beginning to slide.

He jerked his body desperately and his scrabbling right hand caught hold.

For some moments, he hung motionless, listening intently over the loud rasps of his own breathing, then hauled himself upwards. He was thankful for the woollen stuff of his hose as he kneeled on the rough matting, listening once more.

Above his head on the middle galley there were suddenly voices and his heart beat wildly in his chest. He crouched lower against the side of the boat.

'*Merde! Qu'il fait froid!*'

Hosé felt rather than heard the sound of boots stamping on the deck.

He hoped they would move away soon. It was much colder out of the water than in it; his teeth began to chatter. He clamped his jaw tightly and tried to ease his left knee away from a particularly hard knot of rope.

The men above added a few more comments about the weather and their ill-luck in standing guard on this particular shift. There was the stamping of feet again.

'*L'heure de vérifier si ça va avec les chevaux je crois, hein?*' It was the moment they had obviously been waiting for.

'*Plus chaud là,*' agreed the other.

Hosé was sure the man was right; his shivering body also longed for warmth, even from horses. He listened as the footsteps faded then waited a little longer, but there were no further sounds. Very cautiously he climbed up the rope fender and slipped aboard.

The smell from the scuppers was much stronger and he could also hear the oarsmen quite clearly. Punctuating snores was the occasional clank of a leg iron or the slurred mutter of a disturbed sleep.

He looked carefully both ways. To his left was the gavon, the lower level of accommodation; next to it was a wooden ladder giving access to a small outboard stage at the end of a balcony which traversed the boat in front of the carosse on the upper level. There would be another stage and ladder at the far side but they were lost in the blackness beyond the lamp that swung in the middle of the balcony. Usually the carosse was the master's quarters and he commanded the boat from its balcony.

Hosé stared. Was the master in the carosse now? Or had the master of this galley given up his accommodation to the Prince?

There was one way to find out. He started towards the nearer ladder, his feet cold and a little clumsy.

A faint sound caught his attention and he looked up. From the darkness beyond the lantern a man appeared, crossing the balcony.

For an instant Hosé froze, then shrank back, dropping down beside the low rail. He glanced up. The eight-pointed cross was clearly discernible in the lamplight; as was the Knight's sword which gleamed in his mailed hand.

Hosé curled up and lowered his eyes; their whites would betray him even if the rest of him was invisible.

He could hardly endure the enforced blindness.

His ears strained to tell him what the Knight was doing but he could hear nothing except the night sounds from within the apostis.

Then another noise: a slack guy? a loose brail? or a black cloak snatched by the wind?

Hosé scarcely dared to breath. Surely he must hear if the man started to descend the ladder.

Another noise, quite distinct this time; from another direction.

A challenge rang out from the Knight on the balcony and a voice answered him from the deck opposite where Hosé crouched. Hosé risked a quick look. Another guard had appeared and was looking up at the balcony.

The Knight called down to him in French. 'Where are the two men keeping watch?'

'I just saw them in the stables.' The man laughed. 'That horse Ylderim! Thunderbolt by name and thunderbolt by nature. The Pope had better watch out if he doesn't want a hoof in his holy midriff!'

The Knight on the balcony did not join in the joke. 'I thought I heard something over there. If it wasn't them, who was it?'

Hosé had no intention of waiting for them to find out. He rose and slipped over the side.

'Hey!' The cry was followed almost immediately by the clatter of the Knight's boots on the ladder. There was the thud of feet as the other guard ran to join him.

The lamplight had spoiled Hosé's night vision; he dived into the inky blackness.

And struck the water sooner than he had expected; but at least it *was* water.

The Knight had moved fast to raise the alarm. As Hosé reached the stern he could hear shouts and above him figures appeared at the side with a dozen lanterns. He swam as fast as he could around the outermost galley.

A shout overhead told him that the other boats had been alerted.

He took a great breath, dived and swam underwater. When he finally surfaced, he was well clear of the lamplight. The water was choppier and the wind sliced through his wet hair.

He trod water gulping in air and catching glimpses of the quay. What had been a small semi-circle of guards now appeared to be a whole company spread the length of the waterfront, judging from the myriad lights.

He cursed to himself; they were waiting to catch him when he swam ashore.

He continued to tread water thinking. Well, he couldn't stay out here indefinitely. He set off at a steady pace.

It was further than he thought or more likely he was out of practice. His legs began to tire, his arms grew slower, he was forced to stop and recover a little. He floated for a while. Clouds covered the sky now, but even if there had been light, the waves were too high for him to see over. There was more than a chance that he could swim around in circles.

He floated a little longer but he was getting cold; he needed to move again. Just when he thought he would have to make a guess about the right direction a wave lifted him high enough to spot the quayside lights. From this distance, they looked small and harmless, but they showed that the Knights were still there, waiting.

He struck out once more.

Finally, his fingers touched rough wood and he felt his way carefully along the boards. He was nearly there; he only had to get around the other side and he could climb up the piles.

Two pairs of hands seized him and hoisted him out of the water. He struggled to free himself but he was exhausted. He flapped on the deck like a stranded fish.

'Well,' said an amused voice. 'Quite like old times.'

Chapter 8

'I seem to remember something similar fifteen years ago, or more.'

Hosé made the effort to sit up on the open deck of the *Liesabeta.*

'Here.' Cornelius thrust a rough blanket around his shoulders. 'Ugh! What are you covered in?'

'Goose grease; keeps the cold out; some of it anyway.' The words came out jerkily; his teeth were chattering.

'Goose grease?' Jakob laughed beside his father.

'Sh!' Pieter was suddenly urgent.

Hosé had heard it too: the chink of armed men. He pushed the blanket back and struggled to his feet. There was only one place to hide on a boat like this. He slid over the side.

'You keep late hours,' a voice challenged in French.

'Sorry?' Cornelius returned in Catalan.

Hosé clung with his fingertips to one of the crossbeams that protruded through the hull of the cog and wondered how long he would have to stay in the water this time. He clenched his jaw so tight his face began to ache.

The man on the shore repeated himself in a passable Catalan.

'We were wondering about the stir over on the quay. We heard the noises and saw the lights. What's going on?'

The man ignored Cornelius's question. 'What are you doing here? It is a strange season to be sailing.'

'I could say the same thing about you.'

Hosé nearly groaned.

'The Order has important business to conduct. What is your reason?' The Knight's tone was persistent.

'Our business might not seem so important to the likes of you,' returned Cornelius doggedly, 'But it is important to us.'

'What business?' The demand was short.

'Why should it matter to you?' Cornelius could match anyone in that game.

'Why do you not want to tell me? Do you have something to hide?'

'We have nothing to hide.' Cornelius paused. 'But I can't see what right you have to question us. The port officials have that right; the town authorities as well; those I have already answered. The Governor might also have an interest,' he added fairly. 'But you, what right do you have here? You are visitors who have taken shelter just as we have.'

'The Knights of St John,' came the icy reply from a different voice, 'Hold our authority from God.'

In other circumstances Hosé could have been amused: the Frenchmen had obviously not dealt with a Lowlander before.

The boat shifted in the water and Hosé nearly lost his grip.

'*Nee.*' Cornelius was polite but firm. 'You have no right to come on my boat.'

'Damn your impudence.' The Knight was angry. 'We have the right of this!'

There was no longer anything remotely amusing about the situation. Cornelius and Pieter would not stand a chance against armed Knights and Hosé knew realistically the only way he could help them and himself was to stay out of sight.

The boat rocked violently and Hosé lost his hold.

'Seize the boy!'

'*Nee!*'

The scuffling ceased abruptly.

'That's better.' The Knight's voice was slightly breathless but smug. 'Behave yourselves and he will come to no harm; resist and the boy may end up short of one or two of his finer features.'

Cornelius spat out something angrily in his native tongue. The words had a familiar ring; Hosé hoped the Knight had no idea what they meant.

'Now,' put in the other Knight. 'A few simple answers to a few simple questions.'

Cornelius's laboured breathing betrayed his fury.

'Why are you here in Nice, at this season?'

There was a pause but Cornelius was not going to risk anything happening to Jakob. 'We were delayed in Genoa having our boat repaired. Now she is fixed we are on our way to Mallorca for the rest of the winter.' His voice was strained.

'And it is so urgent to get to Mallorca you must sail in a storm?'

There was another slight pause. Cornelius was making his point that he was replying against his will but to Hosé it sounded as if he had something to hide. 'We must help with the building of our new boat.'

The Knight made a contemptuous noise. 'I can see why you would need one; this thing must have been old when Noah built his ark.'

There were loud laughs.

'So,' the Knight was thoughtful, 'A new boat? Such things do not come cheap. You have money.' He paused. 'Or perhaps you have been promised it, in return for some valuable service.'

'What?' Cornelius was astounded.

Hosé was dismayed.

'For helping someone who would dare interfere with the Knights of St John.'

That was far too near the truth, however faulty the reasoning.

'After this I'd be happy to consider it!'

Hosé silently pleaded with Cornelius not to make matters worse.

'But,' the Lowlander added in a more conciliatory tone, 'I have no idea what you are talking about. Nobody offered to pay us for anything. If you must know we had some money from the family business, some we have earned ourselves with hard trading and we will save some of the price by finishing the boat ourselves.'

'So, you have nothing to hide on this tub?'

'As you can very well see,' said Cornelius bitterly, 'There is nowhere to hide anything, or,' he paused, 'Anyone.'

'Nevertheless, we will look.'

The Knight called up to the quay and more feet rocked the boat.

'Take lights and examine every corner of this pile of flotsam.'

Hosé watched the reflections from the lanterns moving on the water around the boat.

'What is this?' The Knight demanded.

'What?'

'Why is there a pool of water here?'

That was where Hosé had been landed and where he had rested for a few, all too brief, moments. He was shivering uncontrollably by now. If the soldiers had stood still and listened they must have heard him, but fortunately, they were still searching every part of the boat, climbing clumsily over the crossbeams, lifting every barrel and peering behind every pile of rope and canvas.

'It probably slopped up when you all came aboard. The bottom boards are flooded.'

'I thought you had this tub repaired. Are you telling me it still leaks?'

'She was repaired and she does not leak,' explained Cornelius carefully, 'But she rides better in high seas with water in her keel. It provides ballast.'

The Knight sniffed. 'Have you found anything?' he called.

Several voices replied in the negative.

The Knight clicked his tongue suddenly. 'Look over the sides,' he ordered. 'The man we are seeking is a swimmer.'

Hosé sank beneath the water and slid under the keel. He hoped miserably that the soldiers would not look for too long.

He shook his head, the blood beginning to pound in his ears. There was a tight band around his chest.

He fumbled clumsily with his tunic; his fingers would hardly obey him.

Very soon he would have to surface for air.

He carefully hauled himself around the stem. He was now in a narrow space between the boat and the harbour wall. His lungs must surely burst. He forced himself to rise slowly. He thought there was no lantern just here; he would have to take the chance. He allowed his face just above the water and let the spent air out against the hull, drawing in cold night air. Under the water, he scrabbled in his tunic again.

'What was that?' The shout was accompanied by footsteps.

Hosé gave a desperate tug. The sodden cloth gave way and he grasped the stick in his numb hands.

He drew a breath and dived once more. This time he did not try to be silent: he did not have the time. He swam as hard as his exhausted body would permit under the keel to the stern.

There he held himself just under the water and put one end of the stick in his mouth. He blew the water out of it and gratefully drew air into his lungs. As far as he could tell the hollow stick was now against the stern post. That was the best he could do at hiding it.

At first it was difficult to breathe evenly; he needed more air than the narrow tube allowed. Very gradually his lungs calmed, his pulse slowed.

But he could still hear the soldiers moving about in the boat.

He began to lose consciousness. The stick drifted out of his slack lips and water filled his mouth. He panicked; his legs struck the boat, his head surfaced.

He spluttered and choked as he tried not to cough.

'Satisfied?' Cornelius's voice was loud and abrupt. 'You must surely believe now that there is nobody else aboard.'

'So it seems,' the Knight was not entirely convinced. 'But I shall leave some of my soldiers here until morning. Perhaps the man we seek might still appear.'

Hosé feared he might. He had got his breath again but he could not stay in the water much longer. Nor it seemed could he board the *Liesabeta* again.

Cornelius began some protest.

'My men,' interrupted the Knight, 'Will stand guard on the quay and your boy can keep them company. You and this other man will stay on-board. Provided there is no "problem", the boy will be returned in the morning.'

Cornelius started to say something but the Knight stopped him. 'Do you understand me, seaman?'

'*Ja*, I understand you very well.' There was no mistaking the enmity in

Cornelius's voice.

Hosé knew this was the moment to go: while the soldiers left the boat and positioned themselves.

There was one last place he might hide; if he could find it in the dark.

He had never been so cold in his life. Even an Anatolian winter had never chilled him like this, right to the very marrow of his bones.

He shivered uncontrollably and tried to sleep, then when he became drowsy he forced himself to his feet because he feared he might never wake up again. He stamped around the narrow ledge trying to restore some circulation. At least he did not need to worry about making a noise; there were only the rats to hear him.

It was pitch black; not even pairs of tiny red eyes relieved the dark.

How long would it be before day broke? How long before there was a glimmer of light in the water at the outfall of the sewer?

He jumped up and down on the spot. His trembling legs barely raised him off the slimy ground, but he did believe he felt just a little less cold. He rested for a while then hauled himself upright again.

He tried to recall every exercise he had ever done: those taught him by the old captain Capello in Urbino; those he had practised with the other boys in Caffa; those used by the janissaries; those he had invented for himself to improve his strength for wrestling; those devised by Isaac to compensate for his "crippled" foot.

Each time he dragged himself up he tried a different one. It distracted him from the dark and the cold if he focussed his mind on something else, and the movement must help; he had to believe that.

He was wearily attempting to imitate Capello for the third time when he thought he saw a faint lifting of the darkness; by the time he had dangled his leg in a weak parody of Isaac's instructions he was sure he was right.

He sat down and rested once more. Not too long or he would go to sleep. Not too long or he would imagine too clearly what he might meet out there.

He really did not want to go into the water again. How could he ever have thought he liked swimming?

He dipped a foot in. Actually, it might be warmer under there; he nearly convinced himself of it and slid in before his treacherous mind suggested otherwise.

He emerged from the sewer and rose to the surface. The first thing that struck him was a hard, cold rain. He muttered a weak curse and looked around, prepared to dive.

The wind was still blowing. It seemed to cut straight through his head, in one ear and out of the other. The grey water was choppy.

But he could see no soldiers.

In fact, he could not see the quay, or the *Liesabeta*; certainly not the galleys, presuming they were still there.

The rain could be as hard and as cold as it wanted!

He let out a weak laugh.

The two watchmen on the galley would have been dismayed to find how helpful they had been Hosé thought as he limped into the stable which housed an ancient mare and half a dozen hens. He kept a respectful eye on the horse as he dipped his hand and drank thankfully from her bucket of water.

He looked hopefully in her manger for oats or barley but there was only hay. His stomach growled.

He was not sure whose stable it was, but it held the promise of shelter while he waited for nightfall.

He climbed the ladder up to the small loft and began to dig into the hay.

A hen looked at him warily but did not move.

Hosé moved carefully towards her, talking softly. She did not move. Could it really be, at this season? He slid his hand out. She stretched her neck and he caught her deftly behind the head before she could peck him. She squawked loudly.

Hosé slipped his hand under her and removed two eggs swiftly before releasing her and moving quickly out of range.

She glared at him but her protests subsided as she fluffed out her feathers and settled herself again on her remaining eggs.

Hosé returned to his bed of hay, burrowed into it then allowed himself to crack the eggs carefully. A raw egg is difficult to eat slowly but he forced himself to pause between the first and the second one; it was a trick he had learned a long time ago.

His luck held: nobody came into the stable all day. At least if they did he did not waken and they did not search the loft.

He met nobody on his way to the warehouse and the building itself was deserted.

He did what he could to clean himself then dragged his clothes on. It would take a lot more to get the sooty mixture off his face but hopefully he could hide the worst with his hood.

His luck ran out as he left the warehouse.

As he secured the side door behind him, he heard that distinctive combination of sounds again: the chink of chain mail, the creak of leather ties, the rasp of an un-oiled hinge in armour.

Not the local watch.

They were passing the end of the narrow alley. At any moment one might turn and see him. He really did not want to explain his presence there, or his condition.

He froze, flattening himself against the wall.

As the last one passed, Hosé turned quickly in the other direction. He ran straight into someone coming the other way.

The struggle was brief. Hosé pinned the body to the ground, his knife in his hand.

There was a gasp. Hosé's hand roughly prevented any further noise.

Only then did his tired brain add together the various clues.

'You stupid little idiot!' He hissed the words. 'You nearly got yourself killed.' He lifted his hand. 'What on earth are you doing here?' The words came out as an angry whisper as he eased himself up. 'Here,' he helped Rab to her feet. 'Didn't you learn your lesson last time?' he demanded.

'The Spanish soldier is not in Nice anymore,' she retorted although her voice was shaking.

'There are other dangerous men around the streets at this time of night.'

'I know,' she spat at him. 'I just met one!'

'What on earth are you doing here?' he repeated his question, tempted to shake an answer out of her.

'I was going to the warehouse,' she answered sullenly.

'At this time? Why?'

She was silent for a moment. 'To look for you,' she answered reluctantly.

'What?'

'You have not been in the office all day. Donna Annette was worried. There were stories that the Knights had been searching the harbour and the port area for someone who tried to board one of their galleys last night.'

And the damned woman had added two and two together with perfect arithmetical accuracy.

'And she sent you to see if I was at the warehouse?' He was incredulous.

'She did not exactly send me.'

'You just thought of it by yourself; out of your great concern for me!' He spoke more cuttingly than he had intended. All he wanted to do was get back to the villa; he was exhausted, cold and hungry.

'I don't care what happens to you,' she flung back at him. 'But she does. And,' she added, 'Isaac would.'

He was taken aback.

'Come on,' he said a little gruffly. 'Let's get out of here.'

He had planned to stay out of sight until after the Knights left Nice; he had not planned to stay confined to bed. The next morning, however, he could not rise from his pallet. Whereas he had been cold before, he now burned and sweated with fever.

He lay back with a groan and tried to think straight but sunk into a restless sleep.

He woke again sometime later with a raging thirst.

As if by a miracle, a hand offered him a mug of some steaming liquid.

He drank thirstily.

He squinted out of swollen eyes. 'Thank you,' he croaked.

A wet cloth was cool on his forehead.

'Rab!'

She turned and he motioned to her.

'Listen; it's important. On no account must the Knights have any reason to connect the van Dammes with me.' His throat felt like old parchment.

She looked puzzled.

'Cornelius might come here inquiring for me.' She frowned. 'But they must all stay away until after the Knights leave.'

She shook her head. 'Why should Cornelius do that?'

'He might want to ask after me.' It would be an understandable curiosity, but disastrous.

'Why?'

'He saw me last night - no, the night before.' Hosé's head was spinning. 'When I was trying to avoid the Knights.' His voice was faint.

She was staring at him.

'Please,' he said. 'Get a message to them; but the Knights must not see; perhaps at the wine shop.' He added, his voice little more than a whisper, 'They must not come here. Do you understand?'

He could see her trying to work it out. Why couldn't she just do it?

'Jakob would be in great danger again.'

'Again? What did you do?'

He shook his head in frustration; his voice had gone completely. He lifted his hands in silent appeal.

She looked at the gesture with some surprise then slowly nodded.

After she left the room he tried to get up but his legs would not obey him. After several futile attempts, he collapsed back onto his mattress. He had to trust she would manage it.

He had no idea how long he slept but the wonderful mug steamed under his nose again and the golden liquid slid down his ravaged throat.

He could only look his question silently.

'It's all right,' she said. She paused. 'They were glad to hear you were still alive.'

Hosé was not sure how long that happy state of affairs would continue; he felt deathly.

He lost count of the days and nights but when he finally woke properly, dawn was just breaking. He could see the grey light around the edges of the wooden shutters. He lay there feeling vaguely puzzled about something. He felt incredibly tired but he thought the fever had gone: his thoughts followed some sort of reasonable order and the outlandish images had faded away. He was no longer desperately thirsty.

He dozed off again for a while, a peaceful sort of sleep.

This time when he woke Rab held the inevitable tisane.

His eyes flew open. 'I know what it is,' he said, his voice weak but working. 'It's quiet. The wind has dropped; the storm has blown itself out.'

She nodded. 'It began to ease a couple of days ago.' She gestured towards the window. 'The galleys are preparing to leave.'

He tried to rise but the effort was too much.

'You need to rest,' she said, offering him no assistance.

'What day is it?'

She told him.

'There are things I need to do.' He succeeded in dragging himself into a sitting position.

'I think they will have to wait,' she said watching him.

He lay back exhausted.

'I will fetch you a bolster if you stay in bed,' she suggested.

He glared at her. 'Some bargain!'

She shrugged but there was a faint gleam in her dark eyes. 'Those are the terms. Take it or leave it.'

'For today,' he finally conceded.

As if he had any option.

He sat up for a while on principle although he soon wanted to lie flat again and sleep. He watched Rab as she moved around the room that had been Isaac's, preparing more tisane on the little burner.

His eyes took in the bowl of water, the lump of yellow soap. They moved around the room to the pile of filthy discarded clothes and stopped at the pot on the floor in the corner.

She turned and he swallowed hard. 'Who,' he asked carefully, 'Has been looking after me?'

'Me, of course.'

He was silent for a while as he considered this. Rab had taken over Isaac's stores and recipes with zeal; Hosé had got used to that and it had not surprised him to find her dispensing teas. But this was something else.

She watched him, grim satisfaction showing plainly as the colour in his face rose over both the pallor of illness and the thick stubble.

'It is not fitting,' he finally managed weakly.

'Who else should have done it?' she asked. 'Would you have wanted some servant who would chatter to the whole world?' Her mouth set, 'Or would you have wanted the Donna Annette to tend to your needs?'

He gulped. 'She didn't, did she?'

Rab regarded him for a moment and finally shook her head. 'Monsieur de Beaumont has become,' she paused as if seeking the right word, 'Most protective.'

Hosé felt a spark of anger for a moment then some amusement. 'He will soon find himself an ex-suitor if he insists on that.'

Rab nodded but said, 'I think not.'

Hosé looked at her curiously.

'But apart from that, Donna Annette thought of a plan.'

He raised a vaguely inquisitive brow.

'It is reported that it is I who am sick. Annette's personal maid comes several times a day to deliver food and water but nobody else is allowed along this passage. The Donna stays away to emphasise the possibility of contagion and also,' she added, 'So she can divert attention from your absence.'

Hosé looked up sharply.

'Two of the Knights arrived the day after you got back.'

'Did they suspect something?'

'The maid did not know the details, but she believes the Donna managed to satisfy them.'

If anyone excelled in the art of verisimilitude it was Annette, he thought.

And who was he to criticise?

'So, what are we going to do with you?'

Hosé opened his eyes and greeted Annette with a sleepy smile.

She pulled over a stool and sat beside him. 'You look positively endearing you know, lying there defenceless.'

He hoisted himself into a sitting position.

On the other side of the room Rab muttered something.

'I am on the mend.' He concentrated on Annette. 'I shall be up soon enough.'

'Possibly,' she said. 'But have you any idea what you look like?'

He was startled; that had not occurred to him. He had no glass or steel mirror; such things were for the wealthy. Two days earlier he had succeeded in shaving himself and although his unsteady fingers had found hollows in his cheeks he had prided himself on his progress.

'You look dreadful,' she said frankly.

'A moment ago, you said I looked endearing.'

She laughed. 'Now I know you are getting better! But seriously,' she continued, 'There is a problem.'

'What? I thought the Knights had gone.'

'So they have. God speed them,' she added, raising her plucked eyebrows. 'But as far as everyone in the villa is concerned, and the rest of Nice to whom the servants will surely have gossiped, you have simply been away on business. Anyone seeing you now will know you could not possibly have been travelling anywhere. Rab on the other hand has supposedly been at death's door but looks in rude good health. So how to explain that interesting situation?'

'I suppose I could stay here a bit longer until I look better,' he said reluctantly. He glanced over at Rab. 'Rab does not need to stay with me. I can manage now. She could pretend she had recovered, couldn't she?'

'Then there would be no reason to keep everyone away from this room.'

Hosé frowned. 'I could go somewhere else,' he said finally.

'Impeccable logic,' Annette smiled. 'Where did you have in mind?'

His mind had been busy with all sorts of things since the fever abated, largely to do with Isaac. He knew for certain now that the Prince was going to Rome. Hosé would follow him there. But only after he had found the Jew.

He silently cursed his weakness. He pondered Annette's question. Where else? Sayf's? The Arab had far too many visitors, even in winter. One of Sayf's many acquaintances? Hosé trusted the Arab but could he be sure of the others?

He looked at the light eyes. 'Where did *you* have in mind?' he asked suspiciously.

She tucked a strand of silver hair back in place and twisted the ring on her thumb until it lay to her satisfaction. 'Somewhere where you can enjoy lots of the fresh air Isaac so recommends, wouldn't you think?' She looked up at Rab who had left what she was doing and moved closer.

Rab stared.

Annette smiled smugly. 'I think you should rest now,' she said to Hosé solicitously. 'So, you are strong enough for some visitors this afternoon.'

'Gaat 't wel?'

Hosé laid a thin hand on Cornelius's brawny arm. *''T gaat wel,'* he returned.

'Do you get sick every time you go swimming?' The Lowlander switched to Catalan.

Hosé pulled a wry face. 'I don't believe I have been seriously ill once since Antwerp.'

He was aware of the ring of faces around his bed. He had tried to make it to Isaac's chair to receive the mystery visitors but had had to admit defeat.

'When you pulled the Englishman out of the water?' Jakob, inevitably, was standing next to Rab.

Hosé looked at Cornelius. How much did the boy know?

'And what Englishman would that be?' Annette was looking very pleased with herself. As well she might, thought Hosé bitterly. She had contrived a situation where she was bound to learn all sorts of things she had long been curious about.

'Master Clough,' said Jakob with obvious distaste.

His father laid a hand on the boy's shoulder. *'Let op.'*

'Ah.' Annette said on a long breath.

Ah indeed.

'I'm sorry I got you into trouble with the Knights.' Hosé tried to change the subject.

'In Amsterdam it was the other way round, *nee*?' Cornelius defeated him.

'Could we talk about that some other time?'

'Oh no,' purred Annette, 'I think now is just the time to talk about it.'

Cornelius looked from her to Hosé and back again.

It was Pieter who intervened. He addressed Annette. 'You thought we might be able to help with something.'

She studied him. 'Indeed I did. Perhaps you still can, but now you have raised the name of Master Clough I think we need to be clear about him first.'

Pieter frowned a little.

Cornelius looked at him.

What would Pieter decide about Annette? wondered Hosé, watching the silent debate.

The big Lowlander, however, was watching Hosé. 'Well?'

Hosé badly wanted to know what the English merchant was doing now and how the van Dammes were involved. He wanted equally badly to avoid talking about the events of fifteen years ago; Annette and Rab already knew far too much about him. He would much rather talk to the brothers alone.

'You still don't think you can trust me?' Annette said quietly.

Hosé was already exhausted; he closed his eyes for a moment and considered her question. 'I have had more than enough proof to the contrary,' he answered eventually, 'But my history is not entirely mine.'

She did not understand what he was talking about.

Cornelius was also staring at him.

Pieter nodded. 'Could you not tell part of it?' he suggested.

Hosé thought again. 'You tell it,' he said finally. 'I am tired and that part you know well enough. But,' he added, 'I should thank you not to name names. They belong to times past and are best forgotten.'

He opened his eyes as Pieter reached the point when the boy he called "Hosé" had left Amsterdam in disgrace.

'But, Papa,' said Jakob indignantly. 'It was not his fault; mother was to blame.'

Cornelius looked rueful.

'I never held that against her,' said Hosé, smiling at the boy. 'You look very much like her you know, when she was wearing the clothes she had stolen from me.'

Rab had an intense expression on her face. 'Your mother once dressed up as a boy?' she said to Jakob.

Jakob nodded impatiently. He could not see why that should be interesting.

Annette had also been listening closely. 'So, you saved the miserable life of that toad Clough.' She stared at Hosé.

'Tell them about your acquaintance with him, Annette,' he said shortly.

She expressed herself in a few unladylike words. She stopped and looked at Hosé. 'Did he know who you were in Moulins?'

Hosé explained about Moulins. 'And no,' he answered Annette, 'I don't think he did recognise me as the boy from Antwerp.'

That had been one small crumb of comfort from the whole damnable affair.

'And now your turn,' he spoke to Cornelius. 'What has he been up to since he was disgraced in Moulins over the Medici business?'

'You must know that he still has considerable wealth and influence in the wool trade. I do not know how much he owns in England, in Norwich, but talking to Thomas I would guess a substantial amount.'

'Where is Thomas by the way?'

'He is in Mallorca.'

'Ah, the new boat,' said Hosé with a small smile, 'Of course. Sorry, please continue about Clough.'

'You will remember that Clough started doing business with Father fifteen years ago; Antwerp is a good outlet for his English worsted. It started off as a reciprocal arrangement but since then Clough has gained more and more control.'

'Over your father?'

Cornelius frowned. 'And over Franz.'

Hosé recalled their elder brother: a gentle young man with an old head on his shoulders. 'He seemed very capable.'

'He was; he is. Van Dammes has been as successful as any of the other Houses. It's taken a lot of the Genoese business and some from the Hanse too. Franz has been largely responsible for that.'

'So?'

'Last year, when Clough came back to Antwerp he wanted to take over van Dammes completely.' Cornelius's frown deepened.

Rebuilding his fortunes after Moulins.

'And how did he intend to do that?'

It was Pieter who answered. 'He proposed marriage to Marije.'

Annette made a small sound.

'Who is Marije?' Hosé asked. His head was beginning to ache.

'Our younger sister. She's nine.'

'That is young.'

'It should have been Tante Liesabeta.' Jakob put in. 'She is older.'

Another aunt? Hosé sank back carefully. 'Liesabeta,' he queried, 'As in *Liesabeta*?'

It was Jakob who spoke again. 'Yes, the boat is named after her and after the Saint, of course.'

Saint Elizabeth. Hosé wondered if it was entirely a good idea to call a boat after a saint on whose special day there had been such a catastrophic flood.

'She might be a woman,' Cornelius said with a cautious look at Annette, 'But Liesabeta would figure out deals that Franz could only dream of.'

Hosé asked. 'So why was it not her?'

'Liesabeta has chosen to marry the Church.'

It might well be a better option than marriage to Clough.

There was a short silence then Annette spoke. 'And the business is to be the dowry?' Disbelief tinged her voice.

Cornelius nodded.

There was something else. Hosé looked at the hard line of Cornelius's mouth. 'But that would disinherit the rest of you. Why should your father have to accept such an outrageous proposal from Clough?'

It was Pieter who finally broke the silence. 'The trouble is Franz.'

Cornelius added obliquely, 'Franz has a wife but they will never have children.'

'She is barren?' Annette asked.

Cornelius did not reply and Pieter stared into some invisible distance.

It took a long time. Annette was the first to draw a slow breath. Hosé's mind lumbered to enlightenment: the custom of the Greeks. 'So, Clough threatens blackmail.' It was a statement.

'And you rescued him.' Annette said again bitterly.

Did she think he did not often consider that?

Cornelius said slowly, 'If Clough had drowned that day in Antwerp many people would be happier today.'

If Allah had some purpose in preserving Clough's life, Hosé thought miserably, it was well hidden. He shook his head. 'But you talked to the Knight of family money for this new boat.'

'You heard that?'

Hosé nodded. 'It was not the best strategy to argue with him, you know.'

'So I told him,' commented Pieter.

'Bloody French knights! Think they can push the rest of the world around,' growled Cornelius.

Hosé could not disagree with that. 'But the good fighter knows when to give ground; it's the winning blow that really counts.' He had learned that the hard way; as with so many lessons, he reflected.

Cornelius looked unconvinced. 'Anyway,' he continued, 'Father could see no way of defying Clough, but he was determined that the man should not get everything. He had certain assets banked outside Antwerp which he reckoned Clough did not know about. He foresaw that Clough would find some way to cut us out when he took over and he wanted us to have some portion before that happened.' He added, 'Pieter and I have never worked in the warehouse. We have carried and traded for the business.'

Hosé certainly could not see either of them anywhere except on the deck of a boat. 'In the *Liesabeta*?'

Cornelius bristled at the gentle mockery. 'No,' he admitted eventually, 'But Clough would certainly regard the *Marije* as part of the business.' He smiled without humour at the double meaning. 'We could hardly sail off with her.'

'The *Liesabeta*,' began Jakob defensively.

'*May seem old fashioned, but she is solid and very well balanced*,' Hosé finished for him in Thomas's serious tone and slightly stilted accent.

'Well she is,' Jakob persisted.

'I know.' Hosé said solemnly. 'I can personally attest to the solidity and cleanliness of her hull. I don't think I noticed a single barnacle.'

Cornelius gave a reluctant smile. 'It seemed essential to move right away from Antwerp,' he continued his story, 'So we headed down the Atlantic coast and then on to Mallorca. Pieter and I had decided that the best way to use the money was to build a bigger boat to trade in.'

'What about Thomas?' Annette asked. 'Where does he fit into this.'

Cornelius repeated what Hosé already knew from Isaac. 'Clough wants nothing more to do with the son of his first wife. He refused to continue paying for Thomas's apprenticeship and he would undoubtedly be happy if the lad just disappeared, forever.'

Jakob's freckled face was flushed with anger. 'But we'll look after him.'

'Thomas is on Mallorca you say?'

Hosé looked at Annette suspiciously.

Cornelius nodded. 'For the moment. When the boat is finished, he can sail with us if he likes; or perhaps he will find other boats to build. That is what he really wants to do.'

'Will you sail for Mallorca soon?' Annette persisted. 'If the weather is good enough for the Knights to leave, presumably you could go too.'

Cornelius nodded. 'Pieter says the weather will hold for the next few days.'

'And the *Liesabeta* might accommodate an extra passenger?'

Hosé let out a groan. 'No.'

'You could visit the island of your birth,' she said brightly.

That was not as funny as she thought.

'And you could get lots of fresh air.' Annette smiled, 'Just what Isaac would order.'

Isaac. She did not know about Isaac.

'What is it?' she demanded as she saw the expression on his face.

Chapter 9

Early Spring 1489
He had fought a rear-guard action of course.

He had managed to delay departure by a day, pleading that he needed to catch up on at least some of the despatches and inform one or two people about the changes.

Pieter had agreed one day would be all right.

Rab looked forlorn as she handed him the packets of tea and herbs. 'I wish I was going too.'

Hosé knew it was not him she was going to miss. 'Annette will need you more than ever,' he said. That would surely meet Isaac's strictures.

She gave him a strange look.

'For dealing with the African trade,' he said. He studied her more closely. 'And there will soon be lots of preparations for the wedding.'

He planned to be in Genoa or even Rome by the time of the event itself; he would not be sorry to miss it.

Rab seemed on the point of saying something.

'What is it?' he asked. 'Is it de Beaumont?' She had mentioned something about him being "*protective*". 'I am sure Annette will still need you.'

'Yes.'

He slowly lowered the letter he had been reading. 'Are you trying to tell me something?' he said. Or trying not to tell him.

The expression on her face was enough.

For a moment, he was startled. 'So, she did it!'

He had been carried out of the villa in a large basket. This had travelled down the steep streets to the harbour in a cart packed with various other packages.

He opened his eyes and slowly stretched, aware of the motion of the boat through the water.

He looked at the mast only a few feet forward of the small shelter. 'What kind of rig is that?'

'Thomas invented it,' said Jakob proudly.

Hosé remembered. He studied the arrangement. The sturdy mast had been reduced to a stump about the height of a man; at the top of it was slung a yard with a large block at its lower end and a lateen sail laced along its length; protruding above the stump, with guys to the stem, was a short, slender mast holding a smaller triangular foresail.

The yard in effect formed the top of the main mast, Hosé realised. 'So the main mast can be raised or lowered, a bit like on a buss.'

'You've seen a buss?' Jakob was impressed.

'I sailed on one, once.' Hosé smiled at the memory of the fishing trip.

'With Papa and Oom Pieter?'

Hosé nodded. 'Help me out of this thing,' he indicated the fur-lined leather sleeping bag, 'And tell me about that block at the bottom.' He thought of something, 'And talk to me in Diets.'

The sail worked well. Hosé was impressed, especially when they had to reach directly into the wind along the mountainous north coast of the island. As they rounded the cape into the great bay of Ciutat de Mallorca, the increasing westerly wind strained at the sail and sped them towards the harbour.

Pieter nodded. 'Tomorrow will be rough,' he said looking up at the scudding clouds. He and Jakob shortened the sail as Cornelius steered them into the sheltered waters of the island's main town.

Hosé unfastened the rope from around his waist. He had recognised the need while they were at sea, but he was not going to arrive in port tethered like a child. He studied the houses climbing up from the water; their whitewashed walls were dull and the hills behind wore a tired look.

'Where is Thomas staying?' he asked Jakob as the brothers made the boat fast.

'The boat builder's sister is a widow with lots of space but little company.' Jakob grinned. 'Thomas says she is like a mother hen, but she feeds him well enough and it is right by the beach where the boat is building, so he doesn't mind too much.'

Hosé nodded; he had a suspicion the second factor mattered more to Thomas than the first.

'It'll be good to have a hot meal.' Jakob on the other hand had a healthy consideration for his stomach.

Hosé grinned; suddenly he felt quite hungry himself.

It was several days before he got to see the new boat; he was still weak and the widow had included this new chick under her ample wings with alarming alacrity and zeal. The contrast with Rab was striking.

He stood looking up at the rounded sides of the boat, supported as it was on large trestles.

The difference to the *Liesabeta* could not have been greater. He laughed at the thought.

Jakob's indignant face appeared over the side.

'I was not laughing at your boat,' Hosé said hastily. 'She looks most impressive.'

'Come up and look properly.'

Hosé eyed the ladder.

He leaned against the rail breathing hard; the smell of freshly planed wood overlaid pitch and new rope. He and Jakob stood in the central well. She was not dissimilar to the carrack he had once sailed in to the Lowlands but the top-sides were lower, especially those of the foredeck. There was still ample accommodation in the stern but Hosé thought he would wait a little while before climbing up to examine the poop deck.

He put his head back and looked up the main mast with its round top already in place. He had no intention of climbing up there, ever.

From the foredeck rose a somewhat shorter foremast.

'Aft there is a small lateen,' Jakob informed him, 'And from the bowsprit there will be a small square sail. She is quite like the *Marije* really although they do not use the word *buyscarveel* of course and Thomas says they do not even talk of a hulk in these parts. He says she is a Marsillian.'

'And does Thomas approve of Marsillians?'

'He thinks Master Joanot is a good boat builder.'

Hosé looked at Jakob quizzically.

'But,' admitted the boy after a moment, 'He thinks the clench work is a poor design.'

'Clench work?' Under Jakob's tuition Hosé's Diets had emerged from some corner of his mind but this was a phrase he did not know.

'The skids,' explained Jakob, pointing at the lattice of narrow timbers that clad the upper part of the sides, to reinforce and protect the hull.

'So, Thomas,' Hosé greeted the boy who emerged from below deck, 'A chance to work on a skeleton-build boat.'

Thomas nodded. He opened his mouth to say more, but a voice from the depths of the vessel bellowed at him. 'Sorry!' he apologised. 'I have to fetch something. See you later.' He swung a leg over the side-rail and they saw him hurrying up the beach towards the workshop.

Two men staggered across the deck with a large piece of timber and Hosé and Jakob squeezed themselves flat to get out of the way.

'*Wat ben jij aan het doen, jongen?*'

The boy jumped.

Hosé lifted a hand. 'It's my fault. Jakob was telling me about the boat.'

'*Goedemorgen*.' Cornelius nodded at him. 'Good to see you out.'

'I definitely needed some of that fresh air!'

'The widow smothering you, *ja*?' The weathered face split into a grin.

'You could put it like that. But,' Hosé moved across the deck, 'I can see you are all busy. I am only in the way. Another day or two and I'll perhaps be of some use.'

He returned Jakob's wave and plodded along the beach. He was certainly not ready to return to the widow's tender care just yet.

It took him some time; he stopped frequently. The view of the bay and its surrounding hills was clear. The storm which had followed them into harbour had blown itself out and now only a stiff chill wind ruffled the waters. His shorn head felt bare without its clerk's thatch and he shivered a little as he walked on. He would find somewhere warmer to sit and rest a while.

He thought he genuinely remembered some things in the port, particularly the impressive Consultat del Mar. Other things he had learned about before he and Isaac first went to Nice, details of the place where he was supposed to have grown up. He climbed slowly away from the seafront. He stopped abruptly as a stone wall came into view. He looked up appreciatively at the long colonnade that surmounted it: the elegant arches were slightly pointed at the top. On top of that was a row of smaller rounded windows, in pairs. Undoubtedly the Almudaina Palace. It was a perfect example of the history of the island, he reflected: bearing both its Islamic and Roman heritage indelibly in its architecture.

For more than three hundred years the city had been Medina Mayurka under the Moors who had constructed this palace for the Banu Ganiyad. They had also built numerous mosques, bath houses and gardens. Hosé grimaced; many of those had been destroyed or built over in the two hundred years since the Catalans had assumed control.

He moved a little and tried to peer around the palace to the nearby cathedral of La Seu. He would have to climb up further to see it, but he did not have the strength for that; and in any case, he was not sure he wanted to see the Christian edifice that had replaced the Moorish mosque; perhaps another day.

And perhaps he might get to see the Castell de Bellver, built by the Catalan kings to defend their prosperous island and city port. Not that they had succeeded: the Catalans had themselves been ousted by the Aragonese.

And under their most Christian influence the Jewish community had been massacred a hundred years before.

Hosé scowled. How were Jews treated in Genoa?

The extermination of the Jews, however, had failed to cure all the Mallorcan ills, he reflected with a twist of his lips. More recently the

Mallorcan farmers had dared to rise up against their Hispanic rulers and been ruthlessly punished.

And just ten years ago, the kingdoms of Aragon and Castile had been united by the marriage of Ferdinand and Isabella. Mallorca and the other Balearic islands were now firmly part of their increasingly powerful joint kingdom.

Hosé frowned. From what Isaac said it would not be long before even Grenada was subsumed into that new kingdom. Moorish strength was spent; Islam would disappear from western Europe.

Although an Ottoman sultan could ensure its security in the east.

And meanwhile Hosé was stuck in Mallorca.

He had nearly done it again.

Fortunately, the difference between '*hij*' and '*zij*' was not so great. The subject was bound to come up of course, but Hosé wished fervently that Jakob would not talk of the wretched girl quite so often.

He had disciplined himself over the past seven years to watch what he said, particularly which language he used; somehow remembering to use "*he*" instead of "*she*" in conversation was considerably more difficult.

He glanced at Pieter; surely he knew the truth. The big Lowlander looked as placid as usual.

And Cornelius? Hosé watched the open face, lit by the lamplight in the wine shop. The younger brother was not stupid, far from it, but he tended to treat life exactly as he found it. He neither saw nor looked for subtleties.

He did not seem to have noticed Hosé's slip. Already onto his third mug of wine, Cornelius began to describe a voyage up into the Baltic Sea one year when the spring thaw had been late. The other drinkers around about fell silent as he caught their attention; the idea of the sea freezing over was beyond their experience and almost beyond imagining. There was a collective sigh of relief as Cornelius related their eventual escape from the great blocks of ice that had threatened to reduce their little boat to splinters.

They were nearly all seamen or fishermen. The sea gave them their living but it also took lives. The sea was the common enemy: nationality or creed quickly faded into insignificance beside the power of that universal reality.

Hosé pondered this thought as men called for more drinks and one broke into a song on the comforts a long-suffering seaman might hope to find in the right port. The words were basically Catalan but strewn with phrases from all around the Middle Sea. It was almost a language in itself, he thought sleepily, as the rest of the company joined in the well-known bawdy refrain. It was a dialect used on myriad waterfronts from Kos to Iskandariya, from Tabarka to Genoa.

'Have you sailed those frozen seas?' The question from an old man sharing the corner roused him.

Hosé shook his head.

'Where then?'

Hosé shrugged. He had prepared some sort of history for himself but he much preferred to avoid the subject: it was less complicated.

'But you are a seaman? You crew with the Lowlanders.'

'For the moment,' he answered shortly, wondering if he should visit the alley outside; that usually worked to break up a conversation.

He was saved from this need by the arrival of three men who pushed into the already crowded room. The singing died away.

'Jaumot, Jofre and young Francesc were taken,' he heard.

'If the waves hadn't suddenly thrown us away from the galliot we would have been taken too.'

'As it was, we were nearly overturned.'

'The boat flooded.'

'We thought to have escaped the pirates only to drown.'

'Pirates? It is too early in the season.'

'You tell them that!'

'Jaumot, Jofre and young Francesc? It will break Aldonça's heart: her brother, her husband *and* her son. Mother of God! It is too much.'

'Where do you think the bastards came from?'

'Oran, Algiers, who knows? What does it matter?'

'Dozens of them on a galliot; all armed to the teeth.'

'Led by a big man with a great black beard.'

There were many of that description raiding out of Africa.

'What of the galliot? Did she survive the seas?'

'We never saw the galliot again.'

'But perhaps Jaumot and the others are still alive?'

'They would be better off drowned than the living death of galley slaves.'

There was a sudden silence The sea and the elements were not, after all, the only common enemy.

Hosé worked with the others on the boat as soon as he could: to escape the clutches of the well-intended widow if nothing else. He gradually managed longer hours but he had no relevant skills so spent most of the time fetching and carrying, and for a while that was demanding enough.

He started to take himself off in the long evenings, joining the others later at the wine shop.

'Where do you go?' Jakob asked curiously.

'To see the sights.'

'But it is nearly dark.'

'Some things are best seen in the dark.'

Jakob's freckled face was puzzled but he caught his father's eye and did not press the matter.

In fact, Hosé had not seen anything much on his explorations although they had given him a good idea of the layout of the town and the hills behind. They had however provided him with the opportunity to check for correspondence from Nice.

There had been two more letters. In the latest Annette wrote briefly and with obvious preoccupation; seemingly nothing of any consequence had happened anywhere.

Hosé was left to conclude that there had been no news from either Rome or Genoa and to reflect with no little bewilderment on the dual effects of matrimony and impending motherhood.

He was still thinking about this as he made his way along the shore to the one place where he had seen anything of interest. He did not see the burly figure come up behind him until it was too late.

Even then he might have managed, if it had just been one against one.

He wiped away the blood from a cut on his forehead, breathing heavily, as he surveyed his captors.

'So.' The tone was definitely not friendly. 'Spying eh?'

'No.' Hosé said emphatically.

The burly man snorted derisively. 'Who sent you?'

'Nobody,' Hosé protested.

The men muttered in disbelief.

'Truly,' Hosé sounded unconvincing even to his own ears.

'You just happened to come along this way at this time of night?'

'Yes.'

'And the other night too?'

Hosé cursed to himself.

'And how many times before that?'

Hosé shook his head.

'Spying!' The second man moved forward.

Hosé watched him warily and shifted his weight slightly.

'Oh no you don't.' The third man had noticed.

'Come to learn our secrets eh?' The burly man turned to the others. 'He certainly needs to learn a thing or two. What shall we teach him first?' He suddenly lunged at Hosé.

The ensuing scuffle was short and left Hosé staggering blindly into a tree.

'No!' He gasped. 'Let's talk about this. I'm sure we could make a deal.'

'A deal?' The third man laughed. 'What could you possibly have that would interest us?'

Still fighting for breath, Hosé suggested something.

'I thought you were here to recover your health?' Cornelius peered at Hosé's face.

'Relapse,' Hosé said shortly.

'Thomas says it will not be long before the boat is ready to launch.' Jakob also stared at the cut and livid bruises but there were other important things to talk about. 'Then we can see how good she really is.'

'It will still take time to finish her, even after she is in the water.' Cornelius warned his son.

'How soon before we can take her to sea?' demanded Jakob.

'By midsummer.'

Jakob groaned.

'But maybe sooner.'

Jakob gulped down the rest of his food. 'Then we mustn't waste time.' He leaped up from the bench and headed out of the door. A moment later he stuck his head back inside. 'And we will have to decide on her name.'

'*Ja*.' Cornelius smiled, but there was a sadness to the usually good-natured features.

Hosé looked at the Lowlander as the boy ran off down to the beach. 'No more sisters?' he inquired.

Cornelius shook his head. 'Jakob thinks she should be the *Katrin*,' he said softly.

Hosé nodded. 'But you?'

Cornelius shook his head again. 'I'm not sure I want to be reminded.'

'You have Jakob's face in front of you all the time.' Hosé pointed out. 'Is that a problem?'

'Of course not.'

'She was quite a person. That is quite a boat.'

Cornelius suddenly looked at him suspiciously. 'Has Jakob been recruiting support?'

Hosé grinned. 'He has mentioned it once or twice.'

'Thomas,' Hosé said softly.

The boy lifted his head from the drawing he had been making, scratching the plan of a boat on a piece of wood. The fingers of his left hand were green from the copper nail.

'Don't turn around.'

Thomas looked at him blankly.

'Listen to those men who are standing by the door.'

Thomas stared at Hosé, his rather solemn face uncomprehending.

'Just listen.' Hosé said quietly.

Thomas frowned in concentration.

'What are they talking about?'

'They're just saying what a lousy place this is because none of the girls.....' He stopped, flushing slightly, then his mouth fell open. 'They're English.'

Hosé nodded; his guess had been right. It was not so surprising, with the sailing season started, but he had learned never to take anything at face value. 'Anything else?'

Thomas listened for what seemed a long time.

'Well?'

'I'm not sure,' Thomas said slowly.

'Not sure about what?'

'It's the accent. I would say at least one of them is from Norwich.'

'No!' Hosé put a hand on his arm as the boy started to turn.

'But I might recognise them.'

'They might recognise you!' Hosé said grimly.

'But how?'

'Maybe because they have been sent to look for you.'

'But...'

Hosé put a finger to his lips. 'Just listen again.' He very much wished he understood what they were saying. He very much wished he knew what they were doing here.

'I think,' said Thomas after a while, 'That one of them is called John.' His face was pale beneath its tan. 'There was a John, the carter's son; he worked sometimes for my stepfather.'

Hosé nodded. 'And the other one?'

Thomas shook his head. 'I don't know; perhaps if I saw him.'

It did not matter that much. It was enough that one of them was connected to Clough.

'How long before the first sea trials?'

Cornelius frowned. 'A week or two,' he replied slowly. 'What's the hurry?'

Thomas looked steadfastly at the bread and cheese that lay uneaten before him.

Hosé hoped the boy would be able to keep the silence he had promised. 'No chance of taking her out today?'

'Today?' Cornelius stared.

'Say this afternoon; just for a trip out around the bay.'

'Why?' The question was not unreasonable.

'Because I would like to.' It was the best answer Hosé could manage.

Cornelius opened his mouth to protest but Pieter laid a hand on his arm. 'I think Hosé is not making an idle request and I think Joannot could be persuaded.'

Hosé was relieved.

Cornelius shrugged. 'Well,' he said, 'I won't say I'm not keen to try her.' He looked at Thomas. 'Lost your appetite *jongen*?'

'I think Thomas needs some time off work,' Hosé said quietly.

'What is going on?' Cornelius shrugged again impatiently as neither Thomas nor Hosé answered him. 'All right. Perhaps someone will explain to me sometime.'

Hosé was tired. He had spent the first hours of the night in trying to answer unanswerable questions. Finally, he had made some hard decisions and slipped out of the house as the first light of dawn was creeping up the sky.

'Why didn't you tell them?' Thomas asked once they were out of earshot.

'Because it's best if they behave today as if they didn't know.'

Thomas looked a little mystified. 'Where are we going?'

'Up into the town. Maybe we can look around the cathedral.'

Thomas opened his mouth and Hosé could see the word "why" forming, but instead Thomas glanced around them and exclaimed, 'This is an odd way to get there.'

'True,' said Hosé grimly, as they picked their way over mooring ropes and fishing tackle.

Thomas looked over the dozens of boats nestling in the port. His eyes rested for a moment on a northern caravel then he spoke accusingly to Hosé. 'John Carter and that other man probably came on that boat. They could easily be looking at us right now.'

'Also true.'

'But last night you did not want them to see my face!'

'That was last night; now things are different.' Hosé put a hand behind Thomas's elbow and gently urged him forward. 'Just keep walking.'

Thomas reluctantly did so.

Hosé smiled sideways at him, 'And perhaps you could talk to me as we walk.'

'What about?'

'How about that boat you have been drawing pictures of.'

Thomas looked dubious but hesitantly began talking. 'I didn't have very long to learn much from Master Richard in Norwich so building the *Katrin* is my only real experience, but I have always looked at boats and talked to people about them: what makes them sail well, how they ride in rough seas, how they reach into the wind, how much cargo they can carry, how many crew they need, things like that.'

Hosé nodded at him. 'Carry on,' he said softly.

'On the one hand, you have the galley, long compared to her width, little freeboard, sleek and fast; but no cargo space worth talking about; vulnerable to high seas and never going to manage on the wide oceans. On the other hand, you have a round-ship like the carrack, lots of cargo space, can navigate high seas, needs a small crew but can wallow for weeks if the wind fails. So, I thought perhaps there was a way to combine the two.'

Or maybe there was a third solution. Hosé recalled Isaac's description of the huge boat from Cathay. But that was for another time; at the moment, he needed to concentrate on other matters.

As they climbed the steep street and turned the corner past the palace, he glanced back. Just the two of them? or were there more? How many to deal with?

He and Thomas made a leisurely inspection of the cathedral but Hosé took little note of the soaring Gothic architecture.

They then made their way down the main street. Hosé bought goats' cheese and olives from the peasant farmers who brought their goods into town; he got a loaf of bread from the baker. Finally, they retraced their steps to the house.

Hosé was relieved to find that the widow had gone on her usual morning round of gossiping. He put their purchases on the table.

Down on the beach once more Hosé looked out at the *Katrin*, moored just off shore. He could see Cornelius and Pieter on the poop deck. He squinted up against the blue sky. 'Is that Jakob in the main top?'

'Yes.'

'Take the skiff and fetch him.'

'What reason shall I give?'

Hosé gave a smile. 'Tell him there is fresh cheese and olives at the house with the midday bread.'

Thomas stared at him but set off.

Hosé watched him reach the new boat then he turned and walked up the beach towards the workshop. Out of the corner of his eye he saw a burly shape pull back behind the widow's house.

'I'm all right Papa, really.'

Cornelius was furious. With the Knights in Nice he had had to contain his fury; now there were no such considerations: he was shaking with rage and reaction. The fulsome vocabulary of the Antwerp waterfront filled the air as he confronted Hosé.

'To put them in such danger, deliberately.'

Hosé looked at him. It was true it had been risky, but it had worked. 'I'm sorry,' he said.

The Lowlander advanced.

'*Nee Papa.*' Jakob protested.

Hosé watched the calloused hands bunch by Cornelius's sides. 'I understand you are upset,' he said evenly, 'But I shall not let you hit me.'

The Lowlander raised his fists.

'And I know my trade as well as you know yours,' Hosé said softly.

Cornelius hesitated. 'You put them in that trap, then abandoned them!'

'You think the Englishmen would have taken the bait if I had stayed?'

'If those other men hadn't happened......' Cornelius could not finish the sentence.

'There was no "*happened*" about it,' Hosé said shortly.

'Who were they then?' Cornelius demanded.

'Some partners in a venture, you might say.'

'Pah! You always talk in riddles or half-truths.'

Hosé flushed as the barb hit a vulnerable spot. He swallowed hard. 'I think it might be more useful if you directed your anger at the real villains.'

Pieter moved forward. 'He is right Cornelius.'

'And you too I suppose, as usual!' He glared at his older brother. 'Sorry,' he said a few moments later. The high colour gradually drained from his face and he clapped Pieter on the shoulder.

He turned slowly.

Hosé grasped the proffered hand.

'So, what happens now?'

'We find out a few essential things from John Carter and his companion,' said Hosé grimly.

Cornelius looked at the distant harbour. 'We should head for shore.'

'No.' The word was quiet but emphatic.

'But it will soon be dusk,' Cornelius protested. 'We need to hand them over to the authorities for attempted kidnap.'

'No,' Hosé repeated. 'That will not put an end to the threat they pose, Cornelius.'

'But.....'

'They didn't come to Mallorca by chance. Someone told them where to look. When that someone learns you are here, with the *Katrin*, he'll try again.' Hosé nodded towards Jakob, 'And he knows exactly what weapon to use.'

Cornelius was silent for a moment. 'But we don't know any of that *for sure*,' he protested feebly.

'They'll confirm it,' Hosé assured him. He turned to Pieter. 'Will the weather be good enough for some sea trials?'

The big man nodded.

Cornelius still hesitated. 'We don't have supplies.'

'Then I suggest we put in to Minorca and find some.'

John Carter cracked easily enough.

Unfortunately, he did not seem to know very much, beyond what Hosé had already guessed: Clough had sent him because he could recognise Thomas.

Why should Clough do that?

Clough wanted his step-son brought home. And the other boy with him.

Why did Clough want the other boy?

Something to do with Clough's business in Antwerp.

And how did Clough know they were in Mallorca?

Carter did not know.

Who was the man with Carter?

Richard Deluce.

What was his part?

Carter swore he did not know.

Hosé turned his attention to Deluce. And knew immediately that this was a much more devious man than Carter.

Well, he would just have to be even more devious.

He leaned over the side of the boat watching the water cream past her hull, considering. 'When you left Antwerp,' he asked Cornelius, 'Did you already plan to come to Mallorca?'

'We discussed it, yes; but we also considered Cadiz or Barcelona.'

'And who did you discuss it with?'

Cornelius pulled a face.

'Carter and Deluce appear to have sailed straight to Mallorca. Can one presume that Clough has sent other men inquiring at Cadiz and Barcelona?'

'I suppose so,' Cornelius agreed dismally.

'He will receive reports from them that you are not in either of those places.'

'So obviously, he will know we are in Mallorca.' Cornelius's voice was flat.

'He will certainly be expecting a report from Mallorca to that effect.' Hosé agreed. 'But suppose that report is also negative?'

'But he'd know it was false!'

'Or one of the other reports was. How would he know?'

'He'd send others to check.' Cornelius was bitter.

Hosé nodded. 'Quite likely. But, while the boat's been building you've been tied to Mallorca; now you can go wherever you want. Clough will have an awful lot more places to search to find you.'

'I suppose so.' Cornelius brightened a little then his face fell again. 'But Carter and Deluce might already have sent a message saying they *did* find us.'

'I doubt it. I think the first time they saw Thomas was when we walked past them in the harbour. I think they followed us immediately and I can't see how they could have sent anyone any messages before Le Bélier and his friends captured them.' Hosé pulled a wry face. 'That was why the trap, with Jakob as an essential part of the bait, had to be laid and sprung straight away.'

Cornelius stared at him. 'You already suspected all this?'

Hosé gave a humourless smile. 'I have learned to accord Master Clough my immediate and most serious attention.'

'But,' Cornelius had a further thought, 'Now there will be no report at all from Carter and Deluce, which Clough will think is suspicious it itself!'

'Eventually,' agreed Hosé. 'So, it would be much more satisfactory to have a false report sent.'

'You could send it?' Cornelius was half hopeful.

'To be credible it would have to be in a familiar hand and in the expected format.'

'But will Carter and Deluce agree to do that?'

'I doubt if Carter is even literate; it is Deluce we have to deal with. And he is no fool.'

Hosé told them what he needed them to do.

'But,' protested Cornelius robustly, 'You can't do that!'

'Oh yes I can,' said Hosé. 'Nothing easier. Just drop them over the side.'

'But is that really necessary?' Cornelius was talking a bit too loudly. Hosé frowned at him. The Lowlander continued in a lower voice. 'If they agreed to write a report to Clough, that would get him off our backs. We could put Carter and Deluce off in Algiers or Tunis and by the time they made their way back to Antwerp, if they made it back, it would be too late.'

'Much safer to dispose of them permanently,' insisted Hosé.

'That would be cold-blooded murder.'

Hosé made an exasperated noise.

'No,' said Cornelius emphatically.

Hosé paused, watching the play of sunlight on the water. Above them a gentle wind filled the new suit of sails. From time to time he heard Jakob and Thomas on the poop deck and felt the boat shift as they adjusted the tiller.

'At least give them a chance.'

Hosé muttered something then signed to Cornelius.

They clattered down into the central well.

'You think they could hear?' asked Cornelius anxiously.

Hosé nodded. 'Just about. Deluce would have been suspicious if it had been too easy. He has to have some reason to cooperate, some small hope he will get away with his life.'

'Will he?'

Hosé did not answer.

Deluce agreed with the right degree of reluctance. Hosé watched him with grudging respect.

The Englishman wrote the message.

'Thomas!' Hosé called the boy. 'Read this carefully and tell me exactly what it says.'

Thomas read it and translated it word for word as well as he could.

It said the right things.

'Now read it again and tell me if there is anything odd about any of the words or phrases.'

Thomas looked surprised but read it through again.

Hosé watched Deluce's face for any reaction; there was none.

'Now again and look at the way the words are written, the use of upper and lower case letters for example. Are they all as you would expect?'

Thomas looked yet again.

Deluce stared at the floor.

Thomas nodded his head.

Hosé moved to Thomas's side and studied the piece of paper. He pointed. 'Those marks there; what are they?'

'It is easy to spot ink if you do not hold the quill quite steady or at the right angle.' Thomas stated the obvious.

'Of course.'

'Is that all?' Thomas inquired.

Hosé looked hard again at the message. 'Yes, I think so,' he said eventually. 'It will do.'

'He reacted to the one about upper and lower case,' declared Cornelius.

Hosé pulled a wry face.' He knows the game too!'

Cornelius scowled.

'Pieter?' Hosé queried.

'I don't think *any* of your questions bothered him.' Pieter said slowly.

'Then we haven't learned anything!' Cornelius said in exasperation.

'On the contrary; we have learned that it must be something else.' Hosé considered for some moments then turned to Thomas. 'Tell me about English spelling.'

'Well,' said the boy doubtfully, 'There are some rules, accepted conventions rather, but people often make up their own spellings; unlike Latin of course which is very precise.'

'There,' Hosé showed Thomas the result. He had copied Deluce's message carefully then picked his way through it with Thomas, underlining certain letters.

Thomas tried to make sense of it. He shook his head.

'Not quite precise enough?' Hosé smiled and changed one or two characters. Deluce had done very well in the circumstances.

'*Noli credere.*' Thomas pronounced. 'Do not believe!' He looked at Hosé in dismay. 'So, it is no use.'

'Quite the opposite; it is very useful indeed.'

'But.....'

'Now it can be rewritten to say the right thing.'

'Will Deluce do that?' Thomas was dubious.

'He won't need to. I can do a good enough copy of his hand.'

Thomas looked at him for a moment, a further question on his tongue.

'Go and help Jakob,' Hosé prevented him.

Perhaps if they had not been so concerned with Deluce and his letter they might have noticed the approaching sails.

Perhaps if Jakob had been in the top instead of at the tiller he would have spotted them.

Perhaps if the galley had not come at them out of the low evening sun they would have had more warning.

But as it was they were totally outnumbered; they never stood a chance.

Chapter 10

The sunlight of a new day moved inexorably down the lateen sail.

Cornelius shifted. The irons already chafed his legs but he hardly noticed; grey despair filled his whole body. He still could not believe such overwhelming disaster had struck, so suddenly and so completely. A few short hours ago, they had been sailing their beautiful *Katrin* and had found a way to outwit Clough. Now Cornelius had no illusions about their fate: the men would be put to the oars. And the boys?

He pulled in vain against his fetters.

Pieter lifted his head and looked at him silently.

If Pieter could offer no hope, there was none. Cornelius ground his teeth.

'All in the same boat now, eh?' Deluce taunted. He had moved from one hopeless situation to another; the irony of it was almost amusing.

Jakob's pale face appeared, rousing from a disturbed sleep. 'Where do you think we are heading Papa?'

What did it matter?

'We have not moved much in the night I think,' said Pieter.

'Perhaps they are waiting for daylight,' Thomas put in.

Cornelius shrugged. 'Perhaps they are waiting for another prize as easy as us,' he said bitterly.

Carter was slumped silent. He had not said a word since they had been taken.

Cornelius looked at the other inert form.

Hosé had put up a great struggle, roaring at their captors in some language Cornelius could not understand, but a blow had laid him out cold.

Cornelius reached out a hand.

Hosé stirred and muttered something.

'Are you all right?'

Hosé groaned and tried to move. The fetters brought him up short. He opened a bleary eye and scowled at the iron bands blankly. He fingered the lump on his head then turned quickly and retched.

He wiped the back of one hand across his mouth and looked around. 'What in the name of.....?' He stopped. He lay back with his eyes closed.

Cornelius watched the irregular rise and fall of his chest.

'Not as clever as you thought.' Deluce jibed.

Hosé was silent. Finally, he sat up again more carefully. 'Anything to drink?'

Cornelius shook his head.

Hosé looked towards the deck. 'Hey!' he called. '*Susadim.*'

There was no reply. He tried again, more loudly and at greater length.

Finally, a figure appeared.

Cornelius stared. In the short action, he had had little chance to study the men who had captured them and the *Katrin.* Now he looked at the full trousers, the wide belt, the turban; undoubtedly just such men had taken Jaumot, Jofre and young Francesc.

Hosé was speaking urgently.

The black moustache lifted. The man smiled and put a leather boot heavily in Hosé's stomach.

Hosé might be fettered but his hands moved in unison. He grasped the booted foot and jerked the man off his feet. In an instant, he had him in a hold which threatened to break the man's neck.

Hosé spoke slowly and deliberately in the language Cornelius did not know.

What could he hope to achieve? There were dozens of them. Cornelius could already hear boots thumping along the deck.

The new arrivals stopped, viewing the scene warily.

Hosé spoke again. His captive groaned as the pressure on his neck increased.

Cornelius stared at the bulging eyes.

There was a brief conversation among the other members of the crew then one of them turned and disappeared.

For what seemed like a long time nobody moved. Finally, another man appeared. A leader of some kind? Cornelius stared at the curved sword.

The leader spoke coldly.

The man next to him suddenly pointed.

Cornelius looked. Hosé's seaman's trousers had ripped, exposing a black mark on his leg.

Then all the men were talking angrily.

This time Hosé was shouted down.

Cornelius caught sight of another figure. This man wore an even bigger turban. He stood watching the scene for some moments then he lifted his hand and there was instant silence. There was a gleam in his eyes as he addressed Hosé and made what sounded like a suggestion.

The other men seemed to like it; there was loud laughter.

'What's going on?' the Lowlander demanded as Hosé released his captive.

'I was just offered a challenge.' Hosé said. 'A chance to put certain matters to the test.'

'A challenge?' said Jakob wide-eyed.

'What sort of a test?' Cornelius demanded.

'The opportunity to redeem myself you might say.'

Deluce laughed derisively. 'Redeem yourself; against all of them?'

'No, just one of them.' Hosé lifted the water bottle that had been brought.

'And if you win?' Deluce sneered.

'Why, freedom of course.'

Deluce stared. 'And if you lose?'

Hosé shrugged. 'You'll see soon enough.'

He stood up and stretched as the irons were removed. 'Ouch. I'm not sure my head is up to this.'

'Can you see anything?' Cornelius demanded.

Pieter shook his head.

There was more loud shouting and cheering. There was a thump that rumbled through the timbers beneath them. There was a collective gasp and a moment's silence, broken by a single roar of rage.

Then Cornelius and the others could hear nothing above the noise of the crowd. Occasionally one voice would rise above the others but the Lowlander had no way of understanding the words.

There was a massive shuffling of feet, moving hastily along the deck, then a crash. The cheering faded.

Now it was possible to catch other sounds: the grunt of straining bodies, the thrash of limbs, heavy breathing.

Another loud thud and the cheering grew again. It increased in volume; victory was surely in sight for someone and that someone was obviously the crowd's favourite.

Jakob looked anxiously at his father.

Suddenly there was a howl of derision and jeering; a single shout of triumph, followed by a moment of shocked silence; a cry and a splash; a few laughs that grew into a swell of mirth and finally cheers.

The cheering faded. The only sounds were the odd rap of booted feet, the occasional call. There was not even any sound from the benches, as the galley remained rolling gently on the sea.

'What happened, Papa?'

Cornelius could only shake his head. Hosé had not reappeared.

'Either gone to a watery grave, may the fish eat him,' said Deluce, 'Or deserted you.'

'He wouldn't do that.' Jakob said stoutly.

At last there was the sound of voices approaching, boots and, yes, the pad of bare feet; Jakob was sure of it. 'Listen, Papa.'

The man in the big turban stood and surveyed the prisoners.

Hosé was with him, his clothes clinging to him, water dripping around his feet.

'Been in the sea, again,' Pieter commented.

Hosé pulled a face. 'The stupid fool couldn't swim.'

'What happened?' Jakob demanded eagerly. 'Did you win?'

Hosé looked at the man in the big turban and seemed to repeat the question. The dark face considered for a moment before he made a solemn reply.

Hosé grimaced. 'Mansur Pasha says I broke the rules.'

Jakob's face fell. 'So, they will imprison you again?'

Deluce laughed.

'No, they will not imprison me again.' He indicated a man who set about removing the fetters from the *Katrin's* crew.

'Hey!' Deluce exclaimed angrily. 'What about us?'

'Mansur Pasha agreed it might be worth taking you back for the slave market.'

Deluce stared then spat at him.

'Although that was not his preferred option.'

Deluce finally understood.

'Save your breath,' Hosé cut through the stream of abuse.

Carter let out a howl.

Cornelius watched the two Englishmen dragged away then turned anxiously to look towards the stern.

'It's all right,' Hosé said. 'The *Katrin* is safely in tow.' He beckoned them to follow. 'Come.' He grinned at Jakob. 'It feels like breakfast time.'

The boy managed a smile although he looked cautiously at the well-armed men who stood aside respectfully as the large turban passed.

Cornelius suddenly stopped and Jakob bumped into him. 'What is it Papa?'

Cornelius stared. A short way off was another smallish galley, but nearer, roped alongside in fact, was a much larger one. On her decks stood more armed men, some in turbans, some in white headdresses with a strange little flap. He had never seen a vessel like this one before but he had heard descriptions; this was no pirate boat; it was a warship.

'Come.' Hosé repeated. 'I'm sure Thomas will enjoy seeing it a bit closer.'

'What's going on?' Cornelius demanded, refusing to move.

'I'm not altogether sure myself, but it will be all right, I promise you.'

Cornelius did not see how he could make any such promise. He stood still, a protective hand on Jakob's shoulder.

'Pieter?' Hosé appealed to him. 'Tell him it is all right.'

The big man smiled his slow smile. '*Is goed*, Cornelius.'

Cornelius still did not understand but he shrugged; Pieter had his own way of knowing these things.

They climbed over to the big galley and made their way to the stern.

'I'll join you shortly.' Hosé pointed their way up the ladder to the carosse. He had a sudden thought and spoke softly to Thomas. The boy looked at his hands in bewilderment but nodded slowly.

The man in the big turban invited them with a gesture to be seated on the large cushions on the floor.

Almost immediately men entered carrying dishes of food which were set on a low table.

Jakob looked eagerly at the feast.

The big turban inclined itself and a smile split the dark face.

Jakob needed no further invitation. '*Lekker*, Papa,' he pronounced.

Hosé entered wearing dry clothes. He looked at home in the baggy trousers and shirt, reflected Cornelius.

'Mansur Pasha is sorry he does not know your language,' Hosé said between mouthfuls, 'But he hopes the meal is to your taste.'

'Oh yes,' Jakob said, then flushed as the others laughed.

When even Jakob had finally eaten enough, the table was removed.

There was a noise at the door and a soldier entered. He saluted Mansur Pasha respectfully and eyed Hosé guardedly. 'I am Ahmed,' he announced in a heavily accented voice. 'You wanted someone who speaks Catalan.'

'It sounds as if you just about fit the description,' said Hosé dryly, continuing to Cornelius, 'I must talk to Mansur Pasha. I shall see you later and perhaps I can satisfy some of your curiosity.' He addressed Ahmed. 'You will please show our visitors around the galley and answer their questions if you can. You will not,' he added carefully, 'Ask any of your own.'

He looked at Cornelius. 'You understand?' he asked in Diets. 'Particularly questions about me.'

Cornelius did not really understand but he nodded anyway.

'*Dank je wel.*'

'Do we have to stay here?' Cornelius looked around the space in the gavon. 'Or are we free to leave?'

'You can go anytime you like,' Hosé replied, sinking down with a sigh.

'And you?'

'I shall stay at least one more night.'

'Why?'

Hosé's eyes gleamed slightly in the lamplight. 'There is a matter of honour.'

'Another fight!' Jakob guessed. 'Can we watch this time?'

Hosé smiled, 'Certainly; provided, of course, that your father hasn't sailed off in the *Katrin* before then.'

'That leaves me any choice?' Cornelius, eyed his son's eager face. He turned to Hosé, 'And how about that explanation you promised?'

Hosé nodded. 'Where shall I start?'

'Start with that fight.' Jakob jumped in.

'If I tell you a few other things first,' Hosé replied, 'You will understand about the fight.'

He explained briefly what Pieter already knew from Master Molfino about Caffa and added some of what followed. He did not mention his father; that was his own affair. Nor did he mention Clough's part in that chapter; that was an affair of state.

'I knew you must be a soldier,' said Jakob triumphantly. 'I said so to Rab.' He stopped suddenly. 'Perhaps I shouldn't have.' He coloured.

'As it happens sh.... he already knows,' Hosé was cross with himself. 'But it is important that as few people as possible know about it.'

'A secret mission,' Jakob breathed.

Cornelius was not so impressed. He frowned.

Hosé looked at him, aware of his problem. 'You accused me of dealing in riddles and half-truths; that hurt, because it is true.'

Cornelius flushed.

'It has to be so. I do not like it,' he regarded the Lowlander seriously. 'But,' he added clearly, 'I serve the Sultan in whatever way that is needed, whatever way.'

'You know the Sultan?' Jakob's mouth had forgotten to close.

'I have met him.'

Cornelius was still unhappy. He understood a little more of worldly affairs than his son. 'And how are you serving the Sultan now?'

Hosé knew what he meant. 'My mission involves no threat to any Christian state.'

Cornelius glanced at Pieter.

'That's the truth Cornelius,' Hosé said. 'I can't promise you the whole truth but I will not lie to you.'

Pieter nodded.

Hosé took a breath. 'The task I was given was to ensure, as far as possible, that Prince Cem presents no danger to the Sultan.'

'Prince Cem? Who's he?' Jakob asked.

Hosé explained.

Cornelius thought about it. 'So how have you been doing that?'

'For the past seven years, the Knights of St John, for their own reasons, have kept the Prince powerless. I have endeavoured to see he stayed so.'

'The Knights?' Hosé could have sworn he saw Cornelius's hackles rise. He also saw growing comprehension. 'So, that was why you were so interested in their galleys in Nice.'

Hosé nodded. 'The Prince was aboard one of them.'

'You saw him?'

'No, but I heard enough to know he was there.'

'Leaving France, heading where?' Cornelius had definitely understood.

'For Rome, where he will be the guest of the Pope.'

Cornelius pondered that silently.

'But what about the fight?' Jakob spotted a gap in the conversation.

Hosé smiled slightly. 'When I was a proper soldier, back in Is..... Constantinople, I was considered pretty good at wrestling. I was the youngest champion my orta, my regiment, had ever had.' In truth, of course, the exceptional circumstances of the time, and his participation in the battle of Yenişehir, had made him almost certainly the youngest janissary ever to be in the orta. Still, however it had happened, he had been proud of that title. He continued more than a little regretfully, 'When I came west I was supposed to be a lame clerk working for the Grimaldi. There was little chance to practice any military skills.' He pulled a face.

'But you beat that man yesterday.'

'There was little chance, as I said. But in Mallorca I happened to meet up one evening with Le Bélier.'

'The ram?' Thomas had been listening as intently as anyone.

'That is his chosen name. He is a farmer, but he also earns money fighting.' Hosé paused. 'He discovered me watching him training.'

'So you fought? That morning you appeared with your face battered!'

Hosé nodded ruefully. 'It was a very short fight. He won.'

'But you had been ill,' Jakob said loyally.

Hosé smiled gratefully. 'I had and I needed to get fit again. I came to an agreement with Le Bélier. I reckoned I had some things I could teach him in return for some hard practice.'

'Things about wrestling?'

Hosé nodded, 'And about a few other things.'

'Such as?' Cornelius demanded.

'The farmers were brutally squashed not so long ago. Le Bélier knows they will have to be much better prepared next time. He trains himself and he also trains others.' Hosé saw Cornelius open his mouth. 'And before you say anything, you should remember that it was Le Bélier and his friends who rescued Jakob and Thomas.'

Cornelius closed his mouth again.

'So, what about the fight yesterday?' persisted Jakob.

'Job, you are like a dog with a bone,' Thomas said.

'Nearly there,' Hosé said. 'When we were attacked, my first thought was pirates but then I realised they were regular janissaries. At that point I demanded to speak to their commander but somebody knocked me out.'

Jakob nodded.

'When I woke up I tried again to persuade someone to listen to me, to let me speak to the officer in charge. Then one of them spotted the orta mark on my leg. Many of the men on this expedition are from my regiment and some of them got very angry, assumed I was a renegade. You will remember at that point Mansur Pasha appeared and he suggested I should be put to the test, wrestling Buyuk 'Brahim who is their current champion. The others thought that sounded like good sport.'

'Had Mansur Pasha recognised you?' Cornelius put in sharply.

Hosé nodded.

'And he thought you were a renegade too?'

Hosé shook his head. 'No. We served together once; he knew better than that.'

'So why did he suggest the fight?'

'It appealed to his sense of humour!' Hosé pulled a face. 'Suddenly it appealed to me too.' He made an apologetic gesture to Jakob. 'I'm afraid it was not the dramatic trial by ordeal it seemed. I knew that even if I lost we would be all right.'

'But you won.'

'I was the final victor.' Hosé smiled at the freckled face. 'At first I thought I could do it by the rules but then my head began to ache and I realised 'Brahim was going to win; so, I decided to bend the rules.'

'What did you do?'

' "*The good fighter knows when to give ground.*" '

' "*It's the winning blow that really counts*!" ' Jakob finished off for him.

Hosé laughed. 'I backed away, until I was right up against the rail. The crowd was jeering and he thought it was all over; he came in to finish me off. As he came forward I flipped him into the sea.' He grimaced. 'Some of the men cheered; some thought I had cheated. Then someone said 'Brahim could not swim so I went in to fish him out.' He added, 'I reckon it was honours even really. A return fight should decide it.'

Cornelius grew serious. 'What are they doing here, in these waters?'

'That was what I wanted to know. Since I left Nice I have not been able to keep in touch with .....things.'

'So, it was just chance?' Cornelius's face wore a pugnacious expression.

'Not exactly. The Topkapi knew the Prince was being taken to Rome. So, it seemed a good idea to have a force somewhere nearby, just in case.'

'In case of what? In case they came across a nice new merchant boat that they could seize?'

'Mansur Pasha was not happy about that; it was not part of the orders.' He looked at Cornelius.

'Of course not. Turkish galleys never take Christian boats or their crews!'

Hosé shrugged. 'Of course they do and the other way around. But they are a long way from home and Mansur Pasha had other orders.'

'Such as?'

'To watch out for a chance to engage the Knights and seize *their* cargo.'

Cornelius considered. He would not care if every Knight went to the bottom of the sea. His animosity faded. 'I expect they reached Civitavecchia ages ago.'

Hosé shook his head. 'Actually, they stayed in Elba for some weeks.' Whilst negotiations on another island were finalised.

He frowned. Negotiations on Lemnos between Hussein Bey and Georges Stomatis, on behalf of the Knights, had reached a new agreement for the new circumstances. The Pope was officially responsible for guarding the Prince, but neither the Sultan nor the Knights were willing to leave the matter entirely to Innocent VIII. D'Aubusson would continue close surveillance and he had promised to keep Bayezit informed. The Sultan however had demanded some direct Turkish presence in the Holy See. In return for an unknown sum, d'Aubusson had promised to arrange the acceptance and protection of an Ottoman envoy in Rome.

'But Mansur Pasha has a report that the Prince has now reached Rome.'

The Turk also had a report of another event. By coincidence, or perhaps not, on the day Cem had arrived in Rome Charles of Savoy had died. Hosé estimated he would have been no more than twenty-one years old. There were many natural causes that carried people off at an early age; but sometimes there were unnatural causes too. Who would stand to benefit from the death of the young romantic duke? Hosé would consider that later.

For the moment, he set about retelling the envoy's description of the entry into Rome. 'The Prince entered the city of Rome by the Portese Gate on a white palfrey.' Would his black stallion Ylderim have seemed too warlike? 'He was met by a deputation of Cardinals, to whom he inclined his head graciously, without removing his turban.'

Cornelius looked blank; the implication of this escaped him.

'Making the point that he owed deference to no one.'

Cornelius nodded.

'On his right hand rode the Pope's nephew, Francesco Cibo, and on his left Guy de Blanchefort, nephew to the Master of the Knights,' he explained. Who had no doubt been appointed by d'Aubusson to continue "close surveillance" of the Prince. 'Behind the Prince came the prior of the Knights' English *langue* and the group of Knights who had accompanied the Prince from France, together with his few remaining followers.' Ironically the Sultan's envoy had been inserted in that same part of the procession. 'Apart from that there seems to have been a regular horde of Pope's officers, Roman nobles, men-at-arms and clerks; even the herald of the King of France.' He chewed his lip. 'An attempt to make the arrival of a political prisoner under guard look like the state visit of some foreign potentate! But it apparently pleased the crowd. The people of Rome turned out in their thousands to see them all cross the St Bartholomew bridge, then process through the Jews Square and the Field of Flowers to the papal palace.'

His audience was silent, trying to picture the scene but since they had no personal experience of the place or of such elevated men it depended a lot on imagination. Judging from his face Jakob's powers of imagination were considerable.

Cornelius on the other hand soon gave up the attempt. 'Will Mansur Pasha head back to Constantinople now?'

Hosé considered his answer. 'Not immediately,' he answered eventually. 'He will wait for new orders.'

'Where will he go?'

Hosé shook his head. 'I can't tell you.'

Thomas had finished thinking of white palfreys, crimson cardinals and papal palaces. 'This galley,' he commented, 'Is really very much like the ones they build in Venice. Ahmed does not know much about boats,' he added.

Hosé was a little surprised: he would have said the man came from the Greek coast somewhere. He shrugged. 'He is a soldier.'

'But you know quite a bit.'

Hosé acknowledged the praise with due gravity.

'What will you do now? After tomorrow, of course.' Cornelius was curious. 'Or don't you want us to know?'

Hosé shook his head. 'You know most things about me by now.'

Cornelius frowned. 'Why did you tell us?' He hesitated. 'Is that not dangerous for you?'

'A lot of it you knew already.' Hosé paused. 'You could not un-know it; the only thing to do was to put the whole picture to you. That way,' he looked around the circle of faces, 'You can see exactly how dangerous it could be for me if you ever spoke of it, to anyone.'

Jakob nodded vigorously.

Thomas nodded slowly.

Cornelius was silent for a long time. There could have been a different way of keeping them quiet.

'*Nee*.' Pieter laid a large hand on his shoulder.

Cornelius swallowed; of course. He knew better than that, like the man with the big turban.

Hosé was looking at them. 'It is a lot to ask.'

Cornelius shook his head. 'No, it isn't,' he said firmly.

It was Thomas who broke the silence. 'Can I ask you a question?' He added quickly, 'About something else. You said I must use my right hand when we ate with Mansur Pasha.' He looked at his hands. 'I've always used my left hand.' He said, 'Even though I was beaten for it when I was little.'

'I'm sorry,' Hosé said. 'I didn't have time to explain.'

'I don't see why it's wrong. It's not *sinister*,' Thomas added a little defiantly.

Hosé shook his head. 'But people tend to suspect what is not the usual.' He added, 'Although it can be quite an advantage in a fighter.'

'But you said.....'

'I was talking specifically about eating. It is the custom ..... it is our custom to eat with the right hand.'

'Why?'

'The left hand is used for personal ablutions so should not also be used for food.'

The boy still looked puzzled. 'I don't see the connection,' he said slowly.

Jakob frowned. 'Rab said Isaac was always talking about such things.'

Hosé nodded. 'Isaac is a great believer in the power of cleanliness.' He smiled ruefully. 'I'm sure Isaac would have seen a direct connection between me getting ill and spending time in the sewers.' He was silent for a moment thinking of the other time he had been in the sewers when he had *not* got ill. The second time there had also been the stable with the hens..... he shook his head. 'But Isaac says as well that these things are complicated; what God has ordered is not to be easily understood by man.' He pulled a wry face. 'Anyway,' he looked at Thomas again, 'That is the custom and good manners demand that you eat with the right hand. I'm sure you would want to be polite.'

'Of course,' the boy agreed.

'But I'm sure you will add it to the long list of things that you puzzle over, eh?' Hosé teased him gently.

The solemn face broke into a slow smile.

'Thomas is always thinking,' said Jakob. 'I wonder his head doesn't burst.'

He looked surprised at the laughter then grinned as his father slapped him on the back.

'So, what will you do now?' Cornelius repeated his earlier question.

Hosé looked at the weather-beaten face. 'The day after tomorrow is Friday,' he said. 'I should like to stay for that.'

Jakob opened his mouth but his father's large hand stopped the question. 'Then?' asked the Lowlander.

Hosé scowled. 'Then I must go to Genoa.'

For the moment, the Sultan's brother must be the concern of the Ottoman envoy; the Sultan's most valued Hebrew servant was Hosé's.

Chapter 11

Midsummer 1489

The city lay huddled by the sea, almost as if the high mountains behind were trying to launch it from the narrow strip of land that ran along the coast.

The master reduced the sails and they moved slowly through the water, past La Lanterna and the western sea walls.

Straight ahead, where the Rio Sant'Ugo flowed into the sea, was the church of San Giovanni with its distinctive bell tower. Generations of pilgrims and crusaders had lodged there on their way to and from their Holy Land. For the past two hundred years, it had been the property of the Knights Hospitaller.

Hosé looked eastward and was still for a moment, looking at the skyline that could not be any other city: the tall buildings with loggias, the bathhouses and the churches, the inns and shops, the banks and warehouses, all with their distinctive air despite (or perhaps because of) the fact that many were cobbled together with stone from other places; the Genoese were ever keen on a good bargain.

He wound his way along the Vicolo Lungo, a street slightly wider than the *carrugi* of the old city. Not far from the cathedral of San Lorenzo he picked out the Doria church of San Matteo, in stripes of Tuscany sandstone and Sardinian white marble. It had been erected to commemorate some crusade in the distant past, in faraway Moslem lands. In present times, and closer by, the Roman Church still held Mohammedans in abhorrence; and Jews.

Hosé grimaced.

The Genoese patois filled his ears. People, carts and mules were making their way in from the countryside, through the gates in the city walls. He moved with them until he reached a piazza, where he bought cheese and olives and drank deep at the fountain.

He moved casually around the market for some time, watching the scene, studying the faces, listening. His gaze turned from time to time to the far corner of the square.

The enclosed space was already becoming hot when he spotted two women arriving.

He made his way through the throng until he could hear what they were saying.

They haggled loud and hard. Finally, they packed the leaf wrapped packages into a basket. And, with a smile, assured the stallholder of the continued custom of the Spinola family.

Hosé's instinct had served him well.

He followed them as they moved on to another stall and negotiated for chickens.

It took quite some time before they had bought all they wanted and by then the basket was so heavy it took both of them to carry it.

Hosé seized the moment. 'It looks as if you need a strong man to carry that for you, ladies.'

'Take our basket then run off with it, will you?' came the sharp retort.

'You are mistaken, entirely. I merely wish to offer my services.'

'For a fee, no doubt.'

'I would like to earn something,' he admitted, his smile white in his tanned face. 'But to be honest with you,' he ignored the snort of disbelief. 'I will happily carry your things for free in the hope you might put in a good word with your employer for some work. I believe I can turn my hand to most things.' He held it out for their inspection.

The younger woman looked with more than her eyes. She examined his brown fingers one by one and traced the calluses on the broad palm. It would never have been taken for the ink-stained tool of a clerk.

The older woman pushed her sharply, impatient; or envious of what once had been. 'We can't stand here all day,' she said. 'Come on then, but there are no promises mind. Taking on ruffians is not for us to say. Although with Signore Spinola being due back there is lots to do.'

Hosé swallowed. But an entrée into the palazzo was crucial.

He resolutely picked up the basket with one hand and offered his other arm to the older woman; she would be the one with influence in the household.

He was correct.

He spent the rest of the day shifting sacks, pots and barrels up and downstairs, along passages and back again, across courtyards, into storerooms. He swept the flagged floors, washed pans at the stone sink. He heard distant voices but could not make out what they were saying and he saw no member of the family. Inevitably, as the newest and most lowly servant, he was then assigned to deal with the foul mess at the base of the latrines.

After that he had to carry water to the wash-house, for the direct conduit was blocked, complained Susanna.

Now why would that be?

He smiled to himself as he thought about water conduits. Had Bertrand de la Forêt finished his fountain? Did Annette bother with such things these days?

Putting those memories aside he crawled around the old stonework and found the problem. At last, the water flowed freely.

As he crawled out he stretched his back gratefully.

He removed his torn shirt and started to wash at the trough in the yard.

'Here!' Bianchetta appeared at his side. 'Susanna says you must put these on and help serve in the hall.' Her voice was a warm breath on his neck. 'After you have made yourself decent.' She giggled. 'What's the use of decent men? I say.' A work roughened finger slid over his hard shoulder and touched the scar on his left arm. 'Got more of those, have you? Out of sight somewhere?'

His skin tingled. 'Maybe.'

As he shaved, his knife as sharp as any razor, he was uneasy. His features would show clearly. Would anyone see a likeness to a boy who had visited the Albergo nearly two decades ago; or to the young woman he was said to resemble, who had now been dead nearly a quarter of a century? It was just one of the risks that had to be taken.

He put on the livery that Bianchetta had brought, the chequered tunic rather tight over his shoulders. He pulled the cap as far down as possible and presented himself in the kitchen.

Susanna looked with scant approval and told him his duties.

He followed two other men and several boys as they took in trenchers and forks, then dishes of food. He deliberately refused to let his eyes wander around the hall. This was not the moment to indulge in pointless and unpleasant memories.

He glanced at the faces around the table as he filled mugs or plates. He did not recognise any of them.

He returned to the kitchen and carried up the next course.

The meal wore on. The extended family finished eating and drinking, the musicians played a final air, the company began to disperse. By now candles were needed to light their way and Hosé watched the little flames disappear. Their steadiness suggested wax: a sign of the Albergo's prosperity and probably a sign of continued trade with Chios. Into his mind came a much grander palazzo with one great lamp above the main doorway and another above the stairs: signs of real wealth and taste.

It was late before he was finished, then he was further delayed by the circuitous route needed to avoid Bianchetta. He finally dropped over the wall onto silent feet and headed for the waterfront.

The wine shops, however, proved to be remarkably quiet and peaceful and their customers remarkably ignorant; at least they seemed to know nothing of those things that Hosé wished to learn.

He made his way back through the dark streets and climbed over the wall.

He was suddenly aware of someone next to him. His weight shifted and he moved swiftly, engulfing the figure securely.

'Ooh, you're as strong as you look!'

'You could get into serious trouble,' he said softly.

Bianchetta gave a little giggle. 'Well, a little trouble can be very enjoyable.'

He relaxed his hold. 'I imagine you can find trouble without even trying.'

Her hand crept up his arm. 'I only look for it in special cases.'

'Like?'

She seemed to ponder the question. 'Not with your weaklings; trouble is best with a good fighting man.'

'And who would you tilt with?' His physical tension was channelling elsewhere. His mind considered.

As a young janissary, he had enjoyed the slave girls that were simply part of life in the orta. In the intervening years, he had lived in a totally different situation, with the safety of his mission demanding abstinence regardless of any principles. At first, in any case, he had been repelled by the behaviour of women in the west, indeed by the women themselves. However, he had discovered over time, to his considerable surprise, that he could like both Annette and Marianne notwithstanding their flagrancy. Although he had taken up pointed suggestions from neither of them.

Here in Genoa, the situation was different again. And there was no reason he could think of, at that moment, to refuse Bianchetta's invitation.

'That's better,' she looked up at him her face close in the darkness. She reached her hands around his neck as she pulled him to meet her.

His body stirred as it sensed the well-filled curves.

Her breathing was fast as she finally drew back and took his hand. He followed, as willing as she.

He was not, however, willing to let her strike a light; even a Genoese servant knew certain things.

'Someone might notice,' he said and felt her shrug.

'No matter; we'll leave it dark. I can find my way.' The chuckle was low in her throat. 'And if you get lost I'll help you.'

Perhaps she was a little too helpful at the end.

The following day he again fetched and carried. His conduct, remembered from that grander palazzo, even won praise from Susanna.

'So, you will be employed a bit longer,' Bianchetta said with a sly smile. 'Although after tonight some things might be more difficult.'

He stared.

'The Master is due back.' She looked at him from beneath dark lashes. 'But he will not stay all night.'

Comprehension dawned: there was an arrangement between her and Oberto Spinola.

'He will also go to the bed of his barren little wife.'

'No children?' Hosé managed.

'Not with her, nor elsewhere that anyone knows about. Suits me!' She grinned and the point of her tongue showed for just a moment.

A shout from Susanna caught her attention and she moved away. 'It's the niece, bad again.'

The niece?

'The Mistress has been calling for things all day. I'll see you later.'

When Hosé had to carry hot water upstairs, the first person he met was a man much his own age, although the gentle planes of his face made him look younger.

'Put it over there.' The words were more a request than an order. He turned and spoke to someone. 'I know you say she will be all right, 'Bella, but I'm not so sure.'

'Bella. Hosé had known it would be, of course, but suddenly his pulse quickened.

A woman appeared. She was also in her mid-twenties but her face was as open as it had been as a girl, Hosé thought. And her mouth still looked like a flower in bud. The light brown hair was hidden now under the seemly coif of a married woman.

'Poor Gianmaria,' said Isabella Spinola. 'Don't look so worried.'

'How is my little Battista?'

There were tiny lines at the corner of the woman's eyes as she smiled. She still found the bright side of life then?

'She will do well enough. Matteo is confident.'

'Are you sure it was wise to dismiss Hubertus Germanicus. He has a good reputation with such matters.'

'Quite wise,' said Isabella Spinola. 'The man's a complete fraud!'

'But does Matteo have enough experience?' Gianmaria looked dubious.

'He has conferred with a learned colleague who confirms both his diagnosis and treatment.'

Gianmaria chewed his lip.

Hosé poured the water carefully into the basin. He exchanged his empty bucket for the full one waiting to be taken away.

As he slowly moved to the door, he glanced at the other people in the chamber.

The young man in the robe of a novice monk would be Matteo.

And the figure propped against the bolster in the stepped bed, her brown hair limp, her face pale, must be the niece, Battista.

Isabella had only one sister, Caterina, once the wife of another Genoese merchant and step-mother to his son. Before Caffa.

Hosé dare not tarry.

As he left the room he noticed the wall painting and drew a quick breath. Next to the Christian Evangelists peering down sympathetically at a martyred Saint Catherine with her wheel, a bishop lifted his hand in blessing.

As Hosé closed the door behind him he heard voices coming up the main stairs.

Was that Oberto Spinola? It had been a long time.

Hosé moved swiftly towards the servants' stairs, head lowered.

'Well, Lorenzo, has Guglielmo Dagna and his tribe sent any more *vitri Ijudaici* from Savona to Nice?'

Vitri Ijudaici? Jewish glassware; was that why Oberto Spinola had been in Nice?

'The Università d'Altare is supposed to hold the monopoly for both making and selling glassware,' was the reply. 'That has stopped the damned Venetians selling their Murano glass, but nothing seems to stop the Jews. They pop up all over the area: not only Savona but Rapallo as well.'

'They come up that way from Tuscany,' was Oberto's comment.

'The Medici have harboured a rats' nest there.' Lorenzo said bitterly. 'A good job Jews are not allowed to stay here in Genoa for more than three days.'

'That's something,' agreed Oberto.

Hosé frowned. So, where had Isaac gone?

Hosé nearly missed Susanna's order.

In the palazzo in Urbino, water was delivered directly to all parts of the household. Federico da Montefeltro had designed it so, a generation ago. Why had others not followed his example?

Hosé mused on this, and other matters, as he trudged upstairs yet again, and sought admission to the chamber.

This time the first person he saw was Oberto Spinola. Hosé's heart hammered.

However, Oberto Spinola was talking to his wife; who was bathing the face of the girl, Battista.

'So, little Matteo,' Oberto's tone was scornful, 'Knows enough to be sure she will be all right.'

'He has studied with the best teachers,' Isabella answered evenly.

'Of course,' said Oberto. 'Along with all the other da Montefeltro bastards.' He looked at his wife. 'It's a pity the family fecundity does not extend to all its members.'

'I am related to them by affection,' said Isabella calmly. 'Not by blood. As you very well know.'

Oberto snorted. 'The Sforzas also do well enough in the procreation business! Her mother,' he indicated Battista, 'Your sister,' he emphasised the point. 'Seems to be managing *very* well.' He turned his glare on Gianmaria, 'While the future of our Albergo, God help us, seems to rest on whatever you and Battista,' he glowered at the bed, 'Can manage to produce. If anything.'

The young man in the robe of the novice monk said doggedly. 'She is improving daily. In a few weeks, she will be very much better.'

Hosé looked as closely as he dared. The slight figure bore little resemblance to his great grandfather, the bull-like Federico da Montefeltro, although there was a determined set to the jaw.

'And a beardless youth knows this for certain!'

Matteo flushed slightly but answered quietly. 'Naturally I consult more experienced authorities.'

Isabella looked at him quickly.

Matteo swallowed. 'There are also books in the monks' library.'

'And what would monks know about the problems of carrying children?' Oberto was cutting. 'About as much as that poxy Hebrew!'

Hosé concentrated on removing the waste water.

'Now you recognise the wisdom of the Synod of Bamberg,' Lorenzo put in slyly.

That was only the most recent example of the Catholic Church's prohibition on Christians seeking help from Jewish physicians. Hosé wrestled in silent anger with the heavy wooden bucket. The Popes might order what they wished; sick Christians would continue to turn to the best in their need.

Oberto looked daggers at Lorenzo then suddenly roared at Hosé. 'Haven't you gone yet oaf?'

Hosé gathered his wits and moved out of the door, keeping his eyes down.

He had no doubt who the "*poxy Hebrew*" was, but what had happened and where was he now? Always the same questions. Lorenzo had said Jews were not allowed to stay in Genoa for more than three days. Did that mean Isaac had been expelled from the city three days after landing? That was months ago; where had he gone?

Oberto Spinola was not there the next day when Hosé was ordered once more to deliver hot water and remove the waste. Hosé was greatly relieved.

He covertly studied the invalid.

Would she be kind to Gianmaria? Her face was strained, but she was raised on her pillows drinking from a cup that Matteo was holding. She looked a little like her mother, Hosé thought, but her features were plainer and definitely kinder. At that moment, she was smiling at her husband.

Would her confinement conclude happily? Hosé had no interest in the fortunes of the Lomellini, but he wished the pair well. They certainly looked much better suited, he reflected wryly, than Gianmaria and Annette ever would have been.

Matteo took the empty cup and laid it aside with a sigh.

' "*Should a boy of sixteen be sighing, my friend*",' Isabella came up behind him.

' "*And mourning the day of his death, when he could be strong in his youth, with his cheek like a rose in the sun?*" '

Hosé froze.

" '*From boyhood my heart has judged me, and so my soul has been bowed, and it placed understanding and learning across it, and cut my soul along wrath.*" ' Matteo looked at her with adolescent melancholy.

" '*What good does anxiousness do you? Be patient, your wound will heal. You moan inside your trouble in vain: What help could you bring with your tear.*" ' Isabella patted his shoulder.

" '*But why should I wait, and how long can I hope, when the day is full, and the end is far, and no one in Gilead knows of balm, for the pain of a plague-stricken man.*" ' Matteo shook his head. " '*My words are driven by worry, my joy in sighing's put out –when I see others laughing my heart splits, for my life as it slips away from me.*".'

What on earth was going on? Hosé frowned. And hastily moved as Isabella looked in his direction. He nearly slopped the bucket.

How could Matteo and Isabella possibly know the verse of Ibn Gabirol, a Jew from Zaragoza, who had died at an early age over four hundred years ago?

And was one of Isaac's favourite poets.

The following day Matteo was not with Battista. As far as Hosé could find out, he was not in the house at all.

'Where is that young monk?' he asked Bianchetta casually.

'Who cares?' she pulled him further into the shadows. 'Come on,' she urged him.

'Why the rush? We can take our time, later.'

'But I don't want to wait until later,' she said.

'Plenty of time later,' he repeated, 'After Signore Oberto has finished.'

'Are you jealous?' She peered at him.

He had been once; but not over a serving girl.

He stopped further questions with simple effectiveness. 'The rest later,' he said. 'Now about that novice. He must be in some religious order.

Bianchetta pouted.

Hosé tried not to show his impatience.

'I don't know about that,' she said eventually. 'They say he studies with the Infirmarian at the San Giovanni hospital.'

Hosé was puzzled. Matteo could surely not aspire to the Order of the Knights of St John: the slight young man would hardly make a warrior monk, quite apart from the fact that he lacked the essential qualification of legitimacy.

'But he has been here, helping with the Signora's sick niece,' Hosé prompted.

'Those from noble families make their own rules.' Bianchetta shrugged. 'He also comes here to escort the Signora to church, when the Signore is away.'

That would be the church of St Luca. Oberto Spinola had once boasted that the church had been founded by an ancestor with whom he shared a name. Curiously, Hosé remembered, another Oberto had also been involved: Oberto Grimaldo.

He almost missed Bianchetta's next words.

'Very devout, the pair of them. For the past year or more they have spent whole days there. In prayer and contemplation, the mistress says.'

"*The past year or more*"? Since Isaac first arrived in Genoa?

Bianchetta looked at Hosé. 'Probably praying for a child.'

That was possible of course.

A few days later Oberto left again for Rome.

And Matteo returned.

If Bianchetta was right, he would escort Isabella to church the following day.

Hosé needed to follow them. Servants, however, were not given time off, except for religious festivals. If Hosé left the palazzo without permission, it would certainly end his employment.

He slipped over the wall after leaving Bianchetta's hospitable arms for the last time and spent the rest of the night hiding in the dark alleys of the city, keeping a very keen eye and ear open for the watch.

He hoped Isabella and Matteo appeared. He did not fancy spending too many nights this way.

He had just about given up hope when he saw them emerge from the house. Apparently, Matteo was regarded as sufficient escort: no servants accompanied them, nor men-at-arms.

The pair walked, without hurry, through the streets. Hosé kept them in sight and watched them approach the door of the Spinola church. They did not look around.

With the last warning notes of the church bell a few other people hurried in. Hosé kept close behind a sturdy man and even sturdier woman.

As they entered the gloom, he moved to the back, where common folk would be expected to stand. A quick check revealed that, thankfully, there were none he knew. He barely noticed the ritual. His eyes were on the figures in the Spinola family seats.

At the end, he continued to watch them; otherwise he might easily have missed their disappearance. They left their seats, and started towards the back of the church and the main door. But the next moment they had gone.

There must be a side door, through which they had slipped with what, to Hosé, looked like a well-practised manoeuvre.

He pulled back as far as he could, as the rest of the congregation departed. Just when he thought it was safe to move, a shadow interrupted the early morning sunshine, and someone entered.

Hosé froze. Even with the light behind, he recognised the figure instantly.

Lorenzo Spinola walked to the front of the church.

Hosé peered intently as Lorenzo approached the place where Isabella and Matteo had disappeared. Surely, he had arrived too late to see them?

Hosé held his breath.

The priest reappeared. And for some time stood talking to Lorenzo.

Hosé could not hear what they were saying but he studied them carefully. Was the priest deliberately shielding the door? Hosé could not tell. Was Lorenzo particularly interested in it? He did not appear to be. Although he did seem to be asking a lot of questions.

A boy hurried in the main door, his bare feet pattering on the stone floor as he ran up to the priest and gasped out some message.

Apologising profusely, the cleric hastened towards the main door, shepherding the boy, and Lorenzo, before him.

Hosé waited.

Finally, he moved quietly to the front of the church and found the side door.

He grasped the iron handle, slipped through and found himself in a short passage which led to what was obviously the vestry.

He looked around the small room. He could see that its stone shelves held the accoutrements of Christian worship. Several robes hung on pegs. Otherwise it was empty.

He stared.

Isabella and Matteo had come this way. He had not seen them re-emerge. He spotted the small door and put his ear to it.

Then opened it cautiously.

It gave access to and from a narrow alley that ran down the side of the church. It was a common enough arrangement, allowing the priest to come and go without using the main door.

But why would Isabella and Matteo use it? And why so furtively?

They would not have turned towards the main street; that would have made no sense. Hosé headed the other way. The alley turned a sharp corner, ran around the back of the church, then turned once more down the far side, back to the main street.

He had obviously missed something. He retraced his steps. And there it was, behind the east end, almost hidden by a plant that had taken root in the crumbling stonework: a small opening.

Hosé stepped through.

The passageway was overhung by so many creepers it was almost a tunnel, and so narrow he sometimes had to edge sideways.

At one point, it breached one of the old city walls, before finally emerging in the dilapidated remains of a monastery. Ancient black stone columns, headed by square capitals, were in poor repair, but nevertheless still supported a double-storey cloister.

In the open area enclosed by the cloister there were the faint traces of paths, even the outline of what might once have been a fountain in the centre. But there was no sign that feet still trod those particular ways of contemplation.

Hosé did not tread them either. He followed the cracked stone flags to the far side until he came to a door at the base of a ruined bell-tower: a door small but decidedly *not* ruined.

After a brief moment, he grasped the handle.

It turned easily and the door swung on well-greased hinges to reveal the foot of a spiral staircase. Hosé closed the door quietly behind him and climbed upwards, his feet fitting the hollows worn in the steps. He came to a small platform where a slit-window gave enough light to see that it was impossible to climb any further: collapsed masonry blocked the way. Another small door, however, gave quiet access to the upper storey of the cloister.

Part way along the first side there was a heavy door, boarded up, the heads of the nails dulled by time. He put his ear to it and was surprised to hear the muffled but recognisable sound of men's voices, chanting.

The monastery was not completely abandoned.

However, any monks still living there obviously did not use this part, nor use the way Hosé had come.

He thought about this quarter of the city and suddenly realised he knew where the main entrance was. He frowned. What was the monastery called? He could not recall. But it was certainly not San Giovanni, indeed nowhere near it, which was a distinct relief. Perhaps Bianchetta had got it wrong; or been misled.

He shrugged. And walked on.

Yet another door. Again he listened: more faint voices, but a different quality.

Down another staircase to an open doorway lit by bright daylight.

He risked a look. In an enclosed courtyard, in the sunshine, beds of plants were laid out in tidy rows. Already bees were busy in the warm scented air.

'Here, 'Bella, for you.' It was Matteo's voice. 'The Sweet Balm is beginning to flower but there are still plenty of leaves.' There were steps on gravel. 'Fortunately, the African Mint is still fine; I'll pick some and make tea.'

African Mint was Isaac's favourite drink.

'I think we should drink it inside.' Isabella's figure crossed the doorway.

'Duke Federico had al-Razi in the Urbino library.' It was Matteo's voice. 'In manuscript, of course!' He continued, 'My teacher was not happy with those parts where al-Razi gives accounts of his own treatments and finds fault with Galen.' There was the distinct sound of pages turning. 'You have made many notes in the margins.'

A cup clunked gently on a wooden table.

'This was only printed a couple of years ago. You must have got hold of one of the first copies. Where did you get it?'

Hosé drew a breath and listened to the long pause.

'Did you buy it? Did someone give it to you?'

What did it have to do with Matteo?

'It must have cost a lot of money.'

And where would a Jew get that much? Hosé could almost hear the next question.

But Isabella surprised him. 'What would you like to do today? It will soon be too hot to work in the physik garden. Would you like to discuss something? Or will you teach us some more poetry?'

Hosé leaned back against the wall. She was talking as if coaxing a sick child.

What was going on?

He no longer had any doubt that Isaac was there, just a few steps away. But what had happened to him?

His mind turned over all sorts of likely, and unlikely, explanations as the voices continued. Apparently, Isaac had decided he would like to hear some more of what Petrarch had to say about Cicero.

Hosé listened impatiently.

Finally, there was the noise of benches scraping.

'I'm afraid we have to go now,' said Isabella. 'But Matteo will return soon with something to eat.'

Hosé ran back up the stairs, around the cloister and ducked out of sight, breathing hard.

Footsteps went the other way, towards the bell-tower and disappeared.

How soon would it be before Matteo came back with the food?

The door into the herb garden still stood open.

Hosé drew a breath of the aromatic air and walked across the gravelled path.

Chapter 12

The old Jew looked at him with an enquiring smile.

'Isaac.' Hosé took one bony hand and squeezed it.

The Jew nodded and lifted a finger of the other hand. And you?

Hosé's heart sank.

'It's Hosé. Don't you know me?'

The gaunt face lifted and the sunken eyes regarded him solemnly for a long time. Slowly the physician shook his head.

'You were in Nice,' Hosé said. 'We were working together for the Sultan.'

There was a faint gleam.

Hosé seized the tablet and thrust it into Isaac's hand. 'Tell me you remember.'

Isaac frowned and finally wrote: Bayezit.

'Yes, yes, Sultan Bayezit. You left Nice sailing for Islambul, to see the Sultan.'

The Jew looked blank.

'But you are in Genoa.'

Isaac nodded.

He knew that at least.

'What happened to you?' Hosé asked urgently.

The Jew wrote some words on the tablet. Matteo says I fell down the stairs. I don't remember.

Hosé stared at him. 'But you remember lots of things,' he protested. 'Like Ibn Gabirol, al-Razi, Plutarch.'

Yes, some things I remember. The Jew shook his head.

'You remember different languages. You write in Genoese and you understand me in Turkish.'

Isaac's face brightened and he nodded.

Hosé seized the tablet. Do you remember how you lost your tongue? He wrote in the shorthand they had always used.

Isaac could read it. But the answering marks said he could not answer the question.

Hosé told him.

The Jew's face slowly fell. How could I forget that?

'Do you remember when your donkey ran off near Aleppo, and Mansur, Nasr and I, we found you, nearly frozen to death? I saw Mansur recently. He is Pasha now.' Hosé gabbled on.

He stopped as he saw the distress on Isaac's face.

He could find the key to unlock the memories. He was sure of it, but it would take time. He would take Isaac away and then they would have all the time it needed.

'Does Matteo stay here with you at night?'

Not always. Isaac was relieved there was a question he could answer.

'Will he stay tonight?'

He may stay with Battista. She is….

'Yes, I know about Battista.'

The Jew nodded. But she is getting better Matteo says.

'Did you tell him how to treat her?

Isaac nodded.

'So, your medical memory is still there?'

A lot of it I think. Maybe there is more.

'There are just some things you don't remember.' Hosé smiled at him. 'Tonight, we'll leave here and I can tell you about other things. It'll remind you, I'm sure.' He spoke confidently.

Isaac stared at him. Why do we have to leave here?

'Because it's not safe.'

Matteo and Isabella have been very good to me. Isaac smiled. I am perfectly safe here.

But I'm not! The words remained unspoken.

'This is a sanctuary.' The words were quietly but firmly spoken.

Hosé spun around.

'You!' Matteo stared at him. He looked at Isaac then back. 'You come in here frightening a sick old man. How dare you?' The young face coloured with anger. 'Get out!' The slight shoulders squared under the rough cloth. 'Get out now; right out of the quarter.' He advanced on Hosé. 'In fact, you would be advised to leave the city, immediately.' He paused, 'Before I speak to Oberto Spinola.'

Hosé had moved back a little. Suddenly he smiled. 'You won't do that.'

Matteo flushed.

'I don't understand half of what's been happening, but I do know Signore Oberto Spinola would not tolerate a Jew staying in Genoa for more than three days. Isaac has been here a good deal longer than that and it's my belief that you and Signora Isabella have been responsible for that.'

Matteo's face fell. After a moment, he demanded. 'How do you know anything about Isaac anyway?'

Hosé indicated the basket in Matteo's hand. 'Suppose we all sit down and share the contents of that. We can talk while we eat.' He grinned. 'And you got it wrong. "*My words are driven by worry, my joy in sighing's put out – when I see others laughing my heart splits, for my life as it slips away from me.*" That's the first verse, not the last.'

Matteo gaped. 'You know Ibn Gabirol too?'

'I had the same teacher.' Hosé looked at Isaac. There was a look of recognition; but that might just be for the poem. 'He should learn *The Field*, shouldn't he? It offers more hope to a dispirited youth.'

Isaac stared at him.

'Who are you?' Matteo's first question was hardly surprising.

'I am Hosé.'

The youth bristled.

'Sometimes called Hosé de Mallorca.'

'You speak like a Genoese.'

Hosé swallowed a piece of fresh bread and ignored the comment. 'I have worked with Isaac for a good many years.'

'You are also a physician?' Matteo looked dubious.

Hosé laughed. 'Hardly. I have been Isaac's assistant, his clerk, his guard.'

Matteo looked at him. 'The last part I can well imagine.'

Hosé shrugged.

'And you were with Isaac before he came to Genoa?'

'Yes.'

'In Nice?'

It would be easy enough to know the *Santa Giovanna* had come from there.

Hosé nodded.

'But Isaac was travelling alone.'

'There were two men supposed to see him safe. Obviously, they did not do what they were paid for,' Hosé said bitterly, and looked at Isaac in the vague hope of an explanation. The Jew shook his head. 'Isaac took ship from Nice heading for Tunis, but I understand the *Santa Giovanna* diverted to Genoa.' Hosé paused. 'Where Isaac left her in the company of Oberto Spinola.' He looked at Matteo.

'Oberto had got talking with Isaac on the voyage.' Matteo paused. 'Oberto Spinola is a man of many contradictions.'

Hosé thought that was one way of putting it.

'Often he is arrogant, ruthless even, but.....,' Matteo's voice tailed off. He tried again. 'He has been married to 'Bella for six years.'

Hosé knew that.

The youth coloured slightly. 'There have never been any children.'

Hosé knew that as well.

'They have frequently been apart, while Oberto has been serving as a condottiere.' The young face flushed more deeply, 'But when he is here he is as,' he hesitated, 'As loving as ever.' He hurried on, 'And I mean loving; he cares for 'Bella you know.'

The remnants of old feelings stirred.

'They consulted several physicians but nobody was able to help.'

'So Oberto resorted to seeking advice from a Jew,' Hosé finished for him.

Matteo flushed a deeper shade at the tone.

'I'm sorry,' Hosé repented a little. 'You have shown yourself to be of a broader mind than most in your Church.'

'I know what my Church says about the Jews,' said Matteo. 'But I find I must question that, along with many of its teachings.' The young face creased almost with pain. 'I have learned so much from the infirmarians and been privileged to serve the sick. But there are other matters I have not been able to accept, although I have tried! The Brother in charge of the novices says such questioning is false pride and must be surrendered to the greater wisdom of the Church.'

'But?' Hosé's eyes gleamed slightly.

'But I had the run of the great library in Urbino when I was growing up.'

Hosé imagined it held even more books by then than when he had seen it.

'Duke Federico collected works by many people: Italian, German, Greek, Arabic, Persian, even Hebrew. And he read them all or had them read to him. He believed knowledge was to be found everywhere on God's earth, not just among the Christians.' Matteo hesitated. 'I have discovered that many Churchmen, even those who call themselves scholars, have no knowledge of these books. Nor wish to.' He paused again. 'Can it be wrong to seek knowledge, wherever that knowledge is to be found? Including knowledge that can help heal.'

'But is that knowledge of God or of the Devil?' Hosé asked. 'Can a mere mortal understand the difference? Or question the wisdom of a God who has visited afflictions on His sinful people? Should, in fact, a physician seek to heal? Is that not flouting God's will and purpose?'

Matteo was startled. 'You can't think that!'

'I don't,' Hosé said grimly. Allah had not made a disease without appointing a remedy for it. 'But I know the arguments.'

Matteo looked at him curiously. 'Yes, that is exactly the conflict I have been faced with.'

'It makes for a much easier life if you do not question things.' Hosé looked at him sympathetically. 'But perhaps you could tell me a bit more about Isaac and Oberto Spinola.'

'I understand Oberto invited Isaac to stay a couple of days until the *Santa Giovanna* was ready to leave port. He asked him to see 'Bella.'

'The childlessness obviously being her fault.' The words came out more sharply than he intended.

'Oberto has always assumed that was the case,' Matteo replied carefully.

Even Bianchetta could see otherwise!

''Bella says Isaac was most thorough in his questions to her and,' he added pointedly, 'About Oberto.' He smiled at the Jew. 'She was most impressed by his manner and knowledge.'

Naturally.

'Isaac suggested certain herbs that would ensure a regular flow of her courses, but he did tend to the opinion that the problem lay with her husband.'

The Jew suddenly lifted his tablet. Did 'Bella get him to take the tincture?

Matteo nodded.

Hosé looked at him. 'Did Oberto know about it?'

Matteo shook his head. 'He is still adamant that he is not at fault.'

'He did not like Isaac's diagnosis,' Hosé said sourly, 'So in classical style he abused the messenger?'

'No,' said Matteo quickly. 'It was not like that. Isaac was to board the boat again but he slipped going down the stairs and banged his head severely. 'Bella did not know what to do. She knew Oberto would not have a Jew in the house, would probably not even let him stay in Genoa, even though he was injured. But,' he looked straight at Hosé, 'She was determined to look after him until he was recovered.'

Hosé nodded; of course.

'She came to find me and asked for my help. We brought Isaac here.'

'And the Church happily received a Jew into its care?'

Matteo avoided his eye for a moment. 'We have not mentioned his race. 'Bella and I come here when we can. Otherwise a very old infirmarian helps.'

We help each other! Isaac wrote the words with a smile.

'Of course, it has been easier when Oberto has been away in Rome,' Matteo added.

Hosé chewed his lip and looked at Isaac; what to do for the best?

Isaac for the moment felt secure where he was. Hosé was a virtual stranger. Could he really take the Jew away?

At the same time Hosé was convinced he could help Isaac recover his memory, if anyone could.

No, they would have to stay in Genoa. But Hosé had burned his boats at the Spinola palazzo; they would never have him back. And even if it had been possible, he reflected, it would not serve the purpose: he needed to be with Isaac.

Matteo interrupted the silent debate. He spoke almost shyly. 'Would you be able to stay here with Isaac? It would answer best, wouldn't it?'

Hosé started.

But there was another problem: 'Bella. He did not think she had recognised him so far, but if they were to meet here with Isaac that state of affairs was not likely to continue.

He rasped a hand around his chin. It was not only a face that was distinctive; there were mannerisms, the way a person moved.

And if, when, she did recognise him?

It was a strange time. There were no locks and no guards but Isaac was confined by his malady, and Hosé by the fear of discovery or recognition.

They inhabited a sheltered and fertile little oasis, Hosé reflected.

The weeks passed as he sought to find the key to Isaac's personal prison. They spent hours in talk, Hosé recounting hundreds of incidents from their common past. Isaac listened with interest and relearned the facts.

Somehow, he wrote, I feel what you say is true but I cannot actually remember these things happening.

Often, they spent time studying and discussing books that Matteo or Isabella brought.

Sometimes they tended the garden, with the old infirmarian. The bent old monk apparently accepted the whole odd situation without question. Any curiosity was reserved solely for his beloved herbs: their qualities, their preparation and their use.

His extensive knowledge and experience informed the notes and illustrations Hosé added to the herbal Isaac had started.

Isabella brought news of the wider world. Isaac merely took a polite interest and misunderstood Hosé's restlessness.

You can still exercise, the Jew commented, and made some suggestions.

Hosé stared at the tablet then at the old man. Did he remember making just such suggestions before?

Did I? Isaac shook his head sadly.

One day Isabella paused in the herb garden as she was about to leave. She looked at Hosé and his heart sank. She put out her hand and he was forced to take it.

'Battista is very much better,' she said.

'Good,' he said shortly. 'But I can take no credit for that.'

'No,' she considered him. 'But you could perhaps help her with one thing that frequently bothers her.'

He looked at her warily.

She gave her sweet smile. 'Battista often wonders what became of her brothers.'

He withdrew his hand and on its broad palm lay a small figure, a bishop lifting one hand in blessing.

'Which brother?' He stared at the figure.

'She wonders about the boy her mother grieves for, but also about the older one, her half-brother.' Isabella's voice was gentle. 'As do I.'

He was silent.

'Perhaps you no longer have any regard for such things,' she pointed at the bishop.

In one sense, she was right; such images had no place in his life.

But in another way, she could not have been further from the truth. 'You have the same picture on the wall of your room,' he said.

'It means a lot to me,' she said simply.

He swallowed. 'Is Oberto away?'

She recognised the oblique connection. She smiled a little. 'My husband is a man of many contradictions.'

'Matteo used the same words,' he said wryly.

She continued serenely, 'Although he may be hard with others he has always been considerate of me. Ours was an arranged marriage of course, but in his way, I believe he loves me.'

'Do you return his affection?' Hosé asked carefully.

'I have grown to respect and value him for what he is,' she replied. 'We deal together very well.' She looked at him frankly. 'I know of his philandering.'

He drew a quick breath.

She put her head on one side. 'Bianchetta has been strangely subdued these past weeks,' she said.

Hosé kept a straight face.

'But hers is not the only bed Oberto shares.' Isabella's voice was calm. 'There are surely others in Rome. Men are like that I suppose. Duke

Federico undoubtedly loved both his wives dearly but.....

'Still fathered several bastards.'

Isabella looked at him seriously. 'Whom he loved and reared, and whose own children, and grandchildren,' she said evenly, 'However begotten, are some of the most worthy people I know.' A small crease spoiled the smooth brow. 'The teachings of the Church and the realities of life are sometimes difficult to match.'

'No wonder you and Matteo are so close!'

'Yes, I could not imagine life without him,' she underlined her point, then added more speculatively, 'Perhaps the Church sets the ideal standard but man cannot help but fall short of it.'

'Not even the Church's appointed Vicar apparently.'

Another small frown. 'It is true there is much talk of the Pope's nepotism.'

'Nepotism?' Hosé queried. 'They are the Pope's *nephews*?'

She shook her head, but in sadness not disagreement. 'Matteo and I talk of such things and wonder how they can be, but what can we do about them?' She answered her own question. 'The only person I can really take responsibility for is myself; other people must see to their souls. And if they fall short who am I to condemn them? Christ forgave sinners. Can I do less than try to do the same?'

Hosé looked at her. 'To try and follow directly the teachings of your Christ rather than the example and commands of your Church sounds dangerously close to what some would call heresy, 'Bella. The Holy Inquisition has investigated people for much less. You and Matteo should be careful who you share such dangerous thoughts with.'

'I am,' she smiled at him.

He flushed.

She said softly. 'And will you share something with me? Will you tell me of Battista's brothers, both of them?'

'Oberto would be interested to know that too.'

She smiled again. 'I do not share dangerous thoughts with him.'

The weeks grew into months. Another new sailing season got under way.

Hosé knew they should leave Genoa. He put the matter to Isaac.

The Jew was still for a long time. Finally, he wrote on his tablet. I realise that the longer I stay here, the more dangerous it is for Isabella and Matteo.

Hosé nodded. 'You would be safe in Islambul. The Sultan would ensure you received the best of care.' But even as he said the words he wondered if the first part was true: Isaac would be easy prey to enemies that he could no longer recognise.

Isaac paused. I believe what you say about the Sultan but I cannot actually remember him. He shook his head. Perhaps if I met him again..... The words tailed off. The old Jew looked at Hosé. Would you take me to him?

That was another decision Hosé had to make. He should go to Rome but the Sultan would also expect him to look after Isaac.

Perhaps if he could learn more, more than reached Isabella's sheltered ears, he would know what to do. He would go down to the waterfront in the evening.

The wine shops were busy. Polyglot seamen from all around the Middle Sea drank and sang, gossiped and whored. Hosé moved from one wine shop to another, listening and talking, keeping a sharp eye open for anyone he might know, particularly from the Spinola household.

Genoese boats often put into Civitavecchia. From there came news of the exotic prince who was often seen these days in Rome. In the day, he rode his great black stallion with a company of knights and men-at-arms; in the evenings, he walked the streets giving alms to the poor. They said that was part of his heathen faith.

Hosé took a small sip of the tart local wine.

It seemed there were Turks everywhere these days. They had been seen in Florence and Milan as well as Rome; and not only on the land. Many seamen claimed to have seen Turkish galleys off the coast of Africa, around Sicily, even up into the Venetian sea.

Hosé wondered what degree of exaggeration to factor in.

Trade with the remaining Genoese outposts in the east had been good: the Knights on Rhodes were protecting the area against further Ottoman incursions.

Mind you, that meant trade for the Venetians was also thriving. Large gobbets of spit hit the filthy straw on the floor.

Hosé made for another bar. It was getting late; already the more respectable citizens of the city had headed for home; soon even the seamen would stagger away into the night.

'Psst! Hosé!'

He stopped, instantly alert. His first thought was Bianchetta but she was not likely to be out in these parts at this time, then he recognised the treble voice.

'Jakob?' he said softly.

The boy appeared at his side. 'I saw you go into the wine shop but I did not dare go in there by myself so I waited for you to come out.'

'By yourself? What are you doing here anyway? Where is your father? Where is the *Katrin*?'

'She is moored down at the quay.' The boy answered the last question.

'You should not be out on your own.' Hosé took him by the arm and moved as men in various states of drunkenness emerged from the door.

A girl in a very low bodice thrust her face in his and made a suggestion.

Hosé waved her away. 'Come on,' he said to Jakob, 'Let's get you back to the *Katrin*.'

The boy followed him for a short way then pulled up. 'There are things you should know before we get there.'

Hosé stopped. 'What's happened? Clough?'

Jakob's face was pale against the darkness of the harbour. He shook his head.

'What have you been doing?' Hosé prompted him quietly as the boy remained silent.

'We have been trading with the *Katrin*, ever since she was properly finished. We went to Marseille, across to Algiers. She is a lovely boat, handles beautifully; even Thomas says so.'

'Is Thomas with you now?'

Jakob nodded.

'So still the same crew.' Hosé said lightly.

Jakob paused. 'We put into Nice a couple of weeks ago.'

Hosé stiffened. 'Signora Annette?'

'She is well enough,' said Jakob quickly.

'Rab?' Hosé should have thought of her first.

Jakob nodded miserably.

'What's the matter with.....him?'

There was a long silence but when Jakob spoke there was no mistaking the first word. 'She is on the *Katrin*.'

Hosé waited.

Jakob lifted his face. 'You are not surprised. You knew, didn't you?'

'Yes,' he said. 'I knew.' But what had made her give up her disguise? And why was she on the *Katrin*?

'Why didn't she tell me?'

Hosé shook his head. 'Life has been hard for her,' he said, and realised he did not know much about it.

'Now she is in terrible trouble.' The boy's voice shook. 'She jumped into the sea but Papa rescued her. Since then he has kept her shut up in case she tries again.'

'Couldn't the Signora Annette help?'

'Rab refused to ask her. She said it would be impossible.'

What could be so bad even Annette could not help? 'And what is Rab's terrible trouble?' he asked carefully.

'She is going to have a baby.'

'Whose baby?'

Jakob shook his head. 'She won't talk about it.'

Hosé stood thinking hard. 'Why are you in Genoa?' he asked finally.

'Looking for you. We hoped you might still be here or at least we could find out where you'd gone.'

Hosé had quite enough problems with Isaac. He drew a deep breath, then another. Allah knew and ordered all things.

'Let's find the *Katrin*,' he said to Jakob. He couldn't stay long. He had to get back to Isaac.

And to some serious decision-making.

'Rab?' The light from the lamp he held revealed the figure curled tightly in the corner of the cabin.

For a long moment, there was no response. Finally, the girl lifted a drawn face and looked past him at the doorway.

'Isaac is not here,' Hosé said quietly. Rab dropped her head. 'But he is nearby in the city,' Hosé added. 'He had an accident.'

Her head came up more quickly.

'He is well in body,' Hosé continued, 'But he cracked his head. He has lost some of his memory.'

A small gleam lit the dark eyes.

'I have been trying to help him remember,' Hosé said. 'He has relearned many things but he still does not recall them for himself.'

Rab was sitting now, leaning against the wall, although she still had not spoken.

Hosé took a breath. 'Perhaps with more time his memory will come back.' He paused. 'Perhaps a new face would help.'

The gleam flared into a flame, but briefly. 'I am no use,' she said in a very low voice, 'To anyone.'

'Isaac valued you very much,' he insisted.

'That was before.'

'No,' he said, moving forward. She shrank back from him and he stopped, squatting down on the boards a little way from her. 'You had troubles before and Isaac helped you then.'

She shook her head. 'Even Job is disgusted.'

'No, Rabia,' he used her full name. 'Jakob risked the waterfront on his own to come and find me. He still cares for you but he is worried and more than a bit confused. Cornelius and Pieter are also concerned for you.'

'They should have left me to drown,' she said. 'And this too!' She pointed at her belly with its faint swelling. She looked at him, misery mixed with defiance. 'I tried to get rid of it. I looked in all Isaac's books but nothing worked. The only way is to rid the world of myself too.'

He shook his head trying to imagine her desperation. She misunderstood him.

'And don't tell me it is against God's command! What does God care? He will surely condemn me to hell anyway.'

He ignored her judgement of herself. 'Who was it?' he asked.

She was silent.

'Was it Garcia?' he pressed.

She turned her head but he could see the tears which escaped her tightly closed lashes.

'I thought he had left Nice.'

'What does it matter?' He could hardly hear the words.

He thought of the big Spanish soldier. He should have killed him, after all, when he had the chance.

There was a long silence, broken only by the girl's ragged breathing.

Hosé forced his thoughts back from possible vengeance. There were much more immediate matters. 'As you say, what does it really matter? The important thing is that you understand that you have friends, Rabia.' He saw the disbelief again. 'Friends who want to help.'

'Isaac might have helped,' she said. 'He could have got rid of it. Now it is too late.'

'Whether he would have helped in that way or not I don't know,' Hosé said. 'But we have to face matters as they are.'

'We?'

'Yes, we. The van Dammes. Me.'

'You?'

'Me,' he answered quietly.

'What has it got to do with you?'

'Several things. I know that Isaac would want to help and I have to do that for him. For myself I know what you did for me when I was ill.' He paused. 'And I believe I also have to do something for the child.'

She stared uncomprehending.

He could not explain further.

'A bastard begot by the Devil!'

'It is not at fault, whoever else might or might not be.' He prevented her interruption. 'It should be properly cared for,' he said deliberately. 'It and you.'

'How?' she demanded angrily.

He was sorry he had to leave; anger was definitely a step in the right direction.

'I must go back to Isaac now,' he said.

Her face drained of its colour.

'But I shall be back soon; when I can arrange things.'

'Will you bring Isaac with you?'

He nodded. He rose and hesitated as he picked up the lamp. 'Do I need to take this away with me?' he asked.

'Or will I set fire to the boat and burn everyone on board, you mean?'

That was what Cornelius had feared.

'I won't do that.'

No, she would not do that to them.

She dropped her eyes. 'But perhaps it would be better to keep the door barred.'

'Just for the time being,' he agreed seriously. He suddenly smiled. 'Until you learn to swim. It is almost impossible to let yourself drown, you know, once you can swim.'

Her head shot up as she gaped at him.

'What did you say to her?' Cornelius asked curiously. 'We couldn't get a word out of her; not even Jakob.'

Hosé said dryly. 'I think I just sparked a tiny bit of interest in living.' He followed the Lowlander across the central well. 'I wish I could stay longer but perhaps that is enough for tonight. I promised I would be back and I promised to bring Isaac with me.' He stopped. 'I'm making some pretty big assumptions, Cornelius.'

In the lamplight, the weathered face broke into a smile. 'Not so big.'

'Where had you actually planned to go?'

The heavy shoulders lifted. 'Where would you like to go?'

Hosé shook his head. 'I'd been considering where to take Isaac but I hadn't decided anything. Now there is Rab too. I need to think about it.'

You had an interesting evening last night? Isaac thrust the tablet at him.

'You could say that,' Hosé replied absently.

And you will take me to Islambul?

Hosé shook his head. The new problem needed a different solution.

But we agreed it would be best to leave.

Hosé nodded, 'Best to leave Genoa.'

Then where shall we go?

The all-important question. 'We shall go with friends on their boat and find somewhere safe.'

What friends?

'Perhaps you will recognise them,' said Hosé hopefully. Or maybe Rab.

Footsteps on the gravel caught his attention. Isabella and Matteo entered.

The young man looked worried.

'What is it?'

'It may be nothing,' said Matteo but without confidence.

'Lorenzo wanted to accompany us to church,' said Isabella.

Hosé looked at her. 'It is the Spinola church after all,' he commented.

'Of course,' she said. 'He attends on a Sunday. But not during the week.'

'He was there the day I followed you two,' Hosé said. 'Although,' he added with a small smile, 'He did not arrive until after the service had finished.'

Isabella did not return his smile. 'There was something about the way he spoke.' She shook her head. 'But then he speaks as if everything he says has a hidden meaning.'

Hosé nodded in understanding. 'But he did not come with you?'

Isabella shook her head. 'In the end, he said he had business to attend to. He would come with us another day.'

'There is no chance he followed you?' Hosé grimaced. 'As I did.'

'I do not think so,' said Matteo with a frown. 'We have taken greater care since then.'

'Is there any reason Lorenzo might have become suspicious?'

Matteo shook his head. 'He was up much earlier than usual.' He frowned. 'Although he seemed to have had a late night of it.'

Hosé felt the unwelcome cold prickle at the back of his neck. 'Where would he have been having this late night?'

Matteo shrugged. 'I don't know his haunts.'

Hosé looked at Isabella without much hope.

She surprised him. 'He and Oberto often go to the wine shops along the waterfront. They say that is the best place to hear about the things that the ships' masters never tell them.'

The prickle turned into a shiver.

'I was there last night,' he said quietly. 'Perhaps he saw me, though I thought I had kept a good lookout.' There had been a lot to distract him.

Isabella looked at him curiously.

'It is time for me and Isaac to leave.'

Matteo opened his mouth to protest but Isabella put a hand on his arm. 'We have done what we can.' She smiled at the Jew. 'To keep Isaac here longer would be self-indulgence. In Genoa, he can never really be safe.' She looked at Hosé. 'He will be in good hands.'

Hosé hoped she was right. 'If Lorenzo is getting suspicious then the sooner we leave the better.'

'Have you made arrangements?' Isabella asked softly. 'Do you have a way of leaving immediately?'

He nodded.

Again, Matteo was prevented from speaking. 'It is best not to ask,' she said firmly. She looked at Hosé, 'But do you have everything you need? Can we provide anything?'

'No,' he answered. 'You have done more than enough.' He paused, 'Although if you could keep close to Lorenzo for the rest of the day that would make me feel easier.'

'Now that *is* asking rather a lot,' Isabella replied gravely.

Hosé looked at her in surprise then flushed at the twinkle in her eye.

She chuckled. 'And tomorrow we will positively insist he join us for mass at San Luca.'

Matteo had gone ahead to check the way was clear.

Hosé took Isabella's hand. 'I think he belongs here,' he said, placing the little bishop in her small palm, 'But it was good to make his acquaintance again.'

'I shall treasure him, perhaps more than before.'

'Thank you,' he said with difficulty, 'For all you have done for Isaac.'

'He has done so much for us.'

He swallowed. 'And all you have promised to do.'

She smiled. 'That,' she said, 'Will be a pleasure I never expected to have.'

He lifted her hand in the western fashion as he had long ago.

Chapter 13

July 1490

Date palms, olive trees, apricots, carobs, figs, grapes, grenadines, wrote Isaac, but no lotus flowers.

Rabia looked at him in bewilderment. 'What are lotus flowers?'

'Oh yes,' said Thomas, 'I remember. Ulysses almost lost his men when the beautiful maidens of the island fed them lotus flowers.'

The Jew nodded his approval.

'What happened?' demanded Jakob.

'The men were so intoxicated that Ulysses found it almost impossible to make them return to their boats,' said Thomas.

'Who was Ulysses?' asked Rabia.

'He was the hero of a story by Homer.'

'A story?' said Jakob.

'Who was Homer?' Rabia asked.

'An ancient Greek.'

Trees provided welcome shade in the courtyard of the *menzel*, flowers made splashes of colour as Isaac continued the day's lesson.

It was Jakob as usual who asked if it was nearly time for lunch.

Isaac frowned at the face with its summer freckles. You know the rules. You have to finish the morning's tasks properly first.

Jakob pulled a face. 'Papa never *used* to be so fussy.'

'Learning things can be useful,' said Thomas seriously.

'But there are much more useful things to learn about than ancient Greeks,' Jakob protested; for instance, how to use a sword or wrestle as Hosé taught them.

'That was only part of what Isaac was telling us about,' Rabia jumped to the Jew's defence. 'He was describing the history of the island and this part of Africa. It is easier to understand about a place and its people now if you know what happened before.'

Thomas nodded agreement.

Jakob looked unconvinced.

'Djerba is so different from Nice. Here most people are Kharidjite Moslems but Jews are allowed to live in peace at Hara Seghira and attend their synagogue at El Ghriba. Christian traders come and go. Visitors like us are welcomed.' The wonder still sounded in her voice. 'How did that come about?'

Jakob frowned. 'Yes, it is special I suppose,' he said grudgingly.

Tomorrow we will go into Sedouikech to the market, wrote Isaac, a more practical lesson. He smiled at the undisguised delight on the boy's face. But we have not finished with today yet!

'Desperate cases demand desperate remedies.' Hosé said defensively.

You know Hippocrates.

'I know that much,' Hosé said. '*You* taught me.'

Isaac nodded, watching the figures in the shallow waters. It is not proper.

'Nor is being driven to suicide,' Hosé said grimly. 'Which is the lesser sin?'

The sunken eyes turned towards him. You mistake me. I was not condemning. Actually, I believe it was just the right remedy in the circumstances. He paused. Moreover, I have begun to think that swimming can be helpful in pregnancy. He chewed the end of his stylus. Swimming out in the sea like this is not acceptable in any society I know of, but perhaps there could be private pools for girls and women. He nodded. I shall make a note of it.

'In al-Razi? I cannot believe he has a relevant chapter in his book!'

The Jew smiled. No, I don't believe he does, but there is still some space on the end papers. He wiped his tablet and stared across the lagoon.

The *Katrin* moved gently under their feet.

'What is it?' Hosé asked eventually.

The girl, Rabia. Her face reminds me of someone.

'Perhaps from Nice,' said Hosé hopefully.

The Jew shook his head. I don't think so; from a long time ago. He frowned in concentration. The thought came to me when I was in the synagogue last week. The words of the service were so familiar. I imagine I heard them in my boyhood; in Córdoba, you said?

Hosé nodded.

I could almost hear someone else saying the words and I could almost see another synagogue. And I could almost see other faces. He shook his head in frustration.

Hosé hesitated. 'I could never really understand why you formed such an attachment to Rabia in Nice.' He remembered his less than worthy thoughts on the matter. 'And when you left on the *Santa Giovanna*,' he continued, 'You asked me specially to look after her.' Which he had failed to do. He continued doggedly, 'Maybe you recognised her or something in her from an earlier time.'

Isaac thought hard.

'You said you never had children, no daughter.' Hosé prompted with all the information he could recall. 'There was just your wife.' He frowned. 'I think you said you had known her from when she was a girl.'

Rachel. The letters appeared on the tablet. Was that her name? Isaac's face lightened.

'I don't know,' said Hosé gently. 'I don't think you ever told me.'

Sedouikech, like the other villages scattered across the island among the palms and ancient olive trees, shone like a white jewel against the blue sky; the houses with their rounded domes sparkled in the sunlight.

In the colourful market place were stalls selling all sorts of local produce. Faraj proved herself an expert at bargaining.

Rab watched the older woman with grudging admiration.

Hosé had recruited Faraj to accompany Rab outside the menzel. The girl had been furious. The knowledge that propriety demanded it and that Hosé was right did nothing to lessen her anger or her resentment. Fortunately, Faraj had put Rab's ill humour down to the vagaries of pregnancy.

Faraj was a local woman of middle age. She had no children of her own and had been widowed for some years. She lived in the nearby village but agreed to come and stay at the menzel until the spring.

She watched hawk-eyed as the fruit seller wrapped the goods in palm leaves then smiled a little as Jakob pointed at something on the next stall.

'What are those?' the boy demanded.

Faraj said something in Arabic.

'They are camel muzzles,' Rabia translated, her eyes shining.

'Camels? I haven't seen any camels here.'

'Nor have I,' said the girl, 'But I've seen them before.'

'Have you ridden on one?' Jakob demanded.

She nodded. 'I went on a long journey once with my parents.'

Jakob gaped.

'With a caravan?' Thomas used the word carefully.

She nodded again. 'There were more than fifty animals. The *mahgribs* are skilled at handling them.'

'Mahgribs?'

'Men from the west of Africa. Mahgrib means where the sun goes down.'

Isaac nodded at her. The boys should learn Arabic.

Jakob pulled a face. 'Not more lessons to fit into the morning,' he protested.

The Jew shook his head. No, he wrote, I cannot teach you to speak it but if Hosé and Rabia use it you will learn.

'Perhaps we should not start with the word "camel" though,' said Rabia looking at him.

The Jew laughed.

Jakob looked bewildered.

'There are many, many words for "camel" in Arabic!' She explained the joke to Faraj.

The woman's lined face creased in a smile.

'Camels.' Thomas had been following his own thoughts. 'I saw some in Algiers. They can go across the desert without needing to drink and can carry four times as much as a horse.'

Isaac smiled at Thomas's unfailing concern for facts and figures.

He waved his group on to the next stall where fishing baskets were piled. Maybe another week we can go to Guellala. I am told that it has been the centre for ceramics and pottery since the time of King Midas.

'King Midas?' then Jakob groaned, as he realised he had given Isaac his opening.

Rabia nodded curtly at Hosé as she entered the room.

He returned the nod and lay back again on his sleeping mat by the doorway. 'Jakob and Thomas have made good progress with Arabic while we have been away,' he commented.

'Faraj has helped,' she said neutrally.

Hosé sighed to himself. Allah had set him a hard exercise; or perhaps he had brought it on himself; as usual.

He watched as she pulled her robe over her head. The bulge of the baby was still neat but definitely more distinct, sitting oddly, he thought, on what was essentially the body of a girl. He suddenly wondered how she would manage the birth. It was a hazardous business for any woman.

She turned at that moment. 'You promised,' she said, pulling her under-shift around her.

He swallowed the pointless protest.

He was no more reconciled than she was. It had simply seemed the only option. The people of Djerba might be blessedly tolerant, but Rabia's state would hardly find acceptance. There was nothing to be done about the pregnancy, the only answer was for her to be married.

'And I am supposed to suddenly find a husband?' she had demanded bitterly.

'Perhaps you do not need to search very far,' he had answered shortly.

She had stared at him uncomprehending. 'You?' she had said at last.

He had nodded. 'For appearance only,' he had added dryly.

Her face had been fixed. 'No marriage bed.' It had not been a question.

He had shaken his head.

'Promise.'

'I promise.' That had not been one of his worries.

It still wasn't, but the trip to Tunis had added others to a growing list. He frowned, pulling rather too hard at a loose thread in his mat.

'Did Cornelius and Pieter find goods?' she asked.

He was too absorbed in his own thoughts to notice the small olive branch the question represented. 'Yes.' The trip had been very successful; for them.

'So, they can go trading with the *Katrin*?'

He nodded. There was a long silence. The soft light from the small lamp showed her back as she curled on her mat, facing away from him.

He knew perfectly well, of course, the question she had not asked. What he did not know was the answer. The van Dammes would sail out of the Ajim channel, up across the Gulf of Gabès and round into La Goleta, the fortified port of Tunis. Their course was perfectly clear, he thought a little bitterly.

What was not clear was what would happen to Isaac, Rabia and himself; and the baby.

He had taken responsibility for this child, out of some sense of justice that still defied proper explanation, even to himself. He was well aware that as a kul his only responsibility was to the Sultan. The news in Tunis had reminded him of that; as if he needed reminding.

An earlier thought nudged itself back into his mind. He regarded the slender form. Could he talk to Isaac about it? Would the Jew even remember the relevant details?

He turned back with determination to the news he had learned.

'I wonder how Annette is.'

The words made him jump. He had not expected her to speak to him again, and certainly not of the person he was just thinking about. Although he realised it was not unreasonable; if she had been following the same train of thoughts as he had.

'I was going to tell you tomorrow,' he said at last.

She half turned. 'You heard something?'

'Yes,' he admitted.

'Well?'

'She had a difficult pregnancy,' he said.

'And?'

'An even more difficult labour,' he said, 'But,' he added a little too hurriedly, 'In the end she produced a fine child. They are both reported to be well.'

She nodded. Of course, she saw the parallel: she was sharp enough.

'And?' she asked eventually, 'Was it a boy or a girl?'

'A boy.'

There was a long silence again. 'She will be glad.' The genuine pleasure for Annette did not quite cover the other tone in her voice.

Yes, Annette would be happy, he thought.

And there had been similar news from a different quarter. Isabella's letter from Genoa had informed him pointedly that with the birth of a boy to Battista and Gianmaria the name of Lomellino would carry on for another generation.

Hosé had no interest in that, even in the choice of name, although he wondered what the man who was the child's grandfather might feel about it. Hosé had sent a despatch to Islambul. Ironically the Sultan's dragoman was the one person Hosé would trust absolutely to act against anything the Vizier might contrive. The Vizier had earned the interpreter's undying enmity the moment he chose to work with William Clough.

Hosé pondered uselessly, yet again, on what the Englishman might be doing now. He did not really think that the merchant would have given up his search for the van Dammes, nor did he think Clough would have abandoned work for the Vizier. Both ventures promised too much reward: to the Englishman's pride *and* to his pocket. Not to mention any other ventures he might have contrived.

In her letter, Isabella had given other family news: of Matteo, of Oberto, of Lorenzo. But nothing about Bianchetta. He winced inwardly.

The other letter, that she had forwarded, contained news of much wider import.

'Hosé, what will happen?'

'What? When?' He stalled.

She turned to face him fully, pulling herself up on one elbow.

'If I, we, survive.' Her voice was remarkably steady.

'I can't tell you what I don't know,' he said frankly.

'You'll cross that bridge when you get there?' she said. 'Or perhaps you will not have to cross it at all?'

That was the thought that had been nudging his mind. 'That is not what I hope for,' he said evenly, and he thought it was the truth.

'But it would make your life easier.'

He said wearily, 'I have long ceased expecting an easy life.'

'What is it?' Hosé put a hand on Pieter's arm.

The big Lowlander said softly. 'There is something about the sky.'

Hosé looked up at the thin veil that had come over during the day. It hardly looked threatening.

'The wind is from the other direction.'

Hosé turned his face to the south and felt the breeze welcome on his face. Practice that afternoon had been hard: Jakob was getting good and Thomas was improving. 'So?'

'I am not sure but something is in the air.'

A boyhood memory stirred in a corner of Hosé's mind.

'It is hotter,' continued the big man. 'And it is much drier.'

That was true. Already Hosé's shirt was no longer sticking to his back.

'A strong wind is coming perhaps.'

As if in response to the words, a gust hit them, blowing sand up off the beach into their faces.

'The siroc?' Pieter queried, almost to himself. 'But that is not usual in the autumn.'

Hosé's memory suddenly released a graphic picture. 'Once in Tabarka when I was a boy there was a violent storm, carrying so much sand it was almost impossible to breath. It lasted for several days and when it finally blew itself out, there were flattened trees strewn around and the splintered remains of fishing boats all along the shore.' He frowned. 'The people there called it the *arifi*, so thirsty it pulls the moisture out of every living thing.'

'We must talk with Cornelius,' said Pieter.

There was nowhere more sheltered that they could have taken the *Katrin*, even if there had been time.

Cornelius dropped the spare anchor and the three men managed to hitch ropes to a couple of what they hoped were substantial palms. By the time they had finished, the branches were already swaying wildly, the ringed trunks bending in the strengthening wind.

Sand stung their eyes.

'Come on,' urged Hosé, heading up the beach.

Cornelius stood peering out at the boat, tossing on the white capped waters, leaning over as if to protect herself from the storm. Her main mast dipped towards the sea. The mooring ropes were taut as a crossbow wire.

If one of those snapped it would kill anyone in its way, thought Hosé. 'Come on,' he repeated. 'If we stay out here we will only endanger ourselves as well.'

'Will she be all right?' Cornelius demanded of his brother.

Pieter shrugged. 'I cannot know that; any more than any man.'

'We should get back to the house,' said Hosé.

'*Kom* Cornelius.' Pieter laid a hand on his brother's shoulder. 'We can do no more here.'

The menzel had seemed ideal, set a little way from the village but within a short distance of the beach. Like the other houses on the island it was solid, its domed form hugging the ground. Like many houses throughout the Islamic lands its outer walls were windowless, protecting the privacy of the household. They also protected against the elements: the glaring sun of summer and now against the violent storm. Even the open courtyard in the middle of the building was sheltered from the worst of the blast, with only the very tops of the shade trees being whipped by the wind.

Hosé thankfully dropped the bar into place as Cornelius and Pieter shut the heavy door behind them.

It seemed suddenly very quiet, too quiet.

'Jakob!' Cornelius called, moving along the passage towards the kitchen.

He returned in a few moments. 'There is nobody here.'

'What?' Hosé stopped shaking the sand out of his clothes. 'Nobody?' He looked incredulously at the Lowlander.

'I have looked everywhere. They have all gone.'

'Gone?' Hosé repeated stupidly. 'Where could they have gone?'

'How should I know?' Concern added an edge to Cornelius's voice. 'It is dangerous out there.' A gust of wind roared through the trees nearby and rattled the door. Cornelius stared at the solid timbers as if he might look through them. 'The boys should have been back ages ago.'

Jakob and Thomas had been sent home while the three men had worked to secure the boat. It was only a few minutes' walk and that had been a couple of hours before.

'Isaac, Rabia, Faraj? Were they planning to go anywhere?' Hosé had not seen them that morning: he had gone straight from prayers to the beach.

'They didn't say anything,' Cornelius said, frowning. 'But,' he added, 'The weather did not look bad first thing.'

'They would surely have noticed the storm getting up and come home.'

'Perhaps they were taken unawares and sought shelter somewhere,' put in Pieter.

'But then where are the boys? Where could they possibly have gone between the beach and here?'

'Perhaps they came here then went out again,' said Hosé.

'What for?'

Hosé shrugged. 'Is there any sign they got back?'

Cornelius turned quickly. He was back in a few minutes. 'They ate something in the kitchen.'

Jakob had definitely been behaving entirely as expected at that point. Hosé might almost have smiled.

'Is anything missing?'

'What sort of thing?' demanded Cornelius impatiently.

'I don't know. Anything that might suggest why they left or where they went.'

The three went to different parts of the house. Cornelius's voice recalled them. 'The axe is not here.'

'Why would they want an axe?' Hosé frowned.

'The trees will fall down by themselves in a wind like this,' said Cornelius listening to the thrashing of the palms.

'Maybe one already did.'

'What?' Cornelius stared at him.

'Maybe one fell down and they wanted the axe to chop it up.'

'Why?'

'I have no idea,' said Hosé. 'Any other suggestions?'

The wind howled again. There was the crash of something hitting the roof and a thud outside.

'If they went out in this they could be anywhere.' Sand had sifted in around the door frame. 'It was already hard to see when we got back.' Cornelius lifted his head as a new sound reached their ears. Rain had started to fall, suddenly and in torrents.

'It'll wash the sand and mud down,' commented Hosé, 'But it will hardly improve visibility.'

There was another thump from somewhere and something slammed into the door.

'We have to go and find them,' said Cornelius.

Hosé chewed his lip. It was dangerous out there, but what bothered him more was that it would be almost impossible to know where to start looking.

Pieter suddenly held up a large hand. 'Listen!'

'What?' Cornelius turned.

There were more crashes and then unmistakeably another thump on the door.

Cornelius and Pieter grasped the bar and the door blew inwards almost knocking them aside.

Rabia was carried in on the blast nearly losing her footing. Her hair, now part grown, swung loose around her head. She had hitched her robe up and long scratches showed on her legs.

Behind her, just visible through the dense cascade, were Jakob and Thomas. They had threaded the handle of the axe under Isaac's armpits and were using it to carry him between them.

Hosé and Cornelius rushed out and took the insubstantial form, carrying it into the house. The Jew appeared lifeless.

'What happened?'

Rabia was kneeling beside Isaac. She did not reply.

Hosé turned impatiently to Jakob. 'What happened?' he repeated.

It was Thomas who got his breath back first. 'We had just finished eating, Jakob and I, when Rab came in. She said Isaac had been hit by a tree. We went to help.'

The girl was trying to rise.

'What on earth were you doing out there anyway?'

She was very pale under the grit and grime. 'Should get some rosemary; might help.' Her words came in strangely abbreviated phrases.

Suddenly she stopped, half way between kneeling and standing, then with a great effort finally straightened up. 'Fetch it,' she said, moving with great deliberation.

Jakob watched her go with a frown. 'She said they all walked to the village this morning. Faraj wanted Isaac to see her sister who had broken her arm. It had not healed properly.'

Thomas put in, 'Isaac had to reset it.'

'He gave the woman some poppy extract,' said Jakob 'And afterwards he said Faraj should stay until her sister woke again properly.'

'Why didn't Isaac stay himself?' Hosé was puzzled.

Jakob chewed his lip.

Rabia reappeared with a small bottle and sank down next to the Jew.

A pungent odour filled the air as she loosed the cork.

Isaac did not move.

'How did this happen?'

The girl drew a sharp breath. 'Half way home, a tree came down. Struck Isaac.'

She turned a drawn face to Pieter. 'Perhaps some water,' she said. The big seaman went off towards the kitchen.

'And he was knocked out?'

She was waving the bottle under Isaac's nose again, but with no more effect.

'Couldn't move the tree,' she answered, skipping the direct answer to his question. 'Came to fetch help.'

'We knew you were all busy with the boat,' said Jakob, 'And Rab said it was not far so we grabbed the axe and went with her.' He looked at his father a little apologetically. 'Perhaps we should have left you a note or something.'

'Yes, you should,' said the Lowlander with feeling.

'We managed to chop off some of the branches then we could lift the trunk,' said the boy undaunted. 'And we carried him home. He isn't very heavy.'

Hosé grasped the bowl of water from Pieter and splashed its contents over Isaac's face.

There was no response.

Rabia drew another sharp breath. Hosé looked at her aghast then down at the inert form of the physician and back again.

'Isn't there anything else we could try?'

She shook her head mutely.

She started to rise. 'Too late,' she muttered.

Hosé stared at the old physician willing him to open his eyes, then at the two brothers.

'Cornelius?' Hosé appealed.

The seaman shook his head.

'Pieter?'

The big Lowlander shrugged his broad shoulders. He knew many things of nature but not about this.

Hosé did not know about it either, but he had helped with lambing on the farms. That had to be something; didn't it?

Chapter 14

The English cloth merchant looked around at the busy city which lay enclosed securely in its great walls on the slope behind the bay, with the mountain of Montjuic to one side.

It was bounded by its two rivers. Even in the bright spring sunshine both were equally insalubrious. The thin mouth lifted in a rare smile as the man recalled their local names: the *Merdança* and the *Cagallel*, the Shit stream and the Turdbearer. That made them no different from most ports, even the ones on the western seaboard which had the benefit of high daily tides to remove some of the rubbish. And, in a way, he reflected, that was almost a mark of success: the inevitable consequence of human activity in manufacture and boatbuilding and above all in trade.

The city could claim to have the oldest stock exchange in Europe in the Llotja; and it was not just old, it prospered. He thought of the Pere Arbei near the waterfront with its huge single arcaded room and flat-beamed ceiling.

Nearby the chimes of the Capilla Marcus sounded. The man walked slowly down the Carrer Montcada looking at the palaces that lined both sides. They were not dissimilar to those that could be seen in a dozen other cities around the Middle Sea, but here they were on an altogether grander scale.

As he drew near the beach, he stopped and looked at the church that stood there. The Santa Maria del Mar, finished some hundred years earlier, looked uncannily like an ark turned sideways on to the harbour. But in a city founded on boat building and fishing that was not inappropriate, he thought.

He turned along the coast towards the massive battlemented watchtower that stood guard over the huge stone sheds that had been built about the same time as the church, but were of considerably more interest to the merchant than any holy edifice. The sheds housed the Drassanes, the boatyard of Barcelona.

It was some years since he had last visited the place, but the yards seemed as busy as ever and there were even one or two familiar faces among the building *mestre* and *menestral.* Yes, Ramon remembered the inquiries about a vessel being built for brothers from Antwerp; and yes, he was sure he would have known about them if they had been here.

And so, the main point of Clough's visit was dealt with in a matter of moments. Still the merchant talked to him a little longer; it was always good to gather news and information. How was trade?

The boatyard was busy, Ramon confirmed. 'There is always something to fix with a mill, a boat and a woman.' He grinned, but his face grew more sober as he added quietly, 'But politics are harder to mend and not so profitable.'

Clough looked at him enquiringly.

'For ten years, we suffered internal war as King Joan struggled to gain authority. For another ten years, he struggled to keep that position. For the past ten years, since he died, we have been ruled by a king and queen who have far bigger fish to catch than Catalonia.'

Clough nodded: King Ferdinand of Aragon and his Queen Isabella of Castile were intent on the elimination of the last Moors and Jews from the Iberian Peninsula. In spite of being brought up in a monastery Clough had little interest in religion, except, of course, when it impinged on trade. Wars could disrupt trade, as Ramon had implied, but they could also be a source of good deals, if one had the right goods to sell at the right time.

'And life for you?'

The question brought Clough's thoughts back. He shrugged.

'Dealing in some mighty fine woollen cloth these days,' suggested Ramon, who obviously did not limit his interests to boat building.

Clough nodded. Links with the flourishing cloth trade in Barcelona were a logical extension to the personal alliance he had already formed between Norwich and Antwerp, and the cargo he had brought with him on the *Marije* had been very well received.

'What will you load for the return voyage?'

It was an obvious query but Clough preferred to be the one asking the questions. 'I have various options,' he answered smoothly, 'But I will not be returning to the Lowlands just yet. Perhaps I will call here on the way back.' And before the man could ask "on the way back from where" he offered his hand. 'It has been good to see you again. I trust the boatbuilding will continue to flourish.'

'Must you leave so soon? I am sure my wife would be honoured to offer you supper.'

Clough forced a look of regret. 'Unfortunately, I already have an appointment.'

'Then when you return, I hope,' said Ramon.

'You are most kind,' Clough avoided committing himself.

His dinner was a good deal plainer than Ramon's wife would have produced, Clough reflected, as he tucked into the fish supplied by the waterfront wine shop, but then the company was a great deal more colourful.

His reflections turned to the main point of his trip. So, the damnable van Dammes had not been in Cadiz, nor here in Barcelona.

He swallowed the last of his meal with some of the local wine and looked around.

He regarded a trio near the door. They were talking in Catalan as many did in every port around the Sea, but these sounded as if it was their native tongue; locals then? He listened as they talked of the early season catches, the weather, the price of the new rope they had had to buy, the latest reports of pirate attacks from the coast of Africa.

Another couple of men joined the group. A heavily built woman followed them and thumped down an earthenware jug and mugs onto the table.

'It has not been so bad this year,' one of the newcomers added to the conversation. 'Last year some in Ciutat de Mallorca lost their whole family.'

'Like poor Aldonça,' put in his companion. 'They took her brother, her husband and her son.' He took a long drink from his mug. 'She is reduced to begging on the streets.' He shook his head.

Clough was now listening intently. He had no interest in the fortunes or misfortunes of Aldonça, but he did want news from Mallorca. He wanted it very badly.

He waited with growing impatience as the group continued to swap stories on other, much more mundane, matters. At last the three local men rose and left.

'May I?' Clough slid onto an empty stool and placed his own refilled jug on the table. 'Go ahead,' he invited the two men.

They needed no urging. They drained their mugs, wiping the red lees from their chins appreciatively.

'You are from Mallorca?'

The older man nodded.

'Some friends of mine were trading that way last year,' said Clough. 'I expected to see them back in Antwerp before the winter, but they did not return.' He paused and carefully drew a frown on his brow. 'They were sailing in a very old boat and I fear they may have met with some accident.'

'A very old boat from the Lowlands?' put in the younger man. 'An ancient cog?'

Clough did not need to pretend excitement. 'You have seen it?'

'There couldn't be more than one of those things around.' The younger man looked at his companion. 'What was her name?'

'*Elisabet* or something like that.'

'The *Liesabeta*?'

The two nodded.

'And she is safe and sound?' Clough inquired solicitously.

They laughed. 'Not anymore.'

'What?'

'She made a splendid spectacle at the Beltane bonfire.' The men laughed again at the memory. 'Master Joannot salvaged what he could of course, but that was not much.'

'And her crew?' inquired Clough. 'My friends,' he remembered to add.

'Oh, they sailed off in their new boat.'

'They had a new boat?'

The older man nodded, helping himself to more wine. 'Master Joannot had not even had time to finish the sea trials.'

'They left in a hurry?' Clough frowned. Could they have left to avoid Carter and Deluce? How could they have known?

His frown deepened. It did not make sense. Deluce's message had said they had found no trace. Even if the boat and the van Dammes had gone, a few simple inquiries would have provided the information that Clough himself had just learned.

'Perhaps they wanted to make the most of what was left of the season,' suggested the older man with a shrug.

'I really am most concerned about them,' Clough said earnestly. 'Tell me everything you can.'

He was suddenly aware of a big man at the next table who had been listening with undisguised curiosity.

'Yes?' Clough inquired a little irritably.

'There was a funny old boat in Nice the previous year.' The words were slightly slurred but their significance was crystal clear.

Clough looked at the Spanish soldier as he leaned over the side of the *Marije*. He was not at all sure Garcia had told him the truth, or certainly not the whole truth. Clough was certain he had lied about his origins; if the man was from the noble Garcia family in Tineo then Clough was the King of England. But it hardly mattered: other things Garcia had said had seemed enough to justify employing him, for the moment.

The two Mallorcans had given, in exchange for a generous payment, a very full account of the building of a Marsillian boat on Mallorca. They had described the Lowlanders who had commissioned her, the two boys and another man who had appeared with them.

The Englishman had listened with a sense of disbelief that matured into an icy rage. How the devil had that alliance come about?

After that information, the news of the "coincidental" disappearance of two men from a recently arrived northern caravel had made only too much sense.

Clough had the answer to his original question. He did not need to go to Mallorca to discover that the van Dammes had built themselves a new boat there (with what Clough regarded as his money) and had sailed away in it.

But now there was the question of where had they gone. Where might Clough find the answer to that one?

He nodded at the approaching coast. 'We'll be in Nice before nightfall,' he said to the Spaniard. He continued dryly, 'I suspect it would be better if you did not show your face. Am I right?'

Garcia de Tineo swore loudly but nodded his head.

'I'll make sure you are well provided for aboard,' promised Clough. 'And we shall not be staying long.' He could not go to the obvious source of information; he had no wish whatever to renew his acquaintance with the Grimaldo hag. But it should still be easy enough to learn what he wanted to know, elsewhere.

His confidence had been ill placed.

The wine shop whore had started off promisingly then suddenly closed up as tight as an oyster. He cursed silently to himself, smiled thinly and took himself off to the next wine shop.

And the next.

And another.

By the end of the evening he had gleaned only a few straws. He snorted contemptuously at the name of the new Marsillian. Couldn't Cornelius think of anything more original than the name of his long dead wife? The boat had indeed been to Nice the previous year. The two brothers had been aboard and the two boys; no sign of the other man. They had left again. Nobody seemed to know their destination.

Clough angrily made his way back on board.

He watched the harlot as she left the wine shop. Now why would she be up so early? He followed her at a distance as she made her way along the waterfront to one of the larger warehouses, which he was almost sure was the Grimaldo go-down and office.

The woman knocked on the door. A clerk opened it.

Clough was too far away to hear what was said but there were angry words then the clerk slammed the door.

The woman looked around her and Clough ducked back out of sight. When he put his head around the corner again, he could see her leaning against a nearby building. He turned down an alley, picked his way through the stinking rubbish at the back of the next warehouse and slid quietly towards the street again.

He looked out cautiously. The woman was still there and he was much closer to her now.

What was she waiting for?

The answer was not long in arriving. Clough had enough time to recognise the curvaceous figure, somewhat fuller than it had been, but still remarkable. He did not have the time or inclination to inspect her face. He pulled back again, ducking down behind a mound of particularly foul matter.

'Signora, a word with you.' That was the whore.

'Yes?' There was mild curiosity. 'Who are you?'

'My name is Marianne'

'Do I know you?'

The whore gave a short laugh. 'But I know you.'

'That is hardly surprising,' said Annette coolly. 'But what are you doing here?'

'I have something to tell you.' The whore paused. 'In private.'

There was a silence, then sharp orders and footsteps as the two men servants walked a little way away.

'Well what is it?'

'Something I am sure you would want to know.'

'What?'

'It would be worth something to you.'

There was that tinkling laugh and the sound of coins.

'That is not much.'

'There will be more, if it really *is* interesting.'

There was a pause, then the whore said a little reluctantly. 'Last night there was a man in the wine shop.'

'I'm sure there are always lots of men there.'

'This man was a stranger. At least not a total stranger; he was here some years ago.'

'And?' Clough could hear the growing interest in Annette's voice.

'Last time he was here he did not frequent the wine shops. He was a fêted guest at the palace.'

Clough could hear the intake of breath. 'Who was it?'

There was another pause and the sound of more coins.

'It is worth more than that.'

'There! Now who are you talking about?'

'The English merchant who was to have had your hand in marriage.'

There was a most unladylike expletive. It was almost flattering. 'What was he doing?'

'Asking questions.'

There was another oath. 'Must I drag every word out of you?'

'About those Lowlanders who were here last year.'

There was a hiss then a long silence. 'What did you tell him?'

'Nothing.'

'Why not? Did he not offer you enough coin?' Annette scoffed.

'Because he was asking about someone else as well,' came the reluctant answer.

'Who?'

'Your clerk.'

'Rab?' There was considerable anxiety in the word.

'No,' said the whore. 'Hosé.' The word was said with a note of defiance.

Clough clenched his fists. He was not surprised to hear the name but it still made him angry.

'Oh,' said Annette. 'And you did not want to talk about Hosé?'

There was another pause. 'I would not like to get him into trouble.'

'And you think the Englishman meant trouble?'

'He has strange eyes.'

'I know what you mean,' said Annette with feeling. There was the sound of footsteps as she paced along the roadway and back. 'So, you told him nothing.' It was more of a statement than a question. 'Although he will try and ask others no doubt. Well we'll see about that.' She turned again. 'You did well to come and tell me.'

Clough finally made it back to the boat and changed his filthy clothes.

They matched his humour, he thought with a scowl.

'So, you learned what you wanted?'

The Englishman regarded the soldier icily. No, he had not. He had learned nothing he did not already know or could have guessed and, unless he was very much mistaken, it would only be a short time before a company of Grimaldo men-at-arms appeared at the harbour to prevent him finding out more.

'Who is Rab?' He threw out the question.

The silence finally registered and he turned.

'Is there something you would like to tell me?' he inquired softly.

It had taken a long time but Clough thought he had cajoled or forced most of the story out of the reluctant Spaniard.

He was not bothered by the man's morals, or lack of them. Such things had long ceased to count in his view of life, if indeed they ever had. His main interest, as always, was how they might be used to Clough's advantage and this tale showed considerable potential for that; considerable potential.

He would enjoy working out the best options.

The boat began to move through the water as she left the port.

'What is our destination, *Meneer*?'

Clough had been considering that.

'Genoa, I think,' he replied. Someone recalled the Jew boarding a Genoese boat. And Clough thought it worth visiting La Superba anyway: to test the waters on other matters.

At Genoa Clough found one or two people who thought they remembered the *Santa Giovanna* returning from a trip to Nice a couple of seasons ago. Nobody was certain and nobody remembered seeing anyone of Isaac's description.

The seamen in the wine shops of Genoa obviously knew their boats. Clough threw out another query. It produced half an answer: the *Katrin* had indeed been there, the previous year. However, nobody seemed to know where she had been bound when she left.

Clough scowled in frustration. Still, if she was recognisable in Genoa, the *Katrin* would be equally noticed in any other port. He would send inquiries all around the Middle Sea. Sooner or later he would get news.

He chewed over his other findings. Was it simply coincidence that the Jew and the Lowlanders had both headed for Genoa? It had not been at the same time and, in any case, what connection could there be between them?

The answer to that was as troubling as it was obvious: the "clerk". He was certainly involved with the Jew and had apparently been on Mallorca with the van Dammes.

Clough thought over that for some time.

He let his mind turn to the equally unsolved puzzle of why the Jew and the "clerk" had separated. Where had the Hebrew been going?

He shook his head. Too many questions.

What did he know for sure? There was one thing certain at least: sooner or later the "clerk" would make his way to Rome, since that was where the Prince now was.

Clough himself would like to go to Rome, but he recalled with the familiar angry resentment that he had first to re-establish his financial security and that lay in Antwerp.

And there were still the other consequences of that wretched Medici business. Although times were uncertain in Florence its ruling family still had considerable power. Did it stretch as far as Rome these days?

He might at least get a definite answer on that. Lorenzo Spinola could surely give him the latest news.

Spinola had provided some very useful information.

Clough chewed over the unpalatable part: it would be unwise yet for the Englishman to venture into either Florence or Rome, although there was a distinct hint that conditions were changing.

His thoughts returned to the "clerk", who had managed to thwart at least one of Clough's attempts to get his hands on the Prince and ruined Clough financially by the denouncement to the Medici bank. For those things alone Clough wanted redress. Now it seemed certain the man was aiding the van Damme brothers, who were sailing around the Middle Sea in a substantial part of Clough's capital assets.

At present, Clough could not follow him to Rome, but the talk with Spinola had suggested an alternative idea.

Chapter 15

End Sept 1490

Of course, it was nothing like lambing.

Hosé looked at Rabia with considerable respect.

Relief and, yes, exhilaration were coursing through him. Events had unfolded with an intensity and speed that had left him with a feeling not unlike that after the battle at Yenişehir.

Rabia moved cautiously. For a moment she regarded the wizened features of the baby, then lifted her dark eyes. 'It seems we have both survived,' she said.

Hosé smiled ruefully.

'What?'

'I was thinking of sheep.'

'Sheep?'

'My only previous experience of the birthing process!'

She stared at him. 'Sheep?' she repeated.

'When I lived on the farms, I worked a lot with the sheep. I liked them, even though they were so stupid and got themselves into no end of unnecessary trouble.' He was lost for a moment in his memories and missed the glint in her eyes. 'If there is a difficult way of lambing, a sheep will surely find it.' He looked at his broad hands which had been considerably smaller then. Thank God Rabia had had no such difficulties.

'So, to you I am like a troublesome ewe?'

He looked up quickly. 'Of course not.' Nothing like. He recalled how remarkably she had managed. He opened his mouth and shut it again as he met her hostile gaze.

He looked at the child instead. 'He wants to suckle.'

She watched the tiny questing mouth but made no move.

'He needs encouragement,' he urged her. 'Now.'

'Is that what you did with the lambs?'

He was sorry he had mentioned sheep. 'The ewe usually manages that bit quite well for herself,' he said, more sharply than he had intended.

He watched as she still hesitated. 'I know you never wanted this child,' he said. 'He has been forced upon you by Garcia, and,' he admitted, 'In a way by me. I have tried to help up till now and I will do whatever I can for the child for the future, but right now I cannot offer him what he needs. You have to do that.'

'It could go to a wet-nurse,' she said.

He shook his head. 'It will be hours before it will be safe to find one.' The storm was still raging outside. 'He,' he emphasised the word slightly, 'Needs sustenance before that.'

He dipped his little finger into the pitcher of drinking water and offered it. The baby's eyes remained closed but his mouth reacted immediately.

'He needs more than water.'

Rab was silent. She could hardly gainsay that.

'He was fathered by Garcia,' Hosé felt his way, 'But he is somebody different. I owe my father my body but I go my own way in life. You may resemble your mother but you are not her.' He stopped.

She was very still.

The baby began to grizzle.

She lifted him slightly but made no move to feed him.

'Remember what Annette said? When you did not want to treat my knee?'

She looked at him resentfully.

'You managed that,' he said. 'You faced your fears.' He paused uncertainly.

She was silent.

'What is it you really fear?' he asked.

She stared for a long time at the far wall and the baby's mewling grew louder. She did not seem to notice.

Hosé ripped a piece of cloth and soaked it in water. The baby sucked at it eagerly. Not wine this time, he thought, but it worked temporarily. The cries gave way to a soft snuffling.

She looked down. 'Did you do that for the lambs too?'

'No, for my brother,' he said shortly.

'You have a brother?'

'I had.'

She looked at him curiously. 'What happened to him?'

Why did everyone ask that question? 'I don't know.'

She was surprised by the tone of his voice.

'What would Isaac say to you now, if he could?' Hosé changed the subject.

'How is he?' she avoided answering.

'Cornelius thinks his colour is better.'

'Good,' she said.

'And what would he want to hear, when he comes round?' Hosé persisted.

'I know that!' she said. 'But I can't, not even for Isaac.'

'Can't? Won't? What are you afraid of? That you might actually grow fond of the child?'

She stared at him. 'I'll never…..' She stopped. 'It's not that.' She lowered her eyes. 'I don't think I could bear it,' she muttered. A shudder shook her body.

'Listen,' he said. 'I have an idea how Garcia treated you.' Marianne had been pretty explicit.

'You have no idea!' she snapped. 'How could you? You're a man.'

'Obviously! And because of that I know how it should be.'

She glared at him.

'Did your father treat your mother badly?' He was clutching at straws. He had no idea; anyway, intimacies would have been kept private.

But her face softened. 'Of course not.' She was silent again for some time. The baby was beginning to stir again.

'How can I not think of Garcia every time his getting touches me?' she asked finally.

So, that was it. Hardly surprising.

'What will his name be?'

She stared. 'I hadn't thought.'

'Perhaps if you give him his name it will help you see him as his own person.'

She nodded, but without conviction. 'What name should it be?' She looked at him curiously. 'What is your name? Your proper name?'

He almost smiled at the way she phrased it, but it was a question better not answered; not at this moment anyway.

He shook his head. 'He does not have to have my name,' he prevented her interruption, 'Any more than he has to have Garcia's. He needs a good name of his own.'

She pondered this and he was glad she did not pursue her question.

'But it would be alright to give him the name of a good man, wouldn't it? It would give him an example to live up to.'

'Of course.'

She looked down at the baby. 'Then he will be Ishaq,' she said. The child chose that moment to open his gummy mouth and bawl.

Hosé smiled and Rabia lifted the baby tentatively.

Hosé watched as girl and child struggled together.

'I can't,' she said over Ishaq's roar.

Hosé's hand engulfed the small head and firmly guided Ishaq's outraged red face. There were a couple of muffled protests then the baby found what it needed.

Rabia looked down with terrible fascination as the tiny jaws worked furiously.

'I think the others would like to meet Ishaq,' Hosé said later. He had said the traditional prayer and the baby lay quiet. 'Would that be all right?'

'Of course.'

Hosé reached to take the child.

Rabia shook her head. 'I'll bring him.'

Hosé stopped. 'You should rest.'

'Why? Do the ewes rest after lambing?'

'Don't be silly.' She must see there were limits to the analogy.

'I'm not,' she said. 'I feel like stretching my legs.'

He looked and saw she was serious. He shrugged and offered her a hand.

She ignored it and rose a little awkwardly to her feet.

'It might be better ....' He began.

'No, really. It just feels a bit funny; the balance is different.'

Well it would be, he supposed.

She took a breath, shifted the baby to her other arm and walked across the room.

Jakob greeted them warily. The pregnancy had already put a distance between him and Rabia; that had been a step in life that he could not follow. Now the birth emphasised the difference.

Thomas stood back a little, looking appraisingly at this new being with its perfect but tiny fingers, its mop of black hair and snub nose. Hosé could almost see him making a mental list.

Cornelius turned and came towards them. He regarded the child for some time, laid a tentative and calloused finger into the little fist and grinned as it was seized.

'His name is Ishaq,' Rabia said carefully.

There was a laugh.

Hosé stood stock still. 'Isaac?'

The physician's eyes were open and although there was a deep crease of pain on his forehead he was alert.

Hosé sank to knees beside the Jew. 'Isaac?' he said again.

Isaac groped weakly with one hand.

'Where is his tablet?' Hosé looked at Jakob.

Rabia moved close and the old Hebrew managed a smile. He pointed at the child with a gnarled finger. She held out Ishaq for his inspection.

The bony finger traced the features and lifted the tiny fists then pointed at Rabia making a query sign.

'I'm fine,' she said.

Isaac reached for the tablet Jakob had brought, but could not form the letters.

'Later,' said Hosé. 'You can ask all the questions you want, later.'

'How is your head?' asked Rabia. 'Here,' she thrust the baby at Thomas.

Thomas took the child as if it was an egg, a very fragile egg.

'No,' said Jakob impatiently, 'Not like that.'

'So, you are an expert?' demanded Thomas with unusual heat.

'Cornelius,' Hosé said. 'You must know at least that much!' He turned his head. 'What do you think?' he asked Rabia, looking back at the Jew.

Her fingers moved over the physician's skull. There was a sizeable lump on one temple, colouring fast, but she did not think it was too bad.

He tried to shake his head then stopped, pointing his finger instead.

'Is the pain inside your head?'

The finger assented.

She hesitated. 'Your memory?' she queried.

Isaac stared at her for a moment then closed his eyes.

She looked at Hosé. 'It's possible,' she said. 'He said it is rare but ……'

'Isaac is a very rare creature,' Hosé put in with feeling.

A bony finger wagged feebly at him but the sunken eyes stayed shut.

Faraj regarded Hosé in shocked silence.

It was a good thing she did not know the rest of it, he thought. She assumed Isaac had assisted in the delivery and nobody had corrected her.

The physician had more or less been back on his feet by the time the woman returned to the menzel with the end of the storm. His headaches were also improving. Unlike his temper, reflected Hosé sourly.

'But it is not right.' The woman looked at him. 'A husband removes himself at this time.'

'Not this one,' he replied shortly.

'If you are there I cannot sleep with your wife,' she said. 'To assist her with the child in the night.'

'We …..she can manage,' he said. 'How is your sister?'

Faraj looked troubled. 'She is suffering,' she admitted.

'She needs your help?'

'But, I suppose,' she said reluctantly, 'Your wife will keep quietly to the house for the next weeks and the physician will take good care of her.'

The second one of her assumptions was certain, he thought. He had a lot more doubts about the first. However, he nodded.

'Perhaps I could come over for part of each day,' she brightened with the thought.

That would be welcome. Jakob's bargaining skills at the market were only slightly better than Thomas's efforts in the kitchen. As for laundry, a baby added a dimension that Hosé would not have believed possible.

The bony fingers touched Hosé's arm. He reluctantly looked at the Jew.

We need to talk.

Hosé could think of many other things he needed to do more. 'The van Dammes are getting the *Katrin* ready to sail. I promised to help them.'

They have plenty of help. Isaac pointed at the Marsillian. She had come through the storm with remarkably little damage and now they were beginning to stock her. Jakob had just rowed out with more supplies and these were being hauled on board.

Another figure was in the skiff. Hosé narrowed his eyes and stared across the shining water of the lagoon.

She will be all right, Isaac scribbled. She is hardly more than a child herself. She needs to be active.

Hosé nodded. His eyes returned to the boat.

And the baby will be safe enough. That was your main worry, wasn't it?

Hosé made an impatient gesture. He hated it when the Jew could read him so easily.

Isaac's fingers were insistent. You think they will not all care for him?

Hosé was silent.

The Hebrew cleaned his tablet. The more she can do for herself the less she will resent the child.

Hosé frowned at the words.

But, the Jew wrote again, I think that is not so much of a problem now.

Hosé still did not commit his thoughts to words.

You have achieved much.

Hosé shrugged. 'Does your head hurt?' The gaunt face was pinched.

Isaac tried to smooth the lines away with his fingers. The return of memory is remarkably painful, he wrote with a grimace. Both physically and otherwise.

Hosé stared at him.

That is surprising is it not? The stylus paused. At first in the cloister I worried and worried about who I was, where I had been going, what I had been doing. Then as the weeks passed and I could recall nothing I began to accept that I had no past and could plan no future; all I had was the present. And, you know, I enjoyed that: every day with no worries, only endless hours of study or work in the garden.

Isaac stopped. He looked up at Hosé. Or conversation with the most kind and cultured people.

'Until I arrived?'

I think you fitted into the company remarkably well.

Hosé looked at the words.

Almost like part of the family.

Hosé did not respond.

Are you…? The Jew erased the words. Were you part of the family? Isaac looked at him quizzically.

Hosé shrugged.

The Jew chewed the end of his stylus for a few moments. Why did the Chief White Eunuch not point out to the Sultan that you were from the Genoese community in Caffa?

Because Hosé had initially been separated from his peers and when he had become a kul saw no reason to correct the Chief White Eunuch's misapprehension. It had seemed an insignificant detail in the much greater need to keep his polyglot skills from notice.

Isaac persisted. Were you a Spinola once?

'No.'

So, which family did you belong to?

Hosé hesitated.

I do not command an answer.

Hosé pulled a face.

I think we have moved beyond that. You have had to take command of yourself. And that is even harder, is it not?

Hosé nodded.

And yet that is the true test. To do something because it is ordered is one thing, to do it out of choice is much more.

Hosé was silent.

You have had difficult choices to make these last months. The Jew looked at him. Like marrying Rabia.

'There was nothing else to do. And anyway, it is not a real marriage.' He flushed. 'She is hardly more than a child. You said so yourself.'

And you can repudiate it any time? Isaac looked quizzical.

A husband did not have to give reasons for divorcing his wife. Isaac knew that. Hosé nodded.

And where would that leave her?

Hosé would deal with that situation when it arose.

A kul has no family; his only loyalty is to the Sultan.

Hosé winced as his words were quoted back at him.

That is why a kul is forbidden to marry.

Hosé traced a pattern in the white sand with a brown foot. 'It does not change my loyalty to the Sultan.'

And you will explain that to him?

Hosé said quietly. 'I sometimes wonder if I will ever return to Islambul. Who knows what will happen?' He looked the Jew in the eye. 'But if it came to it I would plead my cause with a clear conscience.'

The Hebrew nodded. And the child?

'He is no blood of mine.'

So why are you so protective of him? We have established that it is not out of any romantic feelings for Rabia.

'Hardly.'

Then why? Isaac insisted. He looked intently at the younger man. Out of obligation to what I asked of you.

Hosé moved uncomfortably. 'Which leads to another question doesn't it? Why are you so involved with the girl? Is it to do with your wife?'

Isaac shook his head. No, that was a false trail.

'What was her name incidentally?'

Leah. The Jew erased the name quickly. No, Rabia has nothing to do with her. He paused. She is the granddaughter of a man I knew well when I studied in Fez.

'Does she know this?' Hosé asked.

The Jew nodded. We realised it when we talked of the town and people we knew there.

'What happened to her?'

Isaac looked at him. She has not told you?

'She talked of a Turk called Kara Hasan.' Hosé pulled a face.

Isaac acknowledged the irony.

'She has not explained what happened or how she met Garcia de Tineo.' He waited curiously.

But Isaac shook his head. I think it is not my part to tell of that. She will tell you herself.

Not that it really made any difference.

Isaac regarded him for some time. Finally, he wrote. Tell me about Isabella.

Hosé glared at him but the question was inevitable.

Isaac smiled a little sadly. You see why my head hurts?

Hosé sighed. 'You no doubt now remember about the dragoman.'

Isaac remembered all right.

'His second wife was Caterina Sforza. Isabella is her sister.'

Hosé nodded.

And Matteo?

'Isabella virtually brought him up in his early years. She regards him like a younger brother, although they are not related. He is a Montefeltro, the bastard son of a bastard grandson.'

Isaac looked at him sharply. Was that part of your concern for Ishaq?

'Being a supposed Grimaldo bastard for the past years has made me think,' Hosé admitted.

And?

'And nothing,' Hosé replied a little too quickly.

And Battista? Isabella called her a niece. The daughter of Caterina?

'Born after Caterina fled from Caffa,' Hosé confirmed.

So, fathered by the dragoman, Isaac wrote. Your half-sister in fact.

Hosé shrugged.

And which family did the dragoman belong to?

'He was Guido Lomellino.'

The same family as Gianmaria?

'But no blood relation.'

Isaac frowned.

'Gianmaria's family was adopted into the Albergo because his uncle was remarkably successful at producing olive oil.' Hosé half smiled, 'A very valuable asset to any merchant family.'

Isaac nodded. The marriage of Battista and Gianmaria makes very good sense then, from the Albergo's point of view. Their child will continue the family, assuming Oberto Spinola cannot do so. Hosé avoided the Jew's gaze. It makes more sense than Gianmaria marrying Annette! The bony hand paused. Rabia tells me you heard from Nice. It is good news.

Hosé agreed. He added a few of the other things about Nice. Nice was a much safer subject.

Isaac waited until he had finished. And Isabella?

Hosé drew a sharp breath. The old devil was persistent.

The Jew looked inquiringly. Did she recognise you?

Hosé obliterated the lines he had drawn in the sand with his toe. 'Yes.'

Isaac stared at him. But not her husband?

Hosé shook his head. 'I was only in Oberto's company briefly.'

Isaac chewed the end of the stylus. She would not betray you, of course.

Of course not.

He looked at Hosé again. Was there something between you?

'Would you believe that of her?'

The Jew shook his head. I know she is a most honourable woman. But, he paused, she also longs to give Oberto a child.

'I have always held 'Bella in the greatest respect,' Hosé said evenly. 'Our meeting again has not changed that.' He swallowed. 'Our communion is of the soul and the mind, not the body.'

Isaac studied him.

'That is the truth.'

I don't doubt it. But how much of the truth?

'As much as you need!'

Isaac nodded. You didn't by any chance get news from her, when you were in Tunis?

Hosé made an exasperated sound. 'I suppose you don't command an answer to that either?'

The Jew grinned. But I would be interested! He listened as Hosé gave him the facts. So, the child is another Guido Lomellino?

'The name was Battista's choice,' said Hosé tersely.

Will her father like that?

Hosé shrugged.

You have informed him?

Hosé nodded. 'I wrote to him.' He added quickly, 'I do not want any connection with him, as my father. He belongs to another part of my life. But we must work together for the Sultan.'

And this news will help the Sultan?

'Of course not!' Hosé spotted the glint in the Jew's eyes too late. 'If you must know I wrote to him mainly so he could look out for you.'

Me?

'At the time, it seemed as if you would return to Islambul without your memory. You would have been easy prey for the Vizier.'

Isaac accepted that. An interesting situation, he commented.

That was one way of putting it.

Is there anything else I would be interested to know? Isaac's deep-sunk eyes gleamed.

Hosé reached inside his shirt. 'Isabella forwarded another letter.' He passed it to the Jew.

Isaac looked at it. From the Topkapi? He read for some time, his face grave. His finger pointed to one page: Pope Innocent had written to the kings of Europe saying that Prince Cem had promised to withdraw from Constantinople and all of Rumelia, if he was reinstated as Sultan.

Hosé nodded. 'It might just be enough to persuade the Christian sovereigns to support the Pope's ambitions.'

The Jew frowned. The Sultan fears so.

'But still he cannot accept the idea of removing his brother from this earthly tangle.'

Can you think it would?

Hosé shook his head. The Sultan was dedicated to the good of the empire and the people in it, but his personal affection for his younger brother was unwavering. 'Will the Pope have the support of the Knights?'

Isaac shrugged. D'Aubusson sold the Prince to the Pope for a cardinalate. He no longer holds the hostage.

'Although de Blanchefort and some of the other Knights still accompany the Prince.' Hosé told the Jew what he knew of the Prince's new life in Rome.

Isaac pondered that. The Knights have been paid handsomely by the Sultan for years to keep the Prince "safe". They have used much of the money to fortify their base on Rhodes. Power has been kept evenly balanced. Perhaps d'Aubusson now feels it is time to try and tip the balance in his favour.

'Could it happen?'

That would depend largely on how much other support the Pope can gather.

'And on having the Prince to put up as a figurehead.' Hosé could not resist.

Isaac ignored the bait. You will go to Rome.

Hosé should have been there a long time ago.

When?

'When I have made arrangements for you,' Hosé replied. 'Put you on a boat that is guaranteed this time to go directly to Islambul.' He looked out at the *Katrin*.

Isaac followed his gaze and raised a grizzled eyebrow. They are willing to sail that way?

Hosé smiled. 'Jakob and Thomas were delighted at the suggestion.'

And Cornelius?

'Not exactly delighted,' admitted Hosé, 'But he was persuaded in the end.' The Lowlander had driven a hard bargain.

Isaac nodded. And Rabia and the child?

Hosé frowned. 'There are various options.' Not very many. 'I haven't decided yet.'

You haven't decided? What does she think?

Hosé stared at him.

'What?' Hosé turned.

'We need to talk.' The girl repeated.

He scowled. He had already heard those words once too often that day.

She hesitated at the look on his face. 'The *Katrin* will sail soon,' she persisted. 'And you will go to Rome.' She looked over at where the baby lay, snuffling a little. 'And we both survived.' She looked up at him, 'There *is* a bridge to be crossed.'

'Ishaq is just going off to sleep.'

She made an impatient noise. 'Then we could talk somewhere else.'

'Tomorrow,' he said.

'No!'

'Sh,' he said, although the child now lay still.

'Please,' she said with an obvious effort.

He brought his eyes back from the baby to the girl. He flushed slightly. She should not have to beg.

Chapter 16

The sand remained warm beneath their feet. The sun had dropped out of sight but colour still filled the sky. In the bay the *Katrin* rode peacefully at anchor, and from further out voices of fishermen carried across the water as they set about their night's work.

Hosé indicated the *Katrin's* skiff which was drawn up the beach. Rabia sat with her back to the boards and clasped her hands around her knees.

He squatted down nearby, not quite facing her.

There was an uncomfortable silence.

'I wish it did not have to change,' she said vehemently. 'It is nice here, with Isaac, Jakob, Thomas, Pieter, Cornelius.'

He noted the order with interest. 'And Ishaq?'

She looked at him. 'Yes,' she said quietly. 'Even Ishaq.' She looked out towards the Marsillian for some time. She opened her mouth then swallowed. 'It is difficult sometimes,' she said eventually. 'Always having to think about him and do things for him.' She let sand dribble between her fingers. 'But it's strange.'

Hosé waited.

'I've got used to having him around. Like now, sitting here without him seems odd. I wonder if he is all right, if he has woken up.'

'They know where to find us.'

She nodded. 'He smiled today,' she said. 'Really smiled.' She paused. 'It was like a gift, the only thing he could offer.'

Hosé was sorry he had missed it.

'And there was something else. For a moment, he looked so much like my grandfather.' She looked up. 'But you were right.'

He was glad to hear he had got something correct.

'There are glimpses of other people.' She hesitated. 'Even Garcia.' She hurried past the name, 'But Ishaq is definitely himself. How can that be? At just a few weeks?'

'God is great.'

She looked at him. 'You are a strange man.'

Hosé shrugged. He was not sure he wanted her to expand on that.

'In Nice you were so....' She stopped. 'But here it is different I suppose.' She half found the answer to her own question.

'Yes, it is different living in the Dar al-Islam,' he said with feeling.

'I wouldn't have expected that to mean so much...'

'To a Turk?' he finished for her.

She avoided his eye but nodded. 'In Rome,' she said, 'You will be back in the Dar al-Harb.' She looked at him curiously.

'It is necessary,' he said shortly.

There was a silence again.

'What about me and Ishaq?' she said finally.

Hosé watched the now darkening sky. 'Do you have family? In Fez or anywhere?'

She stared out at the sea. 'What decent family would want a whore?'

'Whore? That is a harsh word.'

'It is the right word,' she said bitterly.

'Not if you were compelled.'

She was quiet.

'God forgives and is merciful. Should a family do less?' He waved away an insect. 'Did they throw you out because of Kara Hasan?'

'No,' she muttered.

'Then what happened?'

The words were low. 'I couldn't go back.'

'But it was not your fault.'

She sniffed.

'How old were you?' She was hardly more than a child now.

'Old enough, for some men.'

'Could you tell me about it?'

'What concern is it of yours?'

'You and Ishaq *are* my concern, in case you hadn't noticed.' Perhaps he should not have added the second part, but she looked at him and nodded slowly. 'Tell me about your family,' he said quietly. 'About the grandfather Isaac knew, about your parents.'

'My grandfather,' she began then stopped, as if the memory was painful. She took a breath and started again. 'My grandfather was a scholar. In his youth, he even studied with Ibn Khaldun.'

'Ibn Khaldun?' Hosé tried to recall where he had heard the name.

'Have you read his Kitab al-Ibar?'

Hosé frowned; the title meant nothing to him. 'Ibn Khaldun?' he repeated to himself.

'One of the greatest historians of all time.'

Then Hosé remembered: *The names of perfumes, fruits, birds, or flowers to indicate the letter or forms different from the accepted forms of the letters....* Had that been the second lesson on ciphers, after the Book of Jeremiah? Or had that been Julius Caesar? 'Isaac certainly knows his work,' he said dryly. 'It was not only history Ibn Khaldun wrote about.'

She looked at him curiously.

'Tables of letter frequencies.'

It was her turn to frown. 'Annette talked of those.'

'No doubt Isaac included those in her education too.' He peered at her. 'Did he not teach you about ciphers?'

She shook her head. 'I wanted to learn other things from him.'

'Tell me about the Kitab al-Ibar.'

She thought for a moment, clearing more recent events from her mind. 'It is a history of the world. It took him all his life and there are many volumes, including his introduction on Muqaddima.'

'Muqaddima?'

'Ibn Khaldun studied and wrote about all the things that different peoples have done, including the old Romans, and he saw a pattern in how certain parts of the world and their peoples have been powerful and prospered at certain times, then fallen to other peoples and cultures.'

Hosé thought about that. He had a hazy idea about the old Roman Empire, he knew a bit about the empire of Byzantium, he knew considerably more about the Ottomans. His eyes narrowed. 'What else did he say?'

She told him what she remembered. 'He spent the last twenty years of his life in Cairo,' she concluded. 'There was too much fighting in Morocco. He couldn't find the peace to go on with his work.'

That would have been when Isaac returned to Córdoba.

'There are still great scholars working in Egypt,' she said. 'My mother talked of Jalal al-Suyuti. He has also written a history: not of the whole world, just of Egypt. But he claims that his books are read in all the countries from Syria to Takrur.'

'So, your grandfather studied history?' He could barely see her features by now, but he sensed she was more at ease.

She replied promptly. 'My grandfather was a doctor.'

'Ah.'

'He studied the writings of the great Arab physicians, he made many discoveries himself, he taught the students in Fez.' She grasped another memory. 'At the Qarawiyyin mosque or at the Bu Inaniyya madrasa.' She stopped again. 'Of course, he could not teach me there because I was a girl.' There was regret in her voice. 'But at home he would answer my questions.'

'And your father followed the same profession?'

'No, he was a trader.'

Hosé's eyes narrowed.

'He followed his uncle. He traded the routes between Fez and Cairo.'

'Was your mother from Cairo?'

'Why do you ask?'

'Your colouring.' She was dark but not that dark.

'Yes,' she said, 'My mother came from Egypt.' Another short painful silence. 'From a family where there were many learned women, well respected for their writing skills and their devotion.' She added a little defiantly, 'She said there was no impropriety in a woman learning for *whatever is in heaven and earth celebrates the praise of Allah.*'

Hosé half smiled to himself. It was a phrase he often pondered. 'And she taught you?'

The girl nodded.

'And your father?' he guessed, 'Did he also teach you?' Rabia had been able to make herself very useful to Annette and to the family business.

She nodded again. She had been the only child born of her parents' marriage. Her mother, she said, had sometimes suggested that Rabia's father should take a second wife who might provide the sons that were lacking, but he had kept putting off the matter. He had taken great pride in his daughter and he loved his wife dearly.

Hosé was glad that the girl had known that.

Rabia continued quickly. 'My mother said there was no reason for her to stay at home with just me. She would much rather travel with my father. She loved to see different places, to learn new things and she said I should learn about them too.' She added evenly, 'So that one day I would be a help to my husband.'

Hosé grimaced. 'So, you often went with your father when he traded. Is that how you came to be in Oran?'

She nodded. 'We had gone to Oran before with him. Some said it was not safe, there were rumours of pirates, but my father said we would not go near the coast.'

Hosé watched as the stars began to glitter overhead. Just above the dark silhouettes of the palms a half moon was rising.

'The pirates had somehow heard of our caravan. They came inland and lay in wait.' She hugged her knees more tightly. 'My father's men fought bravely but the Turks,' her voice shook, 'Slaughtered everyone.'

'But not you.' Even to him that sounded crass.

'It would have been better if they had,' she said in little more than a whisper. 'What was there left worth living for?'

He had no answer to that.

'My parents were dead and my grandfather was in Fez. How could I ever get there? And if I did, how could I ask him to accept me, after what had happened?'

'Perhaps you misjudge him.'

'No,' she said, 'My grandfather is a good man. That is part of it. He would have shown charity. But then what? I would have been kept in seclusion, protected from public opinion.' She continued in a flat voice. 'The man I was supposed to marry, when I reached womanhood, a fellow trader of my father's, would not have wanted me, nor any other man.'

'Your status is different now.'

He could just see the shrug of her shoulders.

'But you are going to Rome. You would not accompany me to Fez.'

That of course was true.

'It would seem a fantastical tale.' She paused. 'They would find it hard enough to accept that I was even still alive, never mind married; to some unknown and absent man! How should I answer questions about you?'

That was undoubtedly a problem: the truth would not do. She was probably right. Fez would not provide the solution.

'How did you end up in Nice?'

'For half a year Kara Hasan kept me on his boat as they raided up and down the coast.'

Hosé listened as she spoke about the killings and burnings, the celebrations of success, the nights in the suffocating heat of the small cabin. He was not deceived by the flatness of her voice.

'Then they returned to Oran and I managed to get ashore. They were so drunk nobody noticed. I found a Genoese seaman who was willing to take me, for a price.'

She would have had only one currency.

'He was not a bad man,' she added. 'Compared to Hasan.'

Hosé flinched.

'At the end of the season he put into Nice.'

'What happened?'

'He got into a fight with Garcia de Tineo.'

A professional soldier.

'Garcia killed him and took me.' She stopped for a moment. 'I thought Kara Hasan was as bad as it could be. I was wrong.' Her voice dropped. 'By the time Garcia had finished, I thought I would die. I think he thought the same, because he dragged me into an alley and left me.'

'An alley near the Grimaldo warehouse?' guessed Hosé.

She nodded. 'Isaac found me.' Her eyes gleamed for a moment in the darkness. 'He said he could have earned a good living as a tailor.'

Hosé knew of the Jew's deftness with a needle but he could not share her grim humour.

'He took care of me.' She spoke softly. 'And Annette. Those were good months. My body healed but it was much more than that: I could be useful.'

With correspondence or collecting herbs for instance.

'I met the van Dammes and Thomas.'

And she had enjoyed the unimaginable freedom of roaming the cliffs with Jakob.

'The disguise as a boy worked and I took care not to meet Garcia.'

'But you wanted to see Jakob?' Hosé recalled.

She nodded. 'It was too risky. I shouldn't have done it.' She added hesitantly, 'And I misunderstood when you intervened.'

He shrugged.

There was a long silence broken only by the lapping of the sea and the faint rustle of the long palm fronds, black above them.

'I thought Garcia de Tineo had left Nice after that,' he said at last.

'He did. He went to Marseille. But he came back.'

'Why?'

'He had some idea of getting revenge on de la Forêt I think. I did not expect to see him and I did not like to stay in the palace.' She paused. 'Things were different there. Isaac had gone and Annette had married. She was not at all well with the baby. I did what I could for her, but most of the time she just needed to rest quietly. Her husband thought I was a boy and would have thought it strange for me to be with her.'

'So, you ran into Garcia?'

'Literally,' she said bitterly. 'I was passing one of the wine shops when there was a great shouting and he was hurled out into the street. I could not avoid him. I fell over him.' She shuddered. 'He had been drinking but he recognised me. He is a strong man.' She was shaking. 'It was like the previous time all over again and this time I was sure I would not survive. He held me face down. I thought I would suffocate in the muck.' She looked up. 'It is strange that your body resists death, however much your mind might welcome it.' She drew a deep breath. 'Many such thoughts went through my head. It seemed like an eternity. But actually, it must have been quite a short time before some men came out to relieve themselves and saw him. They swore at him and kicked him. They drove him away.' She shifted on the cooling sand. 'I realised I was not going to die. In fact, I had been spared most of his intentions. Apart from dung on my face and a few bruises there was little to see.' She gave a little laugh. 'I heard that he had been chased out of town but I stayed away anyway. And I thought that was the end of it.' She watched as a night bird swooped low over the beach. 'My courses had barely started so their absence did not concern me. I was not sick. In fact, I felt full of energy. I wrote up Isaac's notes, made simples, collected herbs. It was some time before I realised that the fluttering in my belly had nothing to do with what I had eaten.' She continued in a curiously flat voice. 'It would only be a short time before it became apparent to everyone. Annette's part in pretending I was a boy would be revealed; that could destroy her reputation and her marriage. And she was in no condition to defend herself, let alone help me.'

Hosé found it hard to believe that of the strong resourceful woman he knew, but he had to accept that was how Rabia had seen things.

'Then when the *Katrin* put into port I despaired. How could I ever face them with the truth?' She did not wait for an answer. 'You know what happened after that.' She stopped abruptly.

Hosé sat for a long time, the thoughts flying around his head. Gradually several things became clear: one was a certainty about Garcia de Tineo, if they ever met again.

Rabia moved.

'Are you cold?'

'No,' she said. 'Now you can see why I cannot return to Fez.'

He nodded. He could see that; and a lot more. 'You could stay here with Faraj.' That was another option. 'Ishaq would have the company of her sister's children.'

'And me?' she queried. 'I would have the life of a widow.'

'For a while,' he conceded. 'Then if there was no news of me you would be free to marry again.' He paused, 'A proper marriage. You are young, healthy, educated.'

'And obviously fecund.'

Her tone should have warned him but he added, 'And I could provide something for a dowry.' There was still that gemstone among his few belongings.

'That would surely settle matters.'

'You know how these things work,' he said a little impatiently.

'Oh yes, I know how these things work,' she said. 'Traded like a piece of merchandise or a new camel!'

'Actually,' he pointed out, 'You would be in a position to negotiate your own terms, with a man of your choice.'

She was silent for a moment, considering. 'That's true,' she said at last.

'But?'

'I don't want to marry anyone,' she said fiercely. 'I don't want a "*proper marriage*" as you call it. I don't ever want a man to use my body again.'

'All men are not like Kara Hasan, or Garcia de Tineo. You said your father loved your mother.'

'Their life was different. Can't you see?' she demanded. 'I can't just forget about what has happened. It is part of me.'

He was silent. Yes, he could see her point, but he had hoped she would feel differently and solve some of his problems. It was fortunate that Rabia could not see his expression, he thought, as he smiled wryly at himself.

'Ishaq will need feeding soon.'

Of course. He had not realised how much time had passed. 'You could go with Isaac.' The final option.

'Yes,' she answered. 'I would like that.' She had obviously thought about it. 'I could look after him and help him with his work. I could learn so much more from him.'

Hosé let out a long breath. It was not something he had discussed with the Jew, but knowing how fond he was of the girl Hosé could not imagine there would be a problem. He rose and dusted sand from his clothes.

'But,' her voice halted him. 'I could not live in Constantinople; among Turks.'

He turned. 'Then what other option is there?'

Chapter 17

1491

Their parting came at Messina this time.

Perhaps life had some symmetry, thought Hosé, recalling how he and Isaac had taken passage together from Messina when they first came west, heading for Nice.

The old Jew managed a strained smile.

There was nothing more to say. It had all been said, some of it several times over. Hosé hoisted the pack onto his shoulder and followed Rabia and Ishaq. Neither of them looked back as they rounded a pile of baskets and headed for the boat that would take them to Civitavecchia, the port that served Rome.

Houses, shops, workshops lined the streets as they made their way past the hotchpotch of old and new buildings. At one point, they caught sight of the enormous ruined amphitheatre where ancient Rome had gathered for sports and entertainments.

Rabia said something.

'What about him?' Hosé asked in surprise.

'Not a him, a where,' she said. 'There is a building like this at El Cem. Not as big, but much the same style.'

'That's a long way from Fez, or even Oran. Have you been there?'

'No,' she said quietly. 'My father talked of it. He went that way once, before he married my mother. He was on his way to join the Hajj.'

Hosé pulled a face.

As they drew a little closer to the Colosseum they could see scars where the stones showed bright and sharp. Builders in this modern Rome were not going to bother about quarrying new blocks when there was a great pile like this for the taking.

They passed through numerous squares, round numerous churches; Rabia twisted her head as they passed each one. So many different saints.

They saw the Tevere again, glimpsed in the distance down the roads to their left, before crossing a wide market place with yet another church. Hosé looked at the signs on the buildings. There were many inns in this district for it was the centre for pilgrims and travellers of all sorts. He spotted the picture of a lion on one of them. But an inn would not offer the accommodation they needed.

However, a search of the crowded houses and tenements found few with any space, particularly for folk with a child.

They found lodgings eventually with a baker off the Via del Pellegrino. The man had few words but many children and his wife immediately recognised that one extra crying voice would make little difference, while some income would help a lot. One small attic room was hastily vacated for Hosé, his young wife Roberta and their son Jacques.

Hosé surveyed the cramped space as he lowered the pack. 'We'll look for somewhere better soon,' he said, over the noise of an angry and hungry Ishaq.

Rabia nodded absently as she loosed the lacing on her bodice and Ishaq's howls suddenly ceased.

Hosé looked at the dawn sky then retreated back into the outhouse where he had sought a moment of peace. It was jammed with all manner of oddments that no longer had a place in the bakery: a broken trough, once a testimony to the skill of an unknown cooper; long handled paddles without the long handles; mouldering flour sacks; split wooden boards; cracked pitchers and jugs; old bricks from the oven; not to mention a cart which apparently delivered to inns, wine shops and houses throughout the quarter.

The place was hardly clean but Hosé had achieved a little with his own person and at least he could be attentive. He rubbed at gritty eyes.

He could not kneel as was proper, or speak the required words out loud, but he could face the right direction as he silently addressed the dismal state of his soul.

Outside the boundaries of the Dar al-Islam once more, Hosé recalled one of those treasured conversations with Prince Bayezit. Even then the Prince had tended to the Sufist view: the value of *tasawwuf* compared with *fiqh*. *Fiqh* prescribed the correct conduct in regard to prayers while *tasawwuf* looked to the spirit behind the actions. Hosé could not perform the required actions. How much more important then were his intentions and depth of concentration. In such hostile surroundings, how much more relevant an awareness of and communion with God.

But in his appointed task for his temporal Lord, how much more difficult to follow the final *tasawwuf* injunction: to *live* the prayers in one's morals and manners.

Whatever else their accommodation lacked, it was not fresh bread. The baker and the older children had been up long since.

Hosé and Rabia ate with gusto, then with Ishaq at Rabia's hip they set out through the streets.

They headed for the river.

The bridge was fine and broad. Hosé looked at it with appreciation. It was already fifteen years old but still looked bright and new. They crossed the Ponte Sisto, named for the Pope who had ordered its building, and entered the maze of narrow streets called simply the Trastevere, the far side of the river. Above the buildings, wherever they looked, were the tall fingers of towers, some attached to churches like that of San Crisogono, others with a more military set like the Torre degli Anguillara.

'There are so many churches called after the daughter of Imran.'

He looked at her sharply. She had spoken in Arabic. 'We must both practise speaking like the Romans.'

She pulled a face; that was certainly different from Niçois Genoese.

'And you must not speak of any Imran.'

She knew he was right, but she looked up with interest at the facade of the church where a mosaic portrayed a gentle face looking down at her feeding infant.

She considered the image for some time. After all, she thought, that could be a mother anywhere in the world. She looked down at Ishaq and realised how differently she had come to view him.

In the picture, behind Mary, were ten women holding lamps.

'Why are only eight of the lamps lit?' she said looking closely. 'And why are only two of the women veiled?'

Hosé shrugged.

'Wouldn't it be a good thing to know something of Christian stories?' she suggested.

He shrugged again, although she might have a point.

They walked on and Ishaq slept.

They had come a fair way and the littered pavements of Rome were hard, but there was one place Hosé specially wanted to locate.

They looked up at the huge stone bulk of the Castel Sant' Angelo.

'Is that where the Prince is?'

Hosé nodded; luxuriously accommodated in the upper apartments, no doubt. He stared at the place for a long while, wondering if there was any way he could get inside or at least learn what was happening there.

He shook his head. De Blanchefort would be there, or close by.

And quite possibly Oberto Spinola, serving with Andrea Doria, another member of the Genoese Albergo, in the Papal guards.

They crossed the river once more and made their way back to the baker's.

Next day there was a gusty wind although it threatened to be hot. They set off down the Via del Pellegrino and soon found themselves looking at a huge building site, a palazzo under construction. The part-built stone walls already showed the grandiose layout of the building although it was difficult to imagine the finished structure at this stage. Heaps of stone lay in ordered confusion, dust and rubble covered the ground. There were men everywhere, some hauling the heavy blocks with ropes that looked barely adequate for the task, some carrying timber and pails up ladders at crazy angles. Masons crouched, working with chisel and mallet to dress the blocks.

The stone was different from that being used for the cathedral in Moulins. It was different from that in the walls and barns of Anatolia. Hosé watched with interest.

Voices called orders, other voices swore as loads slipped or as stone or tool struck flesh. A man dressed in a good robe filmed in white was standing on one of the larger blocks and shouting loudest of all.

By his side was a young scribe, scratching notes. His task was difficult with his board balanced precariously in one hand; the all-pervasive grit and dust, aided and abetted by the eddying breeze, made it even harder. He dipped his quill once more and looked in disbelief as the nib split and splattered the rusty black ink over the figures he had just noted. He needed to dig a rag from his pocket to mop up the mess. He needed to find a new pen and sharpen it. He had been short of hands before, now there really was no hope. The board clattered to the ground, the paper detached itself and tumbled lazily in the dirt, the ink well tipped and poured its remaining contents into a small puddle that slowly drained into the earth. The stained rag added an extra leaf to a nearby bush and the new quill set off to reunite itself with a distant parent. The clerk was left holding his pen knife.

The Master builder let loose a stream of abuse and cuffed the young man hard about the head.

Hosé winced in silent sympathy.

'As if there were not enough problems on this job without your idiotic antics. If you want to be a juggler, then go and practise with a troupe of players.'

The clerk scrabbled around retrieving what he could, then hastened after his irate master to another corner of the site.

A few of the tradesmen laughed at the free entertainment before turning back to their work.

'They need extra labourers,' a voice addressed Hosé. 'You look strong enough. Gregorio would take you on. That's him over there.' The man pointed to a figure on the first level of scaffolding.

'Who is building this great palace?'

Hosé was impressed with Rabia's effort.

'Cardinal Raffaele Riario.'

'He must be a very rich man.'

'He knows the right way to make money.' Their informant made a significant gesture. 'Sixty thousand scudi in one night's gambling they say.' His tone was a mixture of admiration and envy.

Hosé glanced at Rabia. She had understood and managed a nod as of approval.

'New to Rome, are you? From the country?'

The curiosity might have been idle but Hosé was instantly wary. 'From Sicily,' he replied. He had thought that would explain Rabia's dark looks and their non-Roman accents.

'You'll do well to learn who are the important people around here: the Riarios for instance: lots of them, lots of influence. Nearly lost it when Uncle Sixtus died, but then many things came to an end back in 'eighty-two. You can say what you like about him, but he had a firm hand. You could go about your business safely in the city when *he* was Pope.' The man was beginning to enjoy his audience. 'He tried his firm hand on some of the other states too: excommunicated the Florentines and the Venetians at different times when they would not come to heel. That didn't work though and he was so furious the apoplexy took him, the gout flew straight to his heart so they say.'

He paused for the expected reaction of awe and delighted horror. Rabia's intense interest was good enough.

'Then, of course, you didn't know who was going to take charge of the Holy See, all the likely cardinals fighting for the votes, paying out for support. It was hell in the streets I can tell you: daylight robbery, violence, arson. You hardly dared venture outside your door.'

Somehow it was difficult to see this man hiding away from the action.

'The Orsini and Colonna took up arms against all Sixtus's "nepots" and whipped up mobs to attack the Riario palaces, while Count Girolamo Riario took refuge up in the Sant' Angelo castle. That was pretty smart because whoever controls the Castel controls the Vatican. The College of Cardinals could not sit and elect a new Pope until the Count pulled out of the castle. They managed to persuade him in the end, with sufficiently generous arguments of course. That's how the Riarios recovered.' He indicated the building with a nod of his head, 'Five years and lots of money to get this far.' The man seemed to think of that amount of wealth for a while. 'Raffaele Riario may back chance to raise his money, but old Sixtus had a more certain method when he taxed the ladies of the night. He wasn't very popular for that but it brought him enough money to squash any protests and to keep order.' He scratched behind his ear. 'Nowadays there's bodies in the streets every morning, nobody to keep watch and nobody to investigate. This Pope adds to his coffers by selling pardons: the greater the crime the greater the price. Even for murder, with enough money, you can buy your way out of your appointment with the hangman at the Tor di Nona.'

Hosé mentioned that they had passed the place on the previous day. It was just across the river from the Castel Sant' Angelo.

The man started to describe the latest body still hanging there but a voice hailed him.

Hosé thanked him for his time and for the information.

They walked on and Rabia asked him about the bits in the man's narrative that she had not understood properly. It was not so much the language as the people and the politics.

She listened intently, a small frown creasing her smooth brow below the unbleached linen of her coif.

Ishaq started to grizzle and Hosé sought somewhere they could sit.

They were in a wide road and here large houses seemed to be built like fortresses, as if their inhabitants expected invasion and war at any time.

'They probably have good reason to,' Hosé replied to Rabia's comment.

They found themselves in the Campo de' Fiori. It was not far from the baker's but they decided to perch themselves by a fountain. The water was cool on their hands. Rabia gave in to Ishaq's vociferous demands, sheltered by Hosé's back, then removed the boy's sodden clouts.

While Rabia finished off the bread they had brought, Hosé took the child. Ishaq squinted drunkenly at the distant sky, thin milk dribbling down his chin. He burped and grinned.

Two apprentices, carrying a length of timber, stared at Hosé. They stopped and one pointed a finger and made a loud comment to his companion. They both laughed.

Rabia moved to take Ishaq.

Hosé shifted the child out of her reach and carefully draped the half-naked form across one substantial shoulder. He pulled out his knife and pared a finger nail with great precision.

The young men looked at the blade in fascination.

Hosé pared another nail. He looked up at his spectators and raised an eyebrow.

The apprentices backed away casually and sauntered off.

Rabia regarded the knife.

'Yes?' he was beginning to recognise some of the signs.

'There have been times when I wished I had a knife like that.'

It was actually only his eating knife. His throwing knife was down his boot and his real knife was snug at his back. But he understood what she meant. 'You have to know how to use one,' he replied, 'Or it is more of a liability than anything else.'

'Is that one of the things you taught Jakob and Thomas?'

He saw the trap and did not answer. She asked the next question anyway.

He hesitated. It was not seemly, but nor was what had happened to her.

They sat for a while as Ishaq enjoyed his full stomach and his freedom; his dimpled legs kicked erratically. His rinsed clouts lay spread in the sunshine.

'It is probably fortunate, after all, that he does not bear the sign of Abraham,' Rabia said, watching the child.

Hosé nodded cautiously.

She had argued very hard on the matter. In truth Hosé had been surprised by her insistence. He had said that it could be done later. Rabia had declared that Turkish customs were barbaric. Isaac had prevented her from going on to elaborate on the point by making the eminently sensible suggestion that the boy should not be circumcised until it was clear where he would be living for the next years of his life.

She glanced at Hosé. 'That must be a danger for you.'

'I must be the most modest man in Christendom,' he agreed wryly.

She nodded but made no further comment.

They watched as visitors to the city rubbed shoulders with those who supplied and made a living from them: bakers and fish mongers seeing to practical needs, curio sellers meeting the demand to carry home tokens or proof of their visit to this city where St Peter had found martyrdom and the emperor Constantine had apparently awarded both the spiritual and temporal foundations of the Christian Church to the first Pope, Sylvester.

More noble Romans made their way towards their large fortified houses, accompanied by servants and men-at-arms.

Cardinals with even more attendants and guards passed through the square, on their way between palace and Vatican. Majestic hats added to their height and to the grandeur of their brightly coloured robes.

Rabia had just finished re-swaddling a sleepy Ishaq when Hosé drew her attention to a procession entering the Campo. In the front were men-at-arms. Hosé looked critically at the matching livery with gold thread decorating velvets that were surely never designed for a battlefield, at gleaming leather boots that had never seen the mud of a campaign. But the shining weapons looked altogether more practical. They were held at the ready too.

Hosé and Rabia joined the small crowd that gathered to watch.

Behind the men-at-arms came a group of clerics in priests' robes of rich black. Clerks carried important satchels with important airs, although totally outclassed by the next men in the procession. These were also churchmen, there could be little doubt, but their robes were not black. Stuff of every colour under heaven was on dazzling show. Scarlet silk bordered cloth of gold, emerald and ultramarine embroidery swirled across ochre grounds, crimson folds failed to cover gleaming white linen and rings on fingers flashed colours of equal brilliance.

In their midst was a figure of more sombre garb and yet his very air of power and authority made him stand out. His gown of deep crimson was not of the brightest hue but outshone all for quality; the silk was of the heaviest and finest available. Gemstones fashioned the long line of buttons reaching from neck to calf. The shoes that clad his feet were of the very best Moroccan leather.

Rabia stared. Into her mind came a vivid memory of the tanners' area in Fez where myriad vats stood under the hot sun, the coloured liquids steaming foully in the stone honeycomb as the tanners cooked and stirred. Tongues of dye licked over the edges of the tanks, mixing and melding into an infinite range of shades. What ingredients, gathered over thousands of miles of sand and sea, had produced this particular hue that so exactly matched the Purple?

The cap sitting snugly in its fringe of thick grey hair was the same colour. It looked simple but it must have taken its maker many hours to achieve the smoothness of a perfect fit, the surface unmarked by crease or stitch.

This man had only a single ring on his hand, but its size and lustre demanded no complement and scorned any competition. The wearer lifted it as he passed and those in the crowd bowed their heads in acknowledgement of the grace shown them.

Hosé and Rabia hastily followed their example.

When they looked up again they could see that he was a man past middle years but not yet sixty. He looked strong, the thick neck perhaps the legacy of a youth spent as a fighting man. Heavy jowls, perfectly barbered, held no wrinkles of age and showed no sign of the overindulgence that patently affected some of the men in front of him. He was a fit man; and handsome.

Behind him came more men-at-arms, a good dozen Hosé counted. 'A cardinal of considerable importance,' he remarked to Rabia.

'Cardinal Rodrigo Borgia.' A woman standing near them had heard his comment. 'Impressive piece of manhood, isn't he? At least six children, probably more, and still at it, so they say.'

The last men passed out of the Campo and the crowd began to disperse.

Rabia looked around them. 'There are less people now. Do they have *sieste* here?'

Hosé nodded absently. He was looking up at a device on the wall. They had reached the corner where the Campo met the Via del Pellegrino.

'Will people be in the wine shops?'

'Some of them.' As they would in Nice.

'Wine is an abomination,' she said watching him.

Along with games of chance, idols and divining arrows. Hosé recognised the reference. And all devised by Satan to stir up enmity and hatred, and to keep the believer from prayer and remembrance of God.

'Even though the *bektashi* teachers say otherwise, don't they?'

He sighed.

'Kara Hasan said they tell the janissaries that wine is allowed,' she insisted.

He shook his head, but not because she was wrong.

He looked for a shaded spot where they could continue the conversation; it was something that needed to be sorted out. He pointed to some stone steps leading up to the remains of what might once have been a temple of some sort.

Ishaq began to grizzle again as they stopped moving; Hosé took him, dangling him between his knees. The boy managed to fix his eyes on a bright flower that was growing out of a crack between the square blocks. He squinted at it and grinned.

'What you say about the *bektashi* is true,' Hosé agreed. He stopped her interruption, 'And we do not need to dispute what the Recitation says. But now we are in the Dar al-Harb and the Unbelievers all drink wine.' He looked at her, 'I realised some time ago that it would look strange if I did not. On top of that,' he said quietly, 'A wine shop is often the best place to hear what is going on and you can hardly sit talking to people in a wine shop without drinking with them.'

'So, that makes it all right.'

'It makes it pretty well unavoidable.'

She was silent.

'You can see that, can't you?' he asked a little impatiently.

'I suppose so,' she said reluctantly.

'But?'

She avoided his eye and watched Ishaq instead.

'I see it a bit like *salah*,' he continued. 'The Recitation also says we should say prayers, but only if it is safe to do so. I would rather not drink wine, whatever the *bektashi* may say.' She looked up. 'But in the Dar al-Harb sometimes it is not safe to avoid it.'

He waited for her to think that through. He turned Ishaq to face the other direction, where a cat slunk into a nearby alley. '*Cum Romanum venio, ieiuno Sabbato; cum hic sum, non ieiuno.*'

'What tongue is that? And what does Sabbat have to do with anything?' she asked.

'It's Latin and the man who wrote it was talking about fasting, not Sabbat.' He gave half a smile. 'The man was a monk and the Christians call him Saint Ambrose.'

'So, you do know something of Christian stories?'

Hosé shrugged. 'I have no idea what he did to be seen as a saint, but what he wrote could apply to many situations.'

'What does it mean then?'

'When I come to Rome then I fast; when I come here – to some other city he visited – I don't.'

She thought about that. 'So, he changed his religious observances to suit the local customs.'

'That's about it.'

She frowned. 'So, the Christians have different beliefs in different places.'

He shrugged again. 'You must know that there are different beliefs and customs within Islam.' He did not want to discuss the *bektashi* again. 'Look,' he said, 'You lived in Nice; it's not as if you did not know what to expect here.' He gave Ishaq his finger. The boy made several unsuccessful attempts to get it to his mouth before finally achieving it.

'It's not that I wish I hadn't come,' she was trying to explain to herself as much as to him. 'Even though I didn't have much choice.'

Hosé was not going reopen that particular debate.

'Rome is actually an interesting place,' she added frankly.

'But?' He was very tempted to use the Turkish word.

'But it was the thought of the wine shops. I mean,' she struggled, 'I knew there would be wine shops. I think I even knew you would have to visit them. But,' she stopped again and shivered slightly.

'Tell me,' he said quietly.

'I hate the smell,' she shuddered again, 'Of drunken men.'

'That is hardly surprising, considering your experience.'

'That's not it,' she muttered. 'Not all of it.'

'What?' He was puzzled.

She directed Ishaq's attention to the flower again, where a butterfly had settled, opening and closing its wings slowly as it sipped nectar. His dark eyes widened with interest for a while then he settled his mouth more firmly on Hosé's finger and concentrated on his sucking.

She pointed. 'That's it.'

Hosé looked down at Ishaq confused. 'What is?'

'Your finger.'

'My what?'

'Your finger. It's clean.'

He stared at her. What was she talking about?

'You got your clothes in Messina. They reek as if some goatherd had helped gut fish, a long time ago.'

He pulled a face.

'But basically, you keep yourself clean.'

He was taken aback, then realised she was right. He had washed his hands when they had stopped to eat, he had rinsed them afterwards. He had tried to wash before observing the *salat-ul-Fajir*. He had got back into old habits during the months on Djerba. For a moment, he was distracted, wondering what else he might not be aware of.

'When you lie down at night, you still smell the same as you did on Djerba.'

'What?' He was jerked back to what she was saying. Fortunately, he thought, most people would not be in a position to observe that!

He almost missed her next words.

'I don't want you to stink of the wine shop.'

Hosé stared at her and she flushed. He bought himself some time, shifting Ishaq to the crook of his arm. 'I don't think it can be avoided,' he said eventually.

'No,' she said. 'I realise that, but I wish it could.' She shook her head. 'That sounds stupid.'

'No,' he said. 'Life is full of things that we would wish otherwise.' He added with feeling, 'Sometimes they are things you can change, sometimes they are not.'

She nodded.

'I have to visit the wine shops and I have to drink wine when I am there, but I can promise you I never get drunk.' He pulled a face. 'Apart from anything else it would be far too dangerous.' To his mission; he had long ago given up much hope for his soul.

Her face lightened a little. She could see that.

'And, believe me, I have become quite skilled over the years at emptying mugs anywhere but down my throat.'

She looked at him for a long moment. 'Perhaps I should see how skilled you are.'

'What?' He was beginning to think he would soon need a new nickname.

'Annette's advice,' she said. 'I hate wine shops so I should make myself go in one.'

She did not look nearly as convinced as her words suggested. 'But maybe women and babies do not go into the wine shops here.' She was almost hopeful.

He felt sure some did, although he was equally sure that the more proper Roman matrons certainly would not. 'You could go back to the baker's,' he suggested. 'I could take you there then go into one of the wine shops by myself.' He glanced at the shadows. 'Siesta will last a while yet.'

She shook her head. 'No, I want to do it, today, right now.' She continued quickly, 'Besides our room will be like the baker's oven itself, at this time of day.' She managed half a smile. 'And it will give us the chance to improve our Roman.'

The talk in the Dancing Bear offered the perfect lesson in both the local dialect and the local gossip.

Hosé was not sure about the female company, but its universal admiration for Ishaq overrode any social niceties.

Hosé settled himself with some sour red wine and listened into the nearby conversation.

He nearly choked and set his mug back on the table.

Rabia raised a dark eyebrow, but his spluttering had nothing to do with the wine.

The names Cristofano di Castrano, also called Magrino, meant nothing to him, but the idea of poisoning the water supply hit him like a blow. He had an instant memory of Clough on the hillside above Nice, exploring the system first installed by the old Romans, a system that supplied the town and the Grimaldo palace, where Prince Cem was then being hosted and fêted.

Could Clough somehow have been behind this similar plot here in Rome? Hosé listened intently. The drinkers were most interested in telling and retelling the gory details of Magrino's death: the Pope's executioners had excelled themselves it seemed. Hosé would have preferred not to hear in quite such detail what happened to a man found guilty of serving the Ottomans. He took a few careful breaths and an even more careful sip of wine as, gradually, the rest of the story emerged.

Magrino had apparently had fears for his immortal soul if he managed to poison the Belvedere spring, where water was drawn for the Papal table. So concerned had he been, that he had shared these fears in the confessional. However, it happened that the man receiving this extraordinary confession was no other than the Pope's legate to Venice, who felt that such a grave threat overrode the usual confessional silence and reported the matter to the Holy Father.

Those were his remains still hanging from the Tor di Nona. They had been there since Spring.

Hosé lifted his mug again and thought about it.

This story spoke of Bayezit's agents supplying the poison and of a handsome payment to Magrino, but Hosé knew that the Sultan would have had no part in a plan that might harm his brother, the Prince. No, it was clear to Hosé that the Sultan's "foot", the Vizier, was behind it. It would have been he who suggested the idea to Clough in Nice and, more recently, used agents to recruit Magrino for a similar plan here in Rome.

Hosé grimaced to himself. The Vizier would not be pursuing such schemes for much longer: Isaac must soon be back at the Topkapi.

He was recalled from these thoughts by his neighbour pushing more wine towards him. He topped up his beaker and concentrated on the new topic of conversation.

The licentious and libidinous pontiff was not in good health, it seemed. Rumours spoke of fits, although these were fiercely denied by the Vatican and Pope Innocent had been seen in the streets, advertising his continuing existence and hold on the Chair of St Peter. Nevertheless, he was not a young man, the company nodded sagely into its mugs and pots, and his days must surely be numbered.

And then what? A question of considerable and immediate interest. A few people made suggestions. Nobody could quite believe that Innocent intended to make his son Pope after him; that was too much.

'The Pope has a son?' queried Hosé.

There was loud laughter. 'You must be new to Rome!' said one man whose clay-spattered clothes declared his trade.

Hosé repeated the line about coming from the south and refilled his mug.

'The Holy Father has at least seven bastards,' said the potter. 'That he has acknowledged, that is,' he added.

'Old Sixtus only ever called his four "nephews",' put in another man who surely did the same work.

'A betting man,' said one red-faced local, returning to the subject of the next Pope, 'Would put his money on Cardinal Roderigo Borgia.'

That name again. Hosé raised his mug.

'Wouldn't they Father Angelo?'

A man in priest's clothes lifted his head at the next table. 'The archbishop of Valencia and Porto, bishop of Mallorca, Carthage, Agria, the abbeys of Subiaco, and the monastery of Our Lady of Bellfontaine, deacon of Sancta Maria in Via Lata and Vice-Chancellor and Dean of the Holy Church.' The words came out in a fluent if slightly slurred flow. Hosé looked at the churchman with interest. Someone who had once served the Cardinal perhaps? Father Angelo took a long swig from the mug in front of him and laid his head down again.

Bishop of Mallorca? Hosé grasped one of the titles. He doubted if the cardinal had ever set foot on the island; not that that would stop him receiving his dues from that and all the other appointments. No wonder he dressed in silk and fastened his gown with gemstones.

Rabia managing to listen, in spite of the cooing from the women around Ishaq, mentioned that they had seen the Cardinal just a short time ago.

Several other people had also seen him and his entourage. One added the information that the Cardinal proudly paraded *his* four children, got on the beautiful Vanozza, late of the Piazza Branchis, owner of a sumptuous villa in the Subarra and proprietor of a well-known and profitable inn on the Via del Orso.

Hosé recalled the wine shop with the lion.

'Not that she lives there,' put in one of the potters.

'Kept in much grander accommodation,' agreed his friend.

There was considerable speculation about her lodgings and her activities there.

Hosé was aware of Rabia's sudden stillness. He tried to steer the conversation to other things. 'We came past the Castel Sant' Angelo,' he put in. 'An impressive place.'

Several heads nodded. 'Much safer for the Pope to be there than in the Vatican, when there is trouble.'

'He can get there easily then?'

Some heads nodded, others were shaken. 'The Castel is not exactly next door,' explained the red face. 'Hey, Luigi!' He hailed a man who had just entered. 'Have you heard any more about that tunnel?'

Luigi turned out to be the workman they had met at the building site. He grinned at Hosé as he settled himself into the space made for him and accepted the mug laid on the table. His huge hands wrapped around the vessel. He drank deeply and finally shook his head. 'Maybe it was only a story,' he said.

'Still it would make sense, wouldn't it? A tunnel between the Vatican and the Castel.'

Hosé topped up his own mug and offered more to Luigi.

Luigi thanked him, but changed the topic of conversation, to matters that obviously interested him considerably more.

Hosé tried, unsuccessfully, to divert him from the latest body found in the Tevere.

Ishaq began to complain more loudly. Rabia retrieved him from the ample lap currently hosting him and rose from her seat.

Hosé nodded at her and they made their farewells.

'Well?' he asked, as they came to the Via del Pellegrino.

She considered. 'I only noticed when your mug spilled. You did that on purpose, didn't you?' She added, 'But I don't think anyone else would have guessed.'

He hoped not.

Chapter 18

Hosé walked past the large villa put at the disposal of the Ottoman embassy and stopped at the end of the road. He recalled with a small shake of his head how the embassy had come to be welcome in the capital of Christendom.

Mansur had described the gift that the Sultan had sent to his Holiness, in addition to the forty thousand ducats in cash. Even holy relics of Christ's Crucifixion had not persuaded Innocent VIII to part with the valuable hostage bought from the Knights of St John, but they had been enough to persuade him to welcome the Sultan's ambassador.

Perhaps Pierre d'Aubusson had also played the part he had promised, but the new Cardinal Saint-Adrien was no more to be depended on than the old Grand Master had been.

Hosé would have loved to have all the latest news from Islambul and to use the embassy communication channels, but the ambassador and his staff would be well watched.

Hosé carried on walking.

He found an oil-merchant who regularly took goods downriver to Ostia, and bought a place for a trip to the silted-up port that had served the old Romans. These days the bigger transports and galleys used Civitavecchia, from where travellers and goods made their way to Rome by road or transferred to smaller boats for the last leg via Ostia and the Tevere, as he and Rabia had done.

Now Hosé wanted to explore Ostia and see what traders were there, traders with overseas business connections.

He spent an interesting couple of days in the little town. There were many buildings that looked just as the old Romans must have known them: bath houses, temples, food stalls with stone counters and benches, even one or two long overgrown public gardens. Hosé peered at bits of surviving wall-paintings and tried to picture the figures there walking the streets of old Ostia, embarking on the boats that must have packed the harbour then, or sitting in one of the gardens in the shade while slaves fetched them wine.

There were some newer buildings of course, but Ostia was now a backwater: the hurly-burly belonged to Civitavecchia up the coast. There they had built sea walls, a tower against pirates, huge warehouses and docks. Civitavecchia not only served the city of Rome, it served the Papacy and was recognised and rewarded for this.

Hosé half wondered whether to seek what he wanted there, where countless boats sailed to all points of the compass.

But then the oil-merchant introduced him to the Ostian trader who handled his goods. Julio might have been fifty, he might have been eighty, with his face wrinkled into myriad lines by saltwater and sun. He had worked the eastern seas, he said, from Corfu to Alexandria. Now he left the sailing to his sons and grandsons while he stayed at home in his villa in Ostia and enjoyed the dates and sweetmeats, the silks and carpets, the wine and spices that others risked their lives to bring across the sea.

'Would it not be easier for you to be based in Civitavecchia?' Hosé asked curiously as he accepted a small brass cup.

Julio's rumpled face creased further as he smiled. 'My sons live there; they are welcome to the place.' He sipped appreciatively. 'Me, I prefer Ostia.'

Hosé also took a sip of the potent brew. The aroma filled his head, sweeping away the cobwebs and bringing sharp memories of the Kiva Han. The hot thick black liquid slid down his throat, almost instantly spreading its energy through his body. Some said it should be forbidden like wine, although Hosé could not see why: its effect was quite different.

Julio waved his hand vaguely. 'Here I fill my house with souvenirs, I have servants who do things the way I like them, my sons bring me the food and drink that I like.' He sipped again. 'And the news from all parts.'

Hosé's instinct had been right. 'And what is the latest news?' he asked.

Julio took another sip. 'In spring Mattias Corvin died,' he said looking at Hosé to see his reaction.

'His Holiness has lost a valuable ally for any new crusade then,' said Hosé with the right amount of regret, adding to himself, with more satisfaction that Prince Cem had also lost the only relative likely to support his pretensions.

'Some say he was poisoned,' said Julio.

'Some said that of the Duke of Savoy. It is a danger faced by those in powerful positions.'

Julio nodded, without too much sympathy.

'Who will succeed Corvin?' Hosé asked.

'Corvin only had the one son, a bastard,' Julio replied.

Totally irrelevant then, unless one happened to be the bastard. 'So, who will become king?'

'Most likely Ladislaus of Bohemia and Hungary. But those who know him say he is a weak man. I doubt the Pope will find much of an ally there.'

Hosé tried to look sorry about that.

Julio's eyes peered at him from within their wrinkles. 'You are widely travelled?' He put the question in Greek.

'You could say so,' Hosé agreed in the same language. 'My father traded.'

Julio nodded and took another sip. 'And you? You are also in trade?'

'In my own way.'

'What do you trade?'

Hosé finished his coffee and set down the beaker. 'Information,' he said evenly.

Julio drained his own cup. 'Now that can be a most valuable commodity,' he said.

'And does not take up much cargo space,' Hosé said.

Julio smiled appreciatively. 'And you have a market?'

'Oh yes.'

'You have just come from Rome with the oil-merchant?'

Hosé nodded watching the man put two and two together: the seed of the idea that Hosé was gathering intelligence for the Papacy had been sown.

'The market there pays well?'

'It will for the right information,' Hosé agreed.

'How well?'

'Very well.' Hosé reached for the purse inside his shirt and counted out several coins. 'That is an example.'

Julio picked up the coins and inspected them. They were gold and bore the Pope's likeness. They would certainly encourage Julio to reach the right answer to the sum.

It was past midnight when Hosé finally climbed up to their room where a small lamp burned. He looked at Ishaq. The boy's eyes were shut, the eyelashes feathered on his cheeks, but his mouth was busy; it would not be long before he woke.

Hosé pulled off his outer clothes and glanced at Rabia. She was curled up beside the child. Night was truly a mantle and sleep a rest, and the day was ordained for work, he thought; except for the mothers of young babes.

Hosé secured employment with Gregorio on Raffaele Riario's new palace.

He had considered presenting himself directly to Signore Bramante, the palace's architect, and offering to replace the unfortunate and inept clerk, but it would be wiser to have a new guise. The more different he looked from the lame clerk known to Guy de Blanchefort and his Knights, the better.

The hard work did not bother him; it kept him fit. It was satisfying to handle stone again and it definitely ensured his hands did not look like those of a clerk.

The fight he had with Gregorio on the first day and occasional brawls with others thereafter added credibility to his new identity.

The only matter that bothered Hosé was one he did not discuss with anyone, although he had long ago reluctantly acknowledged it for himself. It was certainly not something a tough Sicilian labourer was going to admit to.

He tried reminding himself of Annette's advice to Rabia, but it was much easier giving it than taking it, he decided, as he seized the block of stone that had just been hauled to the top level of scaffolding. He wrestled the mass into place, keeping his eyes carefully away from the long drop down to the ground.

They were still living with the baker. The one or two tenement rooms they had found offered no more space, were equally suffocating at this season and were distinctly more squalid. In addition, the rent at the baker's had been significantly improved by the inclusion of free bread.

Soon after their arrival the youngest of the baker's children had developed a high fever which Rabia had successfully reduced with poultices and infusions. She had been lucky that the apothecary on the next street had the herbs Isaac would have prescribed.

Both the baker's wife and the apothecary had been impressed. Lucia had made the offer of free bread, Guiseppe had invited Rabia to come and see him again.

The summer reached its height. The building work continued on the palazzo, although the length of the daily siesta increased. Hosé used the time to visit as many wine shops as possible in his quest for information about the proposed tunnel to the Castel and anything else that related to that building or its celebrated inhabitant.

He also gleaned as much news as he could about the Borgias. Cardinal Rodrigo was already a force in the Church; he could end up being its supreme potentate, inheriting the hostage in the Castel Sant' Angelo.

Hosé learned that the Cardinal's second son, Giovanni Borgia, was in Spain, succeeding at a tender age to family wealth and title, on the death of an elder half-brother. Legitimacy, it seemed, had been no issue.

The youngest children, a boy Gioffre and his beautiful blond sister Lucrezia, lived in the Orsini Palazzo, on the Monte Giardano, with their remarried mother, Vanozza. It seemed that Signore Canale was not as accommodating as her first husband Signore della Croce had been. Such sensibilities, however, had not apparently inconvenienced the energetic Cardinal Borgia: his attentions had already been caught by a younger and even more lovely lady. It was of little matter that she was the wife of Orso Orsini (son of the Cardinal's cousin). Guilia Farnese, and her immediate relations, bathed in the reflected wealth and position of a man likely to become perhaps the most powerful person in the western Christian world. Alessandro Farnese, her brother, even dared to set his sights on the same dizzy heights.

Vanozza's eldest son, Hosé learned, was a youth endowed with the lithe body of his father and the dazzling good looks of his mother. He also had, they said, a sharp intellect. Few people doubted that he had a glittering future, following in his father's footsteps. His first steps had taken him to the Sapienza in Perugia, then on to the University of Pisa, where the teachers received the flower of Italian youth and instructed them in all there was to know; and where canon law, the *sine qua non* for any aspiring man of the Church, was the speciality of the renowned Enrico Decis. With his own generous establishment and magnificent personal guard, Cesare Borgia lived the extravagant life of any wealthy heir.

In spite of Magrino's plot, the Ottoman embassy remained a guest of the Pope and a regular sight in the city. Hosé watched in silent amusement as the local populace gawped in awe and a little fear at the ambassador and his guard of janissaries in their exotic uniform.

Among the crowd another well-built man also watched the Turks. If Hosé had seen him he would have recognised the bearing of a soldier; more, he would have recognised the man himself. Equally Raymond de Glandèves would have recognised *him*. Indeed, that was precisely why de Glandèves, Seigneur de Faulcon and loyal supporter of the Knights of St John, was peering so intently at each member of the Turkish embassy.

But Hosé continued to avoid all contact with the embassy. The system with Julio worked well.

Hosé had already established communications with Nice. He and Rabia eagerly devoured Annette's letters, once again fulsome and dealing in equal measure with commercial-political matters and the scrapes and ailments of her son.

Rabia was less interested in the other correspondence that arrived. There were more immediate matters that attracted her attention. There was an increasing number of times, including evenings, when the apothecary called for her and they visited some sick person in the neighbourhood.

Hosé was not altogether happy about this. He recognised the truth of Isaac's words: *The more she can do for herself the less she will resent the child.* But he worried about the illness she came into contact with, although Rabia protested that she always washed her hands and changed her clothes as the Jew had taught. And she never took Ishaq with her on such visits: in the day, the baker's wife or one of the girls took him; in the evenings Hosé minded the child.

Hosé still worried.

It was late summer before the package they were both waiting for came from Islambul.

It included a note from Jakob that needed plenty of deciphering even though it was not in code.

The voyage to Konstantiniye (he had obviously copied the word from a coin) had been "*quite interesting*" (not as exciting as he had wished then). They had been intercepted off Midilini but Isaac had dealt with the Turkish galley and they had made the Golden Horn without any further problems.

They had docked in Pera and Isaac had sent a message to someone. A group of soldiers had come and escorted him away.

For the next couple of weeks, they had heard nothing more from the Jew but had successfully traded the goods they had brought from Djerba and Tunis, Messina and Kos. Then they had loaded with carpets and stuffs and spices. Cornelius had been happy.

Finally, some soldiers had come again with a note from Isaac. They had been rowed across the Horn and escorted to a house somewhere in the town. (Jakob had expected at least a visit to the palace, evidently, if not an audience with the Sultan himself.)

The old Jew had provided a wonderful feast, though. (Even Jakob's exacting standards had been met.) At the end of the evening he had passed a bag to Cornelius who had looked inside it and grinned.

From one sunburned ear to the other, thought Hosé slightly resentfully.

They had not seen Isaac again but he had organised things for them. There had been a wrestling competition, although the man who won was not as good as Hosé. There had been a display by some janissaries. Jakob had not been able to identify their orta but they had been pretty good with their swords. There had been sipahis who could draw their funny curved bows and fire arrows while facing backwards on horseback. There had been the launch of a new galley which Thomas had admired, although Jakob still thought the *Katrin* was a match for any boat.

They had met lots of seamen from all around the Middle Sea, which the Turks called the White Sea, as well as traders down from the Black Sea.

There were boats from Iskandariya too, and he and Thomas had talked to their crews in Arabic. (Rabia smiled.)

Isaac had said he would send someone to collect this letter before they left port, which Cornelius wanted to do soon so they could trade their new cargo. They would probably head back for Tunis.

Jakob had ended with the word "*Salaam*", in Roman letters, and added a note at the end in a script that might have come from any corner of the earth. Hosé peered at it, then impatiently handed it to Rabia, while he read the other letter from Isaac.

Afterwards he passed it to Rabia. If the girl thought some of the subjects were a little strange she made no comment. The obvious points were that Isaac was safely back; he had talked to the Sultan and the Vizier would be dealt with. And that Hosé should continue to avoid all contact with the Turkish embassy in Rome.

Hosé considered the other, concealed, matters.

He finally became aware that Rabia was waving Jakob's letter in front of his face. She was holding it upside down. That way Hosé could just read the scrawled post script. "*We will definitely be coming back here next year – Isaac secured some sort of trading licence for Papa.*"

She was frowning.

'What is it?' he asked.

'They will winter in Tunis then head east again next season,' she said quietly.

'So?' Hosé's mind was still half on other things.

Her silence finally caught his attention. She had hoped somehow they might come this way.

Wind and rain brought summer to an end, work on the building site slowed down. Hosé was not sorry to work at ground level. He laboured in one or other of the masons' yards for some weeks, but they had their own apprentices to be kept out of mischief.

He helped the baker convert part of his outbuildings into more living space. Lucia was expecting again.

Even so, he had more time to roam the streets.

The Tor di Nona held another body. The cooler weather preserved its broken remains for weeks. Hosé looked at it with dozens of other Romans and with a great deal more personal interest. Under torture the man had confessed to being a Turk. A woman next to Hosé pointed at the shrivelled member displayed prominently as "proof" of this, and made a coarse comment; her neighbour laughed loudly.

But a man might confess to anything when .... Hosé stopped himself following that thought. Had the man really been paid to snatch the Prince; or kill him if that proved impossible?

'In the employ of King Ferrand of Sicily, apparently,' said a voice next to him. 'You and your wife are from there, aren't you?'

Hosé grimaced at Luigi. 'The king would hardly employ me: be more likely to give me the same treatment.' He nodded at the body.

Luigi grinned at the joke and threw an inviting arm in the direction of the Dancing Bear.

Rabia's face lifted with relief as Hosé entered their room.

'Is Ishaq ill?' he asked quickly.

She rocked the fretful child. 'Lucia says it is just that he is cutting teeth.'

Hosé saw the red patches on the round cheeks and hoped the baker's wife was right. Heaven knew she had enough experience, he assured himself.

'He has hardly slept these past three nights.'

And Hosé had been in Ostia. 'Here,' he held out his hands and took the boy.

'I'll go down and brew some chamomile,' said Rabia. 'Guiseppe says it might help.'

Hosé shifted the grizzling infant to his left arm and reached inside his shirt, pushing aside the latest correspondence.

'What is that?' asked Rabia as she returned with the tisane. She removed the object Ishaq had been chewing and looked at it.

'I'm sure His Holiness would be glad to know his image has such healing powers,' said Hosé solemnly.

Ishaq finally went off to sleep. Whether it was the chamomile or the gold coin soother or simply exhaustion neither of them knew, or cared.

Rabia lay down with a sigh.

Hosé was reminded of the letter from Islambul as he removed his shirt. It could wait until the morning.

He stretched out on the other side of the now peaceful child and closed his eyes.

He read the letter through, then from habit started again, although he was sure he had understood everything at the first reading.

'What is it?' Rabia was watching him as Ishaq fed. 'Who is it from?' She could tell it was not Isaac's writing.

Hosé stared unseeing across the room.

'Bad news?' she persisted.

'About Genoa.'

She frowned.

'The.... a correspondent in Islambul says that Clough was in Genoa earlier in the summer.'

'This summer?' She could not see why that was so worrying.

'But inquiring about earlier comings and goings.'

'The *Katrin*,' she said flatly.

Hosé nodded. He hesitated.

'And what else?'

He looked down at the sheet of paper. The dragoman knew Clough had spoken with Lorenzo Spinola but could not know exactly what had been said, although the letter included a number of items that might very well have been discussed. The dragoman had made no comment on the birth of an heir to Gianmaria Lomellino and Battista. He had, however, remarked on the curious news that Isabella Spinola had not only fostered the bastard son of one Bianchetta, acknowledged leman of her husband Oberto, but had at long last quickened with child herself.

Hosé was happy for 'Bella.

He was not happy about the next part.

'Hosé,' Rabia prompted.

He lifted his eyes. 'Clough had a big Spaniard with him.'

Rabia blanched.

'They both boarded the *Marije*, apparently sailing for Antwerp.'

Neither of them derived much comfort from that last bit of information.

Chapter 19

The Twelve Holy Nights proved to be a season for extra Christian celebration that year. Before they ended with the day of Epiphany, Ferdinand and Isabella received the surrender of the last Moorish stronghold in Grenada. News reached Rome early in the Christian year of 1492 and spread quickly across the city. Hosé and Rabia greeted it soberly.

The events in Spain had consequences of many kinds that would show themselves before long in the rest of Europe and indeed the world. That very world was about to be enlarged in a way that most people would have believed impossible.

Freed at last from the gruelling sieges and battles that had absorbed so much money and attention throughout their reign, the Spanish monarchs were now at liberty to look seriously at the persistent and importuning Christoforo Colombo, once of Genoa. The arguments he had been peddling around England, Spain and Portugal for several years seemed credible enough to be put to the proof. If he was correct, then a new sea route to the Indies sailing west from Spain would have value almost beyond measure. All the precious goods that came at present through Egypt and the Levant, at great expense and at the whim of the Saracens, could be shipped freely into western Europe. The profits to the adventurers, the merchants and the Crown would be enormous. Moreover, the Christian monarchs could hope to save for the Holy Catholic Church the souls of all those savages found to inhabit any islands discovered in between.

Hosé's lip curled as Father Angelo pronounced this bit.

The one-time priest and now sot was not the only source of information. Rome was not a seaport, but boats plied up and down the Tevere. Hosé paid regular visits to the wharfs beyond the Isola where they loaded and unloaded, and listened to the talk as he received the packets sent up from Ostia by Julio. He pictured the Atlantic coast of Spain as the boatmen spoke of the caravels which could use the winds of that wide ocean and breast its great seas. It seemed the Spanish would beat the Portuguese to it after all, for da Gama was still making his painstaking preparations for the expedition that would sail south and east in the wake of Diaz. Meanwhile a Spanish fleet of three boats would head south to the Canary Islands and then strike west. They would not try to reach Cathay and Cipangu via the great fishing grounds of the northwest. What would

Thomas think of that? Hosé wondered.

And what would Jakob think of the sipahis who had arrived to swell the embassy numbers and to increase the impressiveness of the Ottoman spectacle parading through the streets? Probably not much, Hosé thought wryly, since they carried their famous composite bows, but did not use them.

Hosé watched the janissaries with more than a little envy: the tough red boots on the paved road; the familiar swinging gait moving the folds of the full trousers, the immaculately folded turbans, the powerful necks above the cotton of their shirts, the sleeveless jackets hanging free of the daggers and knives tucked into each broad sash.

The increased size of the legation was supposed to reflect Constantinople's respect for the Christian capital, mused Hosé, keeping a firm hold on Ishaq's bruised and scratched legs. It would also serve as a reminder of the hordes of highly trained and efficient fighters at the Sultan's disposal.

Ishaq, perched on Hosé's broad shoulders, shouted his approval in the language of a two-year-old Roman. The baker's children had been largely responsible for that part of his education, although Hosé and Rabia also usually spoke to him in the local patois. Between themselves they often used Arabic or Catalan. Some things were simply better expressed that way. Naturally the child picked up words, but Hosé had decided that did not matter since Sicilian was a mixture of many tongues, including both of those, and nobody would think the boy's vocabulary strange; assuming anyone in Rome actually knew anything about the people of Sicily. But one could never be too careful about assuming things, as Hosé often reminded Rabia.

For a moment, the child partly obscured Hosé's face from the sight of the man a little way behind them, then Hosé turned as the cavalcade thundered off down the street.

Raymond de Glandèves drew a sharp breath.

For some time, the Knight managed to keep the man and boy in sight as they moved with the crowd, then they disappeared down a side street.

The burly soldier monk paused, looking down the empty alley. The streets in this part of Rome were a veritable maze and he had little hope of finding them again. He muttered an ungodly imprecation.

However, he now knew for sure that at least part of the curious information in the letter to de Blanchefort was correct. The man he had just seen might look like a robust Roman labourer but it had undoubtedly been the same young man de Glandèves had known in France as the lame clerk, Hosé de Mallorca.

De Glandèves thought about the allegations contained in that letter from Genoa. The Knights had their own organisation for communicating and gathering news but the letter had come from outside that network. It was not special in that: much information, often malicious, was offered to the powerful and wealthy Knights in the hope of harming a personal rival or enemy, or of gaining a reward. But this letter, although anonymous, had offered details that suggested its writer should be taken seriously: details of the Duke of Bourbon's plot to free the Prince that could only have been known to a very few people. De Blanchefort had appointed de Glandèves to pursue the matter. Until today the Knight had failed to discover anything, although he had had the Turkish embassy and their activities closely monitored. Now, at last, he had spotted the man, not *with* the Turkish embassy, but in the crowd watching them.

So how did that fit with the allegations in the letter?

De Glandèves frowned. It was suspicious enough that Hosé should be here in the city where Prince Cem resided. It was equally suspicious that he had drastically changed both his appearance and station in life. The Knight scowled. There had been deception all right.

But to what purpose? The letter had been adamant that Hosé de Mallorca was an agent of the Sultan Bayezit, but de Glandèves had not discovered any contact between the erstwhile clerk and the Turkish embassy.

And the tale of events in Moulins? Enquiries had discovered that to be true. De Glandèves had been outraged. De Blanchefort had been pensive. The clerk had certainly practised deception there too.

But to what end? Any Ottoman agent would surely have taken steps to rid the Sultan, once and for all, of the threat posed by his brother; wouldn't he? Yet Hosé had made no attempts on the Prince's life, in spite of many opportunities over the years. On the contrary he had undisputedly foiled the very real attempt to liberate the Prince at Rumilly.

Who had written the letter, anyway? And with what motive?

De Glandèves shook his head in frustration. He liked to have clear answers. This fog of intrigue was too much for his simple approach to life. He would report what he had seen to de Blanchefort and let him try and answer the questions.

Although the Grand Master's nephew already had much on his mind, indeed the whole of Christendom was in a state of uncertainty.

The Knight shook his head again like an angry dog and began to retrace his steps.

And the child? His thoughts took a different direction. Who knew? Perhaps Hosé's, perhaps a neighbour's. He was a fine-looking boy. De Glandèves had had a good view of him, perched above the heads of the surrounding crowd.

In the early summer, there was suddenly great activity around the Vatican. The Pope was believed dead then miraculously reappeared amid more rumours. Physicians were seen hurrying across the river on the Sant' Angelo bridge. The matter was certainly serious, Hosé thought sourly, when a Jewish doctor was summoned to attend the head of the Roman Christian Church. Not that this Hebrew looked anything like Isaac. It soon transpired that he did not have anything like the skills either.

Matters were becoming desperate. People whispered that the Holy Father was so weak that the only thing that nourished him now was human milk. The Israelite tried to get him to ingest something a little stronger. Unfortunately, the three boys to whom he paid one ducat apiece did not have as much good red blood to spare as the physician assumed. The Jew fled and the Pope died: *Judeus quidem aufugit, et Papa sanatus non est,* as Father Angelo put it succinctly at the Dancing Bear.

On the twenty fifth of July the Holy See became vacant and the jostling for succession to the Papacy became unashamedly overt, even though the obsequies were not concluded until the fifth of August. The following day the Sacred College started its deliberations and few people were surprised by the announcement that Cardinal Roderigo Borgia would be the next Pontiff, taking the name of Pope Alexander VI.

Hosé was certainly not surprised. He had seen the four mules staggering under their loads. He had followed them the night they made their guarded way from the palace on the Banchi Vecchi, home of Cardinal Borgia, to that other palace where Cardinal Ascanio Sforza lived. Sforza's was a valuable vote in the College and Ascanio had a well-established reputation for encouraging others to vote the right way.

For seventeen days, the city had been in turmoil and although the Cardinal Chamberlain had seized all the gates and bridges, his patrols had failed to quell the unrest. Luigi reported with relish that two hundred and twenty bodies had been found during this time.

Work on the palazzo ceased, although the Riarios were not so discomforted by this change of power. Business at the Dancing Bear thrived.

The all-important question, as far as Hosé was concerned, was what use the new Pope would make of his royal hostage. Would his Holiness be any more inclined to release Prince Cem than his predecessor? And if so, at what price.

If Pope Alexander VI could be bought off, then the Sultan might not only be reunited with his brother but at last be able to turn his unrestricted attention to several outstanding matters to the south and east of the Ottoman lands.

For three years, the famous hostage had been lodged in the Castel Sant' Angelo. On those occasions when he had appeared on the streets of Rome, sometimes on foot, sometimes mounted on the stallion Ylderim, he had been accompanied by a force of Papal soldiers, and often by the man Hosé held in great professional respect. Cardinal Saint-Adrien (the erstwhile Pierre d'Aubusson and still Master of the Knights of St John) had contrived that his nephew, Guy de Blanchefort, continue as companion warder to the exiled Prince

Hosé had seen them several times, always at a distance.

In spite of frequent rumours there had been no definite news of the fabled tunnel from the Vatican to the Castel. Hosé had given up hope of that being a chance to get any nearer to the Prince.

As the months then the years passed, a series of more or slightly less unrealistic schemes had teased his mind before being rejected. Although he had heard that one of the Prince's remaining followers, perhaps Nassouh, was free to explore Rome and even Florence and Milan, the Prince himself had been kept in strict custody.

Hosé had chafed and tasted the bitterness of frustration.

Now things might change.

Hosé perused the latest letter from Isaac.

The Hebrew gave details of what the Sultan was prepared to offer to buy off the Pope elect but, Isaac wrote, Lord Bayezit was not hopeful.

Isaac had seen the dragoman recently. The interpreter had informed the Jew acidly that Clough seemed to be in a fair way to rebuilding his ventures. The Englishman had secured control of the van Damme assets in Antwerp, even though the marriage to Marije van Damme had not yet taken place. He had also successfully out-manoeuvred several substantial rivals - sources spoke of irresistible bribes and threats. Clough's company of soldiers had become a well-known, and unwelcome, sight among the warehouses and offices of the port, although the big Spaniard who had trained them seemed to have left.

Hosé wondered where he had gone and why.

His worries increased with the next news.

The Englishman had been venturing into the Middle Sea again. The

Marije had been trading in Genoa and some of her other outposts, in obvious cooperation with Lorenzo Spinola.

Hosé frowned. The fact that Clough still thought it wise to avoid Nice was of little comfort.

However, the news that Clough was once more venturing away from Antwerp revived another idea. Hosé would write about it to Annette. She would surely enjoy working on its execution, he reflected with a grimace.

The *Katrin* had been back in Pera, Isaac wrote finally. Cornelius was making full use of his licence to trade there.

The Jew enclosed a letter from Jakob addressed to both Hosé and Rabia, and a sealed packet with just Rabia's name on it.

Hosé looked at her curiously, but she offered no explanation.

'I'll open it this evening after Ishaq is asleep,' she said and changed the subject. 'We should go soon if we are to have any chance of a good view.'

Cardinal Roderigo Borgia was to be crowned.

It was a hot sunny day and the crowd gathered on the steps of St Peter's was as brilliant as the weather.

Pope Alexander VI took his place in a glorious procession intended to impress both the citizens of Rome and the thousands of visitors gathered there from further afield. All the rich and noble took part in their most ostentatious robes and with their most splendid attendants, guards and servants. Seven hundred priests and prelates wore their ceremonial robes and were escorted by their clerks and lesser officers of the church. The Palatine guard with their great halberds and shining shields warned off the fascinated crowd.

Hosé searched the faces of the *condottieri*.

Of course, the personal guard of Innocent VIII would have been paid off; the new Pope would have chosen his own men. So, where had Oberto Spinola gone? Quite likely back to Genoa to watch the first faltering steps of Bianchetta's son, or to return the windy smiles of his little daughter. Or to try and get a legitimate heir on his wife.

This unwelcome thought was interrupted by a loud cry in his ear. Ishaq had spotted the Turkish horsemen, treading a controlled fierce path down the street. The boy craned his head to keep them in sight and protested loudly as Hosé suddenly sank beneath him.

Twelve beautiful white horses with golden bridles marked the arrival of the centre of the procession, and of the new pontiff. Every common knee bowed to receive a blessing from the hand now carrying the Fisherman's ring upon its lean and strong forefinger.

Hosé avoided Rabia's eye as they knelt, and concentrated on trying to stop Ishaq from talking so loudly about the sipahis.

Finally, the crowd rose to its feet once more and began to disperse. The sound of music and the scent of incense filled the hot air and along every street and at every door were flowers and banners, many with the Borgia device proudly displayed: the Bull was about to run rampant through a meadow left too long untended.

Hosé sat in the Dancing Bear for a while discussing the events of the day with the others, but he left early. Rabia had business with Guiseppe.

The weather stayed as hot and settled as any other summer but the political climate underwent an immediate and drastic change, seen and felt throughout the city. This Pope might dote on his offspring, but that was perhaps the only similarity with his predecessor. In every way, his soundness of body was reflected in firmness of action.

One of the first acts was to bring law and order back to Rome. Murders were no longer ignored, but pursued with vigour and murderers, however wealthy, could not buy grace. The first murderer to be caught had his house razed before his eyes then had the chance for a more lasting view as he was hanged above the ruins.

Inspectors for the prisons were appointed in short order and commissioners charged with swift and severe justice. The Pope himself gave audiences every Tuesday to settle disputes of a distinctly temporal nature.

In contrast to the previous administration, salaries were paid promptly and all receiving them were in no doubt that they were required to earn them.

Work throughout the city restarted on a multitude of projects. The Riarios ordered building to be resumed on their respective palazzos.

The palazzo that was to be the home of Cardinal Raffaele Riario had come on in the two years that Hosé had been working there, although he was grateful that even the more advanced parts were still nowhere near their planned final height.

Much of the bone-coloured travertine stone was scavenged from the nearby ruins of what had once, apparently, been Pompey's Theatre. The otherwise omniscient Luigi had not been sure who Pompey was, but he was sure the man didn't need all that ready-dressed stone anymore, nor the porphyry columns that had been transported with considerable difficulty and now lay like fallen giants awaiting the hour appointed for their resurrection.

Everywhere one looked in modern Rome there were reminders of the city the old Romans had built and lived in. These days there was a population of some thirty thousand people, while ancient Rome had probably been home to over a million. Hosé found it difficult to imagine, but the evidence lay all around in abandoned temples, arenas, villas, ruined gardens and squares, collapsing theatres and public baths, the still discernible pattern of streets and paved roadways.

It was more than seventy years since the Council of Constance had put an end, once and for all, to the controversy as to where the Papal See should be: Rome, not Avignon. A succession of Popes had consolidated this state of affairs and those who held their power and wealth from the same source were creating great new buildings out of the ruins of the old.

One day Hosé managed a quick look at sketches of how Raffaele Riario's palace would look, when it was finished. Signore Bramante had passed them to his current clerk, as work stopped for the day, and the long-suffering man was hanging on to them as if his life depended on it.

Perhaps not quite his life, but certainly his livelihood, thought Hosé, peering at them.

One sketch showed a long façade with flat doubled pilasters between the arch-headed windows.

'Like they have in Florence,' said the clerk. He paused, then carefully pulled out another sheet and put it on top. 'And the proposed courtyard too. Brunelleschi designed the cloisters for Santa Croce in Florence in the same style.' He showed off his knowledge.

Hosé almost smiled, then stared at the drawing. He had seen something very much like it before: a rectangular courtyard to be surrounded by two floors with open arcaded loggias, delicate columns supporting rounded arches. 'Florence, eh?' he said. They looked very much like work he had seen as a boy; in Urbino.

'Brunelleschi's work has inspired many great architects,' said the clerk airily, tidying his precious pile and taking a firmer grip on them.

'It'll take a while to build that lot.' Hosé nodded at the drawings. 'It'll be a few years before the Cardinal can move in.'

'Pope Martin's old palazzo will have to do him for a bit longer,' agreed the clerk.

A considerable number of people could feel reassured about their continued employment.

At the Vatican, the Pope also had building plans: for a tower – not grandiose perhaps, but nice and secure. There were to be improvements too, to the Castel Sant' Angelo and there was renewed talk of the tunnel to connect the two.

Which might be needed rather sooner than later, thought Hosé, as he listened to snippets of news and put them together. Rome was coming to the Papal heel, but other cities and states throughout the long Italian peninsula had merely been waiting to see which way the vote of the Sacred College fell before planning their next moves.

Mischief seeded by Innocent continued to come to fruition. Papal states south of Rome, that were not Innocent's to give, had been handed to one of the bastard sons. This son in turn tried to realise their value by offering to sell them to Gentile Orsini, the contract being witnessed by Cardinal della Rovere. Cardinal Guiliano della Rovere had not been one of the cardinals persuaded to vote Borgia by Ascanio Sforza, for that Cardinal had wanted the papal throne for himself. He did not intend to surrender that ambition, nor did he intend to cooperate with this new Pope.

To the north, the handsome, sly and powerful Ludovico Maria Sforza ruled as "Regent" in the Duchy of Milan. His nickname *Il Moro* suggested a darkness of skin or purpose although, in fact, he was fair of feature. He was quite content for people to believe what they wished about his nature; he had actually chosen the device of the Moro because the mulberry blossomed ahead of any of the other trees. He had seized power in Milan ahead of his young nephew and the boy's even younger Neapolitan bride.

In the far south, the king of Naples protested at the treatment of his daughter and rattled his sword, threatening to march north and reinstate the rightful Duke and Duchess of Milan.

To the northeast, Venice thought this was a remarkably bad notion as it would bring the king within striking distance of their newly acquired mainland territories. Mantua, Ferrara and Siena agreed.

For the moment, the Pope was fortifying the Castel, building up his force of mercenaries, dealing with the various embassies. Hosé could almost admire his statesmanship: if Pope Alexander VI played the game right he would hold the balance of power between Milan and Naples while continuing to strengthen his own position in the middle.

In his first year on the Papal throne, Alexander VI was called upon to balance many matters.

Spain and Portugal were racing neck and neck, across different oceans. Papal bulls tried to pontificate about which territories each could claim, to the satisfaction of neither. An imaginary line, on an imaginative map, gave newly discovered lands to the west to Spain and all those to the east to Portugal.

Hosé frowned. All the voyages confirmed, to anyone with a speck of sense, that the world was *spherical*! Martin Behaim of Nuremburg had even drawn a map showing it so.

Rabia also frowned. She was thinking of the Portuguese heading east. 'What about the people who already live there? Particularly those of the Faith living and trading around the Indian ocean.'

Hosé was a little surprised. 'You know about those parts?'

'Fez is a long way from the sea.' She half smiled. 'You might think that its only remote connection with water comes from the springs that feed the city's cisterns! But Ibn Battuta lived there.' Her smile faded. 'My grandfather knew his writings.'

Of course he did, as did Isaac.

Much nearer home the Pope decided to throw in his lot with Milan, and to cement this alliance he contracted his daughter, the beautiful Lucrezia, to one of the myriad Sforza bastards, Giovanni, Lord of Pesaro.

Pesaro, not far from the mountain fasts of Urbino. Hosé had sailed from its port nearly two decades before, down the Venetian sea. To a new life.

Lucrezia's equally beautiful brother, Cesare, had been summoned to Rome from his studies. Hosé had seen him once in the Trastevere, setting out on a hunting expedition. The first tonsure of the bright auburn hair had been covered with an elegant cap; his jacket and hose had been of fine silk, his boots of softest leather. His armaments had shone in the sunshine as only the best steel did. He had been laughing with his companions as they rode past.

Giovanni Borgia had also returned to Rome. The young Duke of Gandia had arrived in style, to share the family's enhanced fame and fortune. He might not be as handsome as his elder brother but he rivalled him in arrogance, as he paraded around the city with the Pontiff; sometimes in the company of Prince Cem.

The circumstances of the Ottoman pretender had indeed altered, it seemed, with the change in Pope. Cem now rode Ylderim regularly in an exalted group, a prince among princes, a royal and honoured guest.

The exotic Prince might not be the close prisoner he had been, and yet how free was he? Hosé wondered, staring at him.

And what did he talk about with the Pope? Culture, politics, matters of state? Of a common cause against the most powerful of the leaders in Islam?

If Hosé had not been so concerned with these questions he might have taken greater note of the big soldier in the company of Spanish soldiers whom the Papal family favoured to protect them.

Lucrezia's nuptial celebrations were on a scale worthy of a daughter of possibly the wealthiest and most powerful man in Europe. The palace rang to the sound of music and dancing, to laughter and frivolity. There was singing and an uproarious play; there was sumptuous food and wine to weigh down the strongest table, or stomach. The fact that the man in question happened to be the Holy Father, the head of Christendom, and the palace the Vatican, occasioned little comment in a city used to hearing of far greater licence and junketing.

Had Giovanni Sforza's equally illegitimate cousin had anything like it those years ago, when he had taken to wife Caterina, presumed widow of the Genoese merchant Signore Guido Lomellino? Nothing approaching it, thought Hosé.

That same summer Cesare Borgia was raised to the purple, at the age of nineteen. He received his title in the same ceremony that gave a similar one to Alessandro Farnese, also brother to a beautiful sister. The regulars at the Dancing Bear and other unkind citizens of Rome dubbed Alessandro the Petticoat Cardinal in recognition of the connection, but they did not say it too loudly. It was not wise to annoy any of the Borgias or their powerful friends.

Interesting though these Borgia family manoeuvres were, Hosé found it even more interesting to hear of the next passes in the Milan-Naples tourney.

Il Moro of Milan had stolen a march on all the others again and entered negotiations with King Charles VIII of France. Charles of Anjou had a family interest in the kingdom of Naples. Ludovico Il Moro Sforza whispered in the Gallic ear that he would happily consider allowing the French army through Milan to further this interest. If that was not enough of a prize, whispered that same voice, then the most Christian King of France could use the heel of Italy as a base to attack the heathen Turks, to stop their advance in Dalmatia and Croatia, just across the Adriatic Sea. A new Charles the Great could drive the Saracens back into the wastelands of Anatolia, even liberate the Holy Sepulchre!

There was no mention about a French return journey.

Hosé laboured on the Riario palace by day in the sweltering heat and in the evening in the stuffy attic room. He wondered which was more exhausting, as he pieced together the diplomatic moves.

'What will the Pope do?' Rabia was preparing to go out on yet another errand with Guiseppe.

'The King of Naples did not get the promise of help he wanted from Spain, so he is in a very poor bargaining position. I imagine Pope

Alexander knows enough of business to make excellent capital out of the situation.'

'What does that mean?'

'I suspect it means that the Pope will get back entitlement to the states that Innocent tried to give away and probably a nice fat bit of compensation from the Orsini. The usual way to conclude any such deal is to arrange a marriage. Giovanni Borgia has a royal Spanish wife. Cesare is a Cardinal and, although it seems acceptable for a Cardinal to ignore the rule of chastity, it is not yet acceptable to ignore the one on celibacy. Lucrezia has her Milanese Sforza bastard. That leaves Gioffre. How about a marriage between him and a nice Neapolitan princess?'

Rabia nodded absently as she checked the things in her bag.

And all that might have worked out except that the King of Naples was so upset at not getting his own way that he died.

Hosé listened to the melancholy account of the event from Father Angelo, exchanged complaints about work on the palazzo in general and about Gregorio in particular with Luigi, emptied his mug, and left for home.

Rabia had not returned. The small oil light showed Ishaq asleep, with one of the baker's daughters curled up beside him.

Hosé frowned. This was the second night in a row. Rabia had not returned the previous night until after dawn and instead of being tired she had seemed strangely awake, excited almost.

She had said little about the case and Hosé had not asked for details. He stared at the far side of the small room thinking. He was about to wake the girl and send her back down to her siblings when his eyes came to rest on the row of pegs where they hung their clothes.

No, Guiseppe was not in. No, she did not know where her husband had gone. Yes, Rabia had been there and yes, they had gone off together, just the two of them. No, they had not taken Manfredo with them. Yes, that was a bit unusual.

Hosé considered. They had gone somewhere close enough that they felt safe without the servant Manfredo? Or they had not wanted Manfredo with them?

Last night?

A poor woman had dropped down in the street. Guiseppe and Rabia had done what they could for her but she had died.

Where?

Where what?

Where had the woman died? Where was she now?

She had died in Guiseppe's back room. They had taken the body away, of course.

Who had taken it where?

Guiseppe and Rabia had taken it on the handcart. They couldn't have left it in the back room, could they? They must have taken it to the mortuary.

At that time in the morning?

The woman shrugged.

Another house? Another shop?

No, Guiseppe only had the one place. No, he did not have a warehouse; he only dealt in small quantities of herbs and medicines. Oh yes, they did sometimes deliver stuff for him somewhere down near the river.

Somewhere near the Isola?

She didn't know.

It was all a bit strange but perhaps he was making too much out of it.

Hosé walked back to the bakery. Maybe Rabia would be home by now.

There were still only the two children.

He hesitated then left again.

He knew the area alongside the river quite well. At least he did in the daylight. By night it was different.

The shadows in the alleys were so dense he could make out nothing and he retreated to the wider streets. He found himself back by the river which was barely visible in the dark, although he could hear its movement and the rubbing of wooden hulls against each other. There was the occasional plop of a rat; a cat yowled to his right and another answered.

Then somewhere to his right the sound of voices, the thud of feet.

Rabia turned anxiously. Guiseppe was a man past his prime, his breath was coming in gasps and his feet were dragging.

She could hear their pursuers getting closer.

They were now probably a safe distance from the warehouse and its damning evidence, but what possible reason could they give for running through these uninhabited streets at this time of night? And her appearance? There had been no time to see to that.

Guiseppe was a well-known figure in the neighbourhood. If they were caught he would be recognised. And in these circumstances, with her? She had no doubt of the consequences for him.

'Hide here,' she said, pushing him towards a side street. 'Wait until they have gone past then cut around into the Via del Pellegrino.'

Guiseppe drew to a panting halt. 'And you?'

'I'll carry on that way,' she pointed.

'No, no,' he said. 'If they catch you,' he could not finish.

'They won't,' she said with more conviction than she felt. 'I can outrun them.'

'But,' he gasped.

'Go on,' she said urgently. The footsteps were getting very close.

She did not wait for his agreement but fled. Making as much noise as she could, she ducked into an alley. She did not want them to see that it was only one person they were now pursuing. She clattered into a large pot, picked her way over its shards and dived into another opening.

She paused. The men were still following. She waited a moment or two then set off again. There were shouts as they spotted her.

She ran up one street and down another. A dog ran out at her and she hastily turned. The animal followed her, snapping at her ankles. She tried to wave it away but it barked more loudly and she nearly tripped.

Above the yapping and growling she could hear voices.

She tried to kick the animal away but only got bitten for her efforts.

Suddenly she remembered. She managed to reach for her knife. It was a smaller target than she had practised on with Hosé and it was dark. Her first stab caused a loud yelp of pain. She twisted the blade clear and aimed again. There was a whimper and the animal subsided to the ground.

She shoved her knife back in its place and stepped over the body.

'There!'

She turned and ran again.

The alley was a dead end. She stopped, her heart pounding. She scrabbled in the blackness for a way out, or somewhere to hide. She pushed at a door; it did not move.

She ran back the way she had come but she had lost valuable time.

Strong arms wrapped themselves around her and backed her against the wall. Teeth tore the cap from her head and her hair fell over her face, blinding her.

She felt hands dragging at her clothes and opened her mouth to scream.

'A little cooperation would be helpful.'

She gasped. There was a loud sound of ripping cloth. She tried to back away but the stonework was solid.

The man moved against her and she let out a cry.

'Better.'

The man shifted again as he grabbed at his laces. 'Damn it,' he said,

'Don't act the bloody virgin!'

She froze with shock, unwanted memories filled her mind. The bile rose in her throat.

'Come on.' The man's voice was rough.

Suddenly there was light. The torches cast flickering shadows into the narrow alley.

The man swore loudly, the Roman vernacular echoed off the walls. '…. off!' he growled. 'Can't you see I'm busy?'

There was coarse laughter. 'Sorry to disturb you in the middle of such important business.'

'Don't stop because of us,' said another voice.

Rabia felt anger rising out her fear. She began to reach for her knife. A calloused hand caught her wrist.

The man hard against her let out another stream of invective at the intruders.

A third man arrived on the scene, breath rasping. He pushed forward with a lantern, staring at the couple in the alley.

'Got no entertainment of your own?' demanded the bellicose voice near Rabia's ear.

There was no response but the lamp was lifted higher, illuminating the scene.

Rabia flushed as its light exposed her body.

'These aren't them.' The man with the lantern was still trying to catch his breath. 'Did you see anyone go past?' he demanded. 'An older man and a boy?'

'…… off!' The man swore again.

'Too busy,' scoffed one of the others.

His companion spat. 'Fouling the place.'

'Perhaps we should clean it up.'

Rabia felt the man's body tense.

'We should get after the others. Leave this filth where it belongs.'

The man finally let Rabia go and walked to the top of the alley.

He peered out into the main street for a long moment before returning to where she leaned against the wall, trying to pull her clothes around her.

He stopped in front of her. 'I think they've gone.'

She opened her mouth but no words emerged.

He took her in his arms, gently. 'I'm sorry,' he said. 'It seemed the only way.'

She was shaking with relief, with reaction, with something else she could not name. She lifted her head and fell back on anger.

Hosé waited until the words came to a stop. Her command of harbour-side argot was at least as good as his gutter Roman.

'You've made your point,' he said as she threatened to extend the demonstration.

She drew a shuddering breath.

He smoothed the hair away from her face. And paused. The last time he had done that had been the night Ishaq was born and it had grown a lot since then. Of course, he saw it every evening when she untied her coif, but she kept it neatly braided. Now it hung loose, heavy as a skein of silk.

And it was not just her hair that caught the attention of his wondering hands.

She was far too thin for beauty, but she was well-formed for all that. He traced the shape of her, the smoothness of her skin, the line of her hips and thighs, her breasts, small and firm since Ishaq's weaning.

He felt the tightening in his loins.

She shivered under his touch and his hands moved with more purpose.

He had never been quite desperate enough to patronise the myriad whores who plied their trade in the streets. It had been a long time.

He wrenched himself away and struck the wall violently with his fist. The pain helped; a little. He drew in deep gulps of foetid air. Gradually his pulse slowed and he became acutely aware of the stinking alley.

What in the name of the Almighty had he been doing?

Rabia was trembling.

He trusted himself at last to take her hand. The fire had gone now, its flames doused by shame.

She tried to pull away.

'It's all right,' he said a little unsteadily. 'The madness has passed.' He swallowed. 'The fear, the situation, acting as if……' He stopped, thinking of other times. 'The racing of the blood from danger becomes the racing of blood in passion, in lust.' He gave it its proper name. 'Perhaps it is always like that with men,' he tried to explain, to himself as much as to her.

For a long time, she was silent, struggling with her own emotions. Finally, she said, 'I thought you were different.' That had not been quite what she had been thinking, but she had to say something, to try and get things back to normal.

Hosé was trying as hard as she was. He made a sound that was almost a laugh. 'Feet of clay.'

'What?'

'The image seemed perfect if one looked at its golden head. Even its chest and arms were of silver, but its belly and thighs were of bronze, its legs of iron, and its feet of clay.'

'What are you talking about?' She dared to look at him, the whites of her eyes showed dimly as she lifted her face.

'A stone broke the feet and the whole image collapsed. It turned to dust and was carried away by the wind.'

'Who said that?' There was curiosity in her voice.

'King Nebuchadnezzar.'

'King Nebuchadnezzar?' Now she was puzzled.

'He was describing a dream he had, to Daniel.'

'Daniel? Daniel who?' She prodded him.

He was not sure that was a good idea. He caught her other hand. 'One of the old Hebrew Prophets.'

'Isaac!'

'One of his cautionary tales,' he confirmed drily. 'Part of his attempts to improve my education.'

He let her go rather abruptly. He did not want to talk about those months in the cloister in Genoa, and he really didn't want to hold her hands.

'Here,' he pulled his jacket off and put it around her. Fortunately, it reached nearly to her knees, as his other one had, before he had ripped it off her. 'Let's go home.'

They walked in silence for a while, an odd silence.

'Perhaps you would like to tell me what you and Guiseppe were doing.' Hosé spoke at last.

'I don't think you will approve,' she said.

'Does it have anything to do with the sealed packet from Isaac by any chance?'

Chapter 20

It was another year before events finally provoked the Neapolitan marriage, events set in train in France but with direct consequences for Rome and its inhabitants, be they noble or common.

News reaching the Dancing Bear indicated that Charles of France had fixed his unwavering Gallic eye on a glorious place in history and in the Christian heaven. He had dismissed the Neapolitan legate and the hopes of the new king who had sent him. Now he was intent on making more geographical progress.

Pope Alexander had delayed the marriage of his youngest son Gioffre into the House of Naples and not therefore sealed absolutely any alliance, but the French King was determined on more definite proof of Papal sympathy. Charles declared himself King of Neapolitan Sicily and demanded that the Pope invest him personally with the title. The payment for lifting a small piece of headgear onto the Angevin brow was to be considerable, and was, moreover, to be repeated every year thereafter.

Hosé chewed his lip. Rome was caught squarely in the middle, between France and Naples. The army of Naples, massed and prepared, was camped only a very short march from the Holy See. Captain Andrea Doria had been very much involved in that preparation, he'd learned.

While Doria's cousin, and one-time fellow condottiero, Oberto Spinola, had indeed returned to Genoa to consolidate the family, in more ways than one. Although Hosé doubted if Oberto had quite shared the happiness expressed in 'Bella's letter on the birth of their second daughter.

Hosé shook his head and turned his mind back to matters in Rome.

The Pope had put his argument to the Consistory, but they had largely lent ears to the French case. Even Cardinal Ascanio Sforza, comfortably settled into the old Borgia residence, complete with its costly furnishings (and the heavy nocturnal loads of silver), saw the situation from the position of his Milanese brother. Cardinal Guiliano della Rovere always opposed Pope Alexander on principle; he needed to listen to no case at all. He had a clear perception of who would add most force to his particular cause and he had left Rome to put this into practice. He had hastened to Ostia with the Papal mercenaries hastening after him. According to Julio it had been a close-run thing, but della Rovere had been fortunate to find a boat willing to take him to Genoa, from where he had travelled to Nice. There, according to Annette, the Cardinal was almost certainly aiding the most Christian French king in plans that would depose the appointed Vicar of Christ's church if he happened to be standing in the way.

The Vicar made his decision and his stand. Pope Alexander sent his nephew to Naples to crown the Aragonese heir and claimant, and with him went young Gioffre to meet and at last marry his Neapolitan princess.

Hosé may have had knowledge of extra details, but the Roman population was generally well aware of what was happening. Everyone knew that it would not be long before King Charles delivered his reply to this rebuff, and he was likely to deliver it in person.

Throughout the long hot summer people went about their usual business, but with many a glance to the north.

News from the north told of a huge French army preparing to cross the Alps. Thirty thousand soldiers from the military fraternities of Germany, Switzerland and France had been gathered by the young French king. They marched in good order and short time into the state of Milan. Both the kind weather of October and Il Moro favoured the Gallic cause.

Charles VIII accepted Ludovico's invitation to the Castle of Pavia where the putative young Duke of Milan still languished. Perhaps the youthful prisoner saw a futile future in the faces of the two rulers, perhaps something in his captive diet disagreed with him. A very few days after the visit, all hope expired; as did the wretched life of Gian Galeazzo Sforza.

The French King was at Piacenza when the news reached him and he embarked on a public tribute and support for the departed soul that he had never offered the live one. The piety sat well with his proclaimed Christian mission, and would not delay him seriously.

Ludovico made no pretence at regret or delay. He had little difficulty in persuading the Parliament of Milan that he should now officially succeed to the title of Duke (regardless of five-year-old Francesco Sforza, conceived, born and raised in the same captivity as his late father). Once again Il Moro got in first.

The thirty thousand moved inexorably as far as Florence and, although the French King omitted mention of the Neapolitan coronation in his polite note to the Pope requesting passage for the horde en route for Naples, Alexander and his city were deeply disturbed.

The French army was not the only tribulation facing Florence. Piero da Medici may have inherited his father's title but he definitely had not inherited his father's flair or authority: the Medici had been expelled from Florence. For too long the mass of the population had been excluded from the city's wealth, a fact brought increasingly to their notice by the fiery sermons of the monk Savanarola.

Hosé could picture that "I told you so" look on Isaac's face as he heard the news, but the fall of the Medici could have serious personal consequences, as he explained to Rabia.

'You think Clough may come here?' she asked over her shoulder, as she persuaded Ishaq to sit still while she treated the latest cut on his leg.

'I think it is quite likely, especially since he seems to have built himself another sizeable and secure capital base,' Hosé replied sourly.

'Then he won't need the *Katrin* anymore,' she said hopefully.

Hosé snorted. 'He won't let Cornelius and Pieter get away with that.'

Rabia tied off the piece of boiled linen, fastened the distinctly ragged hose and set the boy on his feet. He was big for his four years.

It was not so much that he went looking for trouble as that trouble seemed to find him. He had an insatiable curiosity and that, Hosé had noted with misgiving, always seemed to involve climbing the highest tree or most crumbling wall or most rickety stairway in the neighbourhood, although the baker's girls, set to mind him and their siblings, tried their best.

When roused, he would scrap, but he did not usually start the fights, and he was quick to volunteer his mother to bandage those he beat.

Sometimes she feared she saw something of his father in him, sometimes she saw her grandfather. But mostly she just saw him for himself; Hosé had been right.

She turned. 'Clough has reason to have a grudge against you too.'

He shrugged. He was well aware of that.

'And he can command many people to do his devil's work; like those two he sent to Mallorca.'

Hosé nodded.

'He may have agents all around the Middle Sea looking for the *Katrin*.'

Hosé nodded again. 'He does.'

'You know for sure?' she frowned at him.

'Several have been spotted.'

'Where? By whom?'

'Other agents.' Whose information, passed on by the dragoman, had so far enabled Cornelius to trade unhampered, and profitably. The last letter from Jakob had suggested they might build another boat, a bigger one, one that could face the heavy seas of the Atlantic Ocean. Why should the Portuguese and Spanish be the only ones to trade the new routes? Jakob had demanded.

Rabia cleared away the things she had been using, replacing the cork in the jar of ointment and putting it back in its place on the crowded shelf.

Hosé watched her absently as she took some other things and packed her bag.

His mind was on the French and the Prince. Charles VIII had long proclaimed his wish to lead a new crusade. Suppose he took control of Naples? That would give him the perfect launching place. And how perfectly that would fit with the Prince's pretensions.

If the Pope were forced to hand over his priceless hostage….. Hosé frowned. That would certainly change the situation for him too, considerably.

Rab nudged Ishaq and headed for the door. 'Guiseppe and I may not finish until late,' she said. 'When will you be back?'

Hosé dragged his thoughts to immediate matters. 'I have to go over the river.'

'Can I come, Papa?' demanded Ishaq, seeing the chance of something much more interesting than the company of the baker's girls and the tasks they were required to do.

Hosé hesitated.

'Please,' said Ishaq, in his most persuasive voice. 'I'll be good, I promise.' He ran across the room and took Hosé's rough hand, confident he had argued his point.

Hosé considered the face looking up at him. He had always taken the boy with him whenever he could. It had sometimes provoked comment, a man minding a young child, but a glance at Hosé's expression, and body, had deterred any serious challenge to this odd behaviour.

He gave Rabia a small smile over the top of the boy's dark head. 'All right.'

It was a decision he was to regret for the rest of his life.

It was a fine day as they reached the Ponte Sisto. Small craft jostled for position on the dark waters of the Tevere as they fought to be first under the bridge.

Ishaq pulled Hosé to a halt and listened with mouth slightly open to the raucous arguments floating up from the rival boatmen.

Hosé also listened for a while. One never knew where the next fragment of interesting information would come from. As well as demands for passage and insults regarding parentage, there could be a few words about the goods being carried, sometimes revealing where they had come from or where they were going. In spite of the uncertain times, traffic on the river today seemed entirely normal.

Hosé grasped Ishaq's hand and pushed on across crowded the bridge.

Soon they were on the straight passage that had been cut through the old dwellings and filthy twisting alleys, which was to be part of a new roadway. Pope Alexander had ambitious plans for his city and the Via della Lungara would connect the Vatican directly with the Trastevere.

Hosé explained this to Ishaq as they followed the road past the other Riario palace, which was steadily reaching up towards the blue Roman skies. It was difficult to see what the building would finally look like, obscured as it was with scaffolding, but Hosé thought Domenico's edifice would not be quite as grand as his brother Raffaele's. But who knew when, or even if, either building would be completed? If the present Pope did not manage to handle the challenge from the French king, then many things might change in Rome.

Hosé took a firmer hold on Ishaq's hand, answering the boy's questions as best he could, and picked his way through the lumbering carts and the stream of workmen around the building project.

They headed up the Janiculum hill, through the maze of streets to the tenement Hosé sought. A woman nodded at him then directed a gap-toothed smile at Ishaq, putting a crooked finger to his cheek.

The boy smiled back at her. He was used to female admiration thought Hosé wryly.

'Is Gregorio at home?'

The woman pulled a face. 'Useless piece of donkey shit.'

'Is he ill?'

Gregorio was not a craftsman, not even a member, of one of the official guilds. He organised the labourers like Luigi and Hosé, and often dozens of others. He recruited, he ordered, he abused and he dismissed as he saw fit. The architect was, Hosé suspected, more than a little frightened of the man, but he needed him. And Gregorio had not been at the building site for days.

'Signore Bramante sent me to see him.' Because his clerk had almost fainted at the suggestion *he* might go.

'You are welcome,' she cackled and pointed a finger into the gloomy interior of the building.

Hosé paused a moment, suddenly wondering at the wisdom of bringing Ishaq. Gregorio could be a brutal man, although he had not tried hitting Hosé since that first day.

'He won't hurt you!' The woman saw the hesitation and laughed again. 'Couldn't hurt a fly, the way he is at the moment.'

Hosé nodded.

'But perhaps the boy would find the view prettier out here,' she suggested meaningfully. She smiled again at Ishaq. 'Would you like to sit here with Marietta?'

Ishaq looked hopefully at Hosé.

'All right.' Hosé reached into his bag and pulled out the loaf he had brought with them from home. There was a piece of cheese with it. 'Share these,' he said to the boy. 'And don't wander off, understand?'

Ishaq was already savouring the bread with his nose. 'Yes, Papa.'

At first it was difficult even to see Gregorio. Hosé pushed open a broken shutter and a muttered curse greeted the light.

Hosé turned and stared. 'What happened?'

Somehow, he pieced together the essential details as Gregorio sputtered the words between split and swollen lips.

'Here.' Hosé offered him the mug of water that stood nearby.

The work boss managed a few sips then spat out some unidentifiable globs.

Hosé viewed the man's body, slumped on the floor and still wearing the remains of his clothes. Hosé was no expert, but it was obvious that the left arm was fractured and judging from the way Gregorio was breathing that his ribs were cracked, if not broken.

The man was a mess.

'Have you seen a physician?'

Gregorio snorted. 'Thieving bags of wind.' He mumbled. 'Been in a fight before. I'll mend.' He tried to move but quickly changed his mind.

Hosé sat back on his heels and considered. 'Signore Bramante sent me to find out what had happened to you. He wants you back at work.'

Gregorio tried to move again but lay back with a moan.

'You need help,' Hosé said. 'And even then, it will be weeks.'

Gregorio cursed with commendable fluency. 'Been hurt before,' he repeated.

'Not this bad,' Hosé was sure, and probably when the man was younger. 'That arm needs setting straight or it'll be no use to you.'

Gregorio glared at him from the shadow of two blackened eyes but did not contradict this time.

'I could fetch someone.'

Gregorio groaned then muttered eventually, 'Can't pay.'

There was another slurred string of words from which Hosé gathered that the same gang that had beaten up Gregorio had also stolen what remained of his wages after a hard evening's drinking.

Hosé reached into the leather pocket inside his shirt. 'Signore Bramante suspected you might need an advance.' Gregorio's swollen eyes opened a fraction at the sight of the coins. 'He needs you Gregorio. You know what's what and you get the job done.' Hosé suddenly grinned. 'He might not like you, who would?' Gregorio managed a bloody grimace. 'But his job would be much more difficult without you and he knows it.'

Hosé made his way back outside. Marietta was squatting beside Ishaq playing some sort of game with a handful of stones. Her lined face creased with surprise when Hosé asked if there were a physician anywhere in the area and explained that Signore Bramante's money would pay for one.

'A man as important as that, thinks so much of Gregorio?' This was evidently a completely new idea to her. Hosé suspected the work boss showed little of his few positive qualities towards his wife, only the brutality. The woman considered Hosé's question and named a man who lived a few streets away.

Hosé had another thought. 'While you fetch him,' he said, 'I'll go and get something Gregorio might manage to eat.'

The woman rose stiffly to her feet and went on her errand, still shaking her head slightly in disbelief.

Hosé took Ishaq's hand and considered. There were lots of booths and stalls around the church of Santa Maria della Scala, the centre of the Trastevere, but that was nearly back at the Ponte Sisto. Considerably closer was another solution.

He ducked inside the house and found what he wanted. 'Come on,' he said cheerfully to Ishaq. 'Let's go into the country!'

At the point where the Via Aurelia and Via Mirabilis met was the Porta Aurelia, set in the old walls built long ago by one of the ancient Roman emperors to protect his city on its western side. It was a simple opening but the arch was outlined with large, carefully shaped stones. The ancients had known their geometry, thought Hosé appreciatively. To either side, the walls were punctuated with watch towers of varied form and height, many with cracks in their masonry and edges softened by crumbling stonework. The walls were nothing like those that protected Islambul. A modern army ranged on the hills opposite, with cannon dragged by teams of mules and men, thought Hosé, would make short work of them. Given the chance, they were another thing the present bellicose Pope might attend to, sometime.

'Can we climb up to the top?' Ishaq's question caught Hosé's attention.

'No,' said Hosé firmly. 'We need to go to one of the farms and buy milk,' he added in defence of his decision.

The boy's face fell for a moment then brightened. 'Will they have horses on the farm?'

Hosé gave an exasperated laugh. There seemed some almost devilish irony in the fact that his adoptive son should have such a fascination with both climbing and horses. 'Horses are for the rich,' he answered. 'But, perhaps,' he added, as he saw the boy's disappointment.

Immediately outside the gate were fields planted with strips of crops. Men and women were busy with the late summer harvest, while the younger children guarded the plots from infant siblings and marauding animals.

On an open space beyond the cultivated land were a handful of cows, being herded by a boy only a little older than Ishaq. Hosé asked if he could buy milk.

The boy regarded him for a moment and the pitcher Hosé had brought with him. He suggested a price for filling it.

Hosé laughed. 'I think we'll try a bit further on.' He turned.

The boy revised his offer.

'Maybe,' Hosé considered. He knew the price was still too high but the sheer effrontery of the lad appealed to him, and it was after all Signore Bramante's money he was spending. 'You give my lad here a drink as well,' he countered.

The boy considered. Finally, he nodded and stuck out a hand. He counted the coins carefully then took the pitcher and headed for the nearest cow. He spoke to her with words that made no sense to Hosé, then squatted beside her and started to strip one of her teats into the jug. Once the bony animal half lifted her leg but the boy skilfully avoided it, at the same time protecting the jug and its precious contents.

Hosé watched appreciatively.

The boy stopped and handed over the vessel. Hosé made considerable play with regarding the quantity, assessing how much milk was hidden beneath the froth. He accepted it gravely and passed the milk to Ishaq who drank with great relish, his face emerging with creamy whiskers which he only half removed with the back of one rather grubby hand.

The cow herd took back the pitcher and began milking again, the milk zinging rhythmically into the pot.

'To the top.' Hosé handed it back.

The boy scowled but accepted it without real protest. The rich foam rose to the lip of the jug.

Hosé took it with a smile. 'That should help Gregorio to mend.' He handed over an extra coin.

The boy looked at him in surprise. He opened his mouth to say something but the words remained unspoken at the sound of drumming hoofs. The road was not far distant but the hunting party apparently preferred to ride over the countryside, regardless of the fields and the peasants who tended them.

The boy made a frantic effort to herd his cows out of the way but they bellowed in panic and scattered in all directions. He gave a shout and chased after a couple, his bare feet scattering small stones as he desperately tried to head them off.

Hosé quickly set down the jug and waved his arms at one animal coming his way. Behind him Ishaq copied his actions.

The cow tried to dodge around him. Finally, Hosé managed to guide her back towards the pasture.

He turned and looked in horror. Another cow had headed for the road and Ishaq was pursuing it.

Hosé called out but his voice was lost in the bellows and thunder of hoofs. It was drowned too by the angry yell of men's voices.

Hosé started to run.

Ishaq was still following the cow.

As the noise behind him finally caught his attention, the child stopped. He looked towards the horses. Hosé could not see the boy's expression but Ishaq's stance showed quite clearly that he was in awe rather than frightened.

Hosé yelled again as he tried to force his legs to move faster.

Ishaq stood there for a moment, quite still, then stretched his short arms as far as they would go as a dozen horses galloped towards him.

It was like a terrible nightmare. Hosé's legs felt as if they were made of lead.

From an impossible distance, he saw the two leading horsemen slow their mounts. The one with red gold hair, beneath a jewelled cap, laughed and said something to his companion. The other man, his face dark beneath a snowy turban, replied.

Hosé drove himself forward.

The two men set their heels to their horses.

Hosé could see everything in brilliant detail.

But he couldn't get there.

A soldier, an eight-pointed white cross on the breast of his cloak, shouted something at the men in front of him.

Hosé was yelling again. Why didn't Ishaq move?

The boy stood small but upright, an expression of fascination on his face as the horse loomed over him.

Hosé screamed as the horse failed to clear the sturdy figure, knocking it aside, into the path of the great black stallion.

The party rode on.

Only the Knight paused. Raymond de Glandèves looked down at the small mangled body lying in the dust and shook his head. The young face, remarkably, was untouched. There were even the faint marks of milk around the slack mouth. The boy was somehow vaguely familiar.

De Glandèves stared for some moments, then shook his head. God knew, the peasants had more than enough children.

A man arrived and threw himself down beside the child. The knight, suddenly discomfited by the man's loss, urged his horse forward.

It was several hours before he recalled where he had seen the boy before. That was when he also realised, with a curse, who the man must have been.

He went in search of de Blanchefort.

Chapter 21

Six years before, Sultan Bayezit had nearly managed to buy off King Charles. Now, however, the French monarch had become openly hostile to Constantinople, and the Sultan seriously feared what might happen if Rome, and Cem, fell into French hands.

Pope Alexander had his own fears about the Gallic army. Two days after the feast of St John he sent his Papal Nuncio to Constantinople pleading for an advance on the annual "protection" fee. Forty thousand ducats would pay for a substantial number of extra mercenaries to defend Rome and the Papacy.

Hosé knew from Isaac that the Sultan had immediately agreed. However, weeks passed without any sign of the Nuncio, or the coin.

Late in November a strange tale began to spread. Hosé listened in bewilderment to the story that the Nuncio had been intercepted on his return to Italy, carrying incriminating letters. He had revealed all: that the Pope, the head of the Christian Church, had appealed for help from the Infidel Turk, and that God's vicar had agreed to the conditions set by the Sultan in return for payment.

One condition, apparently, was that the Pope appoint Nicolas Cibo a cardinal.

Why on earth would the Sultan have the slightest interest in the advancement of Nicolas Cibo, Archbishop of Arles? Hosé wondered.

The major demand said to be made by the Sultan was that Prince Cem "*be freed from the tribulations of this life*". Such a move would not, in itself, either surprise or bother those who heard about it, but it did reinforce the point that the Pope had been treating with the Devil, allowing himself to be dictated to by the Saracen.

Hosé sank back on the bench of the ill-lit wine shop and tried to think straight.

Of one thing he was certain: Bayezit would not seek the death of his brother Cem. The Vizier Muhammad had done so, on several occasions. But Isaac's return to Constantinople had been followed, in fairly short order, by a less than short end for the Vizier.

Hosé scowled.

Who had actually seen these letters?

There was little clear information on that from those in the wine shop, or anywhere else that Hosé frequented, although rumour abounded.

Some said that the letters were in Turkish and had been translated at Santa Croce by a man who had lived in Constantinople.

Turkish. Diplomatic letters sent from the Topkapi were in Greek....

Others began to say that the letters were after all in Greek, and they had been translated at Santa Croce by no less a personage than the Bishop of Famagusta.

Greek. Someone had realised their mistake about the Turkish.....

Others again talked of one letter in Latin, the letter about ending Prince Cem's troubled life in return for the fabulous sum of three hundred thousand ducats.

Latin. Conveniently easy to translate into Italian, so everyone could read it.....

And the final "proof" for everyone that the Papal Nuncio's confession was true, was the discovery on his person of the very letter from the Pope to the Sultan.

But why would he have brought that back with him to Italy.....?

Where had the almost unbelievably inept story originated? Hosé asked himself.

Santa Croce. The place in Florence where the Inquisition held its tribunals, home to clerics who would support just such a fabrication, to the best of their apparently limited ability!

And, after all, it was not a total fabrication: the Pope *had* written to the Sultan, and the Nuncio *had* been returning to Italy with (genuine) letters and coin. Somebody had discovered this. And decided to make political capital out of it. And a nice little profit: for the forty thousand ducats must have been seized with the Nuncio.

But who was the "somebody"?

Hosé visited other wine shops, any place where there was gossip.

And learned it had been the Prefect, Captain General of the Church and Lord of Sinigallia, Giovanni della Rovere, who had seized the Nuncio on the road to Rome, and had quite naturally given him into the "care" of his brother, Cardinal Guiliano della Rovere, the Pope's most implacable opponent.

Hosé took a deep breath of the stale cold air.

He frowned again. Had the Nuncio been taken by chance, or had the Prefect known where to find him?

The Nuncio would have landed at Ancona. All the boats arriving at that busy port were taxed, with the money making a nice contribution to the Curia's coffers. Perhaps somebody there had spotted a way to make a nice contribution to their own pocket.

He shook his head. He would probably never know.

The vital question at this point was whether it would make any difference to the position of Prince Cem. On the whole Hosé thought not. The Ottoman hostage was as valuable now as he had ever been, and as much of a threat to his brother, the legitimate Sultan. The Pope surely would not free the Prince from his tribulations, for that would be to destroy a powerful asset.

Hosé's eyes narrowed. But that would only be true as long as the Pope had the asset safe in his own hands.

The Pope may have been short of forty thousand ducats' worth of mercenaries but early in December he declined to let King Charles, with his thirty thousand men, pass through the Papal state. His hope, perhaps, was that the Neapolitan forces mustered nearby would be sufficient deterrent.

But that hope proved unfounded and the horde was not deterred. The people of Rome woke to find the thirty thousand camped outside the insubstantial walls built by the Emperor Aurelius in quite different times.

With the King of France came the discontented barons of the Orsini, the Colonna and the Savelli, and in the jubilant throng came Cardinal Guiliano della Rovere.

Even if Cardinal Riario had wished to continue building his palace he would have been thwarted, for the workers quietly packed their things and made for home, where they used their construction skills to prepare for the invasion. No matter what country they came from, soldiers could be expected to behave the same way and the workmen were determined to protect themselves and their womenfolk as best they could.

Not that Hosé was involved with the palazzo or any of its workers any more. Since the "accident" to Ishaq everything had changed.

Nowadays Hosé avoided all his old acquaintances and all his old haunts. He sought anonymity among the hundreds of vagrants who roamed the city's streets. Rabia had once more adopted the clothes of a youth. Together they pursued the fate of the man whose great black stallion had trampled a small boy.

The Pope accepted the inevitable. From the relative safety of the Sant' Angelo Castel he invited the French king most graciously to pass as he willed. He put the great palace next to San Marco at the royal disposal and sent seven cardinals to greet him.

On the last day of the year, Hosé mixed with the crowd gathered to see the great Gallic arrival. The might of the assembled army held considerable professional interest.

Thousands watched and thousands marched into the city. First came the tall Swiss and German mercenaries, their close-fitting clothes showing off the results of months training and exercising. At least a quarter of them carried the new halberds with their great square blades. These had a long reach and looked deadly, but perhaps they were a little unwieldy. At second glance Hosé decided the soldiers carrying them were up to it. Direct attack would not work against one of those, he thought.

Behind, the rest of the soldiers carried the usual pikes with short swords in their belts.

Hosé did a rough count as they passed. To every thousand pike men there were a hundred arquebusiers. These could do a lot of damage, and from quite a range, but Hosé would have backed the sipahis every time for accuracy and speed.

Behind this vanguard came the French infantry, the officers in steel corselets and helmets, and behind them short squat Gascons humping their arbalests.

More firearms, noted Hosé. The Turks used cannon. They had used them to take Constantinople from Byzantium over forty years ago, before much of Europe had even heard of gunpowder. They were well aware of their deadly effect. However, there had been little development of firearms, to Hosé's knowledge. The janissaries preferred their time-tested weapons, the sipahis rejected the idea completely.

The Christian armies, however, had persevered. The German smiths in particular had been very busy. Hosé looked at the results in front of him and wondered. He would send a detailed report to Isaac.

Two and a half thousand mounted soldiers came next, complete with heavy armour and great maces and lances. With every lancer were three other horses carrying his squire and valets. The other cavalrymen were not so heavily armed, wearing only corselet and helmet, and carrying a longbow. They had discovered the hard way the need to copy the deadly weapon of the English.

A select body of knights shouldered heavy maces, their steel armour covered in the purple and gold surcoat that proclaimed their rank.

Four hundred mounted archers formed the king's immediate bodyguard.

After all this, the monarch himself was a great disappointment. He was a malformed man who looked short even on a horse, thin legs revealed in their golden hose, feet cased in improbably broad shoes.

His face was not unlike a stone grotesque on a Christian church, thought Hosé, looking at the low forehead and huge nose jutting over the loose mouth.

Still the legions poured into the city and the light began to fade. It was quite dark before the rear-guard appeared and that was only visible because of the bonfires that had been lighted along the way.

Swiftly moving horses clattered up the road, the sound of their hoofs nearly drowned by the thunder of the iron rimmed wheels of the gun carriages. Thirty-six there were, although Hosé nearly lost count as one passed him that must have been one and a half times his length and so heavy it threatened to plough up the pavement.

He gazed at the size of its maw. His head would have fitted in there with room to spare.

The turmoil finally ended and the streets began to empty.

So, wondered Hosé, what demands would the small misshapen man in command of this manifest power make?

He was hardly surprised to hear what they were.

King Charles had insisted, naturally, that the French be allowed to pass unhindered through the Roman states to Naples. In addition, he had exacted financial help from the Pope to defeat the Neapolitan army. Moreover, he had insisted on having free access to the Sant' Angelo for his own retreat if that became necessary.

To top it all, as insurance for this Papal assistance, he required two hostages: the Pope's most beautiful son and the Pope's most valuable hostage.

No, Hosé was not surprised. It was a situation Lord Bayezit had feared all along.

A situation that was very much Hosé's responsibility.

They said that the private scene in the Consistory that had been enacted shortly before the Christ Mass had been very affecting, when the most Christian French King had knelt to kiss both the foot and the ring of Christ's Vicar and had sworn the continued unswerving obedience and devotion that had ever been the way of himself and his royal forebears.

Certainly, the public scene at the end of January was most touching. The Pope openly gave his blessing to the King's venture as Cesare Borgia surrendered himself, with his Ottoman companion, into French keeping; together with six fine horses and a string of perhaps twenty pack mules. The Papal prince rode at the right hand of the French monarch; immediately behind was the Turkish prince, mounted on Ylderim.

Hosé stared as the cavalcade made its way down the ancient street that had seen so many leaders great and small over the centuries. On the fleshy face of Prince Cem there was a patent mix of anticipation and anxiety as his circumstances underwent this dramatic change.

Cesare Borgia, on the other hand, looked singularly bright and optimistic. He was a man without a care, Hosé thought bitterly, certainly not for a young boy swept aside in a moment's sport. Life had led the Pope's son to expect only admiration and success.

Hosé's eyes narrowed; or perhaps he knew something that the French king did not.

He and Rabia collected their things and joined the nefarious crowd following the French horde.

At Marino Hosé experienced for the first time a western army on campaign.

He pulled his tattered cloak more closely around his shoulders as the cold of the winter evening penetrated his clothes. He thought longingly of a warm Anatolian *kepnel* as he adjusted the strap of the peddler's case and wandered with his "assistant" through the camp, just part of the hundreds of men, women and children attending the manifold needs of this huge mobile city.

The scene was a seething mass of disorder. Although the army had been on the road for more than three months, and had gathered goodness knows how many before that, there seemed little routine to the camp-making. Picket lines obstructed the lanes between tents, loose mounts were chased across littered areas of mud, voices called loudly for food from men who seemed unused to the vagaries of the campfire, wagons of supplies lumbered into the morass and spilled onto the ground their loads of sacks, barrels and whores.

Hosé pulled Rabia out of the way of a bullock determined not to provide the evening's supper.

Etched in his memory was the plain near Yenişehir, where ordered efficiency had prevailed; where every member of the army knew his job, and did it; where the loudest noises in camp were the whinny of a horse or the bubbling of the regiment's cauldron; where the corps of tent erectors did just that and the corps of bakers had their task down to a fine art; where the objectives of the next day were explained to every fighting man before evening prayers and a good night's sleep. At dawn the cymbals had signalled the order to attack and the white-hatted avalanche had thundered and flowed.

He shook his head at Rabia. He doubted if she would want to share that particular memory. He turned his mind with determination to the job in hand.

They sold needles and thread to soldiers who had repairs to make, they sold a gaudy brooch to a young Frenchman with a sweetheart back in the Auvergne. They made their way steadily towards the walls of the town and the castle where the royal leader of this horde, with his royal hostages, was lodged.

Hosé found them a sheltered corner. The pungent and unwelcome odour of porcine neighbours made him wrinkle his nose.

Rabia shrugged. 'Most men smell as bad.'

Hosé thought of the haphazard latrines that served the thirty thousand, but knew that was not what she meant.

It was always as they lay down to sleep that the empty space between them seemed at its most tangible.

Hosé tried to focus his chilly mind on other things.

By the following night they had reached Velletri.

Partly by good luck and partly because he was looking out for it, Hosé spotted a traveller from the south, complete with small but well-dressed escort. He did not doubt that this was the Spanish ambassador arriving to announce that Ferdinand and Isabella had finally decided to support their Neapolitan relatives and to demand the withdrawal of the French pretender. Hosé did not anticipate that this message would have much effect upon King Charles but he did wonder how Cesare Borgia would react to it.

Hosé and Rabia found a spot where they could see the royal tents occupied by the two hostages and their guards. They took it in turns to keep watch.

Hosé, resisting the urgent need to stamp some warmth into his feet, had almost begun to think he was wrong when there was a movement at the rear of one of the pavilions.

A groom about his business at this time of night? Hosé doubted it. He moved awkwardly on cold legs, to his anxious ears almost as loud as the blundering bullock.

He breathed a sigh of relief as he caught sight of the figure again, moving easily and seemingly unconcerned. The faint moonlight bleached all colour but Hosé would have sworn that the shining locks that showed at the edges of the hood were auburn.

In less than ten minutes they were well away from the small town. Hosé closed on his quarry.

He reached for his knife. One throw and the world would be rid of a powerful and vicious young man.

Then there were the sounds of horses.

Hosé took a deep breath and eased his blade back into its place.

Personal retribution must wait.

The "groom" greeted somebody and took the reins of the horse that had been brought for him. He mounted and started at a good pace heading north towards Rome.

Onto the road behind him came a string of ten heavily-laden mules. Hosé watched as they plodded off in the same direction.

He walked back quietly to where Rabia lay curled in sleep.

He could imagine the panic that the citizens of Rome would feel when they learned that one of the hostages had broken his parole. The revenge of the thirty thousand would be too dreadful to contemplate, for, unlike Cesare Borgia, the citizens did not know that the thirty thousand now faced much sterner opposition from a Neapolitan army reinforced with Spanish troops.

However that all turned out, Hosé's abiding concern was the other hostage still in the hands of the French King.

All day they stayed close to their vantage point, watching the erratic bustle of the army. They saw the flurry of activity around the royal tents.

Boxes and panniers were brought out and opened. Cries of anger greeted the realisation that they were empty. Only half the pack mules had followed the Pope's son back to Rome, but apparently they had carried all the trove.

'What a surprise,' Hosé commented.

What would Charles VIII do about this development?

For another night, they kept watch, turn and turn about.

Finally, a rider in the French King's livery departed with his escort, heading north. A message was being despatched to Rome, not an avenging army.

King Charles, it seemed, had decided to continue with his main aim. The French king and his horde headed south once more.

Hosé scanned the soldiers, guards, attendants who clustered around the departing monarch but could see no sign of the Turkish Prince.

What had happened to him?

He and Rabia continued their vigil.

Her hand attracted his attention. 'There is a small group of soldiers about to leave. That looks like a litter in the middle of them.' She had sharp eyes.

He peered at the figures. A litter? Was the Prince ill? How ill?

He took up the peddler's case and they moved quickly.

'Pretty ribbon?' Rabia approached the captain of the guard. 'Bound to impress any lady, my lord.' She spoke in the accented French of the camp followers.

Hosé hastily dropped his eyes as he recognised the figures gathered around the enclosed litter. He hoped his dishevelled and unshaven appearance looked sufficiently different from the clerk they had once known; or that Nassouh and Sinan would be so occupied with the person in the litter that they did not look at the peddler too carefully.

He shuffled the wares on display as Rabia continued her patter, keeping his head down.

A sharp order rang out and the soldiers reluctantly moved back, forming ranks around the litter. The officer who had issued the order swept his horse to the head of the column, forcing Hosé and the case of goods aside. For a moment he paused, looking Rabia up and down. 'A pretty young man,' he said with a lewd smile. 'But perhaps a little too thin and definitely too upright.' His final judgement brought a snicker from the soldiers.

'A reed knows best how to bend to the wind,' Rabia replied after the smallest of pauses, making her words as suggestive as his.

Only Hosé could see the white of her knuckles.

The man laughed. 'Unfortunately, my sweet boy, I do not have the time to test that out. But perhaps later, if you happened to be in Aversa you might seek out the Duc d'Argentan……'

The cavalcade slowly disappeared from sight.

Hosé looked at Rabia. 'All right?'

'I'm sorry,' she sniffed.

'Sorry? What have you to be sorry about?' Without thinking, he laid an arm around her shaking shoulders.

She shivered. 'It's cold. We should get going.' But it was some moments before she pushed away from him.

At Aversa, they had no chance to approach the French troops but they saw the officer, the Duc d'Argentan. He was talking to a man dressed in the best worsted woollen cloth that Hosé had seen for a long time.

'What is it?' Rabia saw his scowl.

'Clough.'

'What is he doing here? And what is his connection with d'Argentan?'

Hosé shook his head. Since the news from Ostia he had known Clough was once more deeply involved in Italian politics. It was no real surprise to see the Englishman here, but that did not make it any less worrying.

The chatter in the town was also a concern. The health of the exotic invalid was all the talk, although few of those who spread the news could see why the life of one Saracen should be so important.

Hosé knew the answer.

Nevertheless, the gossip continued, the Prince was much improved. The two French doctors who had been bleeding him had been dismissed. The healing draughts administered by the professor from Ferrara had proved much more helpful.

'Professor from Ferrara?' Rabia looked at Hosé.

Hosé grimaced in frustration. There were so many answers he did *not* know.

In spite of the reported improvement to the Prince's health, he was still in a litter as the cavalcade left Aversa.

Unlike the route seething southwards towards the kingdom of Naples, the road taken by the Prince and his entourage was not busy. It led to the town of Capua where Norman invaders had built a castle within the protective sweep of the Volturno river hundreds of years before, in the year before the bastard Norman Duke William had turned his conquering attention to a quite different prize, a short sailing distance from his native land.

Hosé and Rabia passed into the town through the Norman archway. On either side the crenelles of two round towers stood out against the grey sky like square teeth.

The castle of Capua might have been standing for centuries but it looked sturdy enough as Hosé and Rabia did a careful circle of its walls.

Hosé desperately wanted to know what was happening inside, but for once the talk in the local wine shop had little to offer on the subject, although it did confirm that the Neapolitan army under Federico, brother of King Alonso of Naples, had faded away before the Gallic horde, inspite of the Spanish support.

For three days Hosé and Rabia sought a possible way to gain entry to the castle.

On the fourth day, more riders appeared, the unattractive figure of King Charles in their midst. The following day he left again. Hosé peered at the ugly face and tried to read from it anything about the welfare of the Prince.

Was the King leaving confident that the Prince would mend? Or was he leaving because there was nothing left to hope for?

Hosé needed to know. The fate of the Prince was crucial.

And he was revolted by the thought of that fate being in any way in Clough's hands.

He was also revolted by Rabia's suggestion.

'Do you have a better idea?' she demanded, anger masking other feelings. 'Or even any idea?'

At the end of the day, he didn't.

He watched with an icy fury from the corner of the wine shop as d'Argentan settled next to Rabia, large thigh close up against her slim hose.

He watched as the man became progressively more intoxicated and more possessive.

He watched as Rabia's face, beneath its tight cap, grew greyer in the lamp light.

He watched as her eyes grew larger and darker.

He watched as she rose from her seat and followed out into the night.

He slipped out of the other door.

Even then he was almost too late. The duke might be drunk but he was not incapable and he was roused.

Hosé was only just in time to stop Rabia resorting to her last defence as she scrabbled beneath d'Argentan in the foul straw of the stable.

'You can put the knife away,' he said gently.

She looked at the blade for a moment then slowly returned it to its place.

Hosé on the other hand unsheathed his.

It was the first thing d'Argentan saw as he recovered consciousness.

It was an ever-present reminder against his spine as the Frenchman led the way into the castle, past soldiers who were greatly more concerned with keeping warm in the guard room than inspecting the state of their commander (the reek of alcohol, liberally supplemented by Hosé, was plain enough), or indeed the company he had acquired, although the youth looked pretty in a foreign sort of way.

D'Argentan turned along narrow passages and up a stone staircase. Along the corridor at the top, infrequently spaced cressets guttered in the chill draughts, casting as much black shadow as light.

'Stop!' Hosé recognised the voices coming towards them. He slid into a doorway, pulling the Frenchman to cover him. Rabia pressed a hand against d'Argentan's crotch suggestively, although the cold steel of Hosé's blade effectively repressed even the slightest amorous response.

'This is hardly a time for whoring.' Sinan's disgust was patent in his slightly accented French.

D'Argentan made an unintelligible noise, in response to a prod from Hosé's knife.

'Who are you calling a whore?' asked Rabia; she had perfected the camp argot as assiduously as any more recognised language. 'I'm a good boy,' her hand moved slightly. 'Aren't I, M'sieur Duc?'

D'Argentan gasped.

'The King expects you to guard the Prince,' put in Nassouh, his voice rough with emotion, 'Not to indulge your unnatural cravings.'

'Prince?' Rabia's voice sparkled with sudden interest. 'There is a real prince here?'

Nassouh ignored her. 'Whose sickness is getting worse by the hour,' he said angrily to d'Argentan, the words made rough by grief and helplessness.

'Come on,' said Sinan in Turkish to Nassouh. 'The Prince wants to hear if Saadi has finished the letter so that it can go on its way in the morning; if this sodomite is sober enough to organise that by then,' he added contemptuously.

'I do not like to leave him.' Nassouh's worry was patent.

'The Prince will not rest until he is assured about the letter to his brother. Come on,' said Sinan, 'The Englishman promised to fetch us if there is any change.'

Hosé scarcely managed to suppress a gasp.

Still the small round figure hesitated. Then with a last look of contempt at the Frenchman the two Turks moved away.

Hosé was frantically prodding d'Argentan into action when he heard the soft slap of leather soles from the other direction. He pulled the Frenchman and Rabia through the leather curtain behind them.

Chapter 22

The young man making his way along the passage heard the treble voice and the deeper tones. He paused. He was, by now, very closely acquainted with soldiers and their followers, and their afflictions.

His life might easily have taken a different path. He had become a novice at an early age, for surely in Holy Orders he would find the way to understand God and serve the sick. Instead he had found that the Church could not, or would not, answer his questions about God and His purposes.

Even Thomas à Kempis, whose example and works the young man respected enormously and had considered long and hard, had concluded that God's ways were not only mysterious but not to be questioned or discussed.

But Christ's life included healing the sick. He taught that any person ministering to someone in need also served Him. That was a part of Christ's life that the young man could understand and try to imitate.

And although he still suffered many doubts he felt, by and large, that he had made the right decision not to enter the cloistered life, rather to study at the university of Ferrara.

Professor Leoniceno did not see disease as simply the punishment of God. He sought human understanding and earthly remedy for the easement of sufferers, in particular through careful observation. He had sent his most gifted student to catalogue a disease whose trail was marked by painful black pustules, rashes and ulcers, buboes and carbuncles, agonising swollen joints and fever and rotting flesh, and all too often by painful death. There were not many who survived the gruesome symptoms and those who did were broken, often blinded and insane.

Professor Leoniceno had posited that this was a new plague, carried back from the New World that their Hispanic majesties were so enthusiastic about, for its trail seemed to lead from one port to another, from one army camp to another.

The young physician had followed the huge French army of thirty thousand down into the Italian peninsula, treating where he could and making copious and careful notes. Some of the symptoms were reminiscent of plagues already horribly familiar, but this one certainly seemed to have a terribleness all its own.

And he had increasingly found its symptoms among those who were not soldiers, nor whores, nor even of a loose style of living; which added an extra puzzle. It was difficult to see why certain people should be thus struck, being good, honest folk.

Perhaps part of the answer lay in how it spread? Although that was a whole subject by itself and the centre of much angry debate. How did any disease spread? Different diseases seemed to spread in different ways, but were there common factors behind them all?

The young man, whose threadbare gown somehow still hung on him like a clerical habit, had wondered how much he had really achieved of help to sufferers. Of course, he could see the point of the study. How else would man ever get beyond supposition and guesses, if he did not find the evidence to back it up, to promote those logical conclusions that the old Greeks had demonstrated? But it all took so long and there was so much to do and so many illnesses to investigate.

Not all illnesses were new, of course. Many had been around for as long as man, ever since the expulsion from the Garden of Eden anyway: there could not have been any illness in Paradise. The old texts wrote of illness, the old tales spoke of it, many were the efforts that had been made to help those who were ill. And some of those efforts had been effective, he mused. Some doctors had had some success, like al-Razi for instance and in much more recent times that learned Hebrew who had added so many annotations to the printed copy of *Continens.*

In spite of his misgivings and self-doubts, Professor Leoniceno's protégé had become a well-known figure, well-known enough to have been sought out to attend the sick Ottoman prince at Aversa.

And after all, he had plenty of experience of the bloody flux. It regularly swept through any army, especially during summer. How did that spread, he wondered? Did the illness pass from one man to another, or did they all take it from some other common source? From the water they drank, or the food they ate? Or from the air they breathed? That other scourge of the summer campaign, marsh fever, seemed to come from breathing the foul air of the marshes.

What was in that air? He had recently heard of someone in the north, near the great lakes, who had an interesting idea about that. The remarkable lenses that they produced in the glassworks of Venice allowed people to see clearly such tiny things as mustard seeds; perhaps there were even smaller things that were completely invisible to the ordinary human eye, so small they floated unseen in the air. Perhaps one day the glassmakers might make lenses that would show all these things. Perhaps some of these tiny things were what carried illness, like the seeds of certain plants that sailed on the wind looking to settle on fertile soil.

And perhaps that was all nonsense and wild fantasy.

The young physician shook his head and lifted the wooden latch. The heat hit him like a physical blow after the chill of the passage and this was only the ante-room. In the Prince's chamber itself, he knew, no less than three braziers were lit, trying to maintain the warmth of life in the man lying there.

At the moment, all was quiet. The Prince was probably sleeping.

The young man opened the intervening door softly.

The Prince was thirty-six years of age but lying in the great stepped bed he looked twice that. The flesh had drawn back from his cheek bones and his eyes were sunk into dark hollows.

'Master Clough!' said the physician in surprise. 'What are you doing?'

The Englishman turned from the bedside, wiping the irritation from his face. 'The Prince seemed in need of a drink. I thought I would help him.'

The younger man nodded. 'I can do that now I'm here.'

'It's all right. I can do it.' The answer was sharp.

'I have had a deal more practice,' the earnest young face softened.

'Really,' protested Clough, managing a sympathetic tone. 'It is at least something I can do for him.'

At that moment sickness took the Prince and he vomited feebly. At the same instant, a vile odour, lifted by the hot air, issued from the lower part of his stricken body.

Clough drew back, revulsion mixing with a barely repressed anger, but the physician was too concerned with his patient to notice. He moved forward, poured water into a basin and took a fresh cloth that lay nearby.

Finally, the wasted body was restored to some degree of dignity.

'Are you going to get rid of that?' Clough indicated the foul mess in the bowl.

The young man nodded and picked up the basin. 'There is something to be said for a garde-robe opening off the chamber.' He moved towards the curtained opening in the outer wall. 'And thankfully it stinks much less at this season.' He missed the exasperation on the merchant's face as he emptied the basin.

'Do you need more water, perhaps?' Clough asked hopefully.

'There is still some in the bucket. I will refill the pot standing by the brazier so the chill can be taken off it.'

The Englishman watched him, frustration pressing his lips into a grim line.

The Prince moved feebly in the bed.

'I can give him that drink now.' The physician put out a hand for the cup which Clough still held.

The merchant hesitated for a moment then handed it over.

The young man took up a spoon and dipped it into the liquid. He lifted it and sniffed. 'What is it?' he asked. 'It is not the chamomile I brewed earlier.'

'Something Sinan prepared,' came the smooth answer. 'A tea the Prince is especially fond of, apparently,' he added.

The physician sniffed again trying to identify the scent that had caught his attention. 'What is it?' he repeated.

As the Prince began to retch again, the young man hastily put the cup down and tried to catch the thin green stream in a bowl. As he did so his gown swept the cup from the step of the bed. It clattered to the floor and broke, spilling the tea.

The merchant ground out some words in his own language.

'It's all right, I'll ask Sinan to prepare some more,' the young man reassured him, turning back to his patient. The Prince was muttering disjointed words, some in French, some in Italian, some in a language that was presumably Turkish.

'I'll go and … find him myself,' said the merchant tersely.

A few moments later the monk heard the door to the antechamber. Clough was soon back. His mouth dropped open.

'So, *no one in Gilead knows of balm, for the pain of a plague-stricken man*?' Hosé had had time to get over his own surprise at the identity of the owner of the leather sandals. 'Not even you Matteo.'

'What on earth are you doing here?'

'Visiting an old acquaintance.' Hosé nodded towards the bed.

Rabia had been watching this interchange with interest. Now she took a step towards the bed, peering at the human remains there.

Hosé also regarded the man who had been a prisoner for seven and a half years in France and another six in Rome, the man who, for all that time, had been helpless and yet held enormous power simply by existing. 'How sick is he?' he asked Matteo.

'I think he will not last long. He can't keep any food or drink in him. He soils himself continually. He's drying out like an old gourd,' was the quiet answer.

Just then Cem stopped his muttering and turned his eyes towards the people next to his bed.

'*Then are all men restored to Allah, their true Lord.*' Hosé spoke the words and the Prince's face lit for a moment in recognition.

'*Allah is one God. There is no god but Him. He is the Compassionate, the*

Merciful.' The response was barely audible.

Matteo who had recognised nothing but the word "*Allah*" looked from one to the other.

The Prince spoke again, his voice weak but surprisingly lucid. 'Allah knows that in my life I have wanted only to serve Him and my father Mehmet.'

Hosé frowned.

'In the end, I have not been able to fulfil my father's will.'

The supposed will that would have disinherited his eldest son, Bayezit. Hosé's frown deepened.

A question creased the Prince's brow but after a moment he gave up the struggle. Instead he recited, softly but steadily, '*In the name of Allah, most Gracious, most Merciful. Praise be to Allah, the Cherisher and Sustainer of the Worlds: most Gracious, most Merciful; Master of the Day of Judgement, Thee do we worship, and Thine aid we seek.*' His voice suddenly faded. 'That judgement will come soon.' He muttered something about returning his body to Constantinople then his eyes closed.

Rabia broke the silence. '*You shall engage in no affair, you shall recite no verse from the Recitation, you shall commit no act, but God witnesses it. Not an atom's weight in earth or heaven escapes your Lord, nor is there any object great or small which is not recorded.*

'*God's servants have nothing to fear or to regret. Those who have faith and keep from evil shall rejoice both in this world and in the hereafter: the Word of God shall never change.*

'*All glory belongs to God. He alone hears all and knows all.*'

The Prince's eyes stayed closed but a faint flicker of the lids suggested he was listening.

Matteo was also listening, puzzled. He thought the language was Arabic although he could not understand it, then the Prince turned his head feverishly and Matteo moved to wring out a cloth and wipe the dark, wasted face. He grimaced as he trod on the shards of the broken cup.

Rabia bent to clear them out of the way. 'What is this?' she demanded sharply.

'A drink for the Prince. I knocked it over by accident.'

'A drink you made for him?' She was staring at him.

Matteo shook his head. 'Sinan, one of the Prince's servants.'

'One of his servants?' She looked at Hosé.

'What is it Rab?' he asked quietly.

'It has the scent of bitter almonds.'

Matteo stared at her. Of course, that was the smell. He should have recognised it. He looked aghast at the remains of the cup and its contents.

Hosé's eyes narrowed. He had a vivid memory of fresh apricot juice prepared for de Blanchefort's niece and of the woman's screams as the poison administered by a jealous slave had achieved its deadly purpose. 'You are sure Sinan prepared it?'

'Yes,' Matteo replied. 'At least,' he paused, 'The Englishman said so.'

Hosé suppressed an oath.

A frown creased Matteo's forehead. 'You know him?'

Hosé laughed: a short, bitter sound.

'What is going on? What are you doing here? And you?' Matteo turned to Rabia.

Hosé had questions of his own. 'Could Clough have administered poison before this? Could that be why the Prince is sick?'

Matteo thought for a moment then shook his head. 'The Prince was already sick at Velletri. I was sent for at Aversa.'

Hosé nodded. ' "*The professor from Ferrara.*" '

'I have never made any such claim! I have studied physik under Professor Leoniceno of Ferrara, that is all.' Matteo looked shocked. 'But,' he added with asperity, 'I know more than that barbaric pair of Gallic barbers!'

Rab looked up at him with interest.

Matteo returned to Hosé's question. 'And Master Clough only joined the company as we left Aversa.'

'But?'

Matteo's frown deepened. 'The Prince had begun to improve. It is true he then suffered a relapse.'

Hosé scowled.

'Still,' Matteo continued, 'I don't see how Master Clough, or anyone else, could have poisoned him: his servants have been with him constantly.'

'Until today, when the Prince desperately wanted that letter sent.'

Matteo gaped. 'How do you know about that?'

Hosé ignored the question. 'And before?' he mused.

Matteo did not understand. 'Before what?'

'Before Aversa, at Velletri. Could Clough, or someone else, have given the Prince poison?'

Matteo shook his head. 'I can't say. I was not there.'

'When the handsome Cesare Borgia left in the middle of the night, for instance?' Hosé suggested. 'Perhaps a parting gift from one hunting companion to another? The Borgias would not like losing their prize hostage to the French King.'

'I don't know about any of that,' said the young physician. 'The bloody flux suffered by the Prince looks very much the same as I have seen many times among the soldiers. It would be difficult to tell if it was caused by poison or not.' He looked down at the floor in perplexity. 'Why would Master Clough want to poison him anyway?'

Hosé frowned. He had a good idea how Clough had managed to gain acceptance by the Prince's French custodians: through Cardinal della Rovere. The Englishman had managed to be in Ostia just when the Cardinal needed help, needed it very badly.

And Hosé had no doubt that Clough had gone on to prove his value further, with information of the pay arrangement between the Sultan and the Pope. The interception of the Nuncio had indeed not been chance.

But....Hosé cursed to himself. Why assume that Clough was serving *only* della Rovere and the French cause?

'Because Cesare Borgia learned that the Prince, under your care, was rallying. And needed somebody to finish the job.'

Rabia had remained on her knees, busy with the mess on the floor. 'Your foot is still bleeding,' she announced. 'The blood will hopefully wash away any of the poison that might have entered the cut.'

Matteo shifted his horrified gaze from Hosé and stared at her. 'Who are you? And how do you know about such things?'

'This,' said Hosé with half a smile, 'Is Rab.' He added, 'Once student and apprentice to Isaac the physician.'

A mixture of enlightenment and wonder showed on the young face. 'You know Isaac?'

'As obviously you do,' she returned, looking hard at Hosé.

'Matteo helped look after Isaac in Genoa, after he lost his memory,' Hosé told her tersely.

'Yes, 'Bella and I .....'

'Perhaps there will be a time for explanations later,' interrupted Hosé. 'But this is not the moment. I imagine Master Clough will return very shortly.' He lifted a brow at Matteo.

'Good Lord, yes. He said he would fetch more of that drink.' Matteo looked aghast.

'And he will want to do so before the faithful Nassouh and Sinan return from their errand.'

Matteo nodded. 'I suppose so,' he said. 'But I won't let him give it to the Prince,' he added fiercely.

'I'm not sure you would have any say in the matter,' said Hosé seriously.

'What?'

'I have known Master Clough for rather a long time. He is not likely to let something as trivial as a principled young physician get in his way.'

'What can we do then?'

'You go and find Nassouh and Sinan. Get them back here immediately. Tell them the Prince fears he is about to die and he wants them by his side, *all the time.*'

'And you will stay with the Prince? Protect him in case Clough returns first?'

Hosé nodded.

'Promise?' Matteo's trust in people had taken a severe knock.

'I promise.'

Still Matteo looked at him a moment longer. 'I don't know why you are here. I don't even know who you are, not really.'

'Hosé, sometimes called Hosé de Mallorca,' said Hosé with the ghost of a smile.

'But you are Isaac's friend,' said the young man simply. 'So, I believe you.'

There was a great deal more to Isaac than Matteo knew, thought Hosé grimly, but that had no bearing on the sincerity of the promise. 'Go,' he said. 'Now.'

Rabia stood looking at the Prince but spoke to Hosé. 'What will you do?'

'He is not likely to improve again?'

She sniffed carefully at a jug of water then raised the Prince's head and let a few drops fall into his mouth. Her movements were deft.

She felt the Prince's brow then the pulse in his neck. 'His life is ebbing away.'

'How long?'

She shrugged. 'Perhaps a week.' She turned the man's head so that his vomit would not choke him. 'Perhaps only days.'

Hosé nodded.

And so, his mission would end. Just like that, after so many years.

'What about Clough?' Rabia's words broke into his thoughts.

'If he comes back first, I shall kill him,' said Hosé simply. Because of the promise to Matteo, because of all the misery the merchant had caused, because of his greed and because of his attempt on the life of the Sultan's brother.

'And if he doesn't?'

Hosé shook his head. 'I cannot go searching for him. I must let Cem's followers accompany the Prince to the end of his life.' He could not grieve for Cem's death, but Sultan Bayezit would. 'They will offer him what comfort they can. And their presence will certainly prevent Clough trying poison again.' He pulled a wry face. 'Not that it seems necessary!'

'And Matteo?'

Hosé frowned. How good would Matteo be at pretending he still had the same trust in the Englishman?

'He is an earnest and transparent young man, I think,' Rabia said.

Hosé and Rabia joined the gagged and bound d'Argentan in the room behind the leather curtain.

Hosé's knife gleamed, even in the near dark, and the Frenchman's eyes widened.

'Not for you,' said Hosé softly. 'Yet.'

He peered out into the passage. Would Clough appear first or the Turks with Matteo?

It was the merchant. A cup in one hand, he emerged from the gloom at one end of the passage.

Hosé shifted his knife slightly and poised on the balls of his feet. Behind him Rabia caught her breath.

Hosé carefully let the curtain fall and listened to the approaching rapid steps of fine boots.

The Englishman was nearly level with the doorway when there were voices from the other direction. Clough swore viciously and stopped. He ducked sideways and thrust the cup behind the leather curtain, nearly putting it down on Hosé's foot.

A desperate muffled noise came from d'Argentan, quickly cut short.

Clough moved away. 'Is there a problem Matteo?' he inquired.

'The Prince wished his servants to return to his bedside immediately,' Matteo said.

Hosé nearly groaned. The young man's animosity was all too clear. Clough would hardly miss it.

'But of course,' said the Englishman. 'Whatever might help the poor man.'

The Prince's door opened and closed. The only noise in the passage was the occasional splutter from a cresset.

Hosé turned back into the room.

Rabia was examining the slumped figure on the floor. 'It worked,' she said regarding her hands with some satisfaction.

'You haven't killed him I hope.'

She shook her head. 'His pulse is strong.'

'Good.'

Hosé waited behind the curtain. It seemed a long time before the Prince's door opened again.

Hosé recognised the slap of sandals. For a moment, he was sorry it was not Clough come to retrieve the cup.

'What…?' Matteo got no further as Hosé dragged him into the room.

'Who is that?' Matteo stumbled over the body on the floor.

'Our pass into the castle. He will shortly help us leave. You must come too, Matteo.'

'What? I can't do that,' the young physician protested. 'The Prince…'

'Will soon be dead, you said so yourself. There is nothing anyone can do for him.'

'But the Englishman….'

'Cannot touch the Prince as long as there are others with him.'

'But…'

'But,' said Hosé, 'He can touch you.'

'But why should he?'

'Do stop saying "*but*",' said Hosé impatiently. 'He'll realise you suspect him.'

'How…?'

'And he will remove you, Matteo, soon and for certain. I dare not leave you here.'

'*You* dare not?'

'Isaac would not forgive me,' Hosé said. Not a second time.

Matteo still hesitated.

'Nor would 'Bella,' Hosé added more gently. He sensed Rabia's curiosity. That was another thing that would have to be explained, sometime.

Matteo nodded slowly.

'At any moment Clough will arrive at the doorway to pick up the cup he dumped there. We have to go now.' Hosé turned. 'How is the Duc? Awake again?'

'Just about,' said Rabia.

D'Argentan was awake enough to detect the colder touch of sharp steel against his cold back. He staggered along between them.

A sleepy boy brought the horses. He had long learned not to question the strange behaviour of those who commanded him.

'You go up behind the Duc,' Hosé said to Rabia. 'That will look a great deal more convincing than me cuddling up to him.' He pulled a face. 'But please remember, M'sieur,' he addressed d'Argentan, 'That one knife may do as much damage as another.'

Rabia pulled hers from its place and demonstrated the truth of Hosé's words.

The Duc d'Argentan winced.

'And you,' he spoke crisply to Matteo, 'Will ride beside me.'

Matteo looked surprised at Hosé's tone for a moment, then nodded.

The horses' breath formed white clouds. Overhead the stars were brilliant in the frosty air; the beat of hoofs rang out against the old stones.

The guards were even less interested in leaving their shelter than they had been earlier, although they did cast an incurious eye on the young physician as the horses clopped out through the archway.

Once clear of the town they stopped.

Hosé made a show of tying Matteo's hands and bound a cloth around his eyes. 'Now you, M'sieur le Duc.' He did a much more thorough job.

They set off again, this time Hosé with d'Argentan.

Rabia leaned over to Matteo, quietly freeing him.

'What…?' he asked.

She squeezed the frayed sleeve in warning and he lapsed into puzzled silence as Hosé led the way, peering up at the stars each time the frozen road divided.

Two hours later they stopped once more.

Hosé dismounted stiffly and pulled the Frenchman down. 'Time to part company, M'sieur.'

D'Argentan swore between chattering teeth as Hosé placed him on the ground and pulled his boots off. 'You can't leave me like this,' he pleaded. 'I'll freeze to death.'

'I could provide an alternative if you would prefer,' said Hosé easily.

The blindfolded Frenchman gasped as the knife pricked his neck.

'A little desperation can make a man quite resourceful,' said Hosé grimly. 'I'm certain you will manage to get back to Capua, eventually. And you will have plenty of time to think of a plausible story on the way.' He turned, 'But you, Signore Professore, will have to ride a little further before you get your chance. I feel you and the Duc should go your separate ways.' He smiled slightly at Matteo, who was looking rather sick.

It was half an hour before they stopped once more.

Hosé eased himself out of the saddle. 'No offence to you personally,' he addressed the horse, 'But I am much happier on foot.'

Rabia joined him. 'I prefer camels.'

'How about you Matteo?' Hosé asked. 'Are you happy on horseback? That animal should get you wherever you decide to go.'

Matteo started to dismount then slid with a thump onto the frozen ground.

Hosé hurried over to him.

'Just the cold,' the young man said faintly.

Rabia passed practised hands over him. He might feel cold but there was sweat on his face. 'The poison,' she said in a worried tone to Hosé.

There was no question of Matteo deciding to go anywhere.

Chapter 23

* * *

The journey back through the city had been a continuation of the nightmare as Hosé struggled through the hot dusty streets and the crowds of people with his bloody burden.

Ishaq screamed, but Hosé had only one thought: to get the boy home.

After a while the screams became sobs.

By the time they reached the baker's, the boy had fallen silent.

And Rabia had not returned.

Ricardo blanched as Hosé roared at him to find her. Their lodger had never seemed frightening before. The lad set off to Guiseppe's at a run.

Rabia arrived shortly and took one look at her son.

Her face had been pale with what Ricardo had told her, now it went ashen.

Hosé continued to cradle the boy. He looked up at her, pleading.

She knelt slowly beside him and took a deep breath.

Ishaq's eyes fluttered and he let out a faint mewl of pain.

Rabia took another breath and stretched out her hands. They shook slightly as she began to pull aside the torn clothing. Ishaq cried out as she struggled to ease off his hose, as the cloth snagged on something.

Hosé swore as he saw what it was.

The boy's left leg below the knee was smashed to pieces. Some of those pieces stuck out through the torn flesh and skin, gleaming white against the gore.

Incredibly the piece of boiled linen was still in place. Hosé remembered the sturdy limb that Rabia had dressed such a short time ago.

Rabia's hands paused a moment, then moved on relentlessly, revealing the total extent of the child's injuries.

There was the clear imprint of a large hoof, livid on the skin of Ishaq's shoulder. There were other marks on his chest and abdomen which Rabia fingered gently. 'If they are only on the outside they are not so bad,' she said almost to herself. 'If they have damaged the organs inside….' She did not finish the sentence. 'Wrap him up,' she said, her voice a little firmer with the decision. 'He will need all his strength and warmth. No, not his leg.'

Hosé wrapped a blanket around the small form. 'What are you going to do?' he glanced up. 'Rabia?'

She had turned to the door where a row of faces watched mutely. 'Ricardo. Go to the apothecary again and tell him he must come at once. Tell him he must bring all his tools. Do you understand? All his tools.'

'Tools?' Hosé did not understand; the man was not a carpenter. Then he realised. 'What are you going to do?' he demanded again.

'What must be done,' she said. She looked at him. 'The only thing that can be done.' And she explained tersely in Arabic.

'No!' he could not believe her.

'If we do nothing the black rot will set in. Within a few days he will die. There is no way to mend the leg, Hosé. The only way is to remove it. That way he has a chance, a very small chance.'

There had to be something else she could do.

She shook her head.

Ishaq stirred and she took his hand, stroking it gently.

'Can you do it?' Hosé asked at last.

She spoke over her shoulder. 'At least Guiseppe and I understand a little now.'

He pulled a bitter face at the irony. Isaac had started it by sending that extract from Ibn Nasif's Commentary on the Anatomy of the Canon of Avicenna. The Jew had found it in some old books brought to the Topkapi from Cairo and it had set him thinking about how the blood carried life. He had asked Rabia for her comments.

She had studied the document and discussed the subject with Guiseppe. It had been he who had said there was really only one way of finding out more about the workings of the human body. Hosé suspected the apothecary had been surprised, and more than a little alarmed, by Rabia's response.

After the pair had so nearly been discovered, Guiseppe had wanted to give up and Hosé had agreed with him, but Rabia had been keen to learn more. When another opportunity occurred, Hosé and Rabia had had perhaps their first real argument: in spite of their efforts something had changed between them.

'You may know a bit about dead bodies,' he agreed, but Ishaq was still alive.

As if to emphasise the point the boy tried to reach out to his mother, but the movement brought pain and he screamed. Rabia soothed him, urging him to lie still.

She indicated that Hosé should take her place. 'I'll prepare some poppy syrup.'

By the time Guiseppe arrived Ishaq had calmed a little, although his eyes flew open the moment Hosé moved. Hosé settled back by the child and waved a hand at the baker's family. They trooped downstairs, horror and fascination mixed in equal parts. The curtain dropped across the doorway behind them.

The apothecary listened to Rabia as she described the problem and what she proposed. He regarded the smashed leg with dismay and shook his head.

Rabia reminded him what they had learned, how the parts of the leg were disposed, how the muscles and tendons attached to the bones, where the blood vessels ran; how the knee articulated between the upper and lower leg. She described exactly where she proposed to sever the damaged limb.

Guiseppe made one or two grave comments.

She nodded.

The apothecary frowned. 'But the boy is still likely to bleed to death,' he said at last.

Rabia chewed her lip. 'I think there may be an answer to that.'

Hosé looked up sharply.

'Isaac told me once about the Inquisition.'

'What has that got to do with anything?' Hosé spoke more roughly than he intended.

'The Christian church forbids its priests to spill blood.'

'But not to torture those whom they deem heretics,' he retorted. He drew a quick breath as the import of what she had said struck him. 'They use red hot irons,' he said, looking at her, his eyes wide.

'The iron burns the flesh but instantly closes off the blood vessels,' she said, 'So the conscience of the torturer can remain clear.'

Guiseppe was frowning. Rabia had reverted to her native language and Hosé had replied in the same tongue. Now she explained to the apothecary.

He nodded and made a suggestion.

Rabia asked for the bag of tools and picked out one or two.

Hosé felt sick.

She looked at them for some time, turning them round, imagining how they could best be used.

'How will you heat them?' Guiseppe broke the silence.

'The bakery.' Rabia and Hosé spoke the words at the same moment.

'Yes,' said Rabia. 'And it would be easiest to use the baker's big table.'

Hosé always sharpened his blades with great care. A soldier knew his life might depend on it. Now he applied his utmost skill to putting a razor's edge on the tools Rabia had selected. Finally, they were as good as he could make them.

He lifted his eyes and looked curiously at the pile of mouldy bread Guiseppe had gathered.

Rabia reached for the tools and pushed them into the fire she had stoked on the brick floor of the oven.

She turned back to him. 'You remember when you fought Garcia.'

Of course he remembered.

'You knocked him out.'

'Not exactly.'

'No, that's what I mean. You did not hit him but you rendered him unconscious.'

Hosé stared at her. She had noticed that, and remembered it?

'How did you do that; exactly?'

Hosé explained what part of the neck he had sought, how he had applied pressure. He could see where she was leading. 'That was, of course, on a grown man, and it is always chancy. There is no exact recipe for how long to squeeze, to simply cause unconsciousness rather than death.' Or lifelong idiocy.

Guiseppe had been listening with great attention. He had sometimes thought there was more to Rabia's husband than met the eye, but this was not the time to wonder about such things.

For a moment Hosé speculated on how different things might have been if he had forced his fingers into the thick neck of Garcia de Tineo a bit longer; but then there would have been no Ishaq. He looked down at the boy. The feverish spots on the tear stained face were exaggerated in the reflection of the fire. 'Couldn't you give him more poppy?'

She frowned. 'That has the same problems,' she said. 'I have given him as much as I dare already.'

And although the boy's eyes were half closed he was definitely still conscious.

Whatever they did carried risks, enormous risks, but to do nothing was not an option.

All too soon the tools were glowing red hot.

Hosé bent and spoke softly into Ishaq's ear. He was not sure how much the boy would understand but he had always tried to explain the things that happened in the child's life.

'Mama must try and fix your leg.'

The boy stirred. The dark eyes opened wide.

Hosé swallowed. 'And I will make you go to sleep while she does it.' The eyes calmed and Hosé's guts clenched. 'I will put my fingers on your neck and press. Maybe it will hurt a little, maybe you will feel dizzy, but then you should sleep.'

Those eyes regarded him solemnly for a moment. 'Mama will fix it.'

Hosé had never thought of himself as indecisive, but then he had never faced a situation anything like this before.

Rabia snapped at him, betraying her own fear.

Guiseppe spoke gently to her and Hosé glared at the pair of them, seeing how close they were.

He turned back to Ishaq. *My son, I dreamt that I was sacrificing you. Tell me what you think.* He stroked Ishaq's cheek.

Father, do as you are bidden. God willing, you shall find me steadfast.

And when they had both submitted to God's will, and Abraham had laid down his son prostrate on his face, God said to him: Abraham, thus has your dream been fulfilled. And thus are the righteous rewarded.

A bitter test indeed. Hosé placed his other hand on Ishaq's face. '*In the name of Allah, most Gracious, most Merciful. Praise be to Allah, the Cherisher and Sustainer of the Worlds: most Gracious, most Merciful; Master of the Day of Judgement, Thee do we worship, and Thine aid we seek.*' He said the familiar words out loud, regardless of Guiseppe.

His roughened thumb sought the right point on the smooth skin beneath the jawbone and stopped.

He felt Rabia's hand on his shoulder, her strong fingers encouraging. The words from the Recitation were soft in his ear as she repeated them.

Ishaq looked up at them.

Father, do as you are bidden.

Hosé's thumb found the spot; his other hand joined it. He pressed.

He had not pressed long enough. The instant the steel touched his mangled leg Ishaq jerked and screamed.

The time for reassuring words had long passed. Hosé pressed again, more firmly and for longer.

Rabia and Guiseppe did their work then, as fast as they dared, ignoring the stench of roasted flesh. There was a small thud as the severed limb landed on the floor amidst the floury debris.

Ishaq's eyes fluttered and Hosé pressed again on the small neck.

The heat had sealed some of the vessels but blood still flowed when Rabia released the ligature. She tightened it again and stitched, the needle and silk thread shining red in the lamplight. Finally, she was able to pack the bloody stump around with the old bread and bandage it.

Hosé removed his fingers.

Ishaq remained still.

Hosé was convinced he had killed the boy.

Then Guiseppe pointed out the shallow rise and fall of the child's chest. 'Perhaps he is just stunned,' the apothecary suggested dubiously.

It seemed an interminable time before Ishaq began to stir. Finally, the silky eyelashes fluttered, dark eyes stared uncomprehending at the faces around him.

Hosé spoke his name. There was no sign of recognition.

'Stunned,' repeated Guiseppe with little conviction.

The boy moved and cried out. 'Mama's not fixed it!' The anguish was from betrayal as much as physical pain.

Hosé almost laughed with the relief. 'Yes, she has,' he assured the child. 'But it will be sore until it can heal properly.'

'It hurts,' sobbed the boy. He looked up. 'Papa make me sleep again.'

'I daren't do that,' Hosé said gently.

'You are not afraid of anything.'

If only the child knew.

'Mama will make you a tisane.'

By the evening the fever was burning high. Ishaq tossed on his mattress.

Rabia applied wet cloths to try and cool him. She brewed tisanes. Guiseppe fetched others from his store.

In the following days Ishaq protested more and more feebly as Rabia held the cup to his dried-out lips. He brought up most of what he managed to sip. What liquid did pass through his shrunken body dribbled out, discoloured.

His eyes were glazed. The heat from his body was like an oven.

Rabia looked yet again at the remains of his left leg. 'His whole body is so warm I cannot tell whether the wound is over-hot or not,' she said. She put her head down and sniffed. 'But I cannot detect any rot.'

'There are no bright streaks up his thigh,' said Guiseppe.

That was one straw to clutch at.

'Perhaps his other injuries,' the apothecary said tentatively.

The straw disappeared on the equinoctial wind that whistled past the attic roof.

Hosé dripped one more drop of the valerian tea onto Ishaq's parched tongue, then one more. He watched the weak reflex as the boy swallowed. He tipped the cup once more, ever so carefully, allowing just one more drop.

It seemed he had done nothing else for weeks. Anything more than one drop at a time and the boy vomited it up almost immediately. Without liquid the child would die of thirst, never mind any of his hurts.

Eventually the cup was empty. Rabia would bring another with a different brew.

But instead she brought news, bad news.

'How?' Hosé demanded, his brain befuddled with the endless nights without sleep.

'They found out from the cowherd.'

Hosé grimaced as he recalled the events of that dreadful day. De Glandèves! He had recognised the Knight but had been too distraught over Ishaq to care about the implications. Since then, in the few times he had thought of such things, he had hoped the Knight had not recognised *him*. He had shown no sign at the time.

Hosé frowned. 'What else did Gregorio say?'

'It was his wife who brought the warning. The Knights marched in on Gregorio and demanded to know where to find the man who had gone to fetch milk. At first, Gregorio did not know what they were talking about. Nobody had brought any milk for him.'

No, thought Hosé grimly, remembering the pot abandoned in the middle of the field.

'Then the Knights asked more questions. How had Gregorio been injured? How long ago was that? Who had visited him? Who was the boy? Who was the man with him? Then he began to realise.'

'And his wife?' asked Hosé sharply. 'She minded Ishaq while I was inside with Gregorio.'

'She says she did not like the men, but she had liked Ishaq.' A small smile brightened Rabia's drawn face. 'And she feared they meant him harm. She told them there had been no visitors.'

Hosé rasped a hand around his unshaven face.

'She wanted to come and see Ishaq but I said he was too ill.'

Hosé tried to put his thoughts in order. Somehow de Glandèves had recognised who he was, perhaps only realising it later. Somehow, he had traced the cowherd and the boy had remembered the name Gregorio. Somehow in all that rabbit warren called collectively the Trastevere the Knight had discovered the right Gregorio. Very soon he would find out where Gregorio worked and Bramante's clerk would have no reason to conceal who had been sent to visit Gregorio that day. And anyone on the building site could say where that visitor lodged.

He had another thought. 'How many Knights?'

'She said there were two of them, one younger but grander than the other. He did most of the questioning.' She frowned. 'She said he had a curly beard which he pulled sometimes.'

'Guy de Blanchefort!' Of course, de Glandèves would have informed him.

'The Grand Master's nephew, who often rides with the Prince?'

Hosé nodded, often but not on that one dreadful day. Perhaps things might have been different if de Blanchefort had been beside the Prince in the hunting party and not just the Pope's son, the arrogant Cesare Borgia.

'Where did you meet Gregorio's wife? In the Campo?'

Had the Knights followed Marietta? Had the Knights seen her with Rabia?

He glanced towards the doorway as if he expected de Blanchefort and de Glandèves to appear there at any moment.

'There were only the usual people about.' She had understood. 'Some late season travellers and pilgrims. I didn't notice anyone taking a particular interest.'

'And afterwards? Did you come straight here?'

'But I am sure nobody followed me,' she protested.

Hosé looked at the doorway again. 'And Marietta?'

She flushed.

'What?'

'I told her to go to Guiseppe's for a particular ointment.'

Hosé groaned.

'I know what you said about the poppy being dangerous, but you must give it to Ishaq now. We have to leave, immediately.'

'But it might kill him!'

'So might the Knights,' he said grimly.

'He is only a boy, a sick little boy,' she protested.

'Do you imagine the Knights will bother about that? If they get their hands on me they will want answers and they will not mind how they get them.'

She looked at him appalled.

He had realised long ago that adopting Ishaq had made him vulnerable, never mind the complication of Rabia. The prohibition on a kul marrying or having a family made absolute sense. That was obvious now; if it had ever been in doubt.

Hosé had hoped to get away from the baker's without involving any of the family. They would have enough questions to answer and it was best they did not know the answer to the most crucial one.

But as he placed Ishaq carefully in the baker's handcart and began to pile up the loaves again, Ricardo appeared.

'What are you doing? I was about to deliver those.'

'Sorry,' Hosé said.

'Sorry about what?'

'Sorry that I have to do this. Remember that you found me stealing the cart and that I hit you.'

'Hit me?' the boy's eyes widened.

Hosé caught the lad and, giving himself no time to think, landed a blow on the floury head. For good measure, he slapped the unconscious face hard and smeared the blood from the cut lip over the boy's cheek and forehead. He wiped his fingers down the front of Ricardo's grimy tunic.

'What have you done?' Rabia's horrified voice made him turn.

'It looks worse than it is,' he said roughly, 'But it might convince someone of his innocence.'

She bent down.

'No! Leave him. We need to go. Did you get rid of the things? Completely?'

She reluctantly left Ricardo. 'I put all the writing materials and the few bits of paper in the baker's oven and fired them. I raked out the ashes.'

Hosé always committed the important information to memory and destroyed correspondence as it arrived. Now he was thankful for the precaution.

There were only a couple of unopened packets that had arrived the previous day and they were in the cart with the few other things that could not be left or burned.

Rabia had also packed in the herbs and unguents she needed. The rest of her store she had left behind. There was nothing unusual in them, nothing suspicious, but they had taken time and effort to collect. They were very precious to her and she grieved to leave them. She comforted herself with the thought that Guiseppe might be able to use them, provided he was not caught with incriminating evidence of his own. She desperately hoped the tools they used for dissection were in their hiding place.

Then the thought that the Knights might already have followed Gregorio's wife and be questioning the apothecary spurred her to action.

Hosé pushed the handcart via all the narrowest back streets, glancing frequently behind him.

It was a chilly autumn day and although Hosé was soon sweating with the effort he feared he had not wrapped Ishaq warmly enough.

He dared not stop to look.

Finally, they were at the Ponte Sisto. They were by no means the only trades-people crossing the river but they were very exposed. Anyone watching the bridge would be bound to see them, and have no trouble stopping them.

With a last look around and taking a breath, Hosé set off across the bridge.

The last time he had been here, Ishaq had been trotting by his side.

They reached the far bank.

'Hey!' A voice hailed them.

Rabia saw Hosé's hand move to his back. She moved quickly in front of him and looked at the man who had called.

The man wore the uniform of the Pope's guard. 'How much for a loaf?'

As far as she could see he was on his own. 'They are for a customer,' she replied.

'He wouldn't miss one, would he?'

Rabia thought quickly. What would be the best way to handle this, the least likely to arouse suspicion or make the man remember the incident?

'Depends how much you are prepared to pay,' she said. The Romans were as keen on a bargain as anyone.

She haggled with him for a few moments, feeling Hosé's tension behind her, but he had understood what she was doing.

She agreed a price with the soldier and handed over the loaf.

He handed her a coin. 'Worth more!' he said taking a bite and sauntering off.

Hosé watched him go, then turned the handcart, heading for the wharves along the Tevere. Several times he made diversions. At last they came to the oil-merchant's warehouse.

The merchant agreed to his request, although the packages involved were rather larger than usual.

Hosé unloaded Ishaq, still unconscious, his face as white as the flour which had drifted off the loaves, his breath laboured, his skin cold and clammy. Rabia peered at him anxiously.

Hosé left them and took the cart away. When, if, it was ever found, it would be in a place far from the banks of the river, although the river was the obvious way for them to leave the city and de Blanchefort would surely check that eventually.

Hosé was not sure how much Julio believed of his story. The old merchant would undoubtedly accept the point about safety in a Rome facing invasion and war, but to travel with such a sick child rather undid the argument.

However, the old merchant welcomed the little party and immediately put a room at their disposal. His servants fetched a brazier and blankets, hot food and drink.

Ishaq began to gain a little colour as Rabia wrapped heated stones and placed them either side of his body and by his foot. Gradually his breathing became easier.

'The Pope will have much on his mind at present,' Julio commented.

Hosé started. How much did Julio know?

The older man said quietly, 'It would not take a seer to state that with absolute certainty.'

Hosé nodded. Of course Julio was right, anyone could see the difficult position Pope Alexander was in.

'He faces enemies on all sides,' Hosé commented neutrally as he considered how much to say. 'The army of France is in Florence and the army of Naples almost in sight to the south of Rome.'

The wizened face creased. 'But perhaps there is better news for him.'

Hosé looked at him curiously.

'A boat arrived last night.'

In Ostia? And at this time of year? Hosé frowned.

'I am sure it is not her cargo that brings her here at such an unseasonable month. In fact,' the man smiled, 'I know it is not, because a message came to me just an hour ago, asking about boats going up to Rome, for the delivery of an urgent packet.' Julio smiled more broadly. 'To my friend, Marco the oil-merchant.'

For the oil-merchant?

'I replied that they would have time to catch Marco's boat, if they hurried.'

Hosé half rose from his seat.

'But also said,' Julio laughed outright, 'That the packet for Marco could be delivered right here, for its real intended recipient.'

Hosé sat down again and smiled. 'Thank you.'

'It is unusual,' Julio commented, 'To have two such large boats stopping at Ostia. They are too big to get into the harbour and anchoring outside is especially dangerous when the autumn winds and the seas are so uncertain.'

And which seaman could be more *certain* about winds and seas? Hosé's happiness was short lived; as his brain registered Julio's words. 'Two boats?' he queried.

Rabia's tired and drawn face lit up as Hosé told her about the *Katrin.* 'What good fortune,' she said.

Her smile quickly faded as Hosé told her the other part.

The earlier boat had been the *Marije* of Antwerp, which had whisked away the beleaguered Cardinal della Rovere, to the safety of Genoa and then Nice.

'How is he?' Hosé indicated Ishaq.

'He was awake a little while ago. He seems to be recovering from the poppy. He spoke a little. He wanted to see the sea!'

He would surely get his chance soon enough.

'Has he drunk anything? Managed to eat anything?'

'He had a little tisane. He asked for some bread, but after I had softened it for him he did not want it.' She paused. 'Then he began to cry.'

Hardly surprising.

'He said his leg hurt.'

'His leg? Did he mean the stump?'

'No. The lower part.'

Hosé stared. 'But how could it?'

Rabia shrugged. 'Perhaps he still thinks it is there.'

Perhaps he did. The boy had not been in any sort of state to discuss the fact that he now only had one leg, or rather one and a half legs. Hosé and Rabia had hardly talked about it either. The first thing was to ensure that the boy survived. How he would manage was for later.

Hosé looked down at the small sleeping figure. The trip downriver had been hazardous enough, a voyage over the sea was even more so. But they could not stay in Ostia. Sooner or later de Blanchefort would arrive, Hosé was certain.

At least now Rabia and the boy could sail with the van Dammes. That was infinitely better than any other vessel Hosé might have found.

'Me and Ishaq?'

'My task in Rome is not finished.'

'Nor is tending Ishaq!' she retorted.

He knew that. It was an impossible choice.

'I have to go back,' he said quietly.

'And when Ishaq asks for you?' she demanded. 'And you are not there?'

'Don't Rabia. That is not fair.'

'Fair? What is fair in life?' Her eyes blazed at him. 'I never wanted the child. You made me keep him, you made me feed him and care for him, you made me see him for himself, you made it impossible for me to imagine life without him.' She was shaking. 'But for him what really makes life imaginable is you!'

Hosé felt as if she had twisted a knife in his guts. 'I have no choice,' he managed eventually.

'And,' she continued angrily, 'The Knights might find you.'

He shook his head. 'I can keep out of their way. I will not go anywhere near the usual places.'

'It will still be too dangerous.' Life without Hosé was suddenly and totally unimaginable for her too.

The rest of the day passed with agonising slowness. Hosé watched the river anxiously as it brought the day's collection of boats from Rome. He watched the roads for a party of Knights.

He was keen to leave the port as soon as possible but against that was the imperative for secrecy.

Darkness finally fell, concealing him as he rowed out to the Marsillian.

Early next morning the *Katrin* was seen to set sail and point her stem up the coast in a freshening south westerly wind, surely heading for Civitavecchia, or perhaps Genoa, to service the fleet of boats gathered there to carry home the victorious French horde.

Hosé made arrangements for passage on a small boat heading south for Naples.

'The lion's den?' queried Julio.

'His Holiness needs information from that quarter.' And a good many others.

'And the child?' Julio had inevitably fallen under Ishaq's spell.

'I have contacts in the region,' said Hosé. 'My wife and Jacques will stay with them.' He added, 'In the country.'

Julio inclined his head. 'That should help his recovery. I trust the travel will not set him back.'

Hosé fervently hoped so too.

'And any packets that might come for you?' The old merchant inquired.

They were unlikely, but there might be the odd one. 'I should be grateful if you would keep them for me.' And if they happened to fall into the wrong hands, he hoped the codes would be sufficient.

Julio nodded.

The voyage to Terracina was not unduly rough and Hosé spent much of the time answering Ishaq's growing number of questions about the *Santa Anna*, her sail, her ropes and brails; about the winds and the currents; about the birds that wheeled overhead and the coast that passed slowly on their ladboard side.

The fever had abated, the waste passed by the boy's body was beginning to look somewhere near normal, the sea air brought a hint of colour to the sunken cheeks.

More than once Hosé caught Rabia watching them and was stabbed by the reminder of what she had said.

'I bet I could do that,' the child's words caught his attention.

Hosé looked to see what he was talking about and his heart sank. One of the boatmen had climbed the stubby mast to check on a rope.

'I can climb better than any of the other children in the district.'

Hosé swallowed.

'Not now, of course, because my leg still hurts,' the boy continued in a serious voice. 'But when it is better.'

Hosé glanced at Rabia.

She shook her head slightly. It was an ongoing mystery that the boy really seemed to feel that his leg was still there, although he had seen for himself by now that it was not, since Rabia checked the stump and bandages at least once a day.

'Of course,' Hosé forced a smile. Surely bright, even false, hopes were helpful medicine.

The *Katrin* arrived in the small port a few days later.

After the first greetings, there was an awkward pause as Rabia and Jakob regarded each other. In spite of the letters they had exchanged, neither of them had quite imagined the changes wrought by the passing of time. Rabia was a neat Roman matron, Jakob a well-built if somewhat gangling youth.

'This boat is much better than the *Santa Anna*.' An impressed treble broke the silence.

'The *Katrin* is a Marsillian,' Thomas's bass responded with a hint of laughter.

'A Marsillian,' Ishaq repeated the word with relish.

'Would you like to look around her?' Thomas's Italian, like his Catalan, was carefully correct.

'Oh yes,' Ishaq's eyes gleamed.

Thomas looked at Hosé.

'I may, mayn't I Papa?' Ishaq had misunderstood the look. 'Please,' he added as an afterthought.

'Of course.' Hosé moved to pick him up.

'He can take me.' Ishaq indicated Thomas. 'After all, it is his boat.'

Thomas laughed as he lifted the boy. 'It is not exactly my boat,' he glanced at Cornelius. 'But I did help build her.'

There was a short moment of awed silence then the questions began.

'I hope you don't need Thomas for anything,' Hosé smiled at Cornelius. 'I think he will be kept busy for some time.'

Behind them Rabia and Jakob began to talk.

It was Messina yet again where they parted.

Did history repeat itself? Hosé wondered. Not really, he answered his own question. It was he and Rabia leaving the *Katrin* and heading north once more, but everything else had changed.

Last time Ishaq had been with them.

* * *

Now Hosé and Rabia were back in Messina once more, and it was Matteo with them.

They had been delayed on the long road south by the young man's sickness, by the need to avoid the great armies and the many skirmishes that occurred on the fringes, although by spring the fighting was over. The French King had conquered the kingdom of Naples.

Matteo slowly recovered; unlike the Turkish Prince who had finally been freed from the troubles of this life on the twenty-fifth of February in the Christian calendar, shortly after the young physician had left his care to others.

That much news they had gathered for it was common knowledge, but Hosé fretted because he was cut off from any of his usual reliable sources of information. Instead he had to rely on rumours, rumours that said the Prince's body would be carried to Constantinople because his brother the Sultan Bayezit had demanded it, other rumours that said the Pope wanted the remains of his dear friend carried to Rome, still other rumours that described in remarkable detail how the body had been preserved in olive oil and kept in a lead coffin at Gaeta, a few miles north west of Naples.

There were increasingly numerous tales that the Duke of Milan, who had supported the French King in his march south, had now reached agreement with both the Venetians and the Pope to cut off any French retreat. The fleet of boats at Genoa had been attacked.

That part at least was entirely credible and very much what Hosé would have expected of Il Moro.

A few weeks after midsummer, there were reports of a great battle on the River Taro, at Fornovo. The Pope had carefully absented himself from Rome while King Charles and his army marched back through the City. The thirty thousand, their followers and supplies, supplemented by no less than twenty thousand mules loaded with Neapolitan plunder, had not bothered to divert to Perugia in pursuit of his Holiness. They had pushed northwards until they met the forces gathered under Gonzaga of Mantua. Ultimately the French King and many of his soldiers had forced their way through, but the precious cannon, the tents and baggage carts, the spoils of war, had all to be abandoned.

'So, what has the French King's campaign achieved?' mused Matteo. 'Except,' he added half to himself, 'The spread of the *morbo gallico*.'

'Will you take up your studies again for Leoniceno?' Hosé asked.

Matteo looked out across the sickle-shaped harbour, busy in the bright sunshine. The moment had come for his long-delayed decision. Still he hesitated. 'I have learned a lot from the professor. I have learned much from studying for myself. But,' he looked at Hosé, 'I know there are others who could teach me so much more, others,' he flushed slightly, 'Outside Christendom.'

Like Isaac the Jew. 'So?' Hosé asked.

'You have still not provided all those explanations, you know.' Matteo looked at him. 'And,' he continued, 'I think I know why.'

'It is not that I do not trust you,' said Hosé quietly.

Matteo nodded. 'It is like at Capua, isn't it? For my own safety.'

Hosé's expression confirmed it.

'Perhaps you are right. I do not know what you are involved in and I am not wise in the ways of the world. My family all tell me that.' He had a sudden thought. 'Do you know my family? You knew 'Bella, didn't you? From before the time Isaac was in Genoa.'

Hosé shrugged.

'I would like to know.' Matteo smiled. 'I have as much human curiosity as the next man, you know.' He watched as a small boat skulled into the quay. 'About Rab too,' he added. 'She is a remarkable young woman.'

It had eventually dawned on the embarrassed young man that it was not a boy caring for him.

'She is indeed.'

'Will she be going with you? Wherever you are going, that is.'

The answer to the second part was infinitely less clear than the first.

'You will see Isaac?'

Hosé nodded. He hoped for that much.

'You said he is quite recovered. Would he consider taking a student, a Christian student, do you think?'

'I cannot answer for him.'

'Could I come and ask him for myself?'

'It is not a short journey and there are dangers.' It was only fair to warn him.

'Life has dangers wherever one lives, even in a monastery!'

Hosé could see that. 'What about your family?'

'I will send 'Bella a letter. She will understand.'

If only Hosé's own future were so easy a matter.

'Matteo wants to study with Isaac.' Hosé and Rabia sat on the hill above the town, watching the distant sail of a boat.

She nodded, unsurprised.

'I'm sure Isaac will welcome him. With you as well, he will almost have his own school,' Hosé said with an attempt at a smile.

Rabia nodded again but was silent, gazing out over the gleaming waters of the strait.

'You'll be safe with Isaac,' he said eventually. 'Whatever happens to me.'

She turned to look at him then. That was the unknown that hung so heavily between them.

'Now the Prince is dead my mission here is finished,' Hosé spelled it out slowly. 'The Sultan must use me as he sees fit.'

'Because you are his kul,' she said.

'Yes.'

'*A kul owes total allegiance to his Lord.*' She remembered his words exactly. 'And,' she continued softly, 'A kul may have no wife, nor family.'

'You know why I married you. You also know I will free you.'

She was quiet again. 'But I do not wish to be "*free*".' She looked down at their hands, side by side on the short grass: his broad and callused, hers smaller but practical.

Finally, he shook his head. In spite of everything he could not bring himself to say the necessary words.

'We talked about all this before we returned to Rome. I have not changed my mind, Hosé.' She stopped abruptly. 'You have never told me your proper name.'

He hesitated. 'It is Hasan.' He watched her face. 'I'm sorry.'

She considered. 'I'm not,' she said at last. 'You have taught me many things, not least that every Turk is not like Kara Hasan.' She lifted his hand. He tried to pull back but the attempt was half-hearted. 'What will the Sultan do?' she asked.

There were several possibilities. Hosé did not want to consider any of them. He shook his head. 'I don't know. He can order what he pleases.' His scarred thumb moved gently.

The distant boat was clearer now. It was Greek, offering a chance of finding a passage to the east.

Epilogue

'And what of Muid ad-Din ibn al-Arabi?'

Hasan looked up in surprise.

'After all you have told me of your years among the Franks can you still believe that the divine resides in everything and everyone?'

Hasan hesitated. 'It is a thought that has often been in my mind. I believe it must be considered wherever one lives and whatever everyday life brings.'

The great turban inclined slowly. 'Even for a Sultan of the Ottomans.'

'For all men, yes, Lord.'

'There are those who believe I spend too much time on the spirit and not enough on earthly matters.'

Hasan had heard the whispers.

'What do you say to that Ama Hasan?'

Ama. Hasan concealed a grimace. The name was probably as deserved now as it had ever been and as likely to have similar consequences. 'How can I judge that, Lord?'

'Others do,' said the Sultan dryly. 'But you are right, judgement lies with God.'

Hasan opened his mouth then shut it again; not quickly enough.

'Yes?'

'I thought of the Pope, Lord.'

'The Pope?' The black eyes bore into him. 'Speak your thought, Ama Hasan.'

'It would sound impertinent, Lord.'

'That would not have stopped you once upon a time.'

That was true.

Hasan said slowly. 'Pope Alexander is leader of the Holy Roman Church yet there is little to show that he tries to follow the teachings of its Prophet. He is as venal as any other man.'

The Sultan frowned.

'At the day of judgement, I would far rather be you facing Allah than him.' Not of course that he was either. Hasan would face his own considerable reckoning.

For a moment, the dark face was shocked then a small smile lightened the ascetic features. 'From anyone else that would be blasphemous or base flattery.'

Hasan flushed. 'Never, Lord.'

The face was solemn again. 'No, I don't believe you would.' The Sultan looked around the small garden, a secluded corner in the great and populous complex of the Topkapi palace.

'It has been hard for you, all these years, living in the Dar al-Harb.'

It was not a question but Hasan responded anyway. 'Yes.'

'But you have served me loyally.'

'Of course, Lord.'

That intense stare again. 'You say that in spite of all the things you have done which you knew I would not approve of.'

Hasan swallowed. This was the moment of his earthly reckoning.

The Sultan regarded him sombrely and lifted a hand, counting off his fingers. 'You helped one of my brother's followers to escape. You took and used money and gemstones you knew belonged to Prince Cem. You did not reveal that you had re-established links with your blood father and become involved in an old feud, which led to you having to leave the post where you could keep close surveillance over the Prince. When you finally managed to reach his side again he was beyond human help; you failed to kill the man who probably poisoned him and barely prevented a further attempt.'

Hasan said nothing; he had recounted how events had unfolded.

'Furthermore, you married, although you know a kul is forbidden to do so, and were thus diverted from your mission by family concerns.'

Hasan flinched.

'Is that not what I have to conclude from all you have told me?'

It was an all too reasonable conclusion. Hasan bowed his head in acknowledgement.

It had taken a considerable time to tell what had happened over nearly thirteen years. Hasan had tried to show the circumstances in which his decisions had been made. He had feared that his story sounded both fantastical and feeble. The Sultan had listened with grave attention, putting in questions from time to time about the strange ways of the Franks and particularly about his brother's life in the keeping of the Knights of St John.

The only sounds now were the splash of a nearby fountain and the faint hum of insects. The palace was quiet in spite of the activities of the hundreds of people who lived and worked there. In other circumstances, Hasan would have savoured the peace, and the company.

Eventually Bayezit lifted his first finger. 'Before my brother took refuge in Egypt there were Turcomen who robbed him. They then tried to bargain with me, offering their spoils in exchange for exemption from taxes.' He frowned at the memory. 'Do you know what happened to them?'

'Yes, Lord.' Hasan had heard about the executions.

'My brother may have been wrong to challenge my right to be Sultan but he was still a royal prince.'

Hasan wondered about "*royal*". Yes, the man had had royal blood in his veins, but his conduct, in Hasan's opinion, had been far from royal. Hasan accepted that Bayezit had loved his brother, regardless of what had happened, but Hasan could not feel any respect or affection for the Prince who had tried to usurp the throne, who had allowed himself to become a powerful weapon in the hands of the Christians, who had ultimately become a dissolute man.

'There are those who think printing is ugly if not downright ungodly.' The Sultan still had the same finger extended.

A finger expert in beautiful calligraphy.

Hasan drew a breath. He had always spoken his true mind to this man. If he was about to add another black mark to the tally against him so be it. 'I believe printing can be used by man in God's purpose: to spread knowledge and wisdom,' he said quietly.

'But not the word of God Himself.' The words were soft but emphatic.

Hasan suddenly wondered how the Recitation would look in print. He had actually only seen printed Roman script.

'You saw a printing press in France?' The Sultan seemed to pick up the same thought.

Hasan assented.

'Tell me about it.' The tone was neutral.

Hasan spoke of the printer's he had visited in Lyons, of how the books were printed and the great number that could be produced in just a few short hours, some even with pictures and diagrams. He described those he had bought on behalf of the Knights to provide diversion for the Prince.

The Sultan considered that for some time. 'There have been books printed here in Konstantiniye, did you know that?' he said finally.

Hasan had not heard.

'The first was by David and Samuel ibn Nahmias, two years ago, a book containing some of the Hebrew *Code of Law*. There was an intricate decorated letter at the beginning which I asked about. The brothers had brought the woodcut with them. They said it had been made by a Christian silversmith from Córdoba.' Bayezit looked at Hasan. 'Is that not curious? That Jewish printers and a Christian smith should have created printed lettering here in the Dar al-Islam?'

The Sultan had taken that time and trouble, when he obviously had reservations about mechanical writing? Hasan regarded the stern face and wondered yet again at the magnanimity of the man behind it.

'Curious?' He pondered the word. 'Not really,' he continued. 'Considering the welcome you have extended to all those expelled from Spain.'

'Should not all people be able to live in peace together, especially those of the Book?'

'Yes, Lord,' said Hasan with feeling, contrasting in his mind the hatred for Mohammedans and increasing persecution of Jews that he had seen among the Franks.

The Sultan mused again. 'I know Isaac treasures that book.'

Bayezit was not referring to the *Code of Law*, of course. He was talking about *Continens*: the book Hasan had bought for Isaac and paid for with the Prince's money.

'He is always consulting it.' That faint smile crossed the dark face again as he added, 'The margins are not nearly wide enough for all his comments.'

Hasan nodded but did not return the smile. It was not the Jew's appreciation of the book that was in question.

The smile faded. 'Does Isaac know how you got it?'

'I never told him.'

The turban moved. 'When I asked where he had acquired it he avoided my question.'

'Any guilt lies only with me. I never told him,' repeated Hasan.

'He may be old, but he can still add one and one together,' said Bayezit dryly.

Hasan could hardly argue against that.

There was another period of silence. 'And the Prince's man you helped to escape.' The Sultan raised a second finger.

Hasan frowned. Had the Sultan reached some judgement about the money and the book? And what about the gem that he still had? The one he had offered to Rabia as a dowry! He opened his mouth.

'Franck Suleiman you said they called him?' The Sultan continued with deliberation.

Hasan swallowed. 'Yes, Lord. He was born in France but found his way to the Faith before becoming one of your brother's followers.'

'Ah,' the word was soft. 'And the first part weighed more with you than the second?'

Hasan shifted. 'Not exactly. I was fairly sure his escape would not aid the Prince's cause.'

'You were faced, in fact, with a choice between your personal inclination because of your beliefs and political reality,' said the Sultan.

That about summed it up.

'As I have been all my life,' said Bayezit. 'The burden has become ever heavier,' he added.

Hasan was saddened by the pain in the voice and at the same time touched by this confidence.

The Sultan sighed then lifted another finger. 'So, my long-trusted dragoman is your father.' The tone was cool.

'He *was* my father,' said Hasan distinctly. 'After Caffa my life started again. I owe allegiance only to the House of Osman. And,' he added, 'The dragoman has not betrayed your trust, unlike some.'

A slippered foot shifted on the gravel path. 'The Vizier has answered for his treachery.' There was short pause. 'But not yet the Englishman who tried to poison my brother.' The next finger was extended.

Nobody could regret that more than Hasan.

'But someone else had already done the deed.'

Hasan hesitated. 'Matteo is not sure,' he admitted. 'But I believe Cesare Borgia had the reason and the opportunity.' And the ruthlessness.

'Whom you failed to kill.' Another finger.

Another bitter regret.

'The Pope's son.'

Hasan swallowed.

'Who had been Cem's hunting companion,' Bayezit's voice was low. 'And who rode over the child you call your son.'

Hasan would not repeat the part the Prince had played in the "accident". He could understand why the Sultan would choose to believe the blame lay rather with Cesare Borgia.

But Hasan's responsibility for Ishaq was another matter. 'He may not be of my flesh but I am his father,' he affirmed quietly.

The Sultan lifted the last finger. 'You married.'

'Marriage was the only way to save them from a situation which was not the fault of either.' Hasan had not mentioned the other reason he felt responsible for the child; that was hardly relevant. 'It is, however, a marriage in name only.'

The Sultan considered him. 'That is truly the case?'

'I tell you only the truth, Lord.'

'There are few enough who do that.' There was the briefest hint of amusement, 'And this is particularly hard to believe.'

Hasan flushed. It had become particularly hard to maintain.

'So, it does not count as a real marriage then?'

'With your permission, Lord, I would make it so,' Hasan pressed on. 'I am past thirty. By that age many a kul is allowed a wife and family.'

'Many a janissary, perhaps.' Bayezit's face was stern again, 'But you are not a janissary.'

Hasan clenched his jaw. He had been. It had been all he ever really wanted to be.

The Sultan looked at the lengthening shadows. 'It will soon be time for prayers,' he said.

Hasan made obeisance. He would have to wait then to learn his fate.

'We shall talk again about these things,' said Bayezit. 'But first I shall speak to the others involved: Isaac the Jew, the Christian physician who tended my brother and to the woman.'

They were long days. Hasan was not placed under guard but nor was he able to see the others. He had no way of knowing what they said to the Sultan or how that was received.

For himself he felt he could accept the consequences of what he had done, whatever they were, but there was no gainsaying the fact that the fate of others was bound up with his.

The Sultan's face was inscrutable as he bid Hasan rise from the tiled floor.

For a long moment, they regarded each other.

Finally, the Sultan indicated that Hasan should sit. 'If you were any other kul ....'

Hasan waited.

'But,' There was the slightest emphasis on the word, 'You have been involved in a mission of great complexity, in unusual circumstances and,' a slight smile softened the hawk-like features, 'You are not any other kul.' The Sultan continued, 'You served me faithfully in Amasya. You trod the path of study and seeking alongside me.'

'You rescued me from my banishment,' Hasan pointed out.

'*But* that did not make you abjectly grateful!' There was almost a smile. 'Since I have been Sultan I have been surrounded by hundreds, even thousands, who are bound to tend my every need, heed my every command, but not one has offered what you did in those times. I have missed it. I did not realise how much.'

Hasan swallowed.

'The administration of the empire demands that its servants serve it without question and without reservation. But then which servant will dare to question its Sultan?' Bayezit frowned. 'Or tell him the honest if uncomfortable truth? That is a conundrum to which there seems no answer. Yet there is you.'

'You honour me too much, Lord. I have an over-rash nature, that is the root of the matter. That is, after all, why I was banished to that farm in the mountains.' Hasan pulled a wry face. 'I did not mind the harsh conditions or the work, but I missed books, ideas, religious discussion more than I would ever have imagined. To have them again in your household was like the sweetest water being given to someone from the desert. I fear it often loosened my tongue like the strongest wine!' He grimaced. 'Circumstances have changed and cannot come again.'

Bayezit thought about that. 'I believe you are right,' he said eventually. 'There cannot be another time like that, or indeed anyone like you.'

Was that good or bad?

'Which makes it all the more complicated.'

That did not sound promising.

The Sultan looked upwards. The sun shone through the high coloured panes and sprinkled jewels across the ceiling and the tiled walls. Golden motes of dust drifted in the shaft of light, marking its boundaries.

'In spite of what he did, I loved Cemchid, you know.'

Hasan did know.

Bayezit was silent for a while lost in his memories. 'But a Sultan must balance his personal feelings with the needs of an empire,' he continued at last. 'And those demand the total devotion of my servants.'

'You have my total devotion, Lord.'

Bayezit shifted. 'I believe that,' he said slowly. 'After considering what you said, and what the others have told me, I think that you have indeed served both me and God as faithfully as any man could.'

Hasan inclined his head.

'But you have very special talents,' the Sultan continued.

But.

'I still need them at my disposal. The business with my brother is not yet ended. My demands that his body be returned to the land of his birth have so far been refused. I cannot find peace until his earthly remains are fittingly laid to rest.'

Hasan's spirits sank at the thought of going back to Italy but perhaps it would only take a few months. 'And after that is achieved?'

'There are other issues, the Franks threaten us at many points. You have acquired invaluable knowledge on such matters.'

'I will always put myself and that knowledge at the service of my Lord Sultan,' Hasan said. This was the moment. 'But,' he added with determination, 'I wish Rabia and Ishaq to be part of my life too.'

'You *wish*? What right has a kul to wish? What if every other kul had wishes?'

'You said I was not like any other kul, Lord.' Hasan held his breath.

'You are still my kul!'

Hasan bowed his head. So, that was the end of it.

He was aware that Bayezit had left his seat. Hasan hastened to rise to his feet but a hand on his shoulder prevented him. He lifted his gaze and met that of the Sultan. This close he could see clearly the lines carved into the dark skin around the mouth beneath the moustache and the creases of pain between the black brows.

'You are still my kul,' the Sultan repeated, less forcibly. 'But indeed like no other.' There was the ghost of a smile and a sigh. 'You should know that in truth my personal inclination is to reward you, to see you furnished with clothes and property and all fitting goods, as other valued servants are.'

Hasan could hear the word coming.

'But I believe one single gemstone will have to suffice for the moment.' There was gentle irony in the words.

Hasan did not care a whit about Cem's wretched gemstone, nor any other material reward.

The Sultan continued. 'As for the woman.'

Hasan clenched his jaw.

'We talked at some length.' Bayezit sounded slightly surprised by the idea. 'She has quite some learning, even of Sufist teachings.' He reflected on that for a moment before adding, 'She does not wish a divorce.'

Any more than did Hasan.

'If she cannot live as your wife,' Bayezit paused. 'She wishes to devote herself to study and to caring for Isaac.'

The only possible alternative, although Hasan was sure neither she nor the Jew would have mentioned the particular subject of that study.

'No kul may marry.' There were the words again and that finger. The Sultan stared at him. 'I am told that the Franks are much concerned with love. They dress up bodily attraction with high-flown phrases and pretend it is in some way noble. Have you been tainted by your years there?'

Hasan knew the Franks had nothing to do with it. He had seen their dissolute morals and illicit coupling at all levels of society. He only knew what was in his heart.

'What is this love? This earthly love? My father never loved my mother. He never loved me,' continued Bayezit.

Hasan was pained for him. He knew the old Sultan, Mehmet, had been most fond of his Hungarian princess and their son Prince Cem.

'Do any of my wives love me? Or any of my sons?'

'But,' Hasan said quietly, '*You* have loved. You loved your brother.'

Bayezit stared.

'You loved Prince Cem, regardless of what he did.'

The Sultan slowly nodded. 'And your point?'

'Those incapable of love are surely unblessed.'

'You suggest it is a blessing to feel love?'

'I believe so, Lord, even though it may be bound up with pain.' Such as he felt now.

'When it is not returned, you mean?' the Sultan asked.

'Love cannot demand a return,' Hasan said quietly. 'That is a grace.' Although perhaps it only increased the pain.

The Sultan pondered that. 'As we cannot demand that God speak to us but there is unbelievable joy when He does.'

That was a grace far beyond Hasan's experience but he could see the analogy.

There was a lengthy period of silence while Bayezit followed his own thoughts. 'But the woman does return your love, doesn't she? Why else did she go with you, to reach Cem's side?' He did not look for an answer. 'And in so doing rendered me a great service.' He sighed deeply. 'You are graced *and* blessed.'

Hasan knew it. 'Love is a grace and a blessing,' he repeated softly. '*And* it is infinite. The store of love does not diminish the wider it is spread. If I have come to love Rabia and Ishaq as well as Isaac, it does not mean that my love for you is any the less.'

The Sultan lifted one astonished brow then suddenly laughed, a rusty sound. 'Many of my servants have declared their undying loyalty, their respect and allegiance, never their love.'

Hasan flushed.

'You are as provoking as ever, but I think I could not like you so well if you were not.'

Hasan stared. The finger had been folded. Did that mean the Sultan accepted the marriage?

'It is time for Isaac to retire,' Bayezit said almost briskly. 'He wishes to spend his last years passing on his medical skills. He wants to grow his herbs and make his potions, to receive all, including those like the Christian Matteo, who wish to study with him.'

The question continued to fly around Hasan's head.

'Isaac is willing to take the woman and the child. He appears attached to both of them,' Bayezit said. 'Of course, he has tended the child with the utmost care these past months.'

Of course, he had.

'He is a fine boy.'

'You have met him?' Hasan managed.

'Oh yes. He has a lot to say for himself.' The turban trembled slightly. 'He may not be of your blood but he has your ways it seems.'

'He has other ways, all his own.' Hasan grimaced. 'He loves horses.'

'And is a promising rider I am told.'

Hasan started.

'Ah, Isaac has not told you about that.'

No, he had not. The old Hebrew had had little chance to say more than that Ishaq was flourishing.

'He has been learning with a man who breeds fine mounts for the sipahis.'

There was an instant memory of a small child wriggling with excitement as the horsemen with the Turkish embassy clattered along the streets of Rome.

'A certain Nasr.'

'Nasr?' Hasan started. 'The same Nasr who was with us when we found Isaac near Aleppo?'

'I believe so.'

There was surely no man who understood horses better.

'He says the child may ride as well as any other.' The hooded eyes considered him. 'Isaac wishes to move to Midilini.'

Hasan nearly groaned. He had expected the Sultan to say Adrianople, where there was a fine medical school. That at least was within easy reach of Islambul.

Those eyes were still on him. 'Tomorrow you will start preparing to go to Naples.'

So soon!

Lord Bayezit lifted his hand. 'Go! I have other things to do.'

Hasan stared dumbly.

'Are there not things *you* wish to do, before you leave?' inquired the Sultan. The ascetic face was as forbidding as ever but now the gleam of amusement in the eyes above the hawk's nose was quite clear.

They stood facing each other.

What was left of the meal lay on the low table.

'Rab,' Hasan broke the silence at last. 'Rabia,' he tried again.

Finally, she moved and he folded his arms around her, breathing deeply, the scent of her so familiar. For a long moment, he simply held her. At last he lifted a hand and carefully uncovered her hair, watching the heavy braid fall down her back. 'I'm glad you did not cut it again,' he said softly.

'Then I'm glad too.'

His fingers freed the shining mass.

She shivered.

His fingers found her cheek and turned her face towards him. 'This is what you wish?'

'With all my soul!' She caught his hand. 'I wish it for you and I wish it for myself.'

He looked meaningfully at the mattress.

She smiled ruefully at the small figure, curled up securely in his old place.

Hasan pondered the sleeping child. 'Come,' he said, with a sudden grin.

For just a moment Hasan recalled the specially designed basement in a specially built tower in distant France.

Rabia looked at him.

But he shook his head free of the memory, laughed and took her hand.

A dozen lamps shed a soft light on the water which splintered into a thousand glittering drops as their bodies broke the surface.

'It seems such a long time since I last swam,' she said.

That had been in the warm waters off the island of Djerba, nearly six years before, the swell of pregnancy stark on her scarcely adolescent body.

'But I still remember how to do it.' She looked at him sideways. 'You said I would.'

What he had actually said was that if she learned to swim it would be very difficult to deliberately drown herself. It had been a desperate suggestion born of desperate circumstances. It was undoubtedly of questionable morality (like a good many other things he had done) but it had worked.

They swam a few more short lengths then came to a stop.

Hasan reached a gleaming arm over the edge of the bath where a collection of soaps and unguents stood. He picked out a jar.

Rabia tried to take it from him.

He held the pot out of her reach.

She stared at him, colour rising in her wet cheeks.

'I should very much like to,' he said softly.

She quivered at the touch of his fingers, calloused yet incredibly gentle. She watched his face as he smoothed the scented soap over her dark skin.

He put his head to one side, studying the effect of the lather picking out the contours, every bone and muscle, every curve of her lean body. They could keep their plump women, he thought, his hands following their inclinations. Rabia might pass as a boy in suitable clothing, but there could be no such deceit now.

She shivered again and he looked at her. But she shook her head, her black hair shedding drops of water that glittered in the lamplight. 'Don't stop.'

After a while he did stop.

She opened her eyes in surprise.

He took her hand. 'Now it's up to you, Rab,' he said.

In the end, of course, he had done his part.

Author's note

Ylderim continues where *All the Sea* left off, following the fate of the exiled Turkish Prince Cem as he is transferred from France to Rome.

In my note to *All the Sea* I gave some of the reasons I find this period in history so fascinating. The fascination continues and I have enjoyed every moment spent gleaning knowledge of both the wider political and religious landscape, and the details of everyday life in that age.

There are naturally gaps in that knowledge: both because of my personal shortcoming, and because of the passage of time and imperfect historical evidence. However, that has been both a challenge and an opportunity: to fill the gaps with reasonable fabrications and assumptions. I admit to 'embroidering' some known facts to fit the story line, for which I claim author's privilege!

Including as it does the death of Prince Cem, *Ylderim* brings to a close the tale of his unhappy life and doomed ambitions. However, other characters survive and there are a number of threads left hanging, both factual and fictional.

If you are interested to see where they lead, you might like to look out for the next book in the series, *On Two Hills*…..

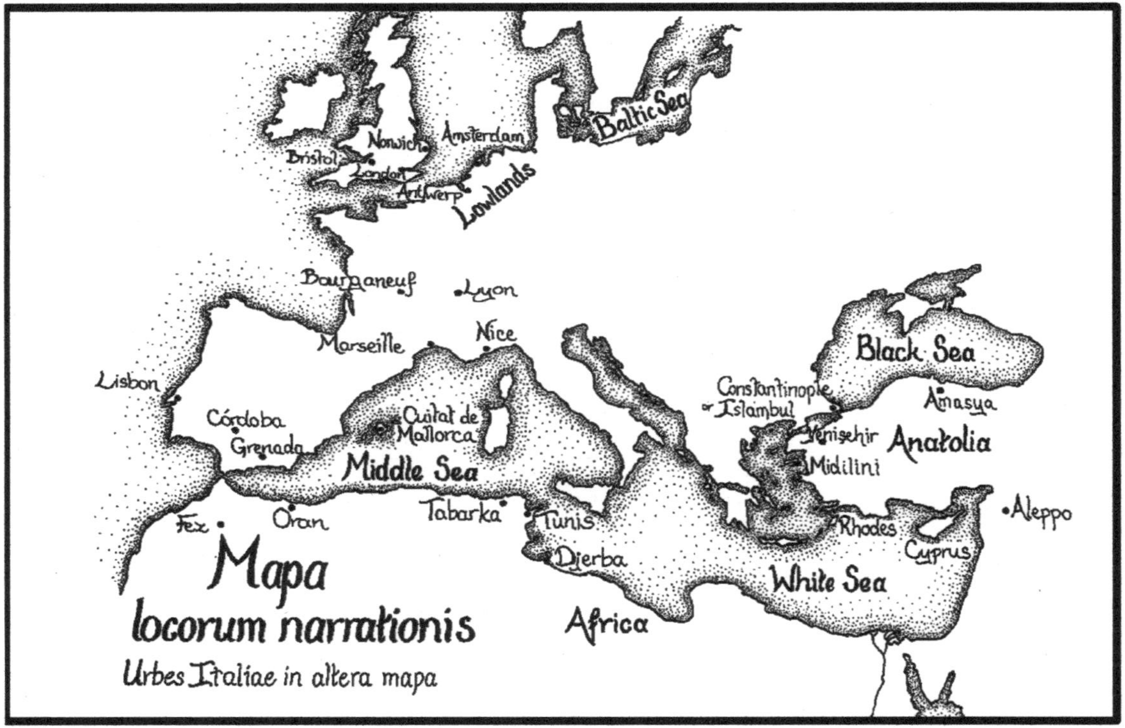
Mapa
locorum narrationis
Urbes Italiae in altera mapa
Baltic Sea
Norwich
Amsterdam
Bristol
London
Antwerp
Lowlands
Bourganeuf
Lyon
Marseille
Nice
Lisbon
Córdoba
Grenada
Ciutat de Mallorca
Middle Sea
Fez
Oran
Tabarka
Tunis
Djerba
Africa
Black Sea
Constantinople or Istambul
Amasya
Yenişehir
Anatolia
Midilini
Rhodes
Aleppo
Cyprus
White Sea

Milan
Venice
Ferrara
Fornovo
Genoa
Pesaro
Florence
Pisa
Urbino
Elba
Civitavecchia
Rome
Ostia
Capua
Terracina
Naples
Urbes Italiae
Messina

DID2113515
#0387 - 050218 - C0 - 229/152/19 - PB - DID2113515